HANG THE INNOCENT

(Based on the Legend of Henry Plummer)

By Daniel Landes

Elemar Publishing

DEDICATION

I wish to thank all of my friends and family members who have given me a variety of ideas as to how I should tell the story of legendary Montana sheriff, Henry Plummer. First and foremost is my wife Martha, who has served as my in-house editor and confidant. Her listening ear and friendly suggestions have helped make this book come to fruition.

Also, I want to express my appreciation to Aaron Toronto, my good friend from Brookings, South Dakota who has supported the writing of this story from its earliest inception. Finally, I am grateful to the History Museum of the Upper Missouri and the local curators in Fort Benton, Montana, who took the time to talk to me regarding my research on the lives of Henry and Electa Plummer.

PREFACE

Historians have had a difficult time separating the legend of Montana Sherriff Henry Plummer from the actual accounts of his life. However, it is undeniable that this man is a central figure in one of the most haunting mysteries of the Old West.

FOREWORD

The first time I heard the name Henry Plummer was during my freshman year of high school in Great Falls, Montana. When my civics teacher described Henry as a young man from the coastal city of Addison, Maine, who traveled to California to search for gold, I found myself curious as to why he was such an important figure in the history of Montana. When my instructor went on to tell our class that Henry had abandoned his dreams of discovering gold to become a sheriff who skirted both sides of the law, I was anxious to hear more.

Years later, after doing my own research, I discovered that many Montanans continue to believe the version of the story my teacher told us fifty years earlier: Henry Plummer upheld the law as a sheriff but broke those same laws as the leader of a ruthless gang called "The Innocents."

Early on, many people's views of one of Montana's earliest sheriffs were based on one of the first published accounts of his life: *The Vigilantes of Montana*, written by vigilante member Thomas Dimsdale. It wasn't until the latter part of the 20th century that skeptics began to reexamine Montana's infamous vigilante era and Dimsdale's book. After reviewing several other eyewitness accounts of Plummer's life, many historians concluded that the young sheriff was simply carrying out his lawful duties when he was falsely accused of being a road agent and a killer.

Despite the contradictions pertaining to Henry's life, *Hang the Innocent* is my attempt to humanize this one-of-a-kind legendary character.

In my telling of the story, I have taken the liberty to create a fictionalized background that details Henry's life as a young boy growing up in Addison, Maine. In addition, I have also embellished Henry's relationships with both his friend Jack Cleveland and his wife, Electa Bryant Plummer. That being said, much of the underlying story is still based on available evidence, including the fact that Henry and Jack fell in love with Electa and that Henry and Jack's friendship ended when Electa married Henry.

Finally, there is the pivotal question as to whether Henry was a law-abiding citizen or actually the leader of a violent gang called "The Innocents." After reading this book, you the reader will need to decide for yourself whether the Montana sheriff was or wasn't an innocent man.

Western States and Territories

1863

PART ONE: INNOCENCE LOST

CHAPTER 1

"When we are children, we seldom think of the future. The innocence leaves us free to enjoy ourselves as few adults can. The day we fret about the future is the day we leave our childhood behind." Patrick Rothfuss

1842

A WEST WIND SIGHS in the branches of several pine trees on an early fall morning in the rural central lowlands not far from the coastal town of Addison, Maine.

Twelve-year-old Samuel Plummer, clad in his father's hand-me-down boots, struts down a rutted country road followed closely by his barefooted nine-year-old brother, Henry. Both boys are dressed in ill-fitted bib overalls and faded red flannel shirts. Despite their dirt-caked faces and disheveled hair, it's obvious the brothers are destined to be fine-looking men someday.

When Samuel and I were young, time stood still. Unfortunately, we were too busy thinking about our own needs to realize how much we loved each other. And like a lot of other boys my age, I had no idea where the path of life would take me. All I knew was I wanted to go the same direction my older brother was going.

Samuel, whose dancing eyes shift as he takes in everything around him, spots a rusty tin can in the middle of the road and gives it a swift kick. His younger brother joins in and they take turns booting it down the road that separates two fields of freshly cut alfalfa.

The wind picks up and begins to whistle through the ryegrass as the mid-morning sun peeks through the branches of a large pine tree.

All at once, a dust devil crosses the road. Samuel keeps walking, but Henry stops, covers his face, and waits for the swirling dust to pass. Henry coughs deeply, rubs his eyes, looks up, and watches carefully as the clouds move rapidly across the sky.

Up ahead, Samuel grows impatient and turns back. "Jesus, Henry! Stop lollygagging!" Henry awakens from his daydream and races ahead until he catches up with his brother. As the boys walk along, the road narrows until they are surrounded by Eastern White Pines and Bigtooth Aspens.

Samuel pulls a peppermint stick from his pocket and shoves it in his mouth. Henry whirls around. "Hey, gimme one of them."

Samuel scoffs. "All I got."

"Come on. Pony up."

Samuel bites down hard on the candy and tosses Henry a small piece. "Beggar." The nub of candy bounces off Henry's chest and lands at his feet. He picks it up, wipes away the dirt, and puts it in his mouth as his older brother turns and looks at the side of the road. "Ain't that a daisy?"

Henry responds quickly. "What? Samuel bends over and picks a daisy out of the tall grass. He holds it up and snickers. "Ya know, a daisy."

"That ain't funny."

Samuel takes a jab at his brother, but Henry jumps back. He shrugs, moves to the side of the road, and lowers his overalls. "Gotta do my necessary."

Henry drops his pants as well. "Me too." Both boys pee designs in the dirt as they laugh.

Samuel snickers. "Got a big secret I ain't tellin' ya."

"No, ya don't...What is it?"

"You'd blab it to Pa."

"Hang me from a tree if I do."

As both boys pull up their pants, Henry takes a step forward and begs with his eyes. "Come on. I'll keep mum, honest."

Samuel trots off and Henry quickly catches up. Finally, Samuel says, "I'm running west. Gonna find me some gold."

Henry argues, "You ain't but twelve. Sides, Pa says you're goin' to work on his boat next month."

"Why ya think I'm leaving? I ain't fishing off no goddamn boat!"

Henry points his finger and shakes it. "If Ma heard you swear like that..."

Samuel grabs Henry's shirt collar. "You keep my words dry, ya hear? Soon as I get a fast gun and a one-of-a-kind horse, I'm ridin' off."

"I'm going too."

"Bullshit. You're nothin' but a hayseed. You'd slow me down."

The wind picks up again just as Henry spots a crystal-clear creek next to the road. He drops to his knees, lowers his head and begins to drink.

Samuel grins. "Ya know, fish shit in that water."

Henry hops to his feet and spits out the water as several cows bellow in the distance. Samuel turns and holds his finger to his lips. "Hear that?"

Henry listens hard as the cows bellow again. "That's nothin' but Pa's cows."

"You ain't hearing right," Samuel whispers, "Most likely Wawenocks." He signals his brother and both boys drop to their knees, and crawl through a field of tall feather grass and into a thick grove of aspens. Samuel jumps up, reaches around to the back of his pants, removes a revolver, and hands it to Henry.

"Keep an eye on this 'til I get back. I'm gonna make a pass at them Injuns."

On bended knee, Henry holds the gun clumsily in both hands. "This here's Pa's gun." Samuel ignores his brother and motions him to stay put as he crawls away.

Henry studies the pistol and then spins the gun barrel. He spots a bird sitting on a nearby tree branch, pulls back the hammer, and aims.

As I held that gun in my hands for the first time, I could feel its power. It was almost as if I was cradling a baby, a small little boy who was depending on me to take care of him.

Samuel reappears and grabs the gun out of Henry's hand. "Ain't Injuns at all. Miners toting bags of gold."

"You stole Pa's gun!"

"Keep your ass down and follow me." The boys crawl along until they reach the top of a grassy knoll overlooking an open meadow. Henry looks down and sees three cows grazing below, not far from a smoldering campfire. Samuel grins, reaches down, and rubs his hands in the dirt. Henry pauses a moment and does the same. His brother whispers, "You scared?"

"I ain't afraid of no cows."

"Cows my ass! Told ya, they's miners with mules loaded with gold and we're gonna steal it all."

With his left hand, Samuel slowly raises the gun and moves it across his line of vision. "Watch my back while I get the bulge on these bastards."

As Henry watches from above, Samuel charges down the hill, fires off five shots and screams, "Lily-livered cowards!"

Two of the cows run into the woods. The third one bellows and stands frozen as Henry joins his triumphant brother at the bottom of the hill. Henry points at the lone cow and his brother's smile disappears when he sees blood oozing from a small hole in the animal's flank.

Before Samuel can react, the wide-eyed cow falls to its knees and onto its side. He realizes what has happened and runs over and sinks down beside the bloody animal. He turns to his little brother and says, "Pa's gonna beat us to death!"

Henry stammers, "I ain't … done nothin'."

Samuel presses his hands tightly on the cow's wound, trying to stop the bleeding. When that fails, he paws the ground and shovels a handful of dirt on the wound. Henry begins to pace back and forth but freezes when he sees his brother's hands are covered with mud and blood. He awakens from his momentary trance and cries out, "I'm going for Pa!"

Not far off, the boys hear twigs break and leaves scatter as two strangers shuffle out of the trees. Their faces are grimy and their clothes are filthy and ill-fitting. Warren Spivey, who looks to be in his late thirties, is big-bodied. His face is unshaven and scarred and he walks with a limp.

Alex Slade is much younger, but it's hard to tell his age because his face is hidden by a scraggly beard and a floppy hat tipped above his eyes that shades his face.

As Warren approaches the boys, he spits tobacco juice at their feet. Behind him, Alex lurks in the shadows of the trees stoking the campfire as the strangers' horses skitter nervously.

The older man grins and steps forward, revealing his brown stained teeth. "What ya little wretches doin'?"

Henry doesn't hesitate. "My brother shot our pa's cow."

Samuel glares at Warren. "On accident."

Warren's eyes darken as he sucks his teeth. "That's my beef ya killed, ya little heathen. Branded it myself."

Samuel locks eyes with the stranger. "That's my pa's cow, Mister."

"Shut your bone box, boy! Find yourself in a hole, best not to dig deeper."

Samuel steps back. "Come on, Henry. Let's go home."

When the boys start to walk away, Warren grabs both of them by their shirt collars and shoves them to the ground. As they cower in the thug's shadow, Henry looks to his brother for an answer. Samuel spots the gun in the grass and snatches it up. He quickly points it at Warren, but the interloper grabs the weapon and twists it out of his hand. He looks back at his partner, who is nervously picking specks of dirt off his shirt. "See there. Ya got my boy all stirred up." Warren threatens to kick Samuel, changes his mind, and pulls both brothers to their feet. He nods and Alex grabs a rope from the ground, shuffles over, and pushes the boys ahead of him. While the older thief saddles his dreary-eyed horse, Alex ties the boys to the trunk of a tall pine tree.

Having finished his job, Alex joins Warren and begins to saddle his own horse. The boys wait until their abductors aren't looking and try to loosen themselves from the ropes. After a brief struggle, Samuel frees an arm, reaches in his pocket, and removes a small bladed penny knife. He begins to cut the rope as he whispers to his brother, "Once I cut us loose, run for home."

Henry says, "I ain't goin' without you."

"Do as I say."

Just as Samuel cuts through the rope, Warren and Alex turn and see that they are about to escape. As the older thief hobbles towards the tree, Alex follows close behind.

Samuel sees them coming, shakes the rope free but drops his knife. Henry picks it up and grips it tightly as he backs away from the tree. Samuel, still tangled in the rope, struggles to free himself, but before he can shed the rope, Warren grabs him and tosses him to the ground. He looks up and nods to his brother. "Go!"

Henry starts to run, but Warren rushes him and snags his belt. Henry instinctively turns and slashes Warren across his forehead with his brother's knife. Warren grimaces in pain. "Ahh! I guarangoddamntee, I'm gonna kill you ya little cocksucker!"

He looks at his brother for an answer and Samuel screams. "Jesus Christ! Get gone!" Henry backs away, not sure what to do as the lawless man presses a hand to his bleeding forehead. As blood runs down his face, he pulls Samuel up from the ground, spits a mouthful of blood on the boy's shirt, and begins to re-tie him to the tree. Then the abuser turns to Alex and points at Henry. "Get dat little snake!" Alex locks eyes with Henry and the frightened boy starts to offer himself up. He thinks better of it and runs off into the nearby trees.

Alex dodges in and out of the pines trying to catch Henry, but Alex trips over a tree root and falls face down in the dirt. He promptly climbs to his feet and takes up the chase again. He doesn't see Henry, but he fires two shots anyway.

Tied to the tree again and having heard the shots, Samuel yells, "Run, Henry!" Warren, who is at wits' end, rushes over, grabs Samuel by the throat, and lifts the boy off his feet by his shirt. As Samuel struggles to breathe, Warren grins as he mocks his young prisoner. "Run, Henry! Run!"

A few moments pass and Alex emerges from the woods. He stands frozen a moment and then begins to pick at his clothes. He looks around, trying to decide what to do. Finally, he spits, lowers his hat, and slogs his way back to camp.

When Alex emerges from the nearby trees, Warren looks at him and his young partner lowers his head. "Let dat piss-ant get away, didn't ya?" Alex's eyes tell him all he needs to know and the intruder spits and elongates the word, "Shh…it."

CHAPTER 2

"There are five types of fear: extinction, mutilation, loss of autonomy, separation, and humiliation." Dr. Karl Albrecht

NOT SLOWING DOWN, Henry makes his way back to the country road and turns for home. On the horizon, he sees his pa, a bearded man in his late thirties. He's wearing a soft hat, and knee-high boots and is seated on a strong horse. Steel jawed William Plummer rides down the hill and stares down at his youngest son. Henry shivers in the shadow of his pa's horse as his father realizes something is wrong. "What the hell? Where's your brother?

Out of breath, Henry talks fast. "We didn't mean to shoot your cow, Pa."

"Where is he? Where's Samuel?"

"South pasture. Two men tied us to a tree. He made me run."

"Get yourself home."

"But I...."

"This ain't no discussion. Now!"

Henry screams out as his father rides away. "He didn't mean to, Pa!" When his father is out of sight, Henry hesitates a moment, circles back through the trees, and heads in the direction he came from.

William rides off. Moments later, he brings his horse to a stop at the top of the hill that Henry and Samuel had charged down only a few minutes earlier. He looks up when he hears several ravens squawking high above. When he lowers his head, he sees Samuel tied to a tree. He rides down the hill past the dead cow and assesses the situation.

Samuel straightens himself as his father slows his horse. "I'm sorry, Pa." William jumps off his horse, just as Henry reaches a grove of tall shrubs not far from the tree his brother is tied to.

While Henry catches his breath, he peers through a gap in the shrubs and watches as his pa walks over and starts to untie Samuel. As William loosens the rope, he studies his son's face. "Who done this?"

Samuel nods in the direction of the trees. "Cattle thieves, but you're baiting their hook."

Out of the trees walk Warren and Alex. William lowers his hand to his belt but realizes he has no gun. Samuel nods at the place in the grass where his pa's gun lays. William walks over, picks up his pistol, and points it at Warren.

The bandit raises his hands and grins at William. Alex steps back and begins to pick at his clothes as he digs a hole in the dirt with the toe of his boot.

The boys' father grits his teeth. "Tie my boy to this tree?"

Warren chuckles. "Tied da knot myself. Yer boy shot that there cow."

"My cows ain't none of yer damn business."

"Best check da brand."

William eyes the fresh brand on the dead cow lying at his feet and says, "We hang cattle thieves in these parts."

Warren spits tobacco juice not far from William's boots. "Not if dere ain't no one ta tell."

"What's that supposed to mean?"

Samuel warns his father. "Pa, he ain't right in the head!"

William turns to his son. "Let me take care of this."

The boy's eyes light up when he looks past his father and sees Warren pull a gun from the back of his pants. Samuel yells out. "Pa, he unshucked his gun!" William pivots back to the smiling culprit.

Warren hisses, "So long... Pa." He slowly cocks his pistol, fires, and hits William in the arm. He recoils, recovers, and pulls the trigger of his gun, but the chamber is empty... click! The outlier chuckles and shoots William square in the chest. The boys' pa falls to the ground mortally wounded as Henry, still hidden in the bushes, grabs his head in disbelief.

Warren turns to Samuel and grins. "Give yer pa an empty gun. Ain't you proud?" With one last burst of energy, William manages to crawl forward and grab the trespasser's leg. He reacts by jumping back and shooting William Plummer twice in the back. "Death got a holt of ya now?" The boys' father lays motionless as Samuel turns away and Henry, still hidden behind the shrubs, lowers his head and begins to cry.

Seeing my father die that way tore a hole in my heart that has never healed. It wasn't until years later that I realized that the crushing sadness I felt, along with the guilt and anger, have made me the person I am today.

Warren signals his cohort. Alex reacts by sliding dirt back in the hole he dug earlier. Then he kicks the ground and makes his way over to the fire pit. He hesitates, grabs a red-hot branding iron from the fire, and heads back to Warren.

Samuel sees the branding iron and begins to flail wildly. Warren grabs him by the neck and shakes him until he stops moving. Samuel gathers himself and snarls. "You killed my father, you fucking asshole!"

Warren pockets his gun and grabs the iron from Alex. "Now dat ain't right. Yer ma teach ya that word? Hold still. Got me some meanness to get rid of. You's about to be claimed."

Alex takes a step forward. "Spivey. He's just a boy."

Warren points the iron at Alex and he steps back.

"Shut the hell up!... And don't be giving out my name!"

Henry watches from the trees as Warren tears open his brother's shirt and slowly places the smoldering metal on Samuel's lower neck. Samuel screams in pain as he smells his own flesh burning.

Still in the trees, Henry sinks to the ground, curls in a ball, and covers his ears. As he cradles himself, he rocks back and forth, sobbing uncontrollably.

Satisfied, Warren waves the branding iron, grits his teeth, and smiles, "How's that filthy mouth? Maybe, if I was ta burn ya every day of yer life, you'd be more respectful."

Warren hands the torture wand to Alex and points at Samuel's neck. "Now he's mine. Says so right there."

As Warren and Alex sit chewing meat cut from the dead cow, a large chunk of meat smolders above the fire. Alex pulls a knife, slices off a piece, and ambles over to Samuel, still tied to the tree. He holds the meat to the boy's mouth. "Chews a little stubborn, but it eats." Samuel reacts by turning his head and throwing up. Warren, who's been watching, spits in the fire and laughs.

Alex starts back to the firepit, but pauses a moment to shoo the flies away from William's dead body. Then he tosses the meat into the trees not far from where Henry is hiding. The boy hesitates, crawls over, picks up the meat, and starts to eat it.

Alex sits down next to Warren, who is picking at his teeth and touching his wounded forehead. The killer belches and grunts. "Time we cut the dust."

Alex leans forward and points at Samuel. "What about him?"

"He's coming with us."

"He ain't in no shape to ride."

"Put the little puke gut on his pa's horse. We're goin' now."

Warren stands, walks over to Plummer's body, and tears off a piece of the dead man's shirt. He wraps it around his wounded head and mounts his horse while Alex shoves dirt on the fire with his boot. Then he leads both his horse and William Plummer's horse over to Samuel, unties the ropes, and helps the grief-stricken boy on his pa's horse.

Warren and his young captive ride away from the campsite as Alex trails behind herding the two remaining cows. In the distance, William's body and the partially eaten cow lay side by side, flies covering their carcasses.

While Warren busies himself shooing flies away from the hunk of meat strung across the front of his saddle, Henry bursts out of the trees and runs towards Samuel and his captors. "Samuel!"

The cattle thieves turn back and spot Henry. Warren growls, "That little shit! Plug him!"

Alex fires twice, each shot meant to scare Henry.

"God damn it! Can't ya hit nothin'."

"I ain't got the balls ta kill no kid."

Warren grabs Alex's gun and prepares to shoot the boy, but Samuel yanks his boot from his stirrup and kicks him in the crotch. As Warren grimaces in pain, Henry stands frozen and finally stammers, "What…should I do!?"

"Forget me! Go!"

Henry hesitates and runs off. Warren recovers, tosses Alex's gun back to him and pulls his own gun. He cocks it and holds it to Samuel's head. "Damn you and your ways."

"Go ahead and shoot. I don't care."

Warren raps Samuel alongside the head with the heel of his pistol and waves at Alex. "The brother? Go end him." Warren smiles at a slumped-over Samuel and says, "I'll collect on you later. You ain't no good to me dead."

Alex turns in his saddle, "That boy...he ain't no danger."

Warren sputters. "Do as I say." Alex begrudgingly turns his horse and rides off. When he reaches a nearby grove of trees, he dismounts and advances on foot to the place where he thinks Henry might be hiding. When he pulls back a tree branch, he sees the nine-year-old crouched down behind a large juniper bush. Alex sneaks up behind him, cocks his gun, and Henry covers his head.

All of a sudden Warren and Samuel hear two gun-shots. Samuel quickly turns and stares in the direction the shots came from. "Henry! Oh, my God!" He bends over his father's saddle and begins to weep as Warren ties his hands together with a small rope.

The two kidnappers and their hostage head down a dirt road as the sun sets in the distant trees. Trailing close behind them with tethered ropes around their necks are the two stolen cows.

CHAPTER 3

Kidnap: "... to seize and detain or carry away by unlawful force or fraud ... " Merriam-Webster

IN A NARROW CLEARING surrounded by elm and pine trees, Warren is seated on a dead tree, cleaning the barrel of his pistol with a small sharpened stick. Not far from him sits Samuel, staring at the ground.

Warren lays his gun aside, removes his hat, and adjusts the bloody bandana covering his forehead. He looks over at Samuel and says, "Asshole brother done dis, ya know." Samuel stares at Warren but doesn't respond.

Not far away, Alex sticks the tip of his knife into the flesh of a rabbit roasting over an open fire as Warren turns and yells, "That fuckin' meat done yet?"

Alex responds in a muffled voice, just loud enough for Warren to hear. "Almost."

Warren pokes Samuel with his cleaning stick. "You's my boy now. Gonna raise ya like Alex over there. What ya think of dat?"

Samuel doesn't answer as he wipes a tear from his eye. Warren continues to badger him. "If'n I was you, I wouldn't fret myself over some kin ya ain't never seein' again, 'cept maybe in yer dreams. Your pa? He a good man?"

Samuel stares at the ground as the scoundrel drones on. "Folks figured my pa to be a proper man, but he was rotten to the core. Pretended he was a preacher. Had'em all fooled. Spoke clean words from the Bible, just so's he could get his hands in their pockets and frequent other men's women. See this?" Samuel doesn't look up, so Warren grabs the boy's chin and lifts his head. Warren points to a mass of scar tissue just below both his eye sockets. He chortles as he pulls Samuel closer to him. "My pa, he got drunk one night and come at me with quicklime. Said he was gonna clean my spirit. Claimed I was impure for lusting my eyes at some gal he favored. Almost blinded me fore I bashed his head in with a rock. People said it was a planned killin', so I lit out."

Warren digs both heels of his boots into the dirt and looks to the sky and cackles. "Ya up there, God? Go on ... strike me down. There's no sinner bigger than me." Warren laughs as he waits for Samuel to say something. When he doesn't respond, Warren keeps going. "No sense in religion. Don't add up. Jesus done all dat healing and what'd them fellers do to him? Strung him up like some bastard outlaw. Me, I'm outlawed for sure. Least when they hang me, my punishment's gonna fit all the sinning I done.... Got nothing to say? Ya look like five pounds of shit in a two-pound bag."

Warren laughs as Samuel looks up and says, "You're going straight to hell, mister."

Warren chuckles. "Okay by me. Most people I know are there already." Samuel gives Warren a sarcastic grin and Warren continues. "What? Ya think you're some kinda angel of God?"

Samuel sneers. "No, but at least I ain't no asshole."

Warren grabs his pistol and raises it to Samuel's head. "You and me's the same ... pa killers." He pushes the gun closer to Samuel's head and the boy responds by backing away and spitting in the intruder's face. As Warren wipes away the spit, he cocks his pistol. "Hell's only half full, boy. You itchin' to stake yer claim?"

Warren pulls the trigger ... click! The chamber is empty. Samuel covers his head and cries as Warren laughs. "Hmmh.

Guess I forgot ta load it; just like you with yer pa. Now stop being so pigheaded and have ya some grub."

Samuel doesn't move, so Warren stands and lowers his gun. He points at Alex, signaling him to bring Samuel some food. "Alex ain't that bright, but he beats talking ta nobody.... Yes sir, took that boy in like I done you. Now and again a man's gotta have someone to bitch and tell what to do."

Alex arrives carrying a piece of the cooked rabbit as Henry removes his oversized boots. Warren reacts. "What ya doin'? Yer feet are gonna get cold."

Samuel responds quickly. "Do I look like I give a shit?"

The miscreant glares at Samuel. "So ya know, run off and I'll chase ya down, cut ya in pieces, and leave ya for to the buzzards to fight over."

Warren walks off and Alex hands Samuel a piece of rabbit.

Samuel begrudgingly accepts it and hungrily takes a bite. Alex waits a moment and nods. "Been spouting his shit talk at you? You'll get used to it."

Samuel speaks with gritted teeth. "Don't wanna get used to it. Sides, you're no better than that bastard. You killed my brother."

Alex lowers his voice. "Just you hold on. Gonna give you an odd truth, but you can't tell that bastard what I'm about to say."

Alex waits for Samuel to make a promise. Samuel finally says, "Ain't tellin' that asshole nothin'."

"I didn't kill your brother."

"You're a liar. I heard the shots."

"I scared him off is all."

EARLIER THAT MORNING

Standing amongst the trees near the pasture, Alex is pointing his gun at Henry's head as the boy cowers. Alex grimaces and lifts his pistol and fires two shots in the air. Henry looks up, confused by what just happened. Alex puts his finger on Henry's chest. "Can ya count to five hundred?"

Henry hesitates and says, "Yes."

Alex continues. "When ya get to five hundred, head for home. Show your face before or after and I'll shoot ya dead." Alex mounts his horse and heads back to Warren and Samuel.

As I watched that man ride out of the trees, I wasn't sure what to do. So, I started to count: one, two, three…. When I got to two hundred, I stopped and ran out of the trees, but Samuel and the two villains who took him were gone.

Henry runs wildly through the elm and dogwood trees. Slowed by thick underbrush, he spots an opening ahead. He instantly exits the trees at a dead run, climbs to the top of a large rock, and looks down over the vast countryside.

In the distance almost out of sight, he spots Samuel and his two abductors just about to top a hill. Too far away for his brother to hear, Henry screams. "Samuel! I'm sorry!" Emotionally spent, Henry plops down, puts his head on his knees, and cries.

Alex finishes his story and Samuel says, "Why should I believe you?"

"Believe what ya want. I ain't no killer. That monster over there is though. His cornbread ain't done in the middle. Better eat up. May be our last meal for a while."

As Samuel starts to take another bite, he pauses. How long you two been ...?"

"Six years."

"If you ain't no killer, why you still with him?"

"Spivey had him a boy 'fore me. Three of us 'til Alex run off. Spivey hunted him down and gutted him like a fish. Not somethin' I'll forget."

"Wait. You were both named Alex?"

"I was Tom, but Spivey give me Alex's name after he killed him."

"He claims he took you in."

"Stole me like he stole you. We ain't nothin' but dirt on a plow to him. You wanna stay above ground, better do as he says. Fightin' it makes it worse."

"Fightin' what?"

Alex doesn't respond and starts back to the fire pit. He passes Warren, who is headed back to Samuel. Warren turns back and commands, "Stoke up some more coffee." When he reaches Samuel, he nods. "You and Alex have been talkin' 'bout me ain't ya?" Samuel doesn't respond, so he grabs his new boy's arm and yanks him to his feet. Samuel tries to break free, but the pain in his neck is too much.

The brute shoves bare-footed Samuel ahead of him as a covey of grouse flies out of the grass in front of them. Alex, who is busy making coffee, looks up and watches as Warren and his new boy enter the dark forest.

CHAPTER 4

"Many men go fishing all of their lives without knowing that it is not fish they are after." Henry David Thoreau

Ten Years Later

THE SEAPORT VILLAGE of Addison, Maine is skirted by large warehouses and wooden docks filled with cargo ships and fishing boats. Men load the boats and skiffs with supplies and repair nets, while others unload lobster, crab, and an assortment of fish.

Several miles out into the Gulf of Maine in rough waters is a seventy-foot fishing vessel. As the wind blows, the ancient craft sways back and forth. Water washes over its deck and hits its side, revealing the boat's name, *Molly Mae*.

Henry Plummer, now a smooth-faced and easy-to-look-at nineteen-year-old, looks uncomfortable in his fishing gear, especially his rubber boots that reach up to his kneecaps. Henry struggles as he helps two older seamen pull a net from the water. An unexpected wave crashes over the side of the boat and surprises Henry by soaking him from head to toe.

He loses his grip on the net and drops ass first to the deck, which garners several guffaws from the older seamen. Henry removes his water-soaked boots as the other men continue to pull in the net. Still seated on deck, he gazes up at the dark clouds in the sky, lost in his own thoughts.

I've always hated fish. Hate the way they smell, hate the way they taste, and hate the feel of their slimy skin.

One of the seamen yells out, "Hey, landlubber! Plummer!" Henry doesn't respond, so one of the seamen exchanges a look with his shipmate as if to say, "What the hell?"

The second seaman chimes in. "Ya gonna help out or not?"

Both men sneer as Henry slowly puts his boots back on. The second seaman rolls his eyes and says to his workmate, "Fucking worthless bull calf!"

Henry coughs deeply, gathers himself, stands up, and joins the two scoffers who are now pulling fish from the net. As he grabs a fish, he spots a soggy piece of paper caught in the net's webbing. He looks at it briefly, folds it up, and puts it inside his left boot.

Having finished emptying the net, the first-time seaman sits alone on a coiled rope as the older seamen disappear below deck. A slow-moving sea crab with large claws that has somehow avoided the net, crawls toward the reluctant fisherman.

Henry spots the crustacean and jumps to his feet. He grabs a pole and approaches the sea urchin. He places the end of the pole under the giant crab and flips it back into the ocean.

Unaware that the boat's captain has been watching him from the window of the ship's cabin above the deck, Henry sits back down on the coiled rope, wraps his arms around his chest, clenches his teeth, and begins to rock back and forth. "Fucking boat! Damn water! Damn you, Pa . . .Samuel."

A few minutes later, below the ship's deck, Henry struggles to keep pace with the other seamen as they toss mackerel, cod, herring, and a variety of other fish in barrels. Although a handkerchief covers his face, it is obvious that the stench of the fish bothers him. Finally, he can't take it anymore, so he covers his mouth, rushes to the ladder, and climbs up to the boat's deck. When he reaches the railing, he throws up, coughs deeply, holds his chest, and sinks to the floor of the boat.

The fishing vessel rocks steadily as the captain, who is on the poop deck, looks through a telescope at the open water. When he lowers his scope, he sees Henry sitting with his back against the rail. The skipper rapidly descends a small ladder, walks over to him, and slaps the young man on the back. "You, okay? You look a little green around the gills."

"Sorry, sir. I just need a moment."

The captain grins as he looks down at him. "Your mother convinced me to take you on ... strong woman."

"Yeah, she is."

Henry tries to stand, but he starts to wobble, so the captain puts his hand on Henry's shoulder and gently pushes him back down. "Truth is, some men are at home on the water. You ... not so much."

Henry thinks about what the captain just said. "I'll get used to it, just like my pa did."

"Your father was a damn fine boatman, but you ain't him."

"Just give me a little more time."

"Admit it. This has been the worst two weeks of your life."

They lock eyes and Henry begs, "I need this job, sir."

"What ya need is to find work on solid ground."

Henry coughs deeply, so the captain pats him on the back. He walks away as Henry lowers his head in disgrace. The captain turns back. "This sea air ain't doin' ya no good either. This is your last ride. It's for your own good."

Four seamen stand on the deck of the *Molly Mae* looking out into the ocean. Two of the men thrust their poles into the water, trying to snag a dead body floating near the boat.

The captain watches as the men hook the corpse and pull it face down out of the water and onto the deck. The dead man is wearing fishing gear similar to that of the other seamen. The captain kneels down and pokes the bloated body as the other men hold their noses.

One of the men appraises the situation. "Looks pretty ripe."

A second man says, "Boots probably filled and sucked him under." Another man grabs the shirt of the dead man and rolls him over. Everyone jumps back as small crabs scurry out of Henry's nose and ears.

Another seaman shakes his head in disgust. "Looks like the Plummer kid who fell overboard last month." Barely recognizable, Henry's face is fish belly white and disfigured.

In a small bedroom, a visibly shaken Henry sits straight up in bed and looks around, trying to recoup from his "death by drowning" dream. He moves to the edge of his bed and looks down at his rubber fishing boots. With his bare foot, he kicks one of the boots across the room. The piece of paper he found earlier in the fishing net is now laying on the floor, so he leans over and picks it up. The banner at the top of the page reads, "Men Rush to California in Search of Gold." He studies the flyer carefully, folds it back up, and puts it in his pocket.

He reaches beneath the mattress of his bed, pulls out his father's old colt action revolver, rotates the gun's cylinder, and points the weapon at the window.

Behind the Plummer family's dilapidated farmhouse stands Henry, who is loading the pistol. Still in his bare feet, he stares at his father's rubber boots that he placed on two of the wooden fence posts that line the back of the property. He cocks the gun, takes aim, and shoots the first boot off of the post. He cocks the gun again, turns his back to the second post, spins around, and fires again. The second boot doesn't move.

Elizabeth Plummer, a slender and weathered woman in her mid-forties, has been watching from the back door of the house. She frowns as she walks over and picks up one of the targeted boots. "These are your pa's fishing boots. What in heaven's name are you doing?"

"What's it look like? I'm shooting holes in them."

"Don't smart talk me. What ya gonna wear when the *Molly Mae* goes out again?"

"Captain gave me the mitten."

"What? Why?"

"Says I ain't got what it takes. Sides, it's nothin' to you what I do."

"Nothin'? What are you talking about? I count on you. You know I just sold the last of our land and cattle. All we got left is this run-down house."

"Bobbing on that water makes me sick ... and those stinking fish. I'm meant to be someplace else."

"Henry, it's just you and me."

Elizabeth starts to cry, so Henry puts his arm around his mother's waist. He takes the flyer out of his pocket and hands it to her. "Take a look."

She takes the flyer and starts to read it. "What is this?"

"Found it floating in the water."

"Why California?"

"'Cuz, Samuel's gonna be where the gold is. And when I find him, we're gonna bring home a shitload of it."

"You watch your language, young man."

"Shit is shit, Ma."

"Your brother's dead or he'd be home by now."

"He ain't dead."

"And how do you know that?"

"The clouds told me."

"Wait. The clouds told you?"

"Yeah, sometimes, they kinda speak to me."

Elizabeth chuckles. "Do you talk back to them?"

Henry grabs the flyer out of his mother's hand. "You wouldn't understand. Sides, I think Samuel sent me this."

She takes a moment. "Samuel sent it ... to you?"

"Why else would it be out in the middle of the water for me to find?"

"Maybe 'cuz someone threw it there. I'm starting to worry about you, son."

"Well, don't."

"It's been ten years. What are the chances?"

"Don't care. Need to look for him. I owe him ... and I owe Pa."

"Not your fault those men killed your father and stole Samuel."

"Ma, you don't know what I know."

"And what is it you know?"

He doesn't answer, so his mother continues. "I don't wanna lose another son."

Henry looks deep into his mother's eyes. "I'm gonna bring him home, so we can be a family again."

Elizabeth stares at her son and her heart melts. "Let me see that again." Henry hands her the flyer and she looks it over a little more carefully this time. As she hands it back to him, she says, "California's a long way. You'll starve or some bear will eat you."

"We'll be home 'fore ya know it. They say finding gold there is like licking butter off a knife."

"Well, right now you ain't got money enough to get a mile down the road."

"Captain found me a job on *The Illinois* out of New York City. Gonna handle mail and other chores. I'm leaving in the morning."

"Another secret. I thought you hated the water?"

"Just have to put up with it one more time. It's my only way to get there." Elizabeth's face suggests she has resigned herself to the fact that her son is going to leave. "You'll be all right, Ma."

Henry's mother offers her hand and he starts to take it, but she points to the gun, so he hands it to her. Elizabeth turns her back to the post, spins, and fires twice. Her first shot knocks the boot off the post and the second one hits it in midair. She blows the smoke from the barrel, tosses Henry the gun, and walks off.

As she leaves, she says, "Keep practicing while I go cook up yer last meal."

Henry's eyes light up. "Chicken and dumplings?"

"Dumplings and vegetables. Dead chickens don't lay eggs."

CHAPTER 5

"Go west, young man, and grow up with the country."
Horace Greeley

AS THE CARGO SHIP, *The Illinois*, makes its way through the rough waters of the Atlantic Ocean headed for Panama, Henry stands on the ship's deck, looking into the distance.

All at once, he leans over the railing, throws up his latest meal, and coughs deeply. He recovers, reaches in his boot, removes the flyer with the California gold story headline, and starts to read. As he refolds the handbill, the wind blows it out of his hand and it falls into the ocean below. He watches it float away, looks up at the clouds, and envisions his future.

In the ship's mailroom, Henry and Jack Cleveland move bags of mail from one side of the room to the other. Jack, who is in his early thirties, looks a lot older. He's burly, his red hair is thinning, and his face is unshaven. When he smiles, his entire face lights up; when he speaks, his voice is loud and his laughter is irritating.

Both men work quickly and with enthusiasm. Finally, they finish moving the last of the bags and simultaneously drop to the floor. As they wipe the sweat from their brows and rest their backs against the mail bags, Jack turns and studies Henry's pale face. He chuckles and says, "Ain't looking so good there, partner. Been eating them shit sardines the cook's been handing out, ain't ya…. the ones covered in red gravy?" Henry starts to gag, so Jack scoots away.

Henry gasps, "Not funny, Jack. I'm 'bout ready to blow my groceries."

As Henry recovers, Jack reaches over, opens a leather bag, and pulls out a ball of yarn and two knitting needles. Meanwhile, Henry removes his boots, takes a journal and pencil from the back of his pants, and begins to write.

Well, I'm on the water again. The worst part about being sea sick for me is that moment just before I throw up. Seems like I spend most of my free time leaning over the railing at the stern of the ship waiting to hurl my breakfast. Thank God this ship isn't as wobbly as a fishing boat or they'd have already buried me at sea by now.

Jack who is knitting what appears to be a scarf, nods at Henry and asks, "What ya got there, some kinda book?"

"Called a journal. Been writing in one since I was a boy."

Henry eyes Jack. "Been meaning to ask. Where'd ya pick up that habit?"

"My grandma, 'fore she passed. Calms my nerves. Wanna give it a try? It ain't that hard."

Jack offers his handy work to Henry, but he waves him off. "Nah, you go ahead."

Henry goes back to writing in his journal, but Jack's curiosity gets the best of him. "What ya tellin' about?

Henry looks up. "Just some random thoughts."

"Random.? That the name of some woman you met?"

"Random. You know, scattered ideas."

The Illinois sways, so Henry lays his journal down. The boat continues to rock and he starts to gag again. Jack grins. "Think on something cheerful, 'bout them nuggets we'll be finding, big as bull's balls." Henry sits up and gathers himself. The boat rocks even more violently, so he grabs his mouth as Jack cowers away again. "Don't send none of that sailor gravy my way."

Jack sees a letter sticking out of one of the mail bags, so he lays his knitting down and grabs it. Henry furrows his eyebrows. "What are you doing?"

Jack hands him the letter, picks up his knitting and begins to knit again. "Read it."

"None of my business. Read it yourself?"

"Don't know how."

"You never learned to read?"

"My pa had me plowing behind a mule's ass soon as I could walk."

Henry grins and says, "Guess it's true what they say."

"How's that?

"All work and no play makes Jack a dull boy?"

Suddenly irritated, Jack points his knitting needle at Henry. "Fuck you, asshole!"

"Easy there, ace. Just something my mother used to say."

"Yer ma don't know me, so don't be calling me dull 'cuz I ain't no damn reader!

"Fair enough."

Jack nods, "Go on, now. Read me some secrets."

As Henry carefully opens the letter, he remarks, "Could get the boot for this, ya know?"

"Christ on a pony! Read the fucking letter!"

"All right! Holster your gun." Henry clears his throat and reads with enthusiasm:

George, the postman ain't brought mention of you for three years now and I sure haven't seen any of the gold you promised to send us. I'm guessing you're dead, hanged, or with another woman by now. I begged you not to ride off, but I don't much care anymore. By and by, I've taken up with Joe Hanson. He takes care of me and looks out for Sally and little George too.

Didn't want people thinking me a whore, so I married him when I found out I was carrying his child. People started asking about me being married to two men, so I got me a lawyer and laid claim you was dead. Probably won't get this letter, so I guess it don't matter how much I account for things. But if it does find you, just know I waited long as I could. Your used-to-be wife, Lisa.

Jack gives Henry a serious look, "Lisa's what they call a gold widow."

Henry grins. "She didn't stay a widow very long."

"You're right." Jack grabs the letter, strikes a match to it, and tosses it to the floor. Henry stomps the letter out as Jack resumes his knitting.

Henry reacts. "What the hell?"

Jack explains. "Lisa whoring around on George like that. He don't need to hear none of that shit."

Henry shakes his head. "There's things in that letter he might've wanted to know."

"Gold's the only gratification George needs."

"Gratification. That's a big word."

"Gal back home give it to me after I pleasured her. Hey, how much gold ya figure we'll be findin'?"

"I'm hoping enough so Samuel and me will need to buy us a mule to get it all home."

"Really think you're gonna stumble on that brother of yers?"

"Be looking for him more than any gold."

"Likely in a bone orchard by now."

Henry turns away. "No, he's alive and I'm gonna find him!"

"California's got a lot of places."

Henry is suddenly pissed. "Always got to have the last word, don't you?" Jack shrugs and there's a moment of silence. Then he says, "Don't give me yer shit 'cuz I ain't got some brother to find."

From the very beginning, my friendship with Jack Cleveland was sharp-edged. There were times when I wished I'd never met the man and other times when I was glad he was around, even it was just so he could irritate me.

Down in the ship's boiler room, Henry, Jack, and a leather-skinned elderly black man shovel coal into the large furnace that powers the ship. The three men are covered with coal dust and Henry is barefooted again. The men finish up, plop down on a pile of coal, and Henry pulls a rag from his pocket and wipes his brow. He grins, "Heard this was one hell of a job, but never figured I'd actually have to work there."

The black man chuckles as Henry looks at Jack for a response. Hearing no reaction, he says, "We still not talking?"

Jack growls, "You wanted the last word."

Henry playfully shoves Jack. "Come on, you know I'm thin-skinned when it comes to thinking 'bout my brother bein' dead."

Henry offers his hand. Jack waits a moment, finally shakes it, and says, "I ain't one to hold a grudge."

The old man chuckles to himself and reaches over and compares his dark-skinned hand to Jack and Henry's hands. "Keep shovelin' this here coal and we's gonna be kinfolk."

The men laugh, but Henry's laugh turns to a cough as he grabs his chest. Jack slaps him on the back and says, "Ya gonna live?"

Henry nods. "Yeah, I'm good."

The black man looks down at Henry's feet. "I's curious. Why ya wear yer feet naked?"

"Cuz I like feeling what's under me…and it brings me luck."

"I hear ya. That, young sir, is what I call a fine answer."

CHAPTER 6

"Gold is worshipped in all climates, without a single temple, and by all classes, without a single hypocrite."
Charles Caleb Colton

IN THE DISTANCE are the snow-capped Sierra Nevada Mountains of northern California. A seasoned old driver guides two oxen pulling a covered wagon down a tree-lined dirt road. Two horses trail behind, tied to the back of the wagon. In the wagon bed, Henry and Jack are seated on two mailbags, half asleep.

All at once, the prairie schooner rocks from side to side. Henry grabs the mail sack beneath him, hangs on for dear life, and blurts out. "Here we go again." Jack chuckles, pulls out a flask of whiskey, and takes a drink. He offers it to his workmate, but Henry waves him off. "Tried that shit once. Tastes like kerosene smells."

"Ya don't drink it for da taste."

As they continue to rest against the bags, Jack notices Henry's pale face and the angst in his eyes as he continues to clutch the bag. "Hug that thing any tighter and you'll have to marry it."

Henry takes a moment and says, "This wagon's worse than a boat." He slides off the bag he's been sitting on and a letter falls out. Jack picks it up, looks it over, and hands it to Henry, who shakes his head. "Hell no. I'm not doing that again."

Jack tosses the letter aside and lights a cigarette. "Can't wait to get to all that gold. How much longer you figure?"

Henry holds up three fingers. "Three, maybe four days."

The driver opens a canvas flap and stares back at his co-workers. "What's burning back there?"

Henry points at Jack. "He smokes when he talks about gold. Well, not Jack himself."

The driver spots the cigarette hanging out of Jack's mouth. "Put it out, for ya burn down my wagon." The flap closes and Henry and Jack laugh.

The sun is setting as the old driver stands next to his wagon gnawing on a rabbit leg. Not far away, Henry aims at a handbill attached to a nearby tree. He fires away, missing his target three times, so Jack walks over and grabs the gun. He looks it over and hands it back. "Forget the handbill. Hit the tree."

Henry fires three more times, hitting the flyer with his last shot. Jack rolls his eyes and shuffles to the wagon, while Henry walks to the tree. He holds up the poster and admires his marksmanship.

With two small mail bags perched on the front of their saddles, the gold seekers ride away from the mail wagon. Not far back, the old wagon driver yells, "Nevada City better be gettin' that mail! Don't you shitheads be tossin' it!"

Jack gives a half-hearted wave and hollers back. "I can see yellow rocks from here!"

The old driver whistles at his oxen. "Them boys ain't gonna find nothin' but dirt."

With the mail wagon in their wake, Henry and Jack ride into the wind as the snow begins to fall. Jack turns to Henry. "How far you figure to Nevada City?"

Henry spits snow. "I think the old man said ten miles."

Jack responds. "He was probably lying."

"Probably."

"You feeling lucky?"

"Just hope Samuel's where I'll be looking. Finding gold be a bonus." Henry digs his heels into the flanks of his horse and gallops off, challenging Jack to catch up.

CHAPTER 7

"I became insane, with long intervals of horrible sanity."
Edgar Allan Poe

OREGON TERRITORY

AS THEIR HORSES TRUDGE through the deep snow, Warren, Alex, and Samuel hunker down in their saddles trying to defeat the cold wind. Despite the large snowflakes that cover their faces, it's easy to see that the ten years have not been good to the two older men. Samuel, however, looks devilishly handsome, despite his scraggly beard and long hair that touches the shoulders of his leather fringed shirt.

Not far ahead, Warren notices smoke billowing from the chimney of a log cabin. He steers his horse in the direction of the small lodge and Alex and Samuel follow suit.

Alex and Samuel sit on their horses outside the cabin and watch as the front door flies open and two barefooted men wearing nothing but long underwear and cowboy hats hobble out.

A moment later, Warren exits the log hut with his gun drawn and hobbles after the property owners. He fires two shots and grins gleefully as the terrified men slog their way through the deep snow and into the trees.

As Warren makes his way back, he notices Alex and Samuel staring at him, so he points his gun at the cabin. "What? Got us a warm place, didn't I?"

The younger men climb off their horses and tie them to a fence post. After they go inside, they kneel in front of the fireplace, and warm themselves as Warren plops down at a misshapen oblong table and chuckles. "Run off like they was scared sheep."

Alex looks up. "Won't get far dressed like that."

Warren grins. "The Lord giveth and Spivey taketh away. Fire up some grub, whilst I look for more takeaways."

Alex argues. "Ain't nothin' here worth eatin'." Warren ignores him and starts to search the cabin as Samuel and Alex look for food.

The three trespassers sit around the table taking turns scooping beans from a mining pan with their large cutting knives. Warren pushes his plate aside and growls, "This all ya could find? Getting fuckin' tired all the time tightening my belt."

Alex sasses back. "Spivey, you chose this place."

Samuel tries to ease the tension. "Found a ripe squirrel. Could cook it up and take our chances."

Warren shakes his head. "Shit! Why's it what I want, I ain't got and what I got, I don't want?"

Alex spits on the floor and says, "'Cuz we got no plan. Been riding for days, looking for nothin'."

Warren wipes his mouth with his sleeve. "Shut the fuck up! You don't know shit."

Warren turns to Samuel. "Go feed the horses. Give'em somethin' better than we got."

Samuel escapes the cabin as Warren turns to Alex. "Real tired of your sassy mouth. Why ya thinkin' yer so smart lately?"

"'Cuz, I got thoughts of my own."

"Best keep them thoughts to yerself. Ya forgettin' who took you in?"

"Ya stole me, you asshole."

"Your folks didn't want ya."

"So you say."

Warren grinds his teeth. "Your pa promised me a three-legged hog and your ma offered to whore herself and throw in a half jug of whiskey if I'd take you off."

"That's a nailed to a tree lie!"

"Yer folks was full of sin and you know it."

"Didn't have to kill them for bein' who they was."

"I burnt down their fuckin' house."

"And they was in it."

"Stop crying. Ya got all ya need with me."

"You don't know what I need."

As Warren warms his hands at the fireplace, he says, "What put a burr under your saddle?"

"Spivey, it's time for a change."

Warren spits into the fire and turns to Alex. "You got your change when Samuel come along."

"That's not what I'm talking about."

"Then what?"

"Way I figure, I should have a say on how things go. Been riding with my mouth shut too long."

Warren growls, "Well, ya figured wrong. If I tell ya to eat shit, you'd better find you a big spoon."

The door opens and Samuel enters the cabin. He brushes the snow off his coat and stomps his boots. When he looks up, he sees Warren and Alex staring daggers at one another. He speaks anyway. "Horses fed. Found some hay hiding under the snow."

Warren turns to Samuel. "Okay. We're heading for Dillon first thing in the morning. Got them a bank. Be easy pickings."

Alex steps forward. "Last bank we robbed, ya almost blew my head off."

Warren chortles. "Lucky I didn't."

Alex says, "We split the take three ways this time."

"Damn you and your ways! I ain't sharing equal with no boys!"

Alex continues, "We ain't boys no more!"

Warren pulls a gun and grabs Alex's shirt and tears it open, revealing a scarred brand on his lower neck. He puts the gun's barrel on Alex's scar. "Ya forgetting this?" Warren points his gun at Samuel as Alex backs away. "Now you! Show me!" Samuel hesitates, pulls down the collar of his shirt, and reveals the brand on his lower neck. Warren fumes, "The day ya ain't my boys is the day ya ain't!"

Samuel tries to change the subject. "When we rob the bank, who does what?"

Warren points his gun at Samuel. "What? Got another rooster in the hen house?"

Alex interrupts. "We just want us a plan is all."

Warren scoops the rest of the beans in his mouth and mumbles, "Best plan is no plan at all."

Warren, Alex and Samuel ride down a snow-packed road headed for Dillon. Just off the trail, they see the frozen corpses of the two displaced cabin owners sitting under a large pine tree. The men are covered with frost and their arms are wrapped around one another in a final embrace against the cold.

Alex and Samuel grimace as they watch a large black bird land on the head of one of the men and begin to peck at his frozen face. Warren pays no attention as he looks straight ahead.

Sitting high in their saddles outside of Dillon, the would-be bank robbers plod their way through the heavy snow that covers the ground and blankets the evergreen trees around them. Warren slows to a stop. Alex and Samuel join him and look at him as if to say, "Now what?"

Warren explains. "We ride in all quiet like. Samuel, you mind the horses while me and Alex empty the bank." Alex glares at Warren, looking for more information. Warren scoffs, "What? We ride off."

Alex snorts. "That's no smarter than a carrot."

"That's all I got, shit face. Ain't nothin' better."

Samuel speaks with soft enthusiasm. "How'd it be if I ride in and look the bank over. Ya know, tell them I wanna put aside some money. Make them show me where they're gonna keep it. Be less trouble if we know what we're up against."

Warren stares at Samuel as Alex nods in agreement and says, "Looking the bank over is a good idea."

"Shut the fuck up!" Warren thinks a moment and turns back to Samuel. "All right. Scout it out. Come back and tell us yer findings, while me and this asshole wait here for you."

Samuel tries again. "What about me helpin' with the robbin' part this time?"

"Not now. Your time will come."

Alex says, "We're all gettin' the same share, right?"

"You can wish in one hand and shit in the other for all I care."

Not giving up, Alex spits and says, "Just want what's mine."

Warren points at Samuel. "Go! Work the plan and get the hell back here. Me and Alex got us a discussion to have." Alex starts to pick at his clothes as Samuel rides off.

Still within earshot, Samuel hears his partners arguing. A few seconds pass and he hears Warren scream, "You're gonna get what I give you ... after all I done for you!"

Alex yells back, "You got a shit memory!"

Just as Samuel enters Dillon, he hears two distant gunshots. He turns in his saddle and looks back. Seeing nothing, he continues his ride into town.

Samuel ties his horse to a hitching post, looks around, and enters the bank. He hesitates a moment when he sees a thirty-something mother and her dim-witted teenage daughter standing at the counter. In front of them is a middle-aged bank manager, Buxton Bailey.

The daughter turns and grins at Samuel as her mother hands the banker some money. She notices her daughter eyeing the young stranger, so she grabs her by the arm and pulls her close to her side. The mother gives Samuel a dirty look, steps up to the counter, and hands the banker a bag of money. "That there is two years of savings, Mr. Bailey. Counting on you to take good care of it."

Buxton smiles as he counts her money. "Nothing safer than this here bank, Ma'am." The banker pulls a key from his pocket, unlocks the drawer behind the counter, and places the money inside it. As the mother and daughter turn to leave, the door closes in front of them. A look of disappointment crosses the daughter's face when she realizes the handsome young man is gone. Her mother sees her daughter's change of expression and thumps her on the head.

Samuel sees Warren sitting on his horse under a pine tree, holding the reins of Alex's horse. He looks around as his shoulders sag. "Where's Alex?"

"He run off. Ain't with us no more."

"That's his horse.

"Don't need it where he's goin'."

"Say where he was headed?"

Warren chuckles. "One place or another." Samuel studies Warren and notices that he has an extra pistol wedged in his belt and that his hands and clothes are dirty. Warren grins at Samuel. "My old man used to say, 'Dance with the devil and ya get burned.'"

"That's funny, my pa always said, 'The devil loves secrets.'"

Warren grins sarcastically. "The devil and me share a lot of secrets." He starts to ride off with Alex's horse in tow. Samuel wipes a tear from his eye and stays put until Warren looks back. "Come on. You wanted to rob a bank. Now's your chance." Samuel considers his options, slows his horse, and joins Warren. As they ride toward Dillon, Warren turns to Samuel. "Got you a new name. Alex Slade. Call all my boys that."

Samuel looks away. "Call me whatever you want, but I ain't your boy no more."

Warren grunts. "What's that supposed to mean?"

Still not turning back, Samuel matter-of-factly says, "You know what it means."

Warren and the new Alex Slade ride into town pulling the old Alex's horse behind them. A stagecoach passes them headed in the opposite direction. The driver, who is wearing a long buffalo robe coat, waves as Warren and Samuel turn away.

Dillon's main street is empty, except for an older couple who are heading home through the snow. When the thieves reach the Dillon bank, Alex ties their three horses to the hitching post as Warren surveys the town. Seeing no one, they put bags on their heads and walk inside.

Buxton Bailey looks up, realizes his place is about to be robbed, and puts his hands in the air. Warren points his gun at the banker and growls. "On the floor, pie eater. Face down."

Buxton does as he's told. While Warren looks out the window, Alex grabs the keys out of the banker's pocket. He jumps over the counter, locates the money drawer, and pulls it open.

Alex's voice quivers. "Nothing. Just a few coins." He rifles through the other drawers, but he doesn't find anything of value. Warren leaves the window, walks over to the banker, and puts a gun to his head. "Where's the fucking money?"

"All I had just rode off for Sacramento."

"In that coach we just passed?"

"There wasn't that much. Been a slow week."

"Gonna be even slower if ya don't fork over some cash."

Warren cocks his gun, so the banker pulls a few bills out of his pocket and lays them on the floor. "Tomorrow's start-up money. It's all I got."

Warren grabs the money and counts it. "Ain't enough here to start a fire."

Alex says, "Can't squeeze blood out of a turnip."

Suddenly angry, Warren shoots Buxton in the leg and the banker screams. "This turnip's got plenty of blood." Then he clubs Buxton on the head and the man goes limp.

As Warren and the new Alex exit the bank, they check the street for bystanders. Seeing no one, they remove the bags from their heads and mount their horses. As they ride off, pulling the third horse behind them, Warren signals Alex and they pick up the pace.

When they reach the edge of town, they look back and see Buxton sitting on the steps of the bank holding his head and talking to the Dillon sheriff, Hewitt Feger, and three local men.

Alex turns to Warren with a concerned look on his face and says, "Shit." They both dig their heels in their horses' ribs and ride off at a full gallop. Warren has trouble hanging on to the third horse, so he lets go.

A mile out of town, Warren's horse steps in a gopher hole and comes up lame. Warren climbs off his horse as Alex circles back to check on him. Spivey assesses the situation, draws his gun, and motions to Alex. "Get off that fucking horse!" Alex does as he's told and the rogue mounts the horse and rides off, leaving his partner standing alone.

As Alex walks along, leading Warren's crippled horse, he turns back and sees four riders approaching at a fast gallop. Sheriff Feger and the three locals circle Alex and the bank robber raises his arms in the air. One of the men jumps from his horse and grabs Alex's gun. He stays behind with the young robber, while the other three men ride off in pursuit of Warren Spivey.

With guns drawn, the posse closes in on Warren Spivey. The brute realizes he has no chance and slows his horse to a stop. He spits on the ground, raises his arms halfway in the air, and gives the sheriff a defiant glare. "Why ya bothering me? On account of some fucking pocket money? Take it." Warren pulls the money from his shirt, tosses it to the wind, and spits on the ground. Two of the men chase the money.

The sheriff grinds his teeth. "Got my hanging rope right here. Either you shut the hell up or I'll hang your ass right now."

At the edge of town, the three-man posse with Warren in tow joins Alex and the fourth posse member. Alex, who is leading the lame horse, looks back at Warren and scowls.

CHAPTER 8

"Wanted—Young, Skinny, Wiry Fellows…not over eighteen.
Must be expert riders, willing to risk death daily.
Orphans preferred. Wages $25 per week.
Apply. Pony Express Stables, St. Joseph, Missouri."
1861 Vintage Poster.

NEVADA TERRITORY – 1859

IN THE DISTANCE, two men traveling in a two-horse-drawn wagon approach a modest log home, a large red barn, and a corral filled with a dozen buckskin, chestnut, and black bay-colored horses. A sign above the corral gate reads: "Buckland Station."

The homestead stands in stark contrast to the flat prairie that is dotted by bunch-grass, low sagebrush, greasewood Indian rice grass, and upland scrub. Pete Buckland, a stocky, leather-faced and middle-aged station manager, is inside his corral feeding his horses when he looks up and sees the wagon approaching.

Dressed in a black three-piece suit, a well-dressed man hands the reins to his assistant and climbs down from his wagon. He walks over to Pete and removes his hat. "Name's Alexander Majors. I'm out of Sacramento."

As Pete sizes up the visitor, he says, "Pete Buckland. What can I do for you?"

Alexander saunters over and leans on the top rail of the corral fence and studies Pete's horses. "Some fine-looking horses you got here."

The visitor puts his hat on again, walks back to Pete, and makes his pitch. "You see, we're starting up a new mail service. Calling ourselves the Pony Express. Be rushing mail from Sacramento to St. Joseph, Missouri in ten days or less. Sure could use your help, Mr. Buckland. Looking to have a station every twenty miles. Got a family?"

Pete leans back. "Yeah. They're in Carson City buying all manner of things I can't eat."

Alexander chuckles. "Well, the pay's a hundred dollars a month, so my riders can change mounts here. I supply the horses and you feed and water them ... horses and my men."

"How many horses would I be boardin'?"

"Six, maybe seven."

"Already got me a contract with the Overland Stage and Freight Company."

"Not a problem. All I'm asking is for you to expand your operation. And like I said, I'll provide the horses."

"Got Paiutes on the prowl. Yer riders will be up against it."

"All my boys know there's an element of danger. That's why I pay a fair wage. Brought a contract for you to sign if you're so inclined." Alexander hands the station manager a legal sized document. Pete removes a pair of bifocals from his pocket, puts them on, and begins to read.

A pale moon shines its light on the bars of the Dillon jailhouse. A few seconds later, a small circle of snow and dirt outside the jailhouse wall gives way. A tin dinner plate emerges, followed by Alex Slade's head. Alex uses the it to finish digging a larger opening and squeezes his way through the hole. Covered in dirt and snow, he uses the plate to make the hole even bigger. Finally, Warren's grimy head pops out, but his torso is too big to fit through the opening. Alex grabs his partner's arms and continues to pull until Warren is finally able to free himself. Alex grabs the plate, tosses it in the air and it sails away like a flying tortilla.

Morning comes and Sheriff Feger ambles into the lockup area with a tray of food. When he reaches Warren and Alex's cell, he looks inside and sees an escape hole with a huge pile of dirt next to it.

CHAPTER 9

"Blessed are the peacemakers, for they shall be called the children of God." Matthew 5:9

HENRY AND JACK ride down a snow-packed road with the outline of Nevada City in the distance. Both men have gained weight, but Henry is ruggedly handsome and sports a Van Dyke beard and mustache. Jack is unshaven, his clothes disheveled, and he looks a bit long in the tooth.

As they ride along, both men look back at Nevada City and shake their heads. Henry removes a badge from his chest pocket, looks it over, and says, "Longest two years of my life." He pauses and throws the badge as far as he can.

Jack speaks. "Can't get over them making you sheriff and me deputy."

"Well, we sure as hell weren't finding any gold."

"Steady pay 'til ya up and shot the wrong fella."

"He had it coming."

They ride silently, taking in the beauty around them until Jack speaks. "Striking it rich north of here, near some town called Bannack. I say we check it out."

Henry looks around. "Which way's north?"

"Gotta be here someplace." Jack turns his horse and heads in the direction he thinks is north. Henry laughs and follows after him. In the distance, they see tall pine trees, fields of yellow and red wildflowers, and the snow-capped Sierra Mountains.

A MONTH LATER

Jack sits on his haunches, leaning over a small mountain stream panning for gold when he hears several gunshots. He puts his pan down, scuttles through a grove of trees, and spots Henry in a wide-open meadow. He watches as Henry spins around and fires three times at a wanted poster attached to an evergreen tree fifty feet away. Henry walks over to the tree, checks the bullet holes in the poster, and smiles. He removes the poster and carefully puts it in his pocket as Jack joins him. "Ya know, I'm getting kind of good at this."

"Yeah. While I'm busting my ass lookin' for color, you're scaring off any chance we got at supper." He gives Jack a hangdog look and his partner continues. "What? We can't get rich shootin' trees."

"I've lost my fire. Let's move on."

"What? We just got here."

Henry's shoulders sag. "I'm getting tired of dipping my hands in cold water for a few flakes of gold. When the fish ain't biting, it's time to cut bait. Come on. Bannack can't be that far."

"Suppose you wanna go now?" Henry grins his answer and Jack shakes his head. "All right. Truth is, I'd kill a priest for a drink."

Henry chuckles. "Good. Let's find you a priest."

My desire to strike it rich diminished considerably as we rode from one mountain stream to another. I guess that's why gold's so valuable. It's so hard to come by that people either give up on it or kill each other trying to find it.

GRASSHOPPER CREEK

Six Colorado Pikes Peak miners are knee deep in a cold mountain stream. Up the creek a little further, one of the prospectors, a burly man with a long red beard, carefully sifts the sand in his pan from side to side. All at once, he stares down in disbelief when he spots a nugget of gold. He grabs it and holds it up to the sun. "Eureka! Got me a solid ass nugget-not no fuckin' flakes!"

The other miners gather round, hooting and hollering. One of them pats the lucky man on the back. "You son of a bitch!"

The burly miner says, "Ya mean rich son of a bitch!

The other miners pan furiously, looking for their share. Another miner yells, "Hey! Found me a big one!"

Still another one hollers, "Christ on a cross! Me too! Thank you, Jesus!"

BANNACK

Two feral dogs wander down Bannack's deserted main street as Ben Girard, terse of speech and hard boiled, sweeps the steps of the Saffron Saloon and Hotel. The dark-haired owner and operator of the establishment stops sweeping when he sees a tumbleweed rolling down the street past him. He looks in the distance and spots the six miners from Grasshopper Creek coming his way.

When the Pike's Peak miners reach the edge of town, they whoop and holler as they hurry their jackasses down Main Street.

Sweet Waters, a blond-haired barmaid, and former prostitute, joins Ben in front of the saloon. "What's all the fuss about, Ben?"

"Appears the Pike's Peakers are wantin' to celebrate."

The miners tie their jackasses to the saloon's hitching post as they continue to laugh and carry on. The red-bearded miner holds up his gold nugget for Ben and Sweet to see as the other men rush into the bar. He turns to Sweet and gives her a toothless smile. "Found us enough gold ta get us whiskeyed up for days. You and yer gals are gonna be awful busy rubbing and tugging. Yes sir, rubbing and tugging."

As the exuberant miner busts his way into the saloon, Ben taps Sweet on the shoulder and says, "We're gonna need a lot more whiskey."

Sweet frowns. "And a lot more whores."

Henry and Jack stand in a mountain stream, panning for gold. Their pants are rolled up around their knees and their boots are laying on the sand next to the creek. Henry carefully removes a few flakes of gold from his pan and puts them in a small leather bag as Jack grins and points to the flakes in his own pan. Henry reacts and starts to sift faster. Jack follows suit and the race is on.

Exhausted, they sit next to the stream putting on their boots as Henry begins to cough. Jack grabs a bottle of whiskey, takes a drink, and offers Henry some, but he waves him off and coughs again. Jack leans toward his friend and says, "You gonna live?"

He ignores the question and says, "Don't know why we stopped here. Could be in Bannack by now."

Jack holds up his bag filled with gold flakes and shakes it. "Don't complain. Least we got enough scratch ta get ourselves stewed."

Henry shakes his bag. "Spendin' mine on a real bed and a smooth face to talk to."

All at once, a bandit wearing a bag on his head walks out of the trees holding a gun. He speaks slowly as if he's not sure what he's going to say next. "Hand them bags over mister … and mister."

Henry looks the bandit over, notices his hand is shaking and whispers to Jack: "Sounds soft, like he's scared."

Jack whispers back. "So why we talking so soft?"

The bandit leans forward. "You fellers bad mouthing me?"

Henry hops up and takes a step toward the bandit. "Just telling my friend here that that there bag is hiding a whole lotta fear. Why don't you walk away 'fore that thing goes off?" Henry takes another step forward and the bandit steps back.

"Stay your ground, mister. I ain't afeared of nobody."

"You're bluffing. Bet you've never fired on a real man, have ya?" The bandit's hand starts to shake again.

Jack interjects. "Careful. Looks as nervous as a whore in church."

"I ain't no whore … ya chawbacon! Gimme them bags!" The bandit shakes his gun, so Henry opens his bag, dumps the contents on the ground, and grinds the gold flakes into the dirt with his bare foot.

The bandit whines. "Why ya go and do that, mister?"

"'Cuz I don't want ya chucking yer life away on account of a few flakes of gold."

The bandit raises his pistol, but before he can get off a shot, Henry draws his gun and shoots him in the foot.

Henry yells. "Stop foolin' around!"

The bandit screams in pain. "Ahh! Jesus! Ya shot me in the foot." The bandit hops around in pain and points his gun again.

Henry aims back. "Let up! Are you lookin' to die?"

The bandit points his gun again and Henry shoots his other foot. The robber screams. "Ahh!" Then he looks down at his boots and complains. "Pa's boots. He's gonna cut off my balls!"

Henry yells again, "Put the fucking gun down!" Frustrated, the robber takes dead aim, so Henry shoots him square in the chest. "Damn you!"

Jack shakes his head, leans over the bandit, and looks for any sign of life. "Deader than a can of corned beef."

"What was I supposed to do? He was aiming at my head."

Jack removes the bag from the bandit's head and Henry, visibly shaken, stares at the young boy's face.

Jack sizes up the situation. "You was right. He's just a kid."

Henry looks down at the boy. "Why'd you have to be so damn stupid?"

"Talk louder. He ain't hearing."

Henry drops to the ground, leans over, and vomits. Jack slaps Henry on the back. "Ya all right?"

Henry takes a moment. "No, I just killed someone."

"Probably won't be your last."

"He kept drawin' on me?"

"'Cuz he was a chuffing idiot. Let the dead be dead. Let's go."

"We can't just leave him lay here."

"I ain't digging no fuckin' hole."

Henry takes a moment. "We'll take him with us to Bannack."

"Ya sure? He's likely someone's kin."

"They deserve to know."

Jack starts to sift through the dirt containing Henry's gold and says, "If no one knows him, maybe we can claim his horse."

Henry looks down at the bandit one last time. "For a moment there, I thought he might be Samuel."

"Why? Is your brother a half-wit?"

"No, but he's left-handed."

CHAPTER 10

"Follow your own path and let people talk." Dante

HENRY AND JACK ride into Bannack. Trailing behind them is the bandit's horse with the young man's body draped over the saddle.

Ben Girard, who is sitting in front of the Saffron Saloon and Hotel, sees the two strangers and strides over and joins them in the middle of the street. Ben looks the newcomers over and then shuffles over to the dead man and lifts his head.

Jack nods. "He fell in love with our gold."

Ben nods back. "Dewey Gunderson. You shoot him?"

Henry responds. "He drew on me."

Jack tries to make light of it. "Sometimes you get. Sometimes you get got."

Henry softens as he asks, "His name's Dewey?"

"Abe Gunderson's boy. Fifteen. Got his gun?"

Jack pulls Dewey's gun from the back of his pants and hands it to Ben. The saloon owner looks it over, spins the revolver's cylinder, and matter-of-factly shows the strangers that it's not loaded. "No beans in the wheel."

Jack says what Henry's thinking. "What the hell?"

"Abe never let him go loaded. Dewey is ... was simple-headed, like his ma. Been sewing a lot of wild oats lately."

Henry steps back. "Big price to pay threatening us with an empty gun?"

Ben looks Henry and Jack over. "So, what's yer story?"

"Looking for some shine like everyone else. Name's Henry Plummer. This here's Jack Cleveland."

The three men shake hands as the saloon owner says, "Ben Girard. Plummer? You the kid sheriff what shot the Nevada City mayor in the foot?"

Henry smiles sheepishly and Ben laughs. "It's all right. I heard he had it coming."

"Yeah. I had my reasons."

Ben looks Dewey over again and notices his damaged feet. "Why'd you shoot his feet?"

Jack chuckles. "He tried slowin' him down. Didn't work."

"When you two rode in, I was hoping you was toting a Spivey or Slade."

Henry perks up. "Spivey?"

"Yeah, we think him and his partner are bushwhacking miners round here."

Henry continues. "Spivey and…?"

"Alex Slade."

"You know what they look like?"

"Always got bags on their heads, but Warren Spivey's a grizzly lookin' fella, and Slade's long-haired and a lot younger."

"If they're all the time hooded, how do you know what they look like?"

"'Cuz they was in the Dillon jail for robbing their bank. Busted out the next day."

Jack steps away. "Come on, Henry. I'm all dried out."

Ben lifts his hand. "Hold on. Town's wanting to hire a couple of lawmen with experience … somebody who can handle a gun. Respectable job … steady pay.

Jack smirks. "Thought you was the law."

"Nah, we run this town by committee. So, what do you say? You two wanna give it another try?"

Henry joins Jack and says, "Nah. Got our fill in Nevada City. We kind of like being on the other side of the law again."

"Well, this ain't no Nevada City, but I hear ya."

Henry grins. "Sides. I'd probably end up arresting Jack every other day."

"And me jailing Henry the other days."

Ben chuckles as Henry begins to cough. "Change your mind, let me know."

Henry starts to walk away but looks back. "If ya need any help hunting down Spivey and Slade, I'd be interested in that."

"Might take you up on it." Ben moves over to two curious townspeople who are checking out Dewey's body as Henry and Jack start to walk away again.

Suddenly, a two-horse-drawn wagon approaches, driven by the local undertaker. The gangly looking man is dressed in a dark suit and is wearing a long brimmed black hat. He climbs down from his death wagon and takes a look at Dewey Gunderson's body as Henry and Jack watch. He approaches and Henry steps back. "You kill Dewey… and so forth?" Henry doesn't respond, so the undertaker continues, "Only a matter of time. Ain't been right in the head lately. Obliged for the business ... and so forth." Henry and Jack notice that when the mysterious man says, "and so forth," he turns his head and talks to his shoulder.

Henry nods. "And you are ...?"

"Ezra Simpson. I bury the dead."

Jack chimes in. "Bone picker. Didn't take you long. You smell him or somethin'?"

"Saw you ride in ... and so forth."

Ezra empties Dewey's pockets and tries to hand Henry a few coins but Henry steps back. "What you doing?

"I share the pocket money with them that brings it."

Henry says, "Don't want none of his money in my pocket."

Jack steps forward, grabs the coins, and stuffs them in his pocket. "Don't bother my pockets any. I'm all about gratification."

When Ben finishes talking to the townsmen, he sees Ezra leading Dewey's horse away. He shouts at Ezra, "You know better. That horse is old man Gunderson's and the saddle too."

Ezra squints, ties the horse with Dewey's body still draped over it to his death wagon, and shuffles back to Ben. "Ben, this here horse is my fair pay for burying Dewey… and so forth."

Ben reacts. "You heard me, Ezra."

Ezra walks back over to Jack and holds out his hand. "Need them coins back."

"Hell no. I ain't givin' them back."

Henry removes two small bags of gold from his horse, hands Jack a bag, and keeps the other one for himself. He walks over to Ezra and points. "Give me your hand." Ezra reaches out a cupped hand and Henry pours several flakes of gold in it. "Bury him good … in a box."

Ezra walks off as Henry sides up to Jack, who frowns and says, "Ain't you somethin'."

Ben interrupts their moment. "You fellas got some tall savings, do ya?"

Jack grins. "Shit! Whiskey and women steal all mine. Pretty boy here sends most of his bacon home to his mama."

Henry coughs loudly and Ben reacts. "That don't sound good. Doc Robinson's just down the street."

Jack adds. "Been nagging him on it since we met."

Henry coughs again and Ben points down the street. "Go on. Don't be your own doctor."

Jack chuckles. "And if he can't help, maybe he'll put ya out of your misery." Henry and Jack slip away, their horses trailing behind.

A moment passes and Ezra rolls away with Dewey's dead body in his wagon, leaving Dewey's horse standing in the middle of the street. Ben shuffles over, takes the animal by the reins and leads him away.

I had put off seeing a doctor all of my life, because I knew he would tell me something I didn't wanna hear.

Inside a small office on Main Street, Dr. Carl Robinson, an older spectacled gentleman, examines Henry's chest with an oversized stethoscope. The doctor lays the scope down and gives Henry a look of concern. "You're what they call a lunger."

Henry looks nonplussed. "A what?"

Jack picks up the scope and looks it over. He puts his hand inside the bugle-shaped end of it. Irritated, Carl grabs the instrument as he responds to Henry's question. "Consumption. You have to give up anything that makes you breathe hard."

Jack chuckles. "No more chasin' long legged women."

The doctor continues. "A spurt of energy now and again is okay, but mining all day is no good. Need to find a softer job."

Jack eyes Henry, who wags his head "no" but Jack ignores him and says, "That man Girard offered us to be the law."

Henry eyeballs Jack. "You got a leaky mouth."

Carl grins. "Might not be so bad. Town's been pretty quiet lately. Smooth wages."

Jack agrees. "Better than any gold we ain't finding."

Henry coughs. "You forgetting Nevada City?"

Carl adds. "This isn't Nevada City."

"That Ben told him the same thing, but he's as stubborn as a mule in the shade."

Henry shrugs his shoulders. "Rather cough myself to death than get shot by some drunken fool."

Jack grumbles. "You'd rather die an inch at a time?"

"Have to agree with Jack here. A slow death is the worst."

As Henry buttons his shirt, "Ain't you two encouraging."

Dr. Robinson hands Henry a bottle and he looks it over. "It's laudanum. It'll lessen your cough."

Henry empties the rest of his gold dust in the doctor's open hand and the two men exit the office. Outside, Henry stops and gawks at a young man who happens to be walking past. "Hey." The young man turns back and Henry says, "What's your name?"

"Elton, Elton Frazier. Do I know you?"

"No, sorry."

Henry nods his apology as Jack shakes his head. Henry takes two steps forward, stops and looks up at the clouds. Jack loses his patience and yells. "Hey!" He waits until Henry turns his attention back to him and scolds him. "What the hell? Where you been?"

Henry ignores the question. "Okay, let's give it a try."

"What ... us being the law?"

Henry nods. "Not backtracking, are you?"

"No, but a few minutes ago you was dead against it."

Henry grins. "Let's chew on it a few days."

"Good. Give me a chance to break a few more laws. Curious. Why the change?"

"'Cuz, I wanna chase down that Spivey and Slade."

"Shit. Ya know them or something?"

"Maybe."

"Got a feeling them boys ain't gonna be easy pickings."

CHAPTER 11

"Never run a bluff with a six-gun." Bat Masterson

IN THE DISTANCE, shots are fired. Henry and Jack look down the street and see a tent with people gathered around it. When they reach the marque, they spot a banner that reads: "England's Greatest Marksman." Tethered to a stake nearby is a coal-black Appaloosa stallion with a white speckled rump. They turn their attention to a tall local man examining a target he just shot at several times. Next to him is England's "Greatest Marksman," dressed in a dark suit and sporting a black derby hat.

As the Brit smiles and prepares to shoot, he signals his assistant to put the target back up. Dressed in a bright red dress, the attractive woman circles the local man's shots with a marker, reattaches the target fifty feet away, and returns to her boss.

The Englishman aims with a deliberate flare and fires five times. Each bullet hits the bull's eye inside the local man's shots. The assistant retrieves the target, shows it to the local man, and he shakes his head and steps back.

Jack studies the Brit as he reloads. The assistant notices his interest, and slides over to him. She winks and addresses Jack with a soft British accent. "Ya look to be a fancy shooter, luv."

The crowd laughs as Jack's face turns red. Seeing his chance to show off, he says, "How much ya wantin'?"

"Five dollars, darling."

"Kinda steep. How's it work?"

The English marksman interjects with his own royal brogue. "Quite simple, Yank. Every shot you place inside my five, a dollar for you. Every bullet I put inside your best, a dollar for me."

Jack begrudgingly hands the assistant a five-dollar gold piece and prepares to shoot. He takes careful aim and fires five times. The assistant removes the target and shows it to Jack as Ben and Henry watch carefully. The assistant circles the five bullet holes and reattaches the target.

The English marksman steps up and fires five quick shots. His assistant retrieves the target and brings it to the front of the tent and shows Jack. All five of the marksman's shots are inside of Jack's bullet holes. Jack grinds his teeth. "Shit. No one shoots that good."

Henry steps to the front. "Give me a try."

Jack scoffs as he steps aside. "Save your money."

The assistant holds her hand out and Henry gives her his five-dollar gold piece. She smiles and says, "Thanks, Sweetie."

Henry readies to shoot as the crowd watches anxiously. He grins, lowers his weapon, and turns to the marksman. "Give me your gun."

The Brit's face tightens. "What? I'll do no such thing." Henry points his gun at the Englishman and he reluctantly hands him his pistol. Henry checks the gun over, aims, and fires four times.

The assistant reminds Henry. "One more, Sweetie."

"No. Bring me that target." She retrieves it and the crowd collectively sighs when they notice there isn't a single hole in it. "Ain't that something ... I was aimin' dead center."

Jack grins. "Not that easy, is it?

The Brit laughs nervously and shuffles his feet as Henry prepares to shoot. "My last shot." Instead of shooting at the target, he aims the pistol at the Englishman's head and fires. The Brit stumbles back, wipes gun powder off his face, and rubs his ears. Henry smiles as he appraises the situation. "Ain't this a daisy. Now you got me curious how you made those holes."

Henry walks to the target, removes it, revealing a thick wooden paneled door with several holes in it. Henry checks the door further and finds a small lever on the side. He pushes the lever down and the door opens. Inside the secret compartment is a dwarf sized man, who is hunkered down. The little man, who is holding a nail, smiles and hands it to Henry.

Henry examines the interior of the panel further and finds a peep hole and five small openings designed to allow the dwarf to punch holes in the target with the nail. Henry looks through the peep hole and pokes the nail through the five small openings as Jack pays a bystander a dollar for a flask of whiskey. Finally, Henry steps back and shouts. "Cheating folks out of their money is against the law, isn't it, Ben?"

The scam artist's voice quivers as he tries to defend himself. "I was assured this town had neither a constable nor gaming laws."

Ben growls. "So, you figured Bannack to be easy pickings?"

"That's not what I'm suggesting, mate."

"I'm not your fucking mate." Ben walks over to check out the secret cabinet as Henry makes his way to the Brit.

Henry sneers. "I've got a suggestion. Give back all the money you stole and get your asses out of our town."

The pretty assistant holds out the bag that contains all the money they fleeced from several local men and Jack grabs it. He removes two five-dollar gold pieces, tosses one to Henry, and pockets the other one. The other victims step forward and call out how much they lost and Jack hands out the rest of the money.

Henry turns to the crowd. "For ya go, we're gonna have us a fair contest. Me and the Brit." He turns to the Englishman. "Outshoot me and you and this gal ride off scot-free."

People voice their disapproval as the marksman considers Henry's offer and responds, "And if I lose?"

Henry points to the marksman's Appaloosa. "That fancy horse over there's mine."

"Nonsense. That animal's pedigree surpasses any money we've collected today."

Ben eyes the crowd. "Look around. These folks are ready to boil tar and pluck chickens … and we got no law to stop them."

The Brit glowers at Henry and then Ben. "What are the parameters of this so-called competition?"

Ben grins. "The parameters are whatever this young man says they are." The marksman considers his options and accepts Henry's offer with his eyes.

The Brit, his assistant, the dwarf, and several townspeople follow Henry to the outskirts of town. Jack lags behind, leading the "fancy" horse and drinking from his flask. Henry stops not far from a fence and turns to the Brit. "Your boots—put them on the posts."

"If you bloody well think I'm going to let you humiliate me by desecrating my own boots …"

Henry turns to Ben. "That tar I smell?"

The marksman reluctantly removes his boots as Jack hands the "fancy" horse's reins to a cow-eyed young girl in the crowd. "Watch him for me." The girl smiles and happily takes the reins.

Standing near the girl is a leather-faced sod buster, Abe Gunderson. Abe watches Henry carefully, but unlike everyone else in the crowd, he doesn't laugh when the dwarf puts his boss's boots on two fence posts.

Henry surveys the crowd, removes his own boots, and explains his rules. "Turn around. Swing back and fire six times. Most holes wins."

"This is ridiculous. My boots are made of the finest Devonshire leather."

"Don't worry. Have a feeling one of them will be just fine."

The Brit looks down at Henry's feet. "And why pray tell did you take off your boots?"

"Don't want these people thinkin' I have an unfair advantage do we?"

The Brit shakes his head in disgust, turns his back, and readies to fire as Henry points to the dwarf. The little man smiles and yells out, "One, two, three!" The English marksman slowly turns and fires six times.

Henry points at the dwarf again and he fetches the targeted boot from the post and hands it to Henry. He checks the boot for bullet holes but can't find any. "See there. Good as new. No holes."

Henry turns his back to the posts and winks at the dwarf, who yells out again. "One, two, three!" Henry whips around and fires six times. The small man retrieves the second boot and puts his finger through six holes. "Six! Six holes!"

People cheer as Henry slides over to the young girl, who has been watching his new "fancy" horse. "Like him, do you?" The blond-haired girl grins ear to ear and nods yes. "Well, he's all yours."

The girl's face lights up. "Really?"

As the lucky young girl leads the horse away, the irritated marksman struggles as he tries to put on his mangled boot. The dwarf tries to help him, but the Brit shoves him away.

Jack takes another drink of whiskey and watches as people surround Henry, pat him on the back, and thank him for getting their money back. Jack, now slightly tipsy, mumbles to himself, "Pretty boy."

Henry and Jack amble down Main Street, lost in conversation when Abe Gunderson steps in front of them clutching a double-barreled shotgun. "You're Henry Plummer."

"Yeah. I know who I am."

"You killed my boy, Dewey ..."

Henry tries to apologize with his eyes as Abe lifts his shotgun and aims it directly at Henry's chest. Abe continues. "... on account of some horse shit gold." Jack steps back as Henry stands frozen, his hand on his gun. Abe grumbles as he cocks his shotgun. "Ya got nothin' to say?"

"He drew on me ... three times."

"He wasn't loaded."

"How was I supposed to know that?"

Abe lowers his shotgun and his shoulders sag. "Go on. Shoot me like ya done him. End the Gunderson name."

Henry doesn't react, so Abe raises his shotgun again and puts the gun's barrel to his mouth. Henry panics. "Hold on! You don't wanna do that."

Tears fill Abe's eyes as he lowers his gun and wags his head. "Weren't much, but he was my boy. Grew him the best I could. Ya had no right." As Abe starts away, he drops to his knees and moans loudly. With sympathetic eyes, Henry and Jack watch as Abe takes a moment, struggles back to his feet and shuffles off.

Didn't wanna kill Abe Gunderson's son, but I did. I made a quick decision and shot Dewey dead. That choice is gonna haunt me for the rest of my life.

CHAPTER 12

"You always fall for the most unexpected person at the most unexpected time and sometimes for the most unexpected reason." Unknown

HENRY WALKS down Main Street, but he stops in his tracks when he sees an auburn-haired woman in a blue-checkered gingham dress unloading a wagon in front of Vedder's General Store. As Lucy Vedder struggles to lift a crate, Henry approaches the wagon and reaches out to help her. She turns back and glares at him, so he steps back. A woman in her early twenties, Lucy is easy on the eyes. However, the despondent look on her face suggests she hasn't smiled in weeks. She looks Henry over and says, "What are you doing?"

"Thought you might need a hand."

"Well ... I don't."

John Vedder, a balding man in his late forties, walks out of the store and approaches Lucy and Henry. "What's going on, here?"

Henry offers John his hand. "I was just trying to help out."

The angry store owner ignores his friendly gesture, grabs another crate from the wagon, and says, "She don't need yer fuckin' help."

"Well, okay then."

From the store steps, John turns back to Lucy. "Hurry up. Don't have all day." Lucy pulls a smaller box from the wagon and hustles off as Henry follows her with his eyes.

Lucy turns back and forces a smile. "Sorry. You meant well. Thank you."

He tips his hat. "Henry, Henry Plummer."

She gives him a half smile. "Lucy."

From inside the store, John yells, "Damn it, woman!" She rushes up the steps as Henry takes a moment and slips away.

Although I had just met her, I could tell Lucy was unhappy. Perhaps it was because her ill-mannered husband was an asshole or maybe she felt trapped in a marriage with no way to escape.

OREGON TERRITORY

Warren and Alex lead their horses through several pine trees lining the Smith brothers' mining camp. After they dismount their horses, they peer through the low-lying branches of a wide trunked tree. When they see Frank Smith and his younger brother Josh exit their makeshift log cabin carrying two bags-of-gold, Warren nods at Alex and they put bags over their heads.

Josh hops up into the wagon and Frank hands his brother his bag. Josh hides both of their savings under the wagon seat while Frank scans the area looking for anyone who might be watching.

From the trees, Warren raises his rifle and aims in the direction of the brothers. Alex reacts by gently putting his hand on the barrel of Warren's weapon and whispering, "You said, we're just gonna steal their gold." Warren shoves Alex away and aims his rifle again.

The brothers, now seated in their wagon, ready themselves to head to town as Frank says, "Did you hide it good? That's my future ya got there."

Josh sasses his older brother. "Mine too, ya fence post!"

Suddenly, a gunshot rings out and Frank slumps over dead. Josh checks his brother and discovers that the top of his skull has been blown off. "Frank! Oh, Jesus! Oh, God!"

Josh grabs the bags of gold from under the seat, but drops one on the ground as he leaps from the wagon. When he bends over to pick it up, a second bullet splinters the sideboard of the wagon. The lone brother stumbles back as the horses rear up and run off, the wagon trailing behind them.

As Josh hurries down a dirt path with a bag of gold in each hand, the gold seekers exit the trees. Warren pulls the sack off his head and puts it in his pocket. Then he raises his rifle and shoots the fleeing prospector in the leg. Josh drops one of the bags, but he's in too much pain to bend over, so he gives up and hobbles off.

Despite his girth, Warren plods after Josh, who is a short distance in front of him. Out of breath, Warren raises his rifle. All at once, he spots the bag of gold on the ground next to his boot. He lowers his weapon and picks it up.

Holding his leg, Josh limps into a grove of pines. He sees a dead tree, finds an opening, and shoves the remaining bag of gold inside it. Not far behind, Warren spots his victim as he's removing his hand from the hiding place.

As Josh hobbles away from the dead tree, Warren approaches. He finds the opening in the tree and hastily pokes his hand inside. As he gropes for the hidden treasure, he is besieged by a swarm of hornets who cover his arm and begin to sting him. "Ahh! Shit!" Despite the pain, he reaches back in the hole and removes the bag. When Alex arrives, Warren is shaking his hand wildly, in obvious pain.

As his partner sucks on his wounded hand, he grabs his rifle with his other one. He groans as he picks up the bags with his now swollen hand. Frustrated, the brute waves his rifle and Alex picks up the bags. "Don't spill none of that! And take that dumb ass bag off yer head." Alex removes the bag, puts it in his pocket, and the thieves resume their chase.

Not far ahead, Josh is sitting on the ground with his back up against a rock, holding his bleeding leg. Warren kicks Josh's bloody leg and the frightened miner screams. The gold thief points his rifle at the bag Josh is holding and snarls, "Might've run faster without them bags weighing ya down."

"Killed my brother on account of some damn fool gold? What kind of animals are you?"

Warren smiles. "Rich ones."

"Ya got what ya want. Leave me be."

Warren grins at Alex and turns back to Josh. "Dead dogs don't bark."

"Wait!" Before Josh can say another word, Warren shoots him in the head.

Alex's eyes widen. "What the hell? He was no threat."

"Check your pants for balls, boy."

Warren looks up at the sky, sees two large scavenger birds circling, and cackles. "Buzzards gonna get their fill today." He spits, leans over Josh's body, and fishes a watch from the dead miner's pocket. He looks it over and tosses it to Alex. "Don't do me no good."

Alex opens the watch and stares at a small photo of what appears to be Josh's wife. Pissed, Alex tosses the watch back to Warren. The rogue shrugs and buries it in his pocket.

Pulled by two weary horses, the wagon carrying Frank Smith's body enters Bannack. A bystander steadies the horses as people gather round. Hearing all the commotion, Ben exits the Saffron Saloon and walks across the street. He looks Frank's body over, shakes his head, and walks away. In the distance, Ezra Simpson, having spotted a business opportunity, climbs into his death wagon.

In the meeting room of the Saffron Saloon, Ben stands ready to address several men, including Henry, Jack, Ezra, and Abe. Three Colorado Pike's Peakers are also seated on a bench in the front of the room.

Ad-lib talk stops when Ben raps his gun on the table. "Listen up! I rode out to the Smith place this afternoon. Frank's younger brother got himself bushwhacked too. Tracks say two assassins."

The red-bearded Colorado Pike's Peaker speaks up. "Steal all their earnings?"

"No other reason for them being dead. Appreciate you Pike's Peakers joining us tonight."

A second miner adds, "Don't put up with gold killers where we come from. We hunt'em down and hang'em straight away."

Ben looks at Henry and Jack. "I hear ya, and until our town gets some lawmen, I'm declaring war on the bastards that killed the Smith brothers. Need a posse. Any takers?"

All the miners grumble amongst themselves as the red-bearded miner responds to Ben's question. "Mark Colorado down as a yes." Other men raise their hands affirming their commitment, including Henry, Jack, Ezra and Abe.

Ben stands up. "Fork your horses. We're goin' now."

CHAPTER 13

"Whenever men take the law into their own hands, the loser is the law. And when the law loses, freedom languishes."
Robert Kennedy

NORTH OF BANNACK near the Bitterroot Mountains, a posse of a dozen men, including, Ben, Henry, Jack, Abe, and three Colorado Pike's Peakers top a ridge.

Trailing behind in his death wagon is Ezra Simpson. The undertaker brings his horses to a halt and surveys the area below as two posse members holding torches light the way so the rest of the entourage can descend the ridge safely.

In the distance, Ben and his men see a man seated in front of a fire. Warren Spivey looks up, sees the approaching posse and reaches for his gun. He realizes he's outnumbered, so he leans back on his haunches and waits as the men circle him with rifles raised.

Henry's eyes narrow when he sees Spivey's face, but he remains silent. Warren starts to stand up, so Ben raises his rifle signaling the scoundrel to sit back down. "If ya wanna stay above snakes, sit yer ass down."

"I ain't done nothing for ya to crawl up on me like this."

"Where's your equal?"

"I don't know what the hell yer talkin' about?"

Ben persists. "Another set of tracks. Right there."

"They was here 'fore me."

"So ya say. Where ya headed?"

"No place special. Just lookin' for gold like most."

Ben gives Warren a sarcastic grin. "Find some did ya?"

Warren chuckles. "Enough to eat regular and ride an unfamiliar woman once in a while."

"Got a name?"

Warren spits on the ground. "Think I'll keep that dry for now."

Ben cocks his gun. "Wouldn't be Warren Spivey, would it?"

Warren spits in the fire, so Ben leans forward. "Couple pricks named Spivey and Slade been thieving around here. You fit the look of one of them."

"Them names ain't nobody to me."

"How 'bout Josh and Frank Smith? Heard of them?"

Warren surveys the gang of men. "Listen, you assholes, I been riding all day. Ain't no crime to stop and get some shut-eye."

Ben continues. "Evidence suggests two cowards murdered the Smith brothers and stole their livelihood."

"I'm on my own."

"Your story's awful thin. Mind if we take a look at your belongings?"

"And if I was to say no?"

Ben smirks and turns to two of his men holding torches. "Light this place up." One of the posse members holds up a torch, while two men check Spivey's saddlebag and his horse.

Ezra walks out of the darkness of the trees, startling everyone. Ben barks. "Jesus Christ, Ezra! What the hell ya doing?"

"Got the back door trots and so forth." Several posse members chuckle as Ezra tightens his belt and joins Henry and Jack.

One of the Pike's Peakers notices a cut mark on the side of a tree, so he raises his torch and spots a bag hanging from a branch. "Something's up this tree, Ben."

"Well, fetch it on down."

The Pike's Peaker lights the tree with his torch as one of the other miners climbs up it. The miner finds a bag hanging from a limb and throws it down. Ben opens it and narrows his eyes at Warren. "Lot more than grub gold here."

"Squirrel all my findings away. Don't keep track how much."

Jack steps forward. "How'd a fat bastard like you get it up that tree?"

"Got my ways. You fellas got the wrong pig by the tail."

Ben stands over Warren. "Show me how ya done it. Climb that tree."

Warren growls, "Climb it yourself."

Ben lowers his gun. "Yeah, well ... I'm not buying none of yer shit talk. What's the chance of you havin' all this gold and the Smiths dying for theirs?" Ben signals one of his men. "Check this cocksucker for more lies."

A posse member frisks Warren and finds a watch in Warren's pocket. He gives it to Ben and says, "Josh and Frank both had watches. Saw 'em looking at them more than once."

Ben looks over at Ezra and the undertaker shrugs. "Wasn't one on Josh 'fore I put him in a box. I claimed Frank's as payment and so forth."

Ben studies the watch. "Well, looky here, J.S ... Josh Smith."

Warren nods. "Yeah, well, I'm ... Jim Spencer."

"Now ain't that handy." Ben looks at the picture inside the watch. "This your woman?"

"Give it to me when we jumped the broom."

Ben passes the watch around, so the other men can see the picture. The last man to get the watch is Ezra. The undertaker stares at the picture a moment and speaks up. "The Smiths left their women back in Kansas." He hesitates, and then hands the watch back to Ben.

Disgusted, Ben looks at the time piece again and tosses it to Warren. "What time is it … Jim?" Warren looks at it and a puzzled look crosses his face. Ben spits and grabs it back. "Lying sack of shit!" He points at two men and hollers, "Tie 'em up!"

Henry studies Spivey's profile as the two men tie the suspect to a tree. The remaining posse members form a circle and begin to voice their opinions as whether Warren is guilty or not. Henry looks away when he sees Abe staring at him. A moment passes and everyone's hand goes up except for Henry's. The red-bearded Pike's Peaker nods to the group and turns to Ben. "All but Henry."

Ben gives Henry a look of disapproval as Warren studies Henry's profile. The saloon owner strides over to the tree where Warren is tied and says, "Wanna change your story?"

"I know the law. I get me a trial."

"Trial's over. Jury decided."

"Shit! That ain't no jury."

"Well, they're all ya get. Come sunup, you've had the biscuit."

The early morning sun breaks through the trees as Warren, Ben, and the rest of the posse sit on their horses under a large pine tree. Warren's hands are tied behind his back, and a rope hangs from a tree limb next to his head. Ben reaches up, grabs the rope and slips the noose around the killer's neck. Warren squirms in his saddle and vents his anger. "You assholes didn't see me do nothin'."

Before Ben can give the signal to hang the assassin, Henry rides up and makes a final plea to save his Pa's murderer. "He's right. No one saw him kill the Smith brothers."

Ben counters. "Had their gold and Josh's watch, didn't he?"

Henry argues. "He deserves a real trial with a real judge. It's the law."

"Bannack ain't got no law. Until we do, I decide who lives or dies."

"This ain't right, Ben."

"You had your say."

Henry backs away as a posse member appears and hands Ben a bag with eye holes. "Found it in the bushes."

Ben holds the bag up for Henry and everyone else to see. He tosses it to the ground, removes a Bible from his coat, and begins to read: "He who covers his sins will not prosper, but whoever confesses them will have mercy ... Any final words, asshole?"

"You saying if I tell you I killed them boys, ya won't hang me?

"No, but might ease your mind some."

Several men chuckle as Warren growls. "I'll see ya' in hell! Be waiting there to kick yer asses!"

A hooded Alex Slade rides out of the trees, sides up to Henry, and puts his gun to his brother's head. He waves his peacemaker at all of the vigilantes and then narrows his aim at Ben. He deepens his voice and says, "Tell your men to toss their guns in them trees ... good and hard or this muck ain't no more."

Ben studies the situation and mutters, "Shit." Frustrated, he flips his hand in the air, and the men throw their weapons into the trees.

Not sure what to do next, Alex gawks at Warren, who is struggling to breathe. His partner looks over at him and gasps, "What ya waitin' on? Get this fuckin' rope off my neck!"

Alex takes another moment and points his gun at a posse member, signaling him to free Warren. While the vigilante removes the ropes from Warren's neck and hands, Henry leans over and whispers just loud enough for him to hear, "You Alex Slade?"

Alex points his revolver back at Henry. "Shut the hell up!" Then he turns his weapon to Ben and says, "All of you, off your horses and remove your boots!"

The men refuse to move, so Alex fires his gun in the air and points his revolver at Ben again. "Do it or this man dies!" Following Ben's lead, members of the posse begin to remove their boots. Meanwhile, Alex grabs Ben's rifle and fires it numerous times at their horses.

As the animals run down the road helter-skelter, Alex turns and points Ben's rifle at Ezra. "You too!" Ezra climbs down from his wagon and removes his boots. Alex grabs the undertaker's rifle from the back of his wagon and tosses it to Warren, who instantly points the weapon at the posse members sitting bootless on the ground. Alex gathers the boots and tosses them in Ezra's wagon.

Next, he ties his horse and Warren's horse to the back of the wagon, while his partner yanks Josh's watch from Ben's pocket. Warren snarls, "Ain't stealin' from me, asshole, even if it ain't mine." Then he spits at Ben's feet and tosses the watch to Alex. "You keep it now! Brings me nothin' but bad luck."

Alex shoves the watch in his pocket and heads for the wagon as Warren aims his rifle at Ben. The saloon owner raises his arms and begs. "No! Don't do it." Warren takes aim at Ben's head, but fires at his left hand instead. The saloon keeper groans, looks down at his bloody hand, and sees that two of his fingers are missing. As he shakes his bloody hand, he growls at Warren. "You maimed me, you son of a bitch!"

The abuser chortles. "That's for my trouble."

Warren climbs in Ezra's wagon, and Alex slaps the reins to the horses. As they ride off, Ben searches for his fingers.

The outlaws roll along in Ezra's death wagon at a fast pace, their horses trailing behind. When they are a safe distance away, Alex rips the bag off his head and glares at Warren. "You owe me."

A few miles down the road, Alex slows the wagon to a stop and they look back to see if they're in the clear. Satisfied, they climb down, untie their horses, and mount up.

As they are about to ride off, Warren raises his rifle and prepares to shoot Ezra's horses. Alex reacts. "Don't do that." Warren grits his teeth, lowers his rifle, and looks at his fellow escapee. Alex holds up his finger, suggesting he has an idea. The young bandit jumps down from the wagon and begins to unhitch the horses. Warren alters Samuel's plan and grabs a jug of whiskey from the back of the wagon. "Leave them horses be.!"

Warren pours the jug's contents on the boots, lights a match, and sets the wagon on fire. As the flames shoot up, the horses squeal, snort, and run off with the fiery wagon trailing behind.

Ezra's wagon burns in the distance as the two escapees come to a road that forks both right and left. Alex checks with Warren. "Where we going?"

"Hell if I know. Sure ain't going right, that's Bannack."

Members of the posse hobble down the road, some barefooted and others in their socks. Ben stumbles along between two men, who take turns holding him up. His hand is wrapped with the bag Warren used to disguise himself. Ben stops, pulls his two bloody fingers out of his pocket, stares at them a moment, and tosses them to the side of the road.

Abe points in the distance, where he sees smoke rising in the air. When they reach Ezra's death wagon, several men take turns throwing dirt on the smoldering flames.

A few minutes later, four men, including Ben, are sitting in the back of the burnt-out wagon Ezra is driving. All of the other men are walking along wearing blackened boots or no boots at all.

The next day, Henry and Jack walk down Main Street. When they reach the Saffron Saloon, Henry signals his friend to wait for him, so Jack plops down on the steps, removes a cigarette from his pocket, and lights up.

When I finally realized that looking for gold might never lead me to Samuel, I decided that being a lawman again might not be such a bad idea. I figured protecting the innocent would also give me the right to hunt down Warren Spivey and Alex Slade if I wanted to. Unfortunately, I don't think Jack saw the prospect of watching over the citizens of Bannack and hunting down my pa's killers the same way I did.

When Henry enters the Saffron Saloon, he finds Ben standing behind the bar counter wearing a black leather glove on his left hand. Henry offers an open hand, and the saloon owner gives him a curious look. Ben gets the message, removes a badge from a nearby drawer, and gives it to him. Henry offers an open hand again and Ben reaches in the drawer, pulls out a second badge, and tosses it to him.

Henry exits the Saffron and finds Jack still sitting on the front steps smoking. As Jack stands up, he spots the badge on Henry's chest. The new sheriff grins, takes the second badge from his pocket, and pins it on his deputy's shirt.

CHAPTER 14

"Never think that war, no matter how necessary, nor how justified, is not a crime." Ernest Hemingway

NEVADA TERRITORY

THE EVENING SKY is lit by the fiery flames of the burning teepees of a small Washoe Indian village. Washoe men, women, and children run for their lives as dozens of Nevada militia soldiers and territorial men, mounted and on foot, chase down their outnumbered prey.

A Washoe warrior runs from the village carrying his severed arm as a mounted militia lieutenant, yielding a bloody saber, closes in on the young warrior. Just as the officer reaches the Washoe brave, the Indian turns and throws his bloody arm, hitting the lieutenant square in the chest. Angered that his uniform is covered in blood, he shoots the warrior in the chest and the Washoe crumbles to the ground.

On the other side of the village, three saddle tramps, an auburn-haired Irishman named Rufus "Red" Murphy, a blond Scandinavian, Nils "Swede" Lindberg, and a brown-eyed Mexican, Diego "Hombre" Sanchez, chase down defenseless Washoes.

They laugh as they crush the natives' skulls with the butts of their rifles. Not far away, other militiamen and Nevada citizens skewer Washoe women and children with their sabers.

As several men continue to mutilate and scalp Washoes, Wenutu, an oversized and chiseled Paiute, and his younger brother, Numaga, approach the battle scene. They dismount and tie their horses to a nearby tree on the fringe of the Washoe village. The brothers crouch down and make their way to a Washoe teepee, where they watch as the massacre continues. After they witness several Washoe women and children being mutilated by the swords and knives of the white soldiers, they look at each other.

Wenutu nods, suggesting they take up the fight, but Numaga disagrees in his native Numic language. "This is not our fight. The Washoe are our enemies. Let them die."

Wenutu responds, "White men kill all Indians not for revenge but for pleasure ... even our women and children!" He waits for a response, but Numaga looks down. Wenutu continues. "Little brother? Did you leave your balls with your woman when we left our village?"

Without warning, the older Paiute runs away from the tent and joins the battle. Not far away, two more warriors succumb to the knives of Red, Swede, Hombre and a young sandy-haired militia private. Having satisfied their lust for blood, the tramps ride off, leaving the young private because he wants to look for Washoe treasure.

Numaga watches as Wenutu softly approaches the private from behind and charges. Catlike, he pulls the young soldier off his horse and onto the ground. The private sits up, but before he can get his bearings, Wenutu cuts his throat. Still hidden behind the smoldering teepee, Numaga tries to summon the courage to join his brother.

After Wenutu finishes scalping the private, he yelps and proudly holds the soldier's flay of hair high in the air. The three saddle tramps simultaneously turn back and watch as the Paiute continues to celebrate his victory. Red spits, raises his rifle, and aims it at Wenutu.

Just as Numaga peeks around the corner of the tent, his brother grins and displays the bloody scalp for him to see. Instantly, a shot rings out and the top of Wenutu's head explodes. Devastated by his brother's sudden death, Numaga lowers his head, slumps to the ground, and begins to groan.

When Red hears Numaga moaning, he turns in the direction of the tent where the Paiute brother is hiding. Seeing nothing, he sides up to his two friends and they ride away.

Numaga covers his face with his hands as he tries to deal with what he just witnessed. He takes a moment, unsheathes his knife, and slashes his chest three times. While he groans softly, he smears his blood on his face and arms.

As darkness envelopes the battleground, a bevy of soldiers head Numaga's way. The Paiute sinks down, scans the area, and realizes his escape routes are blocked.

Avoiding the light from the burning tents and taking advantage of the darkness, Numaga crawls over and lays down next to his brother and the other dead Washoe warriors. He pulls Wenutu's body on top of him and doesn't move.

In the distance, he hears the screams of two Washoe women who are being raped by a hatless scar-faced soldier and the three saddle tramps. Having satisfied their lust, the rapists cackle, exit the teepee and pull up their trousers. The scar-faced soldier doesn't skip a beat as he grabs a burning log from a nearby fire pit. He snickers as he tosses it in the tent, which instantly catches fire.

The desperate Washoe women scream again as they run out of their home with their clothes on fire. They take a few steps and fall to their knees as their deer skinned dresses continue to burn.

Red, Swede and Hombre laugh, while other men turn away in disgust as the women roll on the ground before succumbing to death. Another young private, having witnessed the scene, leans over and throws up. The tramps react by laughing at the youth's softness.

Still not satisfied, the scar-faced soldier bellows to the men around him, "Gonna get me some Indian shit. Anyone coming with me?" No one responds, so he mounts a beautiful black horse and trots his stallion over to the place where Numaga is still hiding under his dead brother. The saddle tramps, who are warming themselves by a fire, watch him ride off and turn away.

When the scar-faced soldier arrives, he steers his horse over the bodies of several dead warriors not far from Numaga. He jumps down from his horse and begins to remove jewelry from the bodies of several Washoes. When he spots the turquoise necklace around Wenutu's neck, he pulls his knife, lifts the Paiute's head up by his hair, cuts the necklace free, and holds it to the light of the moon.

The scar-faced soldier feels a tug on his pants, looks down, and sees Numaga's hand gripping his belt. The Paiute yanks hard, pulls him to his knees, and thrusts his knife deep in the soldier's stomach. Before the rapist can scream, the Indian pulls his knife from the man's stomach and cuts his throat.

Numaga removes his brother's necklace from the soldier's hand and looks to see if anyone has been watching. Seeing no one, he lifts Wenutu by the arms and drags his body over to the dead soldier's mount. He shoulders his brother, drapes his body over the dead man's horse, mounts the stallion, and starts to ride off.

Still sitting by the open fire, the young soldier who threw up earlier sees Numaga riding away. He looks around and realizes that no one else has spotted the Paiute, so he lowers his head and puts his hands to the fire.

As Numaga vacates the camp, leaving both his horse and his brother's horse behind, he looks back and sees several soldiers and locals sifting through the belongings of the dead Washoe Indians.

When he gets a safe distance from the village, he drops to the ground, cuts the billet strap of his new horse's saddle, and throws it to the side. Silhouetted by a full moon, he remounts the horse, takes one last look back, and rides away with his brother's body draped in front of him.

Without warning, a whirlwind of dirt appears and engulfs Numaga, his brother, and the horse. When the Paiute emerges from the dust devil, he has a demonic look on his face.

A Paiute village, surrounded by pine trees and sagebrush, has a backdrop of the Carson Mountain Range roughly fifty miles to the east. The Truckee River, fed by mountain streams, runs freely on the outskirts of the tented community.

As Paiute men and women go about their work re-shaping animal hides, weaving baskets, and cooking wild game on open fires, Numaga enters the village. He sees several familiar faces and is greeted by a dozen barking dogs. Some of the villagers stare when they see Wenutu's body draped over Numaga's new horse.

Inside a dome-shaped earth lodge, Numaga sits across from three Paiute elders, including his father, Winnemucca, chief of the tribe. The stoic men talk amongst themselves and smoke their pipes as Numaga sits silently a short distance away.

Finally, Winnemucca holds out his hand and there is instant silence. In his native Paiute language, he says, "Why did you and your brother leave the safety of our village?"

Namaga is slow to answer. "Because this place is a prison for warriors with spirit."

Winnemucca tightens his face and says, "You fought alongside the Washoe? It was not your fight."

"Our plan was to steal Washoe horses, but when we saw the white soldiers killing Washoe women and children, Wenutu's anger conquered him."

The chief continues. "The Washoe and white soldiers are both our enemies."

"No, Father. Washoe kill so they can steal our horses. White men kill for their own pleasure."

"Why do you live and not my oldest?" Numaga sits silently until his father speaks again. "Did you run like a frightened deer?"

Numaga raises up. "I left so that I can take revenge on the men who killed my brother."

"Wenutu's revenge is mine, not yours."

CHAPTER 15

"Without a family, man, alone in the world, trembles with the cold." Andre Maurois

NEVADA TERRITORY

ATOP A STAGECOACH in the driver's box sits Rut "Stubborn" Long, a fifty-year-old whip, who has worked for the Butterfield Overland Mail Company for twenty years. He's wearing a wide-brimmed gray cowboy hat and a deerskin coat that is covered with trail dust.

Rut slows the coach as he passes the smoldering Washoe village just off the trail. He looks to his right and spots dozens of dead Washoe Indians, who are baking in the sun and covered with flies and pecking buzzards. Washoe mourners, mostly women and older men, circle the dead and cry out as they discover the bodies of their loved ones.

Two middle-aged male passengers pull back the coach's leather curtain, poke their heads out the window, and gawk at the death scene. Rut clicks his teeth and the horses pick up the pace. "Ya wanted to see Indians ..."

An older balding passenger speaks up. "How'd they die?

Rut looks straight ahead. "None of my business."

A second male traveler, a round-faced thirty something, questions Rut as well. "Shouldn't we do something?"

Rut chuckles. "Can leave you here if you want."

The men cower back into the coach and shut the curtain.

BUCKLAND STATION

Pete Buckland is feeding his horses when he notices Rut's coach approaching. The dirt-caked driver brings his rig to a sudden halt as the station owner waves away a cloud of dust.

Maria Buckland, Pete's wife, Sandra, his eighteen-year-old daughter, and Timothy "Buckie," his ten-year-old son, exit the Buckland cabin and greet the coach driver.

Rut, who has a slight limp, climbs down from the coach as Buckie helps his father unhook the hames from the front two horses. Sandra approaches and hands Rut a tin cup filled with water, while Maria slaps the dust off the driver's coat.

The two passengers, dressed in black suits, exit the coach and dust themselves off. The round-faced man looks over and gives Rut a dirty look. Maria escorts the gentlemen to the cabin, while Buckie leads the road weary horses to the corral.

Pete nods. "Right on time, Rut."

"Been here sooner but them dandies got sick on me. Stopped twice so they could air their paunches."

Buckie yells from the corral. "Stubborn, ya see any Indians?"

"Sure did."

Rut leans over and whispers to Pete. "Twenty miles west, saw a whole Washoe village burned to the ground. Dead Washoes everywhere."

"Paiutes?"

"Weren't stuck with arrows. Most likely Ormsby and his men."

Pete lowers his voice. "Thought things was settling down."

"Know how it is," Rut says. "Paiutes and Washoes keep feudin' and the Nevada militia find reasons to kill'em both."

Buckie, who is still in the corral, finishes putting ropes around two fresh horses' necks. "Are you two talkin' about women?"

Rut and Pete chuckle and turn the boy's way as he leads the wagon pullers to the coach. Buckie grins and asks, "Want me to change the other two out?"

"Nah. They've only been pulling since Tahoe."

"Grease the wheels?"

"They're good." Rut runs a hand through Buckie's hair. "Won't be long 'fore you'll be running this place."

Buckie's eyes light up. "Guess what I know, Stubborn?"

Rut gives Buckie a curious look.

"We're getting the Pony Express."

"Ya don't say. Heard they was starting up."

"Pa says they'll be coming here even faster than you do."

Buckie and Rut continue to switch out the horses as Pete approaches with two buckets of water.

Rut nods at Pete. "Pony Express, huh?"

"Signed up two months back. Young fellas riding the mail."

"Good thing they're not toting people or I'd be out of a job."

"Hard to pass on it. Pays a respectable wage."

Rut mouths a wad of tobacco. "How long they stay?"

"Long enough to swap horses. If they need a sleep, I got the barn."

Buckie tugs on Rut's sleeve. "How 'bout them Indians ya saw, Stubborn?"

Rut looks at Pete and winks. "A dozen come at me 'fore I hit the Tahoe station ... feathered my coach high and low, but I outrun 'em." Buckie stares wide-eyed at Rut and the driver laughs. "Nah. I'm shitting ya."

Buckie shoves Rut as Pete starts for the house. "Come get ya some grub. Maria cooked up some elk stew this morning." Rut limps past Buckie and the young boy mimics him by competing to see who can limp to the cabin the fastest. They laugh as they stumble through the front door.

The two passengers look up from their meals and scowl at the driver as he stumbles to the table, secures a chair, and quickly downs a steaming cup of coffee. Rut raises a fork and points it at his customers. "Best watch how much ya eat, gents. Rough road ahead; no more stopping."

The men scoot back from the table, but Maria puts more food on their plates and pushes their dinner back in front of them. "Don't listen to him. This is your last meal 'til you get to Carson City."

Maria offers Rut something more to drink. "Charge your glass, Stubborn?" Rut pushes his cup forward and Maria pours as the passengers start eating again.

The round-faced passenger gives Rut a curious look. "I probably shouldn't ask, but why do people call you Stubborn?"

Maria winks at Rut. "'Cuz, he's too stubborn to slow down."

Buckie adds his two cents. "And he keeps tipping his coach over."

Pete piles on. "How many times now, Stubborn?"

"Hell, I don't know. Leave me alone."

Buckie grins. "Three times."

"One of them times don't count. I was drunk and by myself."

The passengers stare at each other as Sandra brings a pot over to Rut. She ladles stew on his plate and adds her own opinion. "And he's not gonna change, are ya, Stubborn?"

"Sandra, you're getting to be 'bout as friendly to the eyes as your mama over there. Trouble is, ya got her same orneriness.

Sandra smiles, finishes giving Rut his stew, and turns away.

Rut gently takes Sandra's arm. "Hey." Sandra turns back and gives Rut another large helping.

Maria drops a slice of bread on his plate. "Next time you fly off Dead Man's Curve, you might not be so lucky."

The balding passenger looks at Maria. "Dead Man's Curve?"

Rut tries to explain. "Don't know why they call it that. No one's ever died there … yet."

Both passengers push their plates away again as Rut looks the table over for more food. "Mail me some of them creamed peas."

Sandra scoops up a large spoonful of peas and stands over Rut's plate. "Come on … the whole shebang." Sandra plops down the pot of peas in front of Rut's plate.

"Help yourself."

Rut lifts the spoon and eats the peas from the pot.

Seated behind his desk in his new office, Henry is writing in his journal. Jack, who is sitting by the window knitting a red scarf, occasionally looks outside, when he hears a few miners and townspeople walk by.

Being a sheriff in Bannack isn't what I thought it would be. There's a lot more peace and quiet than there was in Nevada City. The only excitement Jack and I get is when a miner gets into a fight over a whore or when some nobody tries to steal another man's gold by cheating in a card game.

Finally, Henry puts his journal in a desk drawer, picks up a stack of handbills from his desk, and thumbs through them. He stops when one catches his eye. He looks over and notices that

Jack is still preoccupied, so he folds the handbill and puts it in his pocket.

Jack puts his knitting aside, rolls a cigarette, and lights up. As he peers outside again, he sees a wagon pull up in front of the Saffron Saloon. The new deputy stands up, presses his head against the window, and watches two hookers exit the saloon. The scantily dressed women appear to be laughing as they pull five miners inside.

Jack takes a long drag from his rollup and turns to Henry. "Ya know, Ben's pretty sure them Smith brother killers is Spivey and Slade. Still think it was them two that done in your family?"

"Like I said before, not sure 'bout Slade. Never got his name or a close look at him. Spivey now, he's got a name and face I'll never forget."

"So, if Spivey's the one, why didn't ya want us to hang him?"

"'Cuz, I need him alive to tell me what happened to Samuel."

"So, when ya talked on him ratin' a fair trial, that was all shit?"

"Maybe. I don't know."

"You're a fool if ya think he's gonna claim a killin' he done a long time ago."

"Not that long to me."

"Might be a while 'fore we see that asshole again."

Henry speaks slowly. "Pa used to say, 'Revenge is a dish best served cold.'" Henry coughs deeply, grabs a bottle from his desk, and swallows a mouthful of laudanum.

Jack returns to the window and looks out wistfully. Bored, he pulls out a flask of whiskey and takes a gulp. "Gonna get me some grub. You coming?"

"Nah, I got something else to do."

"You're plowing that store gal, ain't ya?"

Henry doesn't respond, so Jack continues. "Got you a left-handed wife."

"We're friends is all."

"My pa used to say, 'admire another man's cow long enough, people will figure you're either milking it or wanna steal it.'"

"Lucy ain't no cow."

"Good thing; rustling will get ya hanged."

The Bannack lawmen exit the office and Henry walks towards Vedder's General Store. He looks in the window and sees John and Lucy arguing. He steps to the door and listens as John Vedder screams out: "You ain't going nowhere! And them shelves better be full when I get back or there'll be hell to pay!" John storms out the door as the sheriff steps aside.

Lucy notices her new friend looking around the store, but she doesn't say anything. Finally, she approaches the sheriff, who is eyeing a bolt of fabric. "Looking for something special?"

"My mother's birthday is coming up." Henry notices the sad tone in Lucy's voice, so he gently lifts her chin and studies her face. He sees that her cheek is black and blue. "You all right?"

Lucy removes his hand and turns away, so Henry points at her cheek and says, "He do that?"

"It's nothing. I'm fine."

"You don't look fine. I mean ya look good, but not ..."

"...fine." Lucy smiles and Henry smiles back. "What color?"

Henry gives her a puzzled look. "What color?"

"What color fabric do you want?"

"I don't know. What do you like?"

"Yellow, but it's for your mother."

Henry grins. "Yellow. Yeah, let's do yellow."

"How much you want? How many yards?

"I don't know. Enough to make a dress."

Lucy holds up the bolt of fabric. "She a small woman? Bigger?"

Henry looks Lucy over. "'Bout your size."

"Three yards should be plenty."

"Make it six … in two pieces."

"Six yards? Same color? You sure?"

Henry smiles and nods. Lucy measures and cuts the fabric as Henry watches. They walk to the counter and Henry pays. Lucy hands the material to Henry and he hands one of the pieces back to her. She questions Henry with her eyes and says, "What? You don't want it?"

"Half for you."

Lucy looks Henry in the eyes and says, "No, I can't take this."

Henry smiles. "Sure you can. Make yourself something."

"I can't do that."

"Come on. It's yellow. . .your favorite color."

Henry walks out the door as Lucy stares at the fabric.

PART TWO: THE PONY EXPRESS

.

Pony Express Route
April 3, 1860 to October 26, 1861

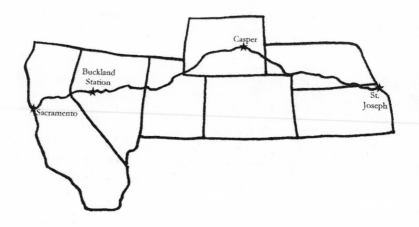

CHAPTER 16

**"People sleep peacefully in their beds at night only because
rough men stand ready to do violence on their behalf."
George Orwell**

NOT FAR from Buckland Station, Johnny Fry, an eighteen-year-old Pony Express rider, tops a hill at a full gallop and speeds his way to his next stop. The pony rider has a pistol strapped to his hip and his horse is equipped with a lightweight saddle. Attached to his rig is a canteen, a bugle, and a small leather mochila.

Pete and Buckie are saddling a fresh horse, when they hear Johnny's bugle in the distance. Sandra rushes out of the cabin carrying ample nourishment for the rider. When Johnny's lathered horse slides to a stop, he jumps down and tosses the reins to Buckie. Sandra scampers over, hands him a bag of food and canteen, and grins. As Buckie leads the horse away, he mutters loud enough for everyone to hear, "This horse is baked."

As Johnny gulps down the water and gobbles up the sandwich, he and Sandra exchange smiles. All at once, Pete lifts Johnny up and puts him on the fresh horse. When the young rider leans over to whisper something in Sandra's ear, Pete slaps the hind quarters of his horse and the animal takes off with the express rider hanging on for dear life. Pete laughs as he yells out, "Don't wanna be late!"

Sandra stomps her feet. "Pa ... you're ... a mean ol' rip." Pete laughs as Sandra speeds her way back to the cabin.

Headed for Carson City, Johnny passes Jane Fields, who is steering her freight wagon toward Buckland Station. Jane is a middle-aged Black woman who stands six feet tall and weighs more than 250 pounds. She's wearing a dusty calico dress, is smoking a large cigar, and has a jug of whiskey propped in the fold of her dress. A large floppy hat sits low on her head and a pistol is strapped to the side of her white apron. As she nears the station, Jane slaps the reins to her two mules and starts singing a Negro spiritual:

Steal away, steal away, steal away to Jesus...
Steal away, steal away home.
I ain't got long to stay here.

Jane arrives at Buckland Station and yanks back the reins to her mules as Pete and Buckie approach her. Both animals react to the sudden tug by snorting and pawing their feet. With a heavy Tennessee accent, Jane yells, "Whoa, Moses! Abraham! Behave yourselves!"

As Pete steadies the mules, he says, "Good Time Jane! Nice to see you. Fed my horses the last of their grain only a few minutes ago."

"Don't give me no shit, Mr. Pete. Ain't my fault I weren't here sooner. Only got word ya needed supplyin' dis mornin'. Rode my big ass sore, just so's ya wouldn't boil a pot waitin'. My poor mules got themselves all lathered up gettin' here."

"I appreciate it, Jane. Glad you made it here safe and sound."

"Yes, sir, safe and sound; yes, I's safe and sound. Buckie, come on over here." Buckie approaches Jane as Pete walks to the back of the supply wagon and surveys the grain bags. Jane gulps down the last of the whiskey, takes a drag from her cigar, and hands it to Buckie. "Go on. Yer pa ain't lookin'. Buckie holds the cigar awkwardly but doesn't try it. "Buckie, you be a lucky chile, yes you's a lucky chile."

Buckie gives Jane a curious look. "Why you say that?"

"'Cuz, ya got your ma's looks and not yer pa's. Only thing he done was plant the seed; yes sir, he planted the seed." Jane crawls down out of her wagon and joins Pete.

The Bucklands start to help Jane unload the grain bags, but she motions them away and wags her finger. "No sir. Sit yer asses down. Ain't dis damn big for no reason." Jane carries two grain bags with ease to the barn and sits them down as father and son sit on a bale of hay watching.

"Pa, you said we're supposed to help womenfolk?

"Yeah, except Jane ain't exactly womenfolk."

The Buckland family, seated around the table eating supper, watch as Jane heaps large portions of food on her plate. She waves her fork and Sandra walks over with a plate of chicken. She starts to give Jane a chicken leg, but Jane spears two larger pieces as Sandra holds the plate steady.

Between mouthfuls, Jane says, "Miss Sandra, now's dat ya got them pony riders coming by all the time, I bet yer tail feathers is high in the air. Is I right?"

Sandra blushes, Buckie grins, Maria frowns, and Pete changes the subject. "Now that we're feeding more horses, we're gonna need ..."

Jane doesn't let Pete finish. "...Shit, Mr. Pete! I see'd all them new horses ya got. I knows yer needs; God damn! Ya think I's blind?"

Maria raises her voice. "Please, Jane! The children."

"I's sorry, Ms. Buckland. Filthy-mouthed master fixed them words in my head and I can't get rid of'em."

Pete continues. "So, a wagon load of grain every week from here on out."

Jane takes a bite of chicken and talks with her mouth full. "That's right, Mr. Pete. Figured that way too."

Buckie pulls the cigar Jane gave him out of his pocket and puts it next to her plate. Jane grins at Buckie. "Boo!" Buckie shrinks back and Jane laughs. "Did I make you shit your britches?"

"I never shit my britches."

Maria stands up. "Pete, are you going to say something?"
Pete curls his lip. "What ya want me to say?"

"There I go again. I's just a sinful old black woman."

Buckie grins. "Ma says you have a dirty mouth."

Jane slaps her knee and laughs wildly.

Maria scolds her son. "Buckie! Do you have to repeat everything you hear?"

Jane pats the boy on the head. "It's all right. Wilder the colt, better the horse. Don't s'pose ya got some giggle water you've been hiding, do ya Mr. Pete?"

Pete hesitates. "No, afraid not."

Maria adds. "This has been a dry home for two months."

"As well it should be...as well it should be."

Buckie gives Jane a curious look. "Why do the Paiutes call you White Crow?"

"'Cuz they think dis here black skin is coverin' dah white woman in me." Jane laughs and slaps the table.

"Pa says you're a runaway slave."

Maria shakes her head. "Buckie, what's gotten into you?"

"It's all right. Boy's got a natural wonder 'bout things. Yes, I's a runaway outta Tennessee. Plowed cotton fields all the day long. If'n I didn't pull hard enough, master beat on me like I's a stubborn mule. Day come when I had enough. Waited my chance and busted Master Field's head open with a rock. That's when I run west. I treats my mules a hell of a lot better than he treated me." Jane reaches over and ruffles Buckie's hair again. Then she grabs the cigar and holds it up. "Mind if me and Mr. Buck have us an after-dinner smoke?" Maria raises her eyebrows and Jane lowers her voice in defeat. "I know. I know. I was just funning wit' ya."

Jane drives her wagon away from the Buckland Station humming another spiritual as Buckie stands alone on the cabin steps watching. He reaches in his pocket, pulls out the full-sized cigar Jane gave him, and puts it to his lips.

At a center table in the Saffron Saloon, Henry, Jack, Gus Franklin, Red Yeager, and Monty Montgomery are playing poker and chipping their teeth. Behind them at the bar, Sweet wipes off the counter in front of Ezra, who is drinking alone.

Back at the poker table, Gus, a one-armed blacksmith, tosses his cards aside with his only hand. "Too rich for my blood."

Red chuckles as he reaches across the table and pulls in his winnings. "Ain't had so much fun since my grandma fell in the well."

Henry scoffs. "Keep stealing our wages, Red, I'm gonna have to jail ya for thievin'."

The lucky man smirks. "Can I help it if I'm having a good run?"

Monty gives Red a shit-eating grin. "Ya sure as hell ain't gonna get rich stealin' from the likes of us."

Gus adds his two cents. "No future in gamblin'. Got himself a bigger plan, don't ya, Red?"

Monty asks, "Going back to findin' gold are ya?"

Before Red can answer, Gus chuckles, "Yeah, only without a pick and shovel."

Monty says, "I know that plan. It'll get ya hanged."

Red reacts. "Maybe we should slow our talk down. Got us a sheriff right here."

As Henry studies his cards, "Considering breaking the law are ya?"

The accused man looks up from his hand. "Supposin' a plan ain't against the law, is it?"

"No, but stealing other people's hard-earned gold is."

"Come on, Plummer. I was..."

"I know, just supposin'. Anyone else supposin' with Red here?" All of the men at the table grin sheepishly as the sheriff leans back and says. "Okay, I'm listening."

Gus tries to change the subject. "Let's play cards."

"No, I wanna hear this get-rich plan unless he's just wantin' to sell us horseshit."

Everyone turns their eyes to Red as he grabs the cards. "My deal."

Henry is dozing behind his desk when he hears the door open. He tilts his hat up and sees Lucy. She's wearing a yellow dress made from the fabric he gave her. He hops up and grins. "Whoa! Nice."

Lucy looks shyly at Henry. "I came here to thank you."

Henry's eyes sparkle. "My God, you look...."

"...Fine?"

"The finest."

They exchange awkward glances until Lucy says, "Well, I'd better go."

"You just got here. You wanna look around?"

Lucy scans the office. "Is there anything to see?"

Henry points to the stove and the coffee pot. "Stove, coffee pot. Two lockups in the back. Come on, I'll show you." Henry leads the way to the jail cell area and Lucy follows. Right away, she notices the cells are empty.

"No lawbreakers today, I see."

"Maybe one." Henry pulls Lucy tightly into his arms and kisses her hungrily.

Lucy enjoys the moment but thinks better of it. She leans back and says, "Mr. Plummer, would you be so kind as to remove your hand from my buttocks." As she straightens her dress, she clears her voice and continues. "Promise me you won't do that again."

Embarrassed, Henry steps back. "Not sure I can do that."

Lucy leaves the cell area and starts for the door as the sheriff follows close behind. She turns back for one last look and Henry's face lights up. At a loss for words, he smiles and says, "I really do like your dress."

As Lucy opens the door, she chuckles. "I noticed."

Elizabeth Plummer is seated at her kitchen table in Addison, Maine. Although her hair has turned silver and her face is lined with prominent wrinkles, she still has the same sparkle in her eyes she had the day Henry left for California. There's a knock at the door. When she opens it, she finds a delivery man, who hands her a package. The man lingers a bit too long, so Elizabeth shuts the door in his face. She opens the package and removes a large piece of yellow fabric. She holds it up and smiles.

It's early morning and the Bannack streets are filled with miners, merchants, and townspeople. Several men whoop and holler as they enter the Saffron Saloon.

Henry is behind his desk cleaning his gun as Jack stares out the window. "Keeping the peace is dull work. I'm gathering dust."

Henry coughs. "Enjoy it while you can. Got a feeling it ain't gonna stay that way." Henry coughs again, grabs the laudanum from his desk, and swallows a mouthful. Following suit, Jack pulls a small whiskey bottle from his pocket, uncorks it, and takes a gulp.

Jack turns back to the window and says, "Thinkin' bout another parley with Irene. Need me some gratification."

Henry sits up. "Ya know every miner in the territory is humping that whore."

"She ain't no whore. She's an adventuress."

"Adventuress?"

"She's got farmer hands too."

Henry laughs. "And that's a good thing?"

"Ever see a farmer milk a cow?"

"Okay, I got the idea."

Jack turns serious. "Me and her got us a plan."

"What kind of plan?"

"Ain't thought it all out yet."

"Ya gotta know, she's got the same plan for every miner in the territory...steal his gold."

"Why ya always doubting what I say?"

"Listen, I'm not trying to mean you. It's the truth."

"Least I ain't samplin' another man's goods."

"We're just sharin' a few harmless kisses."

"Doubt Vedder would see it that way.

Henry looks out the window. "Gonna buy some coffee ... almost out."

"Bullshit! Got plenty of coffee. No matter. Irene's callin' my name." Both men head for the door.

Henry looks to see if anyone is looking and moseys into Vedder's general store. He sees Lucy arranging dry goods on the shelves, but she doesn't see him. He sneaks up behind her and gently kisses her on the neck. She swings around and tries to slap Henry, but he grabs her hand in mid-air and leans in for another kiss. She struggles a moment, relents, and they kiss passionately. Lucy finally regains control, steps back, and adjusts her dress. "I thought we weren't going to do this anymore."

"Been trying my hardest."

"Well, try harder. Why are you here?"

"I don't know. Thought I'd look over any new merchandise ya brought in." Henry pulls Lucy back into his arms and begins to examine the sleeve of her dress. "I like what's in this. It's wrapped so nice. How much?"

Lucy steps back again. "I'm not someone to be bought!"

"Just funnin'. Why you so touchy?"

"'Cuz, John always says he owns me."

"Well, I ain't him. Why'd ya marry that bastard anyway?"

Lucy hesitates and lowers her head. "We're not married."

"Are you messing with me?"

"We never signed any papers or took any vows. Everyone assumes we are, but we're not."

"So why you still with that asshole, the way he treats you?"

"I'll tell you when we have more time."

"Kill someone, did you?"

"No, of course not."

"Rob a bank?"

Lucy frowns. "When we have time."

"I'm not that good at waiting."

"I've noticed."

Henry matter-of-factly locks the front door and pulls the window curtain down. He takes Lucy by the hand and leads her towards the back room as he says, "Closed for lunch."

Lucy starts to pull away. "What are you doing?"

Henry gently takes her hand again. "Come on. It's what we've been wanting to do for a long time. You're not married."

The Saffron Saloon is filled with down-on-their-luck cowboys, filthy miners, and a mangy stray dog that Sweet Waters is trying to shoo out the door with a broom.

In the corner, a hefty middle-aged hooker plays "Camptown Races" on an out of tune piano, while two drunk miners dance. A third man tries to cut in, but the dancing couple pushes him away.

Jack, who is at the bar nursing a glass of whiskey, pulls a five-dollar gold coin from his pocket, dips it in his glass, sucks the whiskey off it and tosses it to Sweet Waters. She grins as she weighs it in her hand and gives Jack a phony smile. "Irene?"

Jack growls. "I ain't here to buy a horse."

Sweet confirms his request. "Take it you're wantin' to be next?"

Jack slams his glass on the bar. "I ain't waitin'!"

Sweet turns her attention to another customer as she mutters to herself. "Sasshole."

A crusty old miner exits a door upstairs above the bar and stands on a landing smiling down at his friends. He turns back and grins at Miss Irene, who is now propped up against her "office" door.

Irene, a haggard but handsome whore in her early thirties, is wearing a red bodice and a black dress that squeezes her body in all the right places. Her cheeks are caked with red rouge and her long curly black hair is disheveled.

As the miner starts to leave, Irene puts her foot up to his backside and gives him a shove. He stumbles down the steps like a drunken sailor and lands ass-first at the foot of the stairs. Everyone laughs as the miner picks himself up, limps over to the bar, and brags to his friends. "Best ride I've had since Old Nelly."

Sweet leans over the counter. "No Nelly ever worked here."

A dirt-faced miner at the bar explains. "Nelly was his favorite jackass."

Sweet walks over and nods at Jack. "You're up."

As the deputy gulps down the last of his drink, the old miner says, "Should be good to go. I wore her down for ya."

Several men chuckle as the old man limps out of the saloon. Sweet waves at Irene, who has made her way down the stairs to the bar counter. The barmaid points to Jack, so Irene walks over, takes him by the hand, and leads him up the stairs as the men at the bar hoot and holler.

Henry has Lucy pinned up against the storage room shelf in the back room of the store. Her skirt is up around her waist as she reaches for something to hang on to. And overly excited Henry pushes up against her as he struggles to remove her knickers. As their passion swells and they continue to grope one another, an avalanche of cans and boxes tumble to the floor.

On a mattress in a small room on the second floor of the Saffron, Jack's on top of Irene. His pants are around his knees and her dress is neatly folded next to her half-naked body. As Irene clutches a five-dollar gold coin, she coldly submits to Jack's advances. Just as the deputy is about to reach the height of passion, there's a knock at the door. He looks up and growls. "Christ Almighty! My time ain't up!" He hears another knock.

John Vedder pounds angrily on the front door of his store. "Lucy! Open the God damn door!"

In the storage room, Henry and Lucy stand frozen in each other's arms, half naked. Lucy has a can of milk in her left hand and her other hand is around Henry's neck. The sheriff starts to cough, so Lucy puts her free hand up against his mouth until he's able to regain his composure. "Go! Go now! Out the back way."

Henry pulls up his pants and rushes out the back door. Lucy gathers herself and scurries to the front of the store as John screams out: "Judas Priest! Open this fuckin' door!"

She slides the metal bolt to the side and John rushes inside. Lucy, still holding a can of milk in her hand, steps back and puts it on a shelf.

"Why was the door locked? How am I supposed to make any damn money?"

"Sorry. I was looking for ... some canned milk in the back."

John points. "Jesus Christ! We got two shelves full of the shit."

Lucy is at a loss for words. "I guess I didn't ..."

"Can't trust ya to do nothin'."

John heads to the till and begins to count his money.

Lucy takes a deep breath. "I need to see Judith about my sewing project?"

John doesn't even look up. "You can see her at that damn sewing circle ya go to every week."

"Need her help on something special I've been working on."

"Are ya deaf? I said no."

Lucy reacts. "John, you don't own me."

John drops what he's doing and rushes over to Lucy. "What did you say?"

"I said, you don't own me.'"

John slaps Lucy's face, grabs her by the throat, and squeezes her so hard that she sinks to the floor. As he continues to choke her, he growls through his teeth and says, "Who owns you? Who the hell owns you?"

Lucy cries out, "Stop, please! You do."

John lets go of her neck. "Damn right I do! Now, get off the floor and clean this place up!"

Henry walks through the door as Lucy struggles to her feet. He stares at her, looking for an explanation. "You all right?"

"I'm ... fine." Lucy rubs her neck and turns away.

"What's going on, Vedder?"

"I can't help it if the woman's prone to fainting spells."

Lucy walks back to the storage room as Henry steps up to the counter. "Give me some of that green coffee."

John hands Henry a bag of coffee and Henry pays. The sheriff pivots to leave but turns back. "If Lucy has another fainting spell, I'll be back, but not for coffee."

"You threatening me?"

"Damn right I am."

Henry walks out the door.

Although Lucy and I continued to see each other in secret, I was no longer burdened by the guilt I had felt for pursuing another man's woman. The only thing left was for me to find out why Lucy had been keeping her relationship with Vedder a secret for so long.

CHAPTER 17

"None of us is responsible for the complexion of his skin. This fact of nature offers no clue to the character or quality of the person underneath."
Marian Anderson

NORTH OF BANNACK, Rut "Stubborn" Long guides his stagecoach around a bend at breakneck speed. Next to him is Malachi Jones, a young man who is clutching a shotgun and has a rifle at the ready.

Inside the coach are three heavy-set middle-aged passengers, two men and a woman, who hang on for dear life as Rut slaps leather to his horses. When the coach reaches the bottom of a steep hill, it slows and Malachi jumps to the ground with his rifle. Rut looks down at the young man as if to say, "What the hell?"

Malachi grins. "Saw a couple deer up top. Gonna get me one. Meet ya up there."

Rut scoffs. "I ain't waitin' for ya."

Malachi runs off the side of the road and into the trees as Rut leans down and addresses the passengers. "Everyone out. Gotta walk up this hill. Horses can't handle your heft."

The passengers reluctantly exit the coach and begin their struggle up the hill, grumbling as they go. Rut slaps the reins to the horses and the coach creeps forward. As he rolls past the despondent travelers, he looks down at them and bellows, "Keep lollygaggin' and I'll be leavin' ya here."

The out-of-shape men and women huff and puff as they try to stay up with Rut and the coach. Halfway up the hill, everyone comes to a halt when two bandits with white bags covering their heads jump out from behind a boulder and step in front of the coach's lead horses.

The passengers raise their hands as Rut grits his teeth. "What you assholes want?"

The older bandit tries to disguise his voice. "The strong box! Throw it on down."

Stubborn reacts. "That ain't gonna happen."

The older bandit aims his gun at the driver. "Ya muddleheaded or somethin'?"

Rut continues. "It's bolted to the floor."

The younger thief speaks up. "Unlock it."

"It ain't got no lock."

The young thief reacts by scaling the coach to check out Rut's story, while his partner climbs inside. A moment passes and the younger bandit leans down and looks through the coach window. "He's not lying. Big ass bolts tying it to the coach."

The older bandit cocks his gun and aims it hard at Rut. "Take your horses up the hill, while we figure this all out."

Rut climbs down and begins to unhitch the horses as the would-be robbers try to decide what to do. Suddenly, in the distance, they hear three shots. The bandits look at one another and then turn to the driver for an explanation. Instead, Rut gives them the low-down on his coach. "Brake ain't gonna hold this coach with no horses."

The older bandit points at a pile of rocks. "Put them rocks behind the wheels."

"Ain't gonna be me."

The older bandit points his gun at the driver's head again. Rut reacts. "Gonna shoot me on account of my bad back?" He points at the passengers. "They ain't doing nothin'."

The older bandit turns and aims his gun at the passengers. "Stop gawking and fetch some of them rocks." The passengers grumble and start putting rocks behind the coach wheels, while Rut finishes unhitching the horses.

With the rocks in place, Stubborn and the passengers start up the hill with the horses. The older bandit assesses the situation. "Got us a coach and no horses."

The young bandit quips. "I say we set fire to it and see if the strong box lets loose."

At the crest of the hill, Rut sees Malachi and waves him over. Malachi tries to explain his failure to kill a deer. "They run off 'fore I could get me a sure shot!"

Rut points at the would-be robbers. "Never mind the deer. See them assholes down there?" Malachi surveys the area below the hill and sees the younger bandit holding a burning stick as he prepares to light the coach on fire. Standing next to him shaking his head is the older bandit.

Malachi turns back to Rut. "Yeah, I see 'em."

The driver points at the bandits. "Fire away."

Malachi hesitates. "Really?"

"You heard me."

Malachi assesses the situation, raises his rifle, and fires twice. He misses badly and the bandits take cover behind the coach. He shoots a third time and hits a rock twenty feet from the coach.

Rut grabs Malachi's rifle. He aims and fires twice, just missing the bandits as they scamper off into the trees. He turns to the passengers. "Back to the coach!" The travelers head back down the hill, while Rut and Malachi follow with the horses.

Rut leans forward in a chair across from Henry as Jack looks out the jailhouse window. Stubborn cackles. "They run off like scared rabbits."

Henry leans forward. "Any idea who they were?"

"Naw. Heads was bagged."

Jack nods at Henry. "Gotta be Spivey and Slade."

Rut grins. "One more thing."

"What's that?"

"If it was them, they're half-wits who don't know shit from wild honey. Gold was there all along."

Suddenly interested, Jack says, "Yeah. Where was it?"

"In my travel bag atop the coach." Rut laughs and turns his back to leave as Jack grins at Henry.

CARSON CITY - NEVADA TERRITORY

Good Time Jane steers her wagon up to the Carson City Saloon and ties a strap to a hitching post. She crawls down from her wagon and walks over to her two mules. "Behave yerselves now ... and try not to shit on dis clean street."

A finely-dressed woman approaches, furrows her eyebrows, and Jane chuckles. The woman lifts her chin and scurries away. Jane calls after her. "Yes Ma'am. I's black as coal and fat as a prairie buffalo." Jane watches as the woman scurries around the corner and then Good Time struts her way into the saloon.

Jane sits all alone at the bar as several men, including the three saddle tramps from the Washoe Massacre, talk amongst themselves at tables nearby. The saloon owner and full-time bartender saunters over and pours Jane a shot of whiskey, just as Red, the Irish saddle tramp, slides up to Jane with an empty shot glass. He raps on the counter. "Hey, bar dog. Gimme a bottle of yer best."

The bartender glares. "I'm the proprietor of this establishment and not a dog."

"Woah, ain't you fancy." The bartender turns his back on Red. "Okay, Mr. Proprietor, I'll take the rest of this bottle."

Before he can respond, the lout grabs the bottle the barkeep left for Jane. The saloon owner holds out his hand and the trouble maker slaps a silver dollar on the counter. Before leaving, the Irishman stares at Jane and turns back to the barkeep. "Why ya servin' her kind anyway?"

The bartender raises his voice. "Good Time ain't no trouble."

The red-headed sot chuckles and gives Jane a cynical smile. "Good Time? Shit ... Why they call you that? My mind's a wonder."

Jane's answer is soft. "Want no trouble, mister."

Red walks over and joins his two friends, Nils, "Swede" and Diego, "Hombre," who have been waiting not so patiently at a table. He pours each of them a drink and says, "Good Time ... my ass!"

Swede snickers. "Don't know. Looks like enough there to keep all three of us busy." The ruffians laugh in unison.

Hombre raises his glass and toasts Jane. "Mucho amor!"

Red slaps Swede and Hombre on their backs and turns and grins at Jane again. "Come on over here, Good Time. We don't bite." Jane stands silently at the bar, so Red stands up and walks back over to Jane. "Gave ya an invite. Ain't polite to ignore a gentleman like myself." Jane doesn't respond, so Red continues. "How 'bout giving us a free touch? Ya got plenty to spare."

The bartender walks up. "Finish your drinks and get the hell out of my place"

Red ignores him. "Never seen a nigger woman naked. How 'bout you fellas?"

Swede chuckles. "Can't say I have. That'd be a whole lot of naked."

Without warning, Red reaches over and squeezes Jane's ass. "Yee hah!"

Jane's face darkens and she backhands the tramp across the face. Red drops to the floor but he quickly jumps to his feet and bull-rushes her. She grabs Red by his shirt, lifts him above her head, and throws him across the room. Red lands on the saddle tramps' table and his friends help him to his feet.

Embarrassed, Red rushes back to Jane, takes a swing, and misses. Good Time grabs him, lifts him off his feet again, and puts him in a bear hug. Eyes wide, she breathes a whisper in his ear. "I's gonna turn ya ta dust, asshole."

As Jane squeezes Red, he gasps for air and his legs flail wildly. His friends rush over and try to pry him away from Jane, but she tightens her grip on Red even more. The bartender approaches, points a shotgun at the two friends, and they back away. He waits a moment and then lays the gun on the bar counter. Then he gently takes Jane by the arm and says, "Let go. It's all right."

Jane gains her composure and releases Red. The buffoon sags to the floor like a bag of potatoes, so his friends try to help him to his feet. Irritated, Red shoves them out of the way.

As the saddle tramps stumble out the door, the bartender trails behind them with his shotgun at the ready. Outside the saloon, the bartender watches as the three troublemakers ride off, Red slumped over his saddle.

CHAPTER 18

"I love a good man outside the law, just as much as I hate a bad man inside the law." Woody Guthrie

A FARM WAGON drawn by two mules speeds down the main street of Bannack and slides to a stop in front of the sheriff's office. Henry and Jack exit their building and wait for the dust to settle.

They see that it's Abe Gunderson, who is slumped over the backs of his two mules holding his bloody leg. Next to him is his wife, Helga, who is rocking back and forth and mumbling incoherently. "Sweet Jesus, sweet Jesus, sweet baby Jesus." Helga wraps one arm around herself and her other hand clutches her torn dress.

Henry speaks first. "What's going on, Abe?"

"Two bastards you freed shot me, stole five of my best cows, and messed up my woman here!"

"What bastards you talking about?"

"That asshole we should've hanged and his side man."

Jack smirks. "Spivey and Slade?"

Abe growls. "That's them. Come up on my place all slow like. Asked ta water their horses. For we knowed it, them Smith killers busted in our place. Tried hold'em back like I use ta could, but Spivey pulled his gun on me. His partner argued the right thing, but that son of a bitch wouldn't listen."

"What right thing did Slade argue?"

"That there's nothin' worth taking and they should go."

"What else?"

"Spivey says, 'No, I got me some needs.' So that Slade says back, 'That's not why we're here.' Then Spivey argues back, 'If'n ya don't want none of this, get the hell out.' So, Slade he heads out the door and Spivey grabs hold of Helga. Tried to fight him off, but he shot me in the leg and clubbed my head. When I come to, the shit-face was ridin' Helga like she was some prize cow. Lucky if she ain't pregnated."

"Slade? Get a good look at him?"

"No, the damn fool kept himself hooded the whole time."

Henry continues. "Better get yourselves over to Doc Robinson's."

When Jack reaches out to help Helga down from the wagon, she recoils and screams. "Ahh! Ahh!" She reaches out, grabs Jack by the hair and tears at his clothes.

The deputy breaks free and jumps back. "Jesus, Mary, and Joseph! Shit!"

Helga hisses in a low satanic voice. "Got no right touchin' me! I ain't no whore! Jesus saves. Jesus saves."

Abe tries to explain. "She's all tangled up. Head weren't on that straight to begin with."

Helga rocks back and forth and gabbles. "Jesus. Sweet baby Jesus. Prick. Prick. Whore. Whore."

Abe turns to Henry. "Killed my boy and now this?"

"Don't be putting what Spivey done on me?"

"Held us back from hanging him, didn't ya?"

Henry ignores Abe's remark. "Which way did they ride?"

"I don't know. South, kinda east."

As Henry and Jack mount their horses and ride off, Abe yells out. "If ya find'em, kill'em hard! Ya owe me!"

Henry and Jack ride along on a high-plains dirt road at a brisk pace as the sun burns brightly. Not too far from the Gunderson farm, they look down at two sets of tracks headed east. Two hours later, the sheriff and deputy spot Warren and Alex up ahead entering Bruce Canyon. When Henry and Jack reach the canyon, they get down from their horses and carefully walk them through the narrow opening.

Warren and Alex, hidden behind a rock on a ridge high above the opening, fire away at the Bannack lawmen as they enter the canyon. Henry and Jack take cover behind a large rock in a narrow ravine below the ridge.

A few minutes pass and Jack scoffs. "Drying up like a piece of jerked meat. Not gonna sit here all day."

Henry spits. "They're bakin' up there same as us."

Several shots ring out and Henry and Jack scrunch low to the ground. As the lawbreakers reload, Jack jumps up. "Ya rapin', chicken shit mudsills! Give us somethin' to shoot at!"

Warren and Alex raise up again and fire off two more shots. A bullet whizzes past Jack. Another one hits a rock nearby and the fragments momentarily blind him. Frustrated, Jack crouches back down behind the rock and rubs his eyes. "God damn it! Stay here if ya want. Them snakes ain't worth dying for."

Henry crawls over. "Lay low and give me your pistol."

"What? Pull in your horns!"

"I'm going up. Try to keep'em busy with your rifle." Jack reluctantly tosses his pistol and Henry sticks it in his gun belt behind his back. Jack readies his rifle as Henry prepares himself.

Jack fires a volley of shots as Henry pops up, zig-zags up the hill, and fires away. When Warren and Alex return fire, the deputy ducks down behind his rock, covers his head, and mutters, "Holy Shit."

Halfway up the hill, Henry trips over a rock, falls flat on his face and his gun flies out of his hand. Warren sees what's happening, steps out from behind a rock, and aims at the young sheriff. Henry sits up, dusts himself off, and yells down the hill. "Jack, you still there?" Warren chuckles, lowers his gun, spits, and aims again. From his knees, Henry reaches behind his back and grabs Jack's pistol. Before Warren can get off a shot, he shoots the heathen in the foot.

Warren screams out in pain. "Ahh!" He looks at his foot and then at Henry. "Son of a bitch! I'd better have all my toes." Warren raises his pistol to shoot again.

"Really?" Henry shoots the scoundrel in the other foot and Warren drops his gun, sinks to the ground, and whimpers as he examines his bloodied boots.

Henry looks at the top of the hill and watches as Alex Slade mounts his horse. Henry takes aim, but before he can fire, Jack rifles a shot. Alex falls from his horse and Henry looks back at Jack and yells, "It's about time!"

When Jack joins Henry, he has a satisfied look on his face. "Rifle jammed. Bet yer glad I got it workin' again?"

Alex, who is bleeding from his head, jumps to his feet and charges down the hill waving a pistol in each hand. In a fit of rage, he fires in every direction. Henry and Jack take cover behind two separate boulders as Warren continues to study his bloody feet.

Out of bullets, Alex throws his pistols and one of them hits Jack on his forehead. Alex starts back up the hill, gathers an armful of rocks, and throws them at Henry and Jack, who remain hidden behind their respective boulders.

When Alex reaches his horse, Jack aims his rifle at the fugitive. Henry steps up, grabs his deputy's arm, and forces him to lower his weapon. "What the hell? I was all set to get my gratification."

"We'll chase him down later. You get a good look at him?"

"Hell, no. I was busy dodging rocks. He did have himself a full head of hair."

Henry turns to Spivey, still sitting on the ground nursing his feet. "Get your ass up, we're riding."

Henry and Jack approach Bannack with Warren Spivey in tow. His hands are tied in front of him with a leather strap. Jack falls back and grins at their prisoner. "That's some partner ya got. Left ya high and dry."

Henry joins the conversation. "How long you two been together?"

Warren growls. "Too long." He studies Henry's face. "Why didn't ya let that posse to hang me?"

"Had my reasons."

Warren looks at Henry's badge. "Heard Bannack got them a sheriff. What's yer name, again?"

"You don't remember me? I'm Henry...Henry Plummer."

"Plummer?"

Henry points at Warren's head. Warren rubs the scar on his forehead and studies the sheriff's face again. "Out of Maine?

"That's right."

Warren takes a moment. "What are the chances? Thought you was dead?"

Henry stares at his prisoner. "Do I look dead?"

Warren spits. "Fucking Slade."

Henry's face tightens. "Lay things bare. What'd you do with my brother?"

Warren grins. "Might recall if I was to be let go."

"Can't do that."

Jack tries. "Go on, let him ride off. But this time, I get a shot."

Warren smirks. "Shit. You can't do that. You're the law now. Hey, I need to make water."

Henry rides ahead and Jack stays back with Warren and growls. "Piss in yer pants for all I care."

When the three men arrive in Bannack, Henry and Jack tether their horses and help Warren off his animal. Ben appears and Henry nods. "Hate to admit it, but you were right all along. This asshole is Spivey."

Ben looks around. "What about Slade?"

Jack steps forward. "Winged him, but that turned him into a wild man and he rode off."

"How the Gundersons doing?" Henry asks.

"Abe's okay. Helga ain't fixable. She's all balled up." Ben furrows his brows. "They'd be a whole lot better if we'd of hanged this asshole."

Henry defends himself. "He still deserves a trial."

Four local men ride up and study Warren's face. The group's leader leans over his saddle and addresses the prisoner. "See ya found one of the brother killers...and Helga raper." The man removes a rope from his saddle and holds it out. "Got us a nice tree all picked out. Time for a good old-fashioned lynching bee."

Henry steps forward. "Not your call. Judge will decide."

A second man speaks up. "That asshole killed Josh and Frank ...we ain't waiting."

Jack draws his pistol. "You heard him. Nothin' to see here. Get yer gratification somewhere else!"

The second man argues. "Shit, Cleveland. You going soft, too?"

The local men stand rigid for a moment and finally slip away as Henry turns to Warren. "Getting tired of saving your ass, Spivey. Lookin' forward to seeing you hang."

Henry and Ben watch as Jack pushes Warren up the jailhouse steps, opens the door, and shoves him inside.

Ben turns to Henry. "Gonna take some time for us to get used to you being the law, but I gotta say I like how you stood up to those men."

"Good, 'cuz I need you and your own to fill in for me and Jack once Spivey is dealt his due."

"Why? Where you going."

"Slade being on the loose aggravates me. I wanna chase him down."

"Know where he's at?"

"No, but I think I know someone who might."

"Good luck squeezing the truth out of that asshole."

Not sure if I'll ever find my brother, but I'm at a place where I just wanna know if he's alive or dead. Brothers don't let brothers wander in the dark.

The Saffron is filled with men and women drinking and talking loudly. No one seems to notice as an elderly, almost blind, territorial judge wobbles into the bar with Sweet attached to his arm. She helps him find a chair behind a front and center table and the old man drops down and farts loudly.

Sweet discreetly waves the air, grabs a beer from a miner at a nearby table, and offers it to the judge. The magistrate grabs the mug and gulps it down in one motion.

Abe and Helga Gunderson are seated at the back of the room with several other weary-eyed sodbusters. Ben, Henry, and

Jack are front and center at a table facing the judge. Next to them is Warren Spivey, whose hands and legs are shackled with chains.

The judge raps his gavel, belches, and everyone laughs. He stares at the curious onlookers and they quiet down. "Spivey, everyone here's convinced you killed the Smith brothers, but figuring you did and knowing you did aren't the same. It pains me to say, but there's not enough evidence to hang you for something all these people think you done."

People boo and jeer and the judge raps his gavel hard on the table. "Tighten your mouths, people! What I do know is you robbed Dillon's bank, escaped, shot Abe Gunderson, and soiled his wife. And one more thing. You and your accomplice tried to kill that sheriff and deputy sitting next to you."

People continue to whoop and holler, so the judge raps his gavel even louder this time. "Spivey, I'm sending you to San Quentin to rust for forty years." The judge raps his gavel a third time as people curse and throw things.

A drunken miner yells out, "The bastard needs to hang!"

Another man hollers, "What about the watch?!"

The judge stares at the crowd and nods. "I know. I struggled with that story, but there's no watch for me to look at." As the crowd boos, the judge signals Sweet Waters. "Another drink, whiskey this time." Several people grumble as they leave the bar, while others go back to drinking and playing cards.

A week later, in front of the Bannack jailhouse, Henry and Jack watch as two hired men help a shackled Warren Spivey into the back of a flat-bed wagon. The men chain Warren's damaged feet to the wagon's floor as he winces in pain.

Henry steps forward and says, "Figured you to hang for sure." Warren simply smiles. "Come clean. Did you kill Samuel? No one gives a shit, but me."

Warren snickers. "Funny thing. My memory started fadin' the day you dry-gulched me."

The guards finish up and prepare to drive off, but Henry holds up his hand and waits for Warren to say something. Finally, the felon grins and then spits. "Tell you what, you find Slade and he'll tell you all ya need to know."

"So, it was Slade that was with you when ya took Samuel?"

"Been me and Slade for more than twenty years."

As the wagon rolls away, Henry follows behind, still seeking more information. "Where do I find him?"

Warren chortles. "Now why the hell would I tell you that?"

"The coward left you high and dry. Twenty-year partners don't do that."

Warren hesitates and chuckles, "Fort Benton. Had us a plan we was cookin' up with the Blackfeet. Better shoot first though. He ain't one to give himself up." The wagon picks up speed, leaving the sheriff in the dust.

Henry starts to cough but tries one more time. "I need Slade alive to tell me what happened to Samuel."

Warren yells back. "Kill Slade for me, and I'll tell what happened to yer brother."

Henry yells back. "Gonna hold you to that!"

The wagon distances itself as Henry returns to Jack, who looks him in the eyes and says, "I hope you know, you were just dancin' with the devil."

CHAPTER 19

"The jealous are possessed by a mad devil and a dull spirit at the same time." Johann Kaspar Lavater

JOHN VEDDER IS COUNTING THE MONEY from his cash register when Lucy comes out of the back room carrying a sewing basket. Adorned in her yellow dress, Lucy has a noticeable bruise on her cheek. "I'm going to my sewing circle, now."

"Don't be late. Got a load of supplies comin' in that need puttin' away." John studies Lucy's appearance. "Why you all the time wearing that yellow dress?"

"Because I like it."

Lucy exits the store and walks down Main Street in the direction of Bannack's only church, but suddenly she takes a turn and heads for Gus's Livery Stable and Blacksmith Shop. When she arrives, she makes sure no one is watching, opens the door, and slides inside.

Gus looks up from his work and walks over to Lucy. He raises his one good arm, smiles, and points to the hayloft. He returns to his furnace and removes a red-hot horseshoe. He places it on an anvil and begins to pound away.

When Lucy reaches the top rung of the hayloft ladder, a barefooted Henry pulls her up and into his arms. They kiss passionately and start removing each other's clothes.

The blacksmith pauses a moment and looks up. He shakes his head as pieces of hay fall through the cracks of the loft. He smiles and then turns his attention back to his work. As Gus rhythmically hammers the horseshoe with his one good hand, he drowns out the sounds of Lucy and Henry's lovemaking.

John is sweeping the floor inside his store when a supply wagon arrives. He looks at his watch, tosses the broom, and hurries out of the store.

The angry store owner paces back and forth on his front walkway as the driver watches. John's face reddens as he peers at the church at the end of the street. Angry, he looks up at the wagon driver and growls, "Leave the wagon here and get ya a drink. Be back as soon as I can."

Laying in the hay in their undergarments, Henry and Lucy continue to cradle one another as Henry gently speaks his mind. "Giving yourself up to Vedder so he'd pay your pa's debt doesn't sound like something you'd do."

Lucy sits up, scoots away from Henry, and starts to put on her dress. "I was desperate. The bank was ready to take our farm." She fastens her last button on her dress and moves back over to her lover.

Henry sighs. "Your family? What do they think of John?"

Lucy's eyes narrow. "They never met him. He rode into town, found me working at our local general store, and made himself out to be a wealthy man. Before I knew it, he convinced me to go away with him. Said if I'd go, he'd ..."

Henry interrupts. "I know, pay off your father's loan."

"Henry, my family was only days away from losing everything." Henry squeezes Lucy's hand and Lucy continues. "The next day John paid off the mortgage and we left that night. My folks still have no idea where I am."

"And you never married?"

"Figured he'd want to, but he's never even mentioned it. And since I don't love him ..."

"And you've stayed with that bastard all this time? He treats you like shit."

"He constantly tells me I owe him."

"Believe me. You're paid in full."

"I've got nowhere else to go."

"You could move in with Jack and me." Henry cuffs Lucy's wrists and holds them tight. "But you'd have to break the law, so's I could arrest you."

Lucy grins. "What sorta law do you think I should break?"

They start to kiss, but all at once, Lucy breaks away. "What time is it?" Henry pats his half-naked body like he's looking for a watch.

Gus, who has been listening in below, checks his watch and yells out, "Five o'clock!"

Lucy scrambles to her feet. "Oh my God! John's gonna kill me!" She straightens her dress and starts to look for her shoes. She finds one but not the other. Henry, who is holding her shoe behind his back, smiles. Lucy grabs his arm and wrestles it away. She puts her shoes on, jumps to her feet, steals Henry's pants, and scampers down the ladder.

Henry is nonplussed as he looks down from the loft. "Hey now." Lucy gives him a sinister grin, throws his pants in the burning fireplace, and runs out the door. Henry slides down the hayloft ladder, grabs some tongs, and pulls his smoldering pants from the fire as Gus chuckles. He climbs into the heated pants and immediately starts to dance in a circle. "Awwh! Shit! Shit! Fish shit!"

Gus laughs as he points at the two large holes in the rear of his young friend's pants. The blacksmith removes his leather apron, hands it to Henry and he puts it on. Half way out the door, he tosses Gus a silver dollar and disappears.

The sheriff soft boots his way down the alley behind the jailhouse. Then he peeks around the corner, makes sure no one is watching, scampers to the front door, and rushes inside.

Jack, who is seated behind the office desk, watches as Henry removes Gus's apron, revealing his fire-tattered pants. The deputy's eyes light up. "Holy mule gravy!"

It's early morning as Henry and Jack load their horses with supplies. Dr. Robinson spots them and crosses the street. "Where you off to?"

Henry yawns. "North to Fort Benton. Looking for Alex Slade."

As Jack tightens the cinch on his horse, he yawns and says, "His idea, not mine."

"Long ways to go. He worth all the trouble?"

As Jack climbs in the saddle, he says, "There's the five-hundred-dollar reward, his pocket money, and his horse. Henry's got his own reasons."

NEVADA TERRITORY

Pete and Buckie are saddling a fresh horse when they hear the sound of a bugle blaring in the distance. Mother and daughter rush out the door with a small bag of food and a water canteen.

Express rider, Johnny Fry, tops a hill in a cloud of dust and approaches the station. He slides to a stop a few feet from Buckie and dismounts. Pete removes the mailbag from his lathered horse and attaches it to a fresh mount.

Buckie steadies the replacement horse as the express rider climbs aboard. He catches his big sister smiling at Johnny and points his finger at her. Embarrassed, Sandra gives Buckie a shove. "Pest!"

Maria hands Johnny the bag of food and Sandra gives him a fresh canteen. The young man starts to say something, but Pete slaps his horse and Johnny speeds away.

As the Bucklands start back to the cabin, Sandra lags behind, watching the young rider disappear in the distance. From the cabin steps, Buckie yells, "Love!" Sandra takes a threatening step towards her brother and Buckie cackles and runs into the house.

IDAHO TERRITORY

On a crisp cold fall day, Henry and Jack, now wearing heavy coats, cross a ridge and see a herd of buffalo on the open prairie. When they reach the bison, the mangy animals don't move, so they ride through the middle of the herd. A few seconds pass and Jack turns to Henry. "I'm curious. Gus ever tell you how he lost his arm?"

"Said when he was a boy, he got it caught in a bear trap and his pa had to cut most of it off."

"Ya believe that?"

"No, but it makes for a good story."

After we made our way past the buffalo headed for Fort Benton, all I could think about was how long it must have taken for the wind, fire and rain to shape the immense prairie that gave those rugged animals a place to live.

Now traveling down a rough road rutted by wagon wheels, Jack interrupts the silence by singing a made-up song to the tune of *Sweet Betsy from Pike:*

Can't find no luck in them cold mountain streams.
God up above has been treating me mean.
If I could find me some nuggets of gold
I'd marry a fine woman before I'm too old.
Singing do rah rah do rah rah do rah rah day.

Henry chuckles. "Didn't know you could carry a tune." The wind picks up and both men hunker down in their saddles. "Wind's got some winter in it."

Black smoke bellows from the funnel of the steamboat, *Emilie*, as it crawls up the Missouri River headed for Fort Benton. An American flag flies above a deck filled with passengers and freight.

Among the travelers are thirty-somethings James and Martha Vail and their children Mary, age six, and Harvey, age four. Not far away is Electa Bryan, Martha's twenty-five-year-old attractive sister, who stands next to a weathered old fur trader talking.

On the bridge, Captain Joseph La Barge oversees a cub pilot who is steering the boat as it approaches the narrows of the Missouri River. The captain speaks with confidence. "River thins ahead. Don't drift too close to the shadows now."

The cub pilot squints. "How long 'til Fort Benton, Captain?"
"Two maybe three days."

Still on the deck below, Martha Jane is holding her son Harvey by the hand, while Electa looks after her sister's daughter, Mary. The leather clad fur trader has made his way over to James at the rail of the boat, where they are both smoking pipes.

The trader finally pockets his pipe, puts a wad of tobacco in his mouth, and snorts. "Tough trail, Mullan Road ... full of Blackfeet. Them heathens are gonna be more interested in yer scalps than any book learnin'."

James responds, "Sounds like you're a man who's had considerable experience with the native population."

The trader pulls up his shirt, revealing two large scars. "Here's my experience. Blackfeet bushwhacked me, stole my horses, and killed my Shoshone woman. Could cook too, hunt … even liked being on her back."

One of the male passengers lets out a scream. "Buffalo!" Men and women alike gather on the starboard side of the boat and watch as a herd of buffalo crosses the river just ahead.

Several other male passengers grab their weapons and indiscriminately fire away. On the other side of the river, five Blackfeet Indians watch the attack, hidden behind a small grove of trees.

One of the passengers wounds a buffalo and it begins to bellow. "Holy shit! Got me one!" There is more shooting, hooting, and hollering as the wounded bison struggle to stay above water.

Martha Jane turns to her sister. "Electa, help me take the children down below." The sisters usher Mary and Harvey below deck as the shooting continues.

As the boat comes to a halt, two men try to pull the now dead buffalo onboard using a rope, but the beast is too heavy. Captain La Barge looks down from the bridge as the chaos grows. "Ya shitheads are gonna get us all killed! That there's the Indians' livelihood you're shooting at!"

A wiry passenger spots a lone buffalo calf that has been swept away by the river's current. Somehow, he manages to rope it and several other passengers help him pull it on board. The calf breaks free and begins to run wildly around the deck. Passengers scream as they try to avoid being run over by the terrified beast.

Incensed, Captain La Barge enters the pilot's house, exits with a rifle, aims down at the calf, and shoots it. The calf bellows, collapses to the deck and dies. La Barge descends the ladder leading to the deck, shifts his rifle, and aims it at the passengers. "Put yer weapons down or I'll throw yer asses off this boat!" The passengers do as he says and lay their guns and rifles on the deck.

While several men murmur amongst themselves, Electa returns from the underside of the boat, looks at the dead buffalo calf and turns to the old fur trader. With stoic confidence, she says, "Appears this boat has its own share of heathens."

As the trader turns to respond, an arrow strikes him square in the chest and he collapses at Electa's feet. Several men yell in unison, "Indians!" The passengers scoop up their weapons and begin to fire indiscriminately at the shoreline.

From the river bank, a dozen Blackfeet warriors take turns shooting arrows from the cover of trees as the boat captain considers the situation. An arrow hits the cub pilot in the leg and he falls to his knees, so the captain returns to the bridge and takes over. Meanwhile, on the deck below, several passengers dodge arrows as the boat slips around a bend in the river.

On the starboard side of the boat, Electa holds the fur trader in her arms until he takes his final breath. As she tries to gather her emotions, an arrow grazes her face and lodges in a post just behind her. She touches her cheek and feels a trickle of blood. With fire in her eyes, she grabs the fur trader's rifle, jumps to her feet, and aims at what appears to be an Indian standing front and center on shore. Instantly, she realizes she is staring into the eyes of a white man, who is disguised as an Indian and aiming his rifle directly at her.

Frozen by her own indecisiveness, the long-haired beauty hesitates until her sister approaches from behind and taps her on the shoulder, and says, "No."

Electa lowers her weapon and glares at her sister. When she looks back at the shoreline, the imposter is gone.

CHAPTER 20

"There is no death. Only a change of worlds." Chief Seattle

TUMBLEWEEDS AND DUST DEVILS make their way across the wide-open Nevada desert and cross Buckland Station. Fighting the wind, Maria exits the family cabin and waits for Pete and Good Time Jane to finish repairing Pete's wagon.

Jane hums a spiritual as she grips the wagon and lifts the axle high enough off the ground so Pete can attach the wheel. Pete grips the spoked sphere, slides it on the axle, and slaps his exhausted helpmate on the back. Jane drops to the ground, leans back against the newly mounted wheel, wipes her brow, and celebrates. "Sweet baby, Jesus! We done it."

Pete grins. "Good Time! You're a wonder."

Maria approaches with a look of concern on her face. "Pete, Buckie's still not back from checking his traps."

As Pete massages his back, he grumbles, "Damn it. That boy's gonna be the end of me."

With worry in her voice, Maria says, "He should've been home by now."

Jane struggles to her feet. "Boy got his self a natural curiosity, a natural curiosity."

Pete growls. "I got no time. I have horses to feed."

Maria persists. "Maybe he stepped in a hole or some snake bit him."

Jane treads over to her wagon and begins to unhitch Moses. "You keep on, Mr. Pete. Me and Moses got nowheres to go. We'll find 'em."

In the open grasslands not far from Buckland Station, Good Time Jane trudges along on her saddleless mule. She reaches down, grabs the jug of whiskey hanging from a small rope tied to Moses' neck collar, takes a gulp, and begins to sing:

There's a balm in Gilead to make the wounded whole.
There's a balm in Gilead to heal the sin-sick soul.
One of these mornings bright and fair, I'm gonna lay down my heavy load. I gotta heavy load.
Gonna kick my wings and cleave the air, I'm gonna lay down my heavy load. I gotta heavy load.

In a forested area a few miles from home, Buckie traipses through the trees, carrying two dead rabbits. He stops near a large pine and finds a squirming rabbit caught in one of his traps. He pulls a knife, leans over, cuts the rabbit's neck, and removes it from the snare.

As Buckie starts for home, he looks over at an open field and spots eight Paiutes on horseback. They're wearing war paint and coming his way. The boy instantly ducks behind the pine tree, drops down, and sits perfectly still.

Numaga, the Paiute leader, is still strikingly handsome, despite the evil in his eyes and the bright red and black war paint covering his face and body. The warrior scans the ground, jumps off his horse, and looks at a pile of muck in the ryegrass. He scoops up one of the horse apples with his fingers and smells it.

Buckie stands up, his back against the tree, and peeks at Numaga as the Paiute leader addresses his Indian friends in his native tongue. "Washoe ... horse shit?" The other warriors snicker as Numaga squeezes the shit between his fingers, revealing several pinon nuts. He picks out a few and throws them at two of his comrades, who duck out of the way. "Pinon eaters. Even their horses eat them." The other Paiutes snicker as Numaga mounts his horse.

Without warning, a dozen screaming Washoe warriors also covered in war paint ride out of the trees past Buckie. They don't notice the young white boy because their eyes are focused on their Paiute enemies.

At close range, several Washoes knock Paiutes off their horses as both sides fire their rifles, shoot arrows, and use their knives and tomahawks to bloody one another.

Still hidden behind the tree, Buckie watches as the gory battle comes to a close and the last Paiute, Numaga, bludgeons and scalps another Washoe warrior. The Paiute licks his bloody knife, surveys the battleground, and spots the two remaining Washoes.

He finds his horse, climbs onboard, and eyes the enemy warriors as they hold up the scalps of two members of the Paiute war party and yell: "Argh! Argh!"

Before he can react, the youngest of the two Washoes fires. The bullet hits Numaga's horse and the animal crumbles to the ground, trapping his leg beneath him. Not satisfied, the young Washoe charges with his lance as the Paiute leader struggles to find his knife.

As the Washoe closes in, Numaga locates his knife, throws it, and hits the charging warrior in the throat. The young man grabs his neck, drops to his knees, and falls to the ground dead.

Somehow Numaga manages to pull himself out from under his horse. He struggles to his feet, hobbles over to the warrior, and removes the Washoe's scalp. He lifts it high in the air and screams, "Puha! Puha!" In the distance, the remaining Washoe mounts his horse and rides away.

Numaga reviews the carnage and sees that all his Paiute friends and the enemy Washoes are dead. He looks closer and realizes that both sides' horses are either dead or mortally wounded. His thoughts are interrupted when he spots Jane Fields approaching in the distance.

When Jane arrives, she rides directly up to the Paiute leader, who is still holding a Washoe scalp in his hand. She climbs off of Moses, studies the Indian's profile, and scans the battlefield. She calls the Paiute by name. "Numaga."

He grunts. "White Crow."

Jane looks around. "This yer doin'?"

Numaga raises the scalp and lets out another war cry. "Ahhh! Ahhh!"

Jane steps back as the Paiute moves forward brandishing his knife. She raises her fist and says, "I ain't afeard of you. Come any closer and I'll lay you out."

Buckie runs out from the trees and yells. "You leave Good Time Jane alone!"

Numaga repeats her name. "Good Time?"

Jane raises her hand. "Buckie, you stay put."

Still clutching his knife, the Paiute tosses the scalp aside and takes another step forward. Buckie rushes the Indian with his knife, but the Paiute disarms Buckie and puts his own blade to the boy's neck. Buckie stands frozen as Jane assesses the situation. "Harm dat child, I'll lay you out."

Numaga removes his knife from Buckie's throat, raises it to the young man's head, and cuts off a large tuft of Buckie's hair. The Paiute lifts the strands of hair high in the air and lets them fall through his fingers. He snorts at his own joke, tosses Buckie at Jane's feet, and grabs a rifle off the ground. He waves the weapon at the dead bodies and points it at Jane and Buckie. "White Crow help Numaga." He points at one of his dead comrades and makes an upward motion with both hands in the direction of the trees.

Jane nods at Buckie. "He wants us to move his friends."

Jane, who has the body of a dead Paiute draped over her shoulders, heads for the trees. Behind her, Buckie is leading Moses, who has two more lifeless warriors on his back. Trailing behind is Numaga, who points his rifle at a tree. Jane understands and rolls the dead Indian from her shoulders and hoists him up and over a low-lying tree limb.

An hour later, Jane and Buckie look back at the pine trees and see the bodies of seven Paiute warriors hanging from tree limbs. Still on the battlefield are eleven dead Washoe warriors.

Buzzards, who have been circling above, drop down and begin to peck at the Washoe corpses. Jane reacts by trying to shoo the birds away as Numaga spits on the ground and smiles. "Coyotes ... birds eat good tonight." He aims his rifle at Jane and Buckie, not sure what to do next. Finally, he mounts Moses, adjusts himself to the width of the mule, and rides off.

Buckie and Jane walk down a road leading to Buckland Station. Jane's clothes and face are caked with mud and blood. Buckie looks up at Jane and smiles. "You're a mess."

Jane touches her face and hands Buckie her canteen. "Pour!" Buckie dumps the contents of the container on Jane's head and bloody water washes down the sides of her face. She bares her teeth and Buckie laughs.

The unlikely pair walk along, headed for home as the blood-red sun sinks below the horizon. Without warning, Buckie stops in his tracks and gives Jane a curious look. "Why'd he have us put them dead Indians in the trees?"

"'Cuz, it gets them closer to da hereafter and keeps the varmints away."

"Think they'll be Indians in heaven?"

"They'll have their place."

"I'm not so sure there is a heaven."

Jane's eyes widen. "I promise there is."

"No one's been there, and why aren't we there already?"

Jane adjusts her hat. "Buckie, you ask the damndest questions."

"Got another one. Why do Indians scalp each other's hair?"

"Don't know. Makes no sense to me."

"Maybe they don't want their enemies to look good in heaven ... I mean if there is one."

Jane chortles. "Now there's a thought I ain't supposed before. Boy, you all the time thinkin'... all the time thinkin'." She puts her hand on the bare spot of Buckie's head. "What we gonna tell yer folks happened to you?"

Buckie looks at Jane and shrugs his shoulders. "They don't need to know nothin'."

Jane laughs. "Gonna know somethin' when they see ya been scalped?" Buckie touches the top of his head and grins as Jane puts her hands to her mouth and whistles loudly.

Not far off, headed in the opposite direction, Numaga rides along on Moses, trying his best to get comfortable. All at once, the Paiute hears a distant whistle. Instantly, Moses bellows, pricks up his ears, rears up, and throws Numaga to the ground. The Indian stumbles to his feet and grabs his rifle, but the mule is already too far away to shoot.

As Jane and Buckie continue to make their way back home, they hear bellowing and snorting in the distance. When they look up, they see Moses approaching at a dead run. When he reaches

Jane, he slides to a stop, brays loudly, and kicks up his heels.

When Buckie and Jane arrive at Buckland Station, Maria, Pete, and Sandra run out of the cabin carrying a lantern. Buckie slips off the weary mule, runs over to his mother and father, and hugs them tightly.

Maria takes hold of her son's shoulders and shakes them gently. "Buckie, we've been worried sick." She holds the lantern up and sees Buckie's new hair-cut, Jane's filthy face, and her blood-stained clothes. "Where have you two been? Ya look awful. And what happened to your hair?"

Buckie grins. "I got scalped."

Maria holds her hand to her mouth in disbelief and turns to Jane. The runaway slave smirks. "He got some story ... some story ta tell."

The Buckland family and Jane walk towards the cabin as Sandra playfully slaps Buckie on the shoulder and says, "Pest." Buckie takes off running, trying to beat his sister home, while his parents take turns staring at each other. When the Bucklands are a safe distance away, Jane lowers her head and begins to cry.

CHAPTER 21

"Whoever loved that loved not at first sight?"
Christopher Marlowe

TRADERS EXIT THE GATE of Fort Benton, leading horses loaded with supplies. Indians and merchants haggle over pelt prices outside the fort as Henry and Jack crest a hill overlooking the Missouri River community. Jack eyes the fort and says, "Doubt Slade's hiding in there?"

Henry counters. "No, but someone might've seen him."

"Not gonna let us in if we ain't got nothin' to trade."

Henry rides ahead as he says, "I've been doing all the figuring lately. You come up with something."

When they reach the fort, a guard standing at the front of the gate raises his rifle as Jack asks, "You in charge here?"

The guard chuckles. "No, Captain La Barge. Him and his boat just got here yesterday."

Jack sits up in his saddle and says, "We'd like to see him."

"He send for you?"

"Nope."

"Then it's not gonna happen."

Jack takes a moment, collects his thoughts, and points at Henry. "Ain't gonna lie and say we been sent for ... but this here's the captain's son, Melvin. He's simple-minded on account he almost drowned being baptized. Preacher let go. Current took Melvin down river a mile for we got to him. Me being his uncle, I thought I'd bring him here so's to meet his pa."

"Are you sayin' La Barge is this man's father?"

Jack nods. "That's right. Yer captain planted Melvin in my sister twenty-odd years ago in Orleans, but the captain, he don't know it. My sister holds no grudges, on account it was a one-time frolic. And since they was both drunk, sister calls Melvin here her whiskey boy."

"That's one hell of a story, mister."

"Didn't come all this way for no reason."

The guard shakes his head and points inside the fort. "Captain's quarters is the first building on the right."

As Jack and Henry ride through the gate, Henry shoves Jack so hard he almost falls off his horse. "Whiskey boy."

Seated behind a desk in his office, Captain La Barge is conversing with James Vail. Next to him is Electa, who has a small bandage on her face. The captain hears voices, the door opens, and Henry and Jack slip past the sentry. They plant themselves in front of the officer's desk and the captain frowns. "Ya know, ya could get shot comin' in here like that."

Jack nods. "Yeah, we really wanna talk to you." Both men remove their hats as Jack looks around. "Never been in a real fort before." The sentry steps up and waits for an order to usher the men out. The captain waves the private away and turns and stares at the two intruders. "Okay, this better be important."

Henry steps forward and shows the captain his badge. "We're out of Bannack looking for a lawbreaker named Alex Slade."

"Not a name I've heard. What's he look like?"

Henry hesitates and says, "Never seen him close up, but was told he could be partnered up with the Blackfeet near here."

Jack adds. "He does have long hair."

Henry coughs deeply and everyone gives him a look of concern. "I'm good. So, no trouble with the Blackfeet?"

"No, they're on the move. Attacked my boat just 'fore we landed. Mainly they stick to killin' and robbin' folks traveling the Mullan Road."

James sits up and gives Electa a worried look as Henry continues. "See any white men with them?"

Electa interjects. "Captain, if I may, I did see a Caucasian male dressed like an Indian on the shoreline."

Henry turns to her. "Get a good look at him, did ya?"

"He was covered with war paint, but I have no doubt that his skin was white."

Jack grins awkwardly. "Did he have long hair?"

"I didn't see his hair." Jack stares at Electa until she turns away.

Henry interrupts their moment. "Slade and his partner did some bad things. Need to find him."

La Barge nods. "Didn't say there were two of them."

"Not anymore. Warren Spivey is on his way to San Quentin."

"Why do you think this Slade is with the Blackfeet?"

"'Cuz, I squeezed it out of Spivey that they had a plan to team up."

"And you believed him?" Henry doesn't respond, so the captain continues. "This Slade, he must be worth some money?"

Henry lifts his jaw. "It ain't the money."

Jack chimes in. "It is for me."

Henry continues. "Guess we'll look around here a couple days and head home by way of Mullan Road. Maybe we'll get lucky and he'll try and rob us."

Jack tries to be clever. "Yeah, him and a whole flock of Blackfeet."

James turns to Electa and then back to the captain. "Sir, I might have an opportunity for these men."

The captain nods at the missionary. "Speak."

"Gentlemen, my family and I are setting up a mission outside of Bannack. If you're planning to return there soon, we sure could use your help with safe passage down that same road."

Henry grins. "Missionaries?"

"Yes, but we can pay."

Henry looks at Jack and his partner shrugs. "Slade ain't payin' nothin' if we don't find him."

Henry nods. "Give us a couple days. If we don't find Slade, we'll ride back to Bannack with you."

James smiles. "God bless you."

Henry offers his hand to James and they shake. "I'm Henry Plummer. This here's Jack Cleveland."

"Brother Plummer … Brother Cleveland, I'm James Vail and this is my sister-in-law, Electa Bryan."

Taken aback, Jack shakes the missionary's hand and says, "In-law?"

"Yes, you'll meet my wife and children later. Thank you. Look forward to you joining us."

As they leave, Jack whispers, "That is one fetching woman. She's gonna beat traveling Slade home."

Henry grins. "Easy. We still might find him."

Jack continues, "Ladiest damn lady I've ever seen."

MULLAN ROAD

James and Martha Jane Vail are seated in the front of their slow-moving covered wagon with Mary and Harvey Vail between them. Electa is in the back surrounded by supplies and Jack trails behind the Vails in a second loaded wagon with his horse tied to the back. Henry pulls up alongside Jack's wagon and his deputy says, "Here I am … in a fuckin' wagon again."

Henry grins. "No more cussing. You're doing the Lord's work … brother Jack."

Jack nods in the direction of Electa. "You been watching how that gal looks my way now and again?"

"Well, you are a curiosity."

"Did you get a whiff of her?"

"What?"

"She smells … I don't know … rich."

"It's called perfume."

Henry looks in the distance, sees a band of Blackfeet Indians, and slowly rides off as Jack says, "Don't be claim jumping now!"

Henry turns back. "What do you care? You got Irene."

"And you got Lucy!"

Henry rides over to the Vail wagon where Electa is sitting. "You doing all right?"

"She moves a strand of hair from her face and says, "I'm fine."

"Just so you know … we got company."

"I assume you're referring to the natives who have been following us?"

"Yeah, stay calm. Don't want you having another run-in with an arrow."

Electa touches the bandage on her face. "How do you know about that?"

"Your brother-in-law told me, Ma'am."

"Electa."

"What?"

"My name's Electa."

"Gotta say, you look like your name should be somethin' else. Where'd ya get that handle?"

"My namesake lived in ancient Greece."

"Some Indians believe ya grow into the name you're given. This Electa, what was she like?"

"If you must know, she started life as a pagan ..."

"Name has ya headed the wrong way, don't ya think? I mean you being a missionary and all."

"First of all, I'm not a missionary, I'm a teacher. Second, if you'd let me finish, I was about to tell you that Electa became a Christian and spent the remainder of her life converting the lost."

"Shit! And I was all set to like her."

"Are you always this sarcastic?"

"Oh, yeah. Sometimes, I'm a lot worse. So, if you're not a missionary, why do you act so religious?"

Electa grins. "You think I act religious?"

"Been watching. It's kinda like you're a priest eyeing Jack and me like we've done something wrong."

Electa says, "Have you done something wrong, Mr. Plummer?"

"Oh no, I'm not answering that one."

Electa smirks. "Tell me, do you believe there's a God?"

"If there is one, he's a mystery to me." Henry takes a moment. "And to be honest, I kinda like it that way. Maybe someday, I'll find out for sure ... or maybe not."

"I'm curious. Where do think you'll go when you die?"

Henry pauses. "Don't know, but what I do know is a whole lot of people who believe there's a heaven are in no hurry to get there." Henry changes the subject. "Teacher, huh?"

"Sister and John have the calling. I'm only helping out until they get settled."

"They seem like good people."

"What about your name?

"Named for my Uncle Henry, who got killed falling off a horse. He was drunk. My uncle, not the horse." He turns and sees Jack giving him the evil eye and turns back to Electa. "Truthfully, Ma'am, I'm ..."

"It's Electa."

"Okay, Electa. So, if you really wanna minister to a lost soul, you might consider Jack over there. He could sure use a smile."

"God's the only one who can judge the condition of your friend's soul."

"Can't speak for God, but Jack's soul is in pretty rough shape."

"You're awfully sacrilegious."

"Sacri ... what? Hell, just show the man some teeth."

Electa turns and looks Jack's way. He grins, waves awkwardly, and Electa smiles back. She turns back to Henry and says, "You happy now?"

"I am happy."

It was at this moment that I realized I was already in love with Miss Electa Bryan. I never meant for it to happen, but it did. And as for Electa, I think she figured she had just met the most arrogant and unruly man on this side of the Missouri River. But for some reason, I found myself hoping she would wanna take on the challenge of taming me.

Henry spurs his horse and heads for the Vail wagon. James greets him with a smile. "Moving along nicely, don't you think? Our arrival should be sooner than I anticipated."

"Yeah, only we got company." James starts to turn, but Henry grabs his arm and points him forward. Then he turns to Martha Jane and grins. "I need to borrow your sister." Before she can respond, the sheriff slows his horse and joins Electa again. He looks to his left and sees six Blackfeet Indians riding parallel to the Vail wagon. A few seconds pass and two of the natives sound a war cry as if they are about to attack. Instead, the warriors ride briskly down the road ahead of the wagons and turn and wait for the Vail party.

James pulls up on the reins of his horses, brings his wagon to a halt, and stares straight ahead as Henry motions Electa to climb aboard his horse. Henry nods at Electa. "Climb on up."

Electa stiffens her back. "What? I don't think so."

"Wanna keep that pretty hair or not?"

Electa resigns herself to the situation and climbs aboard as Henry scoots back behind his saddle to make room for her. As she awkwardly settles into her space, Jack scowls.

Henry slowly rides in the direction of the six Indians, who are still watching him with interest. In the distance, he sees a second band of seven Blackfeet watching from the top of a ridge. One of the men is Alex Slade, wearing war paint.

Henry rides within twenty feet of the band of six, who are now blocking the path of the wagon. He pulls his gun, holds it to Electa's head as she whispers loudly. "What in God's name...?"

"Act like you're scared."

"What do you mean act?"

A moment passes and Henry pulls the gun from her head, puts it to his own, pulls back the hammer, and screams, "Ahh! Ahh!" He laughs, removes the gun from his head, fires a shot in the air, cocks it again and puts the gun back to Electa's head.

The bewildered Blackfeet look back at the second band of Indians in the distance. Alex gives a signal and they ride off and join their comrades. Although a long way off, Henry glares at what he thinks might be Alex, cups his hands, and yells, "Where's Samuel!?" The first band of Blackfeet joins back up with the others and Alex turns his horse and they all ride away.

Electa says, "Who's Samuel?" Henry ignores her and spurs his horse in the direction of the Indians. He thinks better of it, sides up to the Vails, and helps his hostage into the back of their wagon. As he starts to ride away, Electa calls out. "Would you care to explain yourself?"

"Just doing my job."

"By threatening to kill me?"

Henry circles back. "Lot of Indians believe crazy people have evil spirits, so if a lunatic like me kills himself or his woman, they think that wild man's spirit will leave his body and make a home in them."

"How the hell do you know that?"

Martha Jane turns back. "Electa! The children."

Electa lowers her voice and addresses Mary and Harvey. "Your aunt should never say hell with anger in her voice." Embarrassed, she turns back to Henry. "Continue."

"Old Indian fighter told me that, but he was pretty liquored up at the time."

"Why doesn't that surprise me? Just so you know, that man you yelled at was the one I saw from the boat."

"Good to know."

Henry rides over to Jack, who is nonplussed by everything he just witnessed. Henry smiles and Jack says, "Jesus, Henry. That was a whole lot of strange."

"Run 'em off, didn't I?"

"You think that bastard leadin' them was. . .?"

"Yeah, Alex Slade."

CHAPTER 22

"As iron is eaten away by rust, so the envious are consumed by their own passion." Antisthenes

VAIL'S GOVERNMENT FARM AND MISSION is surrounded by pine trees. Centered on the property is a large clapboard-sided house, with a small log cabin not far from it.

Henry and Jack finish helping James unload his wagons. Exhausted, the young missionary leans back against a wagon, lights his pipe, and studies the roof of the main house. "Think maybe you'd be willing to stay on a few days? Roof needs fixing and wood needs cutting 'fore winter comes. Got that extra cabin over there for you."

Henry turns to Jack and his friend shrugs his shoulders. Henry smiles at James. "Guess a few days more won't hurt." The missionary slaps them on their backs and points at the cabin. "Help yourselves."

A few hours later, Electa is seated on a tree stump reading a book to the Vail children, while her older sister hangs clothes on a rope tied to two trees. Jack and Henry take a break from splitting logs, lean back on their axes, and take turns looking at the raven-haired beauty.

Evening comes and Electa is strolling along a bank above Grasshopper Creek near the mission. Henry exits the cabin where he and Jack are staying and sees Electa. He stops for a moment and studies her slender figure silhouetted by the moonlight. He starts to walk away but changes his mind. He sneaks up behind her and clears his throat. "Nice evening, huh?"

Electa jumps back. "God! You startled me!"

"Sorry. Mind if I join you?"

"Okay, for a minute, but I need to get back inside so I can help sister with the chores." Electa finally notices that Henry is in his bare feet. "Aren't your feet cold?"

"I don't mind."

As they stroll the bank of the creek, Electa breaks the awkward silence. "I heard Bannack is the second town to name you sheriff."

"Ahh, Jack. He's not one for keeping secrets."

"Nevada City's a secret?"

Henry doesn't respond, so Electa apologizes. "I'm sorry. I didn't mean to pry."

"Let's just say, we didn't leave there on good terms."

"Must be quite the story."

"One you're itchin' to hear."

"Why would you say that?"

"Strike me as the curious type is all...and maybe someone who likes a little danger now and again."

"I beg your pardon?"

"Saw it in yer eyes when them Blackfeet come 'round."

Electa is unsure what to say. "I was scared to death."

"Yeah, but when your fur was up, you gotta mean look in your eyes."

"You don't know what you're talking about."

"That pagan Electa was ready to fight."

"First, you say I have the eyes of a priest and now I'm a pagan."

Henry grins. "Pagan, priest. That's some mix."

Electa retreats. "This is all nonsense. I need to go."

"Wait. Yesterday, you asked me who Samuel was. He's my lost brother."

"Your brother?"

"I think Slade might know what happened to him." Henry coughs and Electa gives him a worried look. "You okay? That doesn't sound very good."

"I'm fine."

Electa looks at Henry as she prepares to leave. "Well, good night, Mr. Plummer."

Henry squints as Electa realizes her mistake and smirks. "I mean Henry." She lifts her dress and scampers towards the Vail house, leaving the Bannack sheriff standing alone in the moonlight.

As Electa nears the small cabin, she sees Jack sitting on the porch steps rolling a cigarette. As she rushes past him, she says, "Mr. Cleveland, I hope you sleep well tonight.

Jack lights up just as his roommate arrives. Henry, who has a sheepish look on his face, hops up the cabin steps and glides inside. Jack checks the moon, blows smoke at it, and glowers at the door.

As the morning sun peeks over the horizon, Henry and Jack repair a hole on top of the Vail house. Both men sniff deeply as the smell of breakfast emanates from the opening they're trying to patch. Somehow, Jack manages to squeeze his head down through the hole above the kitchen and grins. "Smells mighty invitin'."

The two sisters look up, see Jack's smiling face, and laugh. Martha Jane says, "Come on down. Food's ready."

Jack raises his head and whispers to Henry. "Nothin' better than a meal with perty faces."

The Vail family and their two guests are seated at a table eating hungrily. Martha Jane sees that their visitors' plates are almost empty, so she strolls over with a large stack of johnny cakes and offers them another portion. Before she can serve Jack, he grabs all the cakes and puts them on his plate. Martha Jane's silence is interrupted when everyone begins to laugh. Henry turns to the Vail woman and says, "That's all right. I'm used to it."

The sisters finish cleaning the kitchen and Electa walks into her bedroom. She sits down in front of a small mirrored table and begins to look for something. "Sister, have you seen my brush?"

From the kitchen, "No, I haven't." Electa looks a little longer and gives up her search.

The next morning the Bannack lawmen shake hands with James Vail, tip their hats to Martha Jane and Electa, and mount their horses. As they ride off, Jack takes one last look at Electa. She notices his awkward stare and waves goodbye. Henry grins at his deputy and says, "There you go."

Henry and Jack ride into Bannack, heavy in their saddles. Ben spots them as he exits his saloon and yells, "Any luck finding Slade?"

Jack answers. "No, but found somethin' even more valuable."

Ben lifts his head and says, "Gold?"

"Ain't sayin'. Know how it is ... claim jumpers and all?"

Ben shuffles off as Henry says, "I wouldn't be countin' on somethin' that's not likely to happen."

Jack tightens his teeth. "Oh, it's gonna happen all right."

NEVADA TERRITORY

Johnny Fry blows his bugle as the manager of the Lake Tahoe express station waits with a fresh saddled horse. Johnny arrives in a cloud of dust and jumps down from the worn-out steed he's been riding hard for twenty miles. He looks around for his replacement. "Where's Olson?"

The station manager grumbles. "Claimed he was chased by Paiutes comin' here, so he tossed his bag and rode off."

Johnny frowns. "Shit. Been ridin' forty miles. Buckland Station is another twenty. I ain't had no sleep."

The manager hands him a fresh canteen and a meal bag. "You're all I got." Johnny frowns, jumps on the fresh horse, and gallops off.

A few miles west of Tahoe Station, the pony rider struggles to stay in the saddle as he crosses a rapidly moving river. When he reaches the other side, he leans over and almost falls off his horse.

Still fifteen miles from Buckland Station, Johnny is asleep in the saddle as his horse ambles along. A rabbit crosses his path and his horse rears up, throwing the eighteen-year-old to the ground. He dusts himself off, grabs the bridle of his horse, and slugs his way over to a tree. He ties the animal's reins to a limb, slumps down, leans his back against the trunk of the tree, and falls asleep.

From a distant knoll, Paiute chief Winnemucca, his son Numaga, and a dozen Paiute warriors look down at him. As Numaga readies himself and the other warriors to attack the express rider, Winnemucca signals them to stay put.

Johnny's eyes open when he hears a rattlesnake shaking its rattles only a few feet away. The exhausted rider climbs to his feet, mounts his horse, and rides off as the Paiutes look at one another and laugh.

Struggling to stay in the saddle, the weary young man finally arrives at Buckland Station. A waiting express rider grabs his mailbags and rides off as Pete and Buckie help Johnny off his horse and into the cabin.

Sandra and her mother look up from their food preparation and smile, but their joy turns to concern when they see what condition the young rider is in. Buckie captures everyone's feelings when he says, "Johnny, you look like shit."

Maria grabs Buckie's arm. "Young man, go to your room!"

"Well, he does."

Johnny starts to say something, but faints and falls back into Pete's waiting arms.

CHAPTER 23

"A little bit of sweetness can drown out a whole lot of bitterness." Francesco Petrarch

HENRY ENTERS Vedder's General Store and finds John counting his money. Lucy looks up and smiles. John notices their "special" moment and says, "What ya lookin' for, Plummer?"

Henry turns to Lucy. "Got any of that peppermint candy?" Lucy walks to the counter, removes two peppermint sticks, and hands them to Henry. The sheriff wanders over to John to pay, but before he can lay down his money, John shuts the register. Without another word, Vedder heads for the door with a sack of money lodged in the back of his pants. Then he stops and turns back. "Going to the bank. Think you can handle this place?"

Lucy snarks. "Of course I can."

While Henry waits to pay for his candy, the front door flies open. John steps back and raises his arms high in the air. A hooded Alex Slade pushes the store owner towards the cash register with the barrel of his pistol as he scans the store trying to get his bearings. John manages to hide his money sack under a stack of papers on the counter while the would-be thief isn't looking.

Alex points his gun at Henry. "You. Drop the gun. Kick it over." Henry unholsters his weapon, drops it on the floor, but reaches down for the derringer tucked in his boot. He hesitates and decides not to risk it. Alex notices his strange movement and barks out, "Get your God damn hands in the air!" Henry raises his hands and kicks his handgun over to the trespasser.

John, still behind the counter says, "What you want?"

Alex hisses. "What do you think? I ain't here to steal a can of beans."

"I banked my money already."

"Bullshit!" Alex corners Lucy, studies her profile, and looks back at John. "I take it this is your woman?

Lucy tries to break free, but Alex puts his arm around her neck.

Henry takes a step forward. "Hold on."

Despite the bag on his head, Alex sounds like he might be grinning. "Or maybe she's your woman?

Lucy sneers. "I'm not anyone's woman."

Alex holds his gun even closer to Lucy's head as John tries to decide what to do. "Okay, she belongs to me."

Alex chuckles. "You don't sound so sure about that."

Henry takes another step forward. "Let her go, Slade."

Alex points his gun at Henry. "Shut the hell up! Ya don't know me."

Henry tries again. "Put down the gun or I'll ..."

"You'll what? Shit your pants?"

Lucy turns to John. "Give him the damn money!"

"It's in the bank."

Lucy argues. "Bull shit. I know better."

Alex cocks his gun and aims it at Lucy's leg. "Guess I'm gonna have to give your pretty wife here a permanent limp...I mean, if that's all right with you, John?" Alex cocks his gun. "What a shame. Such a nice leg too."

Henry tries again. "Don't do that."

"You again?"

Henry speaks through his teeth. "Vedder! Give him the fuckin' money!"

John doesn't move, so Henry walks over to the counter, side steps John, lifts a stack of papers and grabs the money. He throws the cash in a bag and tosses it to Alex.

John tries to argue. "You have no right."

Henry gets in John's face. "You're willing to let this asshole shoot her so you can keep some goddamn money?"

Alex chuckles, releases his hostage, and heads for the door as Lucy snarls at John. "What's wrong with you?"

Alex changes his mind, turns back, waves his gun, and reclaims Lucy. Henry tries to intervene, so Alex clubs him over the head. The sheriff falls to the floor and Alex pushes Lucy out the door, as he follows a step behind her.

Outside Vedder's store, Alex grabs the reins of the horse next to his and pushes Lucy up and into the animal's saddle. He pulls a knife from his pocket, cuts one of the reins of the second horse free, and uses the strand of leather to tie Lucy's hands to the saddle horn. He mounts his own horse, grabs the remaining rein, and rides off with Lucy struggling to stay in the saddle.

Henry stumbles out of the store, followed by John. Jack arrives just as the sheriff pulls a derringer from his boot and aims it at Slade in the distance. He hesitates, lowers the weapon, and John and Jack glare at him. "What? I might've hit Lucy."

John looks the two lawmen over and says, "You gonna stand there? Chase him down."

Henry counters. "Worried about Lucy or the money?" John grumbles something under his breath and walks off.

It's early evening as Henry and Jack ride west into a blinding sun. Jack turns to Henry as he shields his eyes. "No sign of them. Be dark soon. Go on back. I'm gonna keep lookin', spend the night if I have to. Meet me here in the morning if I'm not back. Bring Vedder with you."

"Sure it was Slade that stole her?"

"I'm sure."

"That asshole's everywhere." Jack rides off as Henry heads for an opening in the trees.

Alex and Lucy are sitting near a small campfire in a wide ravine, sheltered from the wind. Lucy has her arms wrapped around herself, trying to stay warm, as Alex stirs the fire.

When Alex leans forward, Lucy scolds him. "Take off that bag. It's rude." Alex pulls the bag from his head and straightens his long hair. He combs his scraggly beard with his fingers as Lucy gawks at his handsome profile.

He notices Lucy's half-opened mouth and chuckles. "What? You hungry?" Alex removes a piece of jerky from his pocket and tosses it to her. Lucy studies it a moment, takes a bite, and says, "The sheriff called you Slade. Is that your real name?"

"My name's none of your business."

"I know what you did to Marge Gunderson."

"You mean what Spivey did to her?"

"Saying that makes you Slade for sure." Alex pulls his gun, aims it at Lucy and she scoots back. He glares at her a few seconds, lowers his gun, picks up a blanket and tosses it to her. "Don't be throwing stones. I know you got something going with that kid sheriff."

"Sheriff Plummer and I are just friends."

"Plummer?

"That's right."

"First name?"

"Henry."

"God damn. I knew there was something about him."

Alex, who looks visibly shaken, turns away. Lucy asks, "You know Henry?"

"Saw him a couple times. Didn't know that was his name." Lucy tries to fit the blanket, but it gets all tangled. "You need help with that?"

"How stupid do you think I am?"

"I don't know. We just met."

"I'm not amused. Stay right where you are."

Alex grins. "Just trying to help."

"By kidnapping me and letting me freeze to death."

"Seemed like the right thing ... you being married to such an asshole."

"We're not married."

"He seems to think you are."

"Well, we're not."

Alex walks over and opens his horse's saddlebag. He removes a small bottle, tosses it to Lucy, and she catches it in the lap of her blanket.

"Maybe that'll help."

Lucy quips. "Oh no, I know what this does to a woman's resolve."

"It's all right. I can fend you off."

"I beg your pardon?" Alex chuckles as Lucy tries to think of a witty response. She can't come up with anything, so she says, "Think you're real funny, don't you?" Lucy defiantly pulls the cork from the bottle with her teeth, smells the contents, and takes a sip. She coughs and grabs her burning chest. "Lord! My God!"

When Alex stops laughing, he turns serious and says, "How long ya been friends with Henry?"

"What's a killer like you care who my friends are?"

"Just so you know, I've never killed anyone in my life."

"What about the Smith brothers?"

"Wasn't me that killed them."

"Spivey?" When Alex doesn't answer, Lucy continues, "Okay, how many men have you shot?

"Fired away a few times, but I've been careful not to damage anyone too bad."

"So, you just steal people's money and kidnap women? Lucy takes a bigger drink from the bottle.

"Never stolen a gal before. You're my first."

"Don't I feel special?"

"Behave yourself and I'll turn ya loose tomorrow."

Lucy takes another drink as Alex stands up and walks over and puts another log on the fire. Lucy scoots back and says, "Go back over there."

Alex strides back and sits down again. "Not a problem."

Lucy begins to slur her words. "I'm starting to feel kind of warm. Am I drunk?"

"You might be headed that way."

"If I doze off, you're not gonna take advantage of me are you?"

"No, get some sleep."

Lucy takes another drink, closes her eyes, and slumps over. Alex waits a moment, soft shoes over, and pulls her blanket away from the fire. He adjusts it, so it covers her completely. He considers his options and lays down on the other side of her, not far from the fire.

As he starts to drift off, Lucy takes her blanket and crawls over and snuggles up next to him. He lays perfectly still as she wraps her left arm around his waist and starts to snore softly. Alex smiles and closes his eyes.

Suddenly, Alex sits up and listens carefully. Sensing something is wrong, he walks over to his horse, mounts up, and rides off.

It's early morning as Henry rides out of the trees with Lucy on the back of his horse. She is hung over and has a hard time staying on Henry's slow-moving mount. Up ahead, they see John and Jack, who look relieved to see them.

Henry breaks the silence. "Found her wandering through the trees this morning."

John looks Lucy over. "That asshole do you any harm?"

"He was a gentleman. More than I can say for you."

Henry interrupts their moment. "Come on you two. It's been a long night."

Henry's horse stumbles and Lucy grabs her head and cries out. "Jesus."

John growls. "Why's your head hurt?"

"'Cuz, last night I got myself corned ... and I liked it."

"Sure he didn't take advantage of you?"

"Could have, but he didn't. Why aren't you at home counting your money?"

"Don't sass me."

"John?"

"What?"

"Go boil a shirt."

John spurs his horse and takes the lead as Henry turns in his saddle and grins. "Boil a shirt? Lucy, you're a mean drunk."

CHAPTER 24

**"Falling in love consists merely in uncorking the
imagination and bottling the common sense."
Helen Rowland**

HENRY AND JACK walk down a Bannack side street as the
young girl Henry gave his "special horse" to rides up.

Henry grins. "That's one fine lookin' animal ya got. Did you
give him a name?"

The girl gives Henry a big smile. "I named him Henry
Plummer, but sometimes I just call him Hank."

She rides off and Jack gives Henry a shove. "Shit."

As Henry rolls up his sleeves, he grins. "I'm going fishing."

"Grasshopper Creek?"

"There's no other place."

"See Electa, don't be claim jumpin'."

"Where you at with Irene?"

"You was right. She likes whoring too much. I ain't nothin'
but a walkin' bag of gold to her."

"But you're still seeing her?"

"Man's still gotta water his horse. What about you and
Lucy?"

"Haven't seen her for a while."

The barefooted sheriff is asleep on the bank of Grasshopper
Creek with his boots next to him and his fishing pole between his

legs. Electa exits a grove of trees carrying a basket and sees Henry's horse tied to a tree. She starts to turn back but changes her mind. She makes her way to the creek, spots the sleeping sheriff, and says, "Are you okay?"

Startled, Henry jumps up and his pole slides into the water. He lays back down and puts his hands on his chest. Electa watches as the sheriff starts to look for his fishing pole. Still groggy, he mumbles to himself, "Someone stole my pole."

Electa points. "It's right in front of you ... in the water."

Henry spots the pole but doesn't bother to reach in the water to get it. "You're right. What you up to?"

"Picking berries ... for a pie."

"Sure you're not hidin' out here drinking hooch?"

"I beg your pardon. What's hooch?"

"You know, Firewater, Red Eye ... whiskey."

"Aren't you funny." She changes the subject. "Do you always fish barefooted?"

"It brings me luck." There's an awkward silence as Electa turns away. Henry points at the water. "Hey, you mind?" He starts to cough and Electa gives him a look of concern. Henry takes out his bottle of laudanum and takes a swig. "My fishing pole ... it's right there."

"What do you want me to do?"

"I'm not so fond of being in the water. Maybe you could ..."

"You want me to go in there and retrieve your pole?"

"I'll hold your hand, so you can lean in."

"Thanks a lot."

Electa hesitates, shyly removes her shoes, and takes a couple of steps into the water. Henry reaches out, takes her hand, and braces himself on the side of the bank as she extends her arm into the water. He says, "You almost got it. Just a tad more." She reaches as far as she can, but just as she's about to grab the pole,

Henry's feet slip and they both fall into the creek with a splash. She grabs hold of Henry's arm to pull herself up, but he breaks free and rushes back to the safety of the creek bank.

Electa stands waist-deep in the water, pondering what has just happened. Finally, she sees the fishing pole, reaches into the water, removes it, and plods her way out of the creek. Dripping wet, Electa fixes her eyes on a shaken Henry.

Henry groans. "Shit, I'm sorry! So sorry!"

"Not much of a gentleman when it comes to water, are you?"

"Never a good idea to get too close to a drowning man."

"Did you really think you were drowning?"

"Sure felt like it."

"I thought you grew up near the water?"

"Pa was a boatman, but my brother and I only liked fishing from shore. We both hated not knowing how deep the water was."

"Jack said you've been looking for your brother for a long time." There's an awkward silence, so Electa hands Henry his pole. "Sorry. Your brother is none of my business." She pauses, starts to leave, and turns back. "Tell the truth. Did you let go of me on purpose?"

"No, but I did kinda enjoy seeing you take a bath."

"Henry Plummer, you're a bad man." She playfully throws a handful of berries at him as she leaves.

Once she's out of sight, he picks one of the berries off the ground and eats it. Then he cups his hands and yells out: "Midnight! Same spot! I'll bring an extra pole!"

In the black of the night, four hooded highwaymen wait in the rain by the side of the road as two miners approach leading their pack mules. Guns raised, the gang of four circles the miners, take their gold, and ride away. One of the victims sits down on a big rock and begins to cry.

Only a few miles away, Henry and Electa are back on the banks of Grasshopper Creek fishing by the light of the moon. This time they are both barefooted. A moment passes and Electa feels a fish tug on her line. "I think I've got one!"

Henry grins. "Bring it on in slow like." He grabs a bucket to scoop up the fish, leans over, loses his balance, and falls into the creek.

Electa laughs as Henry stands up, waist-deep, in the water. She says, "You can't stay out of the water, can you?"

He ignores her and lifts Electa's empty fishing line for her to see. "Where's your fish?"

Electa pouts. "Guess he wiggled free."

"Ain't that a daisy. Hold on." He scans the water's surface and dives head first into the creek.

"What are you doing?" Electa waits for Henry to surface, but he doesn't. Worried, she wades into the water to find him.

Henry finally surfaces and gasps for air. He holds up a fish for Electa to see, but it starts to wiggle free. He tries to control it, but before he can, he slips and starts to fall back into the water. Instead, he drops into Electa's arms. As she tries to hold him up, she screams out, "Lord help me, Jesus!"

Henry gains his footing and turns and gazes into Electa's eyes. Still in each other's arms, Electa says, "Thought you were afraid of the water?"

"Yeah, well. After I left here this afternoon, I went home and sat in a water trough. I think it helped."

"You did no such thing."

Henry pulls Electa closer. "Water's not so bad when you have something to hold onto." They kiss passionately until Electa gently pushes him away and says, "What are you doing?"

He grins. "If ya have to ask, I must be doing it wrong."

"You're a bad man, Henry Plummer, a very bad man."

Electa exits the water as the sheriff responds, "I must be. That's twice you've said that."

"I need to go. Sister's gonna wonder where I am."

"Yeah, so where are you?"

"I had a weak moment. I'm going to ask God to forgive me. I suggest you do the same."

"Forgive what? A kiss?"

"For our lusting after the flesh."

"Sorry, but if that's lust, I'm praying for more."

"I need to go."

"Okay. Been nice fishing with you."

As she scampers away, she calls out, "By the way, that fish you found wasn't mine. Mine was a lot bigger."

Jack, who is hidden behind a nearby pine, watches as Electa runs back to the Vail house. Irritated, he uncorks a whiskey bottle with his teeth and gulps down what's left. He takes a final drag from his cigarette, drops it to the ground, and grinds it into the dirt with the heel of his boot.

That first kiss is one I'll never forget. Tasted it in my mouth for three days. I could hardly wait to wet her lips again. I started to wonder what it might have been like for her.

In the early morning outside of Bannack, four hooded highwaymen with guns drawn, wait in the middle of the road for the Overland Stagecoach. Up ahead, the driver, Rut "Stubborn" Long, flies around a corner and aims his coach straight at the

Innocents. Before they can get off a shot, they are forced to dive out of the way. Covered in dust, the Innocents head for their horses as Rut drives wildly down the road as if nothing has happened.

By the time the bandits mount their horses, Rut and his coach are out of sight. The Innocents gawk at one another a moment and ride off in different directions.

Ben enters the sheriff's office and finds Jack cleaning his pistol and Henry writing in his journal. The two lawmen don't look up, so the saloon owner breaks the silence. "Gang calling themselves the Innocents are robbin' night and day. This mornin' they tried holding up Stubborn's coach just north of here, but he outrun them."

Jack growls. "That man's a gang all by himself."

Henry leans into Ben. "Why they called the Innocents?

Ben says, "Hell, if I know. But that's what they're callin' themselves." The saloon owner waits. "Aren't you gonna check it out? Their tracks might lead somewhere."

As Henry puts his journal away, he says, "Jack, why don't you take a look?"

"Why am I the mud end of the stick?"

"You're always complaining about how slow it is around here. It'll give you somethin' to do."

In the darkness of a small bedroom, John sits in a chair near Lucy's bed, watching her sleep. She stirs uneasily, opens her eyes, and sees John. "What the hell are you doing? Go away!

John vaults from the chair and tries to force himself on Lucy, but she fights him off. He persists by ripping open her nightgown, but she manages to break loose. She runs for the door, but John grabs her around the waist. She pivots, kicks him in the groin, and scratches his face. John reacts by pushing Lucy back onto the bed. Then he stumbles over to a mirrored dresser, lights a candle, and checks the damage to his face. He turns back and glowers at Lucy, who now has her blanket up around her neck. "Bitch! Just you wait. I'm gonna get what's mine."

John grabs the burning candle and threatens to set her bed on fire. He thinks better of it and spits the candle out. As he stands in the dark, he hisses, "That flame goin' out's gonna be you." John stomps out of the bedroom. There's a flash of light and Lucy hears the sound of the front door slamming shut.

Jack is headed down Main Street when Ben Girard approaches. The saloon owner questions the deputy with his eyes and finally says, "Any luck?

Jack scratches his head and Ben loses patience. "Finding them Innocents, ya numbskull."

"Oh, yeah ... them. I studied the ground, but I ain't no tracker. Lucky, I found my way home." Jack chuckles and Ben shakes his head as they go their separate ways.

CHAPTER 25

"Violence is the last refuge of the incompetent."
Isaac Asimov

JOHN, HIDDEN BEHIND A NEWSPAPER, is seated in an oversized chair in his living room. He touches the scratch on his face as Lucy makes her way to the front door. She turns back to John and says, "I'm going to sewing circle."

John tosses the paper on the floor and growls, "Need to fill some shelves when ya get back. And don't be all day."

Lucy hurries away from the house and heads in the direction of the church. All at once, she stops in the middle of the street and checks to see if anyone is watching her. Seeing no one, she heads for Gus's Livery Stable and Blacksmith Shop.

Still at home, John enters the kitchen, and spots Lucy's sewing basket. He grabs it and exits the house.

As he marches down the street with the basket in the crook of his arm, an elderly woman walks past him smiling. Embarrassed, he shifts it to his hand and walks faster.

When he nears an alley, he looks down it and sees a black dog trying to mount a smaller white dog. He picks up the pace again and mutters to himself, "Shit."

John arrives at the church and knocks loudly on the sanctuary door. The door opens and he is instantly blinded by the sun's light shining through a large stained-glass window inside the church.

The minister emerges from the light as John lifts his arm and shields his eyes. "John Vedder. What brings you here?"

Still struggling to see, John steps inside and surveys the sanctuary. "Where the hell's Lucy?"

"I'm afraid she's not here."

"So, where's the Goddamn sewing circle?"

"First, let me remind you this is the Lord's house. And as far as the sewing circle, the ladies finished their quilts two weeks ago."

"Two weeks?" John grinds his teeth and stomps out of the church. Back on the street, he passes the alley again and sees the dogs still going at it. Instantly angry, he throws Lucy's sewing basket at them and they run off.

Having reached Gus's livery stable, Lucy opens the front door and sneaks inside. She shades her eyes as she tries to make out who it is that's standing in front of the brightly lit hearth. She whispers, "Hello, Gus?" Gus steps forward, the light from the hearth giving him a celestial appearance. He smiles and points at the loft above.

When Lucy reaches the top of the ladder, she spots Henry, who is sitting on a bale of hay. She smiles and starts to unbutton the top of her dress, but Henry takes her hand and gently pulls her down on the bale next to him. Lucy immediately senses something is wrong.

Down below, Gus hammers away at a horseshoe until the front door opens and Jack struts inside. He looks up at the hayloft and says, "He up there?" Gus nods as a couple of pieces of hay fall through the cracks in the ceiling above him. "Lucy ... or Electa?"

Gus says, "Lucy. You need something?"

"It can wait." Jack turns and walks out the door.

John enters the Saffron Saloon and sees Red Yeager, Monty Montgomery, and Ezra Simpson seated at the bar. Sweet Waters walks over to him to get his drink order as John looks the place over and says, "Any of you see Lucy?"

Red laughs. "No respectable women in here." Sweet slaps Red's hat off his head and the jokester tries to save himself. "You don't count. You work here."

The room turns silent until John continues. "Thought maybe one of you saw her is all."

Jack enters the saloon, walks past John, and sits down next to Red, who says, "Vedder here can't find his woman. Probably should report his loss to the sheriff, don't ya think?"

As everyone laughs, John yells out. "Where is he?"

Jack looks straight at Sweet as he says, "Had some business at the livery stable I think."

Red adds. "Bet he's checking out that fine-looking filly Gus is boarding." John hurries out of the saloon as everyone chuckles. Jack tosses Sweet a coin and she hands him a bottle and a shot glass. He uncorks it with his teeth and takes a drink from the bottle itself.

Sweet rolls her eyes. "I hope Henry shoots all of you."

Jack glares at Sweet, looking for an answer to a question he hasn't asked yet. He re-corks the bottle, puts it under his arm, and side-steps his way out the saloon door.

As John wanders down Main Street, he stops a young couple and asks them if they've seen Lucy. Not getting the answer he wanted, the store owner comes to a stop in the middle of the street and heads directly for Gus's place.

Henry and Lucy are sitting on a bale of hay with their backs to one another, fully clothed. Lucy is crying. "When did you meet … this Electa?"

"Couple weeks ago … when we went to Fort Benton."

Lucy lowers her head. "The missionary woman's pretty sister?"

"So, you know her?"

"They came in the store the other day. Why didn't you tell me you had feelings for her?"

"I wasn't sure ... but now ..."

"Now you're trading me for her ... like I'm some kind of horse?"

"You know better than that."

"You love her?"

Henry pauses. "I don't know ... maybe."

"Did you ever love me?"

Henry lowers his head and Lucy begins to cry. All at once, the door below flies open and John rushes in. Gus sees who it is and begins to hammer on a horseshoe furiously. John grabs Gus's arm, looks up at the loft above, and rushes over to the ladder. Gus yells out. "Trouble comin' your way!"

John tops the ladder as Henry and Lucy stand up. He looks Lucy over and shoves Henry into the hay. "You been fornicating my wife?"

Henry stands up and looks at his gun laying a few feet away. "She's not your wife, Vedder!"

John steps toward Lucy. "You tell him that, you bitch?" John grabs a pitchfork near him and thrusts it at the sheriff, who quickly steps aside. John gathers himself and jabs the fork again, but Henry manages to grab hold of it.

Lucy watches as the men struggle to free the pitchfork from one another. Finally, John whacks Henry on the side of the head with the fork's handle and Henry falls back in the hay. Lucy screams. "Stop it, John!"

John braces himself, steps forward, and prepares to thrust the pitchfork once again. Henry grabs his gun out of the hay and tries to aim at John's feet, but he can't see them. "Don't make me!"

Standing over the top of Henry, John raises the fork high in the air for one final deadly lunge. Henry cocks his gun, hesitates, and shoots John square in the chest. Vedder buckles to his knees, looks down at his bloody shirt, and falls face-first in the hay.

Lucy screams again. "Oh my God!"

As the smoke clears, Henry checks John's body for any sign of life. Finding none, he tries to comfort Lucy as Gus runs out the stable door.

Jack is seated behind the office desk combing his hair with Electa's brush when Gus rushes in. "Come, now! Henry just shot Vedder."

"Sure it was Henry that done the shooting?"

"Not for sure, but Vedder didn't have a gun."

"Fetch Doc Robinson and I'll meet you at your place."

Gus runs off and Jack opens the bottom drawer of the desk. He removes a bottle, pours himself a drink, and toasts the door.

Gus and Dr. Carl Robinson rush through the stable door and find Henry comforting Lucy. Carl looks up at the hayloft. "Vedder up there?"

Henry says, "Yeah, but he ain't breathing." Carl rushes over to the ladder, climbs up, and checks John's vital signs.

Jack, slightly drunk, enters the blacksmith shop. He makes his way over to Gus as Carl looks down from the loft at Henry and says, "Not good. You have a good reason for shooting him?

"Came at me with a loaded pitchfork."

Jack leans forward. "Why didn't ya shoot him in the foot?"

Before Henry can answer, Lucy says, "It wasn't his fault."

Jack continues. "Hope the town sees it that way."

As the doctor descends the ladder, he says, "Jack, you need to lock Henry up."

Henry perks up. "What?"

"For your own good. I'll get the town together and sort things out."

Jack coolly removes the badge from Henry's shirt. "Won't be needing this." As he ushers the sheriff to the livery stable door, he puts the badge on his own shirt.

Several town residents talk amongst themselves in the sanctuary of the local church as Dr. Robinson finishes consulting with the church's minister, steps to the podium, and clears his throat. "Listen up, everyone!"

People ignore the doctor and argue vehemently as an agitator yells out: "Hang the bastard!"

A woman yells. "Lucy's as much to blame as Plummer!"

A second woman hollers, "Adulterers! Fornicators!"

A bearded miner in the back shouts, "Hang 'em both!"

Members of the crowd continue to argue amongst themselves as Carl tries to gain control of the room. "Nobody's hanging nobody!"

Another agitator barks. "Why? 'Cuz Plummer's your friend?"

"Sit down, Clyde! You still owe me for taking that boil off your ass." Several people laugh as Clyde takes a seat. Carl continues, "Friend or not, Henry's gonna get a fair trial! The town owes him that. Jack here is sheriff for now. Now go home." Carl steps back from the pulpit and Jack grips his gun. He holds it steady as people walk away muttering even more insults.

And just like that, the town turned against me.

PART THREE: CLAIM JUMPING

CHAPTER 26

"If you scapegoat someone, it's a third party that will be aware of it. It won't be you. Because you will believe you are doing the right thing." Rene Girard

SACRAMENTO, CALIFORNIA

MEN AND WOMEN riding horses and steering wagons down the main arteries of the city go about their business. Several well-dressed men enter a large five-story brick building with a chiseled stone sign that reads *Sacramento Union*.

As the early morning sun illuminates a fifth-story window newsroom, reporters scurry about shouting snippets of news to one another. Charles Munson, a colorfully dressed dandy and junior reporter in his late twenties, treads lightly over to the desk of senior reporter, Michael Roberts.

Michael, who is in his late thirties, is wearing a wrinkled gray suit and has a mass of fiery red hair piled high on his head. Unaware of Charles's presence, he removes a handkerchief from his vest pocket and begins to clean his glasses. His colleague taps his foot, clears his throat, and says, "Blackman wants to see us."

Michael doesn't look at Charles as he puts on his glasses. Finally, he says, "Okay, give me a minute." He begins to sort through some papers on his desk as the irritated younger reporter continues to wait.

Charles, who can't wait any longer, blurts out, "He fired Amos Fredericks yesterday. We might be next."

The older reporter turns to Charles. "Let's not overreact."

"Neither one of us has written anything of consequence lately."

"Relax. Everything's going to be fine."

Charles begins to pace the floor and then comes to an immediate stop. "When I woke up this morning, I had a premonition. I said, 'Mother, I think I'm going to be sacked today.'"

"And what did your mother say?"

"She said, 'Don't forget to pack your lunch'."

"I've always liked your mother."

"I need this job, Michael."

"Okay, let's find out what Blackman wants before we start cleaning out our desks."

Michael stands and the reporters walk toward the editor's office as Charles chirps away, "Maybe he's gonna give us a raise? It's been a while."

Michael says, "Charles?"

"Yes."

"Shut the hell up."

The newsmen stop in front of an office door that reads: "Felix L. Blackman - Managing Editor." Michael knocks. From inside the office, they hear Felix grumble, "Come in." They enter and sit down across from the stodgy editor, who is smoking a porcelain pipe. Felix, who is wearing a three-piece suit accessorized by a black ribbon tie, looks to be a man in his late fifties. He's a bit pudgy and has a small tuft of hair on an otherwise bald head.

The editor looks down at a document on his desk, touches his remaining strand of hair, and takes a long drag from his pipe.

He lifts his head, exhales, and stares at the reporters. "So, I'm sending you two north to Oregon Territory, to a place called Bannack. Want you to cover Sheriff Henry Plummer's trial and bring me a story that will sell newspapers! Circulation is down."

Michael glares at Charles, suggesting he should keep quiet. The young reporter doesn't take the hint and speaks his mind. "Sir, Oregon is chock-full of barbarians, thieves, and whoremongers."

Felix relights his pipe and grins. "Good. That'll add a little flavor to your story."

Michael interrupts. "When do you want us to leave, sir?"

Felix sucks on his pipe and exhales. "Tomorrow."

Charles reacts. "Wait. Tomorrow?"

"That's what I said. You got something else you have to do?"

Charles looks to Michael for help, but he ignores him and turns back to Felix. "Henry Plummer. That name sounds familiar."

Felix leans back. "He's the young sheriff that got run out of Nevada City last year."

"That's right. He shot the mayor in the foot for beating up a town prostitute."

"How disgusting is that?" Charles says glibly.

Felix chortles. "The mayor's foot or the hooker?"

Michael speaks before his fellow reporter can respond. "So, what did he do this time?"

"Killed a town merchant who caught him in a hayloft with his wife."

Charles quips. "Just to remind you, our expertise is reporting news on the local scene. Covering scandalous affairs in far-away places really isn't our cup of tea."

Felix squints as his face reddens. "I'm not sending you there to drink tea, Munson."

Michael leans over and whispers in his colleague's ear. "It's time to shut up."

Charles whispers back, "We have all the murders we need right here. Why do we need to go north?"

This time Michael whispers loud enough for Felix to hear, "Because Mr. Blackman wants us to and he's our boss." Michael turns back to Felix. "Sir, we'll be more than happy to cover the Plummer trial."

The editor winks. "One last thing. Keep your eyes open for a gang of road agents calling themselves The Innocents. Might be a story there too."

Under his breath, Charles says, "Please, God. Don't let me die in Oregon."

As the reporters prepare to leave, Charles turns and says, "Just so you know, sir, I'm not fond of horses."

"For Christ's sake! Get the hell out of my office!"

Michael gives Felix a half smile and says, "Thank you, sir." The reporters scamper out the door.

When they return to the copy room, Michael gives Charles a look of contempt. "Do you have to say everything you're thinking?"

"No, but the last time I was on a horse, I got a rash so bad I couldn't sit for three days."

"We're not riding horses; they're pulling our coach."

"Still..."

Michael takes Charles by the arm. "It's our first collaboration. Why aren't you excited?"

"Because you're a thief."

"What are you talking about?"

"The French restaurant review last year... you stole it from me."

"The chef poisoned four people with creme brulee and you recommended the place. And I quote, 'Pierre's desserts are to die for.'"

"How was I supposed to know? I had the Brown Betty, which was delicious by the way."

"Why don't we focus on the trip?"

Charles perks up. "What pray tell am I going to wear?"

"I'm sure you'll come up with something. What's wrong with what you have on?"

Charles straightens his back. "This old suit? You really like it?"

Michael walks off, shaking his head as Charles follows him chattering away again. "And you? How are you planning to dress? How about your leather vest? It's very rural."

"What are you, my mother?"

Charles guffaws. "Michael, we both know your fashion choices are atrocious."

Jack and Henry are playing cards through the bars of the Bannack jail cell. Jack throws down a card and gives the former sheriff a toothy grin. "Stole him right out of her pa's barn in the middle of the night."

"Gotta be kiddin' me. That girl really loved that horse."

"Thought about puttin' up a poster: 'Henry Plummer's Been Stolen.' But figured it'd confuse people, you being in jail and all."

Henry turns serious. "What you think? Am I in deep shit?"

"You killed an unarmed man and you were poking his wife. Should've kept your balls in your pants."

"I told you. We were just talking."

"You don't meet up with a woman in a hayloft to talk."

"Vedder is the one who came at me with a pitchfork."

"That's what ya said."

"You don't believe me?"

"Don't matter. There was no one there to uphold your story. Lucy don't count. Henry, ya got too many secrets."

"Lucy's life isn't what you think." Jack waits and Henry goes on. "Can't tell you about it right now."

"I sure as hell ain't hidin' no secrets. Electa's set to teach me readin' and writin'... soon as she's in the mood."

Henry squares his shoulders. "She been round to see me?"

"Hell no, and not likely to either."

Henry looks deep in Jack's eyes. "I told Lucy I don't love her."

"Why ya telling me?"

"'Cuz, I've got strong feelings for Electa myself."

"Well, she's on the shelf and you ain't buying."

"She's not someone who can be bought."

"We'll see about that. My prospects are rising and yers are in the shitter."

"Just 'cuz we both care about her doesn't mean we can't keep on bein' friends."

"Friends don't claim jump!"

"Ya got yer whole life to be an asshole. Why don't you take the day off?"

"Once she's mine, I sure as hell ain't gonna roll her around in no fuckin' hay. Gonna buy me a real bed."

Henry chuckles. "I'm curious. Where ya gonna put that bed?

Jack picks up his chair, throws it against the cell bars, and stomps into the outer office. From there he yells, "Put it wherever the hell I want! Might put it in the fuckin' street!" Henry stares through the bars of his cell and shakes his head.

CHAPTER 27

**"The robbed that smiles, steals something from the thief:
he robs himself that spends a bootless grief."
William Shakespeare, *Othello***

*I didn't know it at the time, but I was about to become famous. The
strangest thing about being well known is that everyone thinks they know
who you are before they even meet you.*

AN OVERLAND STAGECOACH slides around a curve at
breakneck speed. It is dark, but the driver, Rut "Stubborn" Long,
has a lantern burning next to him. Inside the coach are five
passengers who hang on for dear life. The road finally straightens
and Charles Munson leans out the window and tries to say
something to the driver, but the coach is shaking so hard, he
returns to his seat.

A lantern lights the interior of the stagecoach, revealing the
other travelers: Michael Roberts, two thirties-something look-alike
sisters, Hazel and Bernice White, and a handsome Mexican
cowboy, Pedro Gonzales, who is trying to sleep. Michael steadies
himself as the coach continues to roll down the road. "My God!
Why is he in such a hurry?"

Charles mumbles. "Can't hear you. My teeth are rattling too
loud." The coach rounds a corner on two wheels and the
passengers slide up against one another.

Michael straightens his suit jacket and hollers out the window. "Are you out of your mind!?"

Charles turns to the sisters dressed in matching red dresses and raises his voice loud enough so he can be heard. "He never slows down, never stops. We've had to hang our Sunday faces out the window to do our business."

Michael frowns. "Did you really just say that?" The women giggle as the road noise finally diminishes.

The older sister, Hazel, adjusts the bodice of her dress and says, "What takes you two to Bannack?"

Michael explains, "We're covering the Plummer trial."

"The sheriff who killed the husband of a woman he was ..."

Charles finishes her sentence. "Fraternizing."

The younger sister, Bernice, narrows her eyes and says, "Fraternizing?"

Hazel whispers, "It's the gentleman's way of saying screwing, boning, plowing." Bernice giggles as her sister continues, "Let's hope the other men in Bannack are as friendly as the sheriff."

Bernice cackles. "Yes, with lots of gold ... But they must take a bath first."

Hazel agrees. "Of course. That goes without saying. We'll be at the Saffron Saloon, so if you gentlemen ever need ... you know... a good fraternizing."

"Oh, Michael and I don't fraternize."

Both women pat Charles on the leg as Hazel continues. "We're so excited. It's our first time doing the dirty deed for money."

Bernice adds, "But our rates are very reasonable."

Gunshots ring out. Pedro wakes up and looks out the window as the coach picks up speed. "Mierda! Banditos!" The Mexican cowboy pulls a watch from his pocket, puts it in his boot, and blows out the lantern. He grabs his pistol and leans out the coach window. As he fires away, the reporters and sisters cover their ears. Shots are exchanged until Pedro falls back from the coach window. Charles removes the young cowboy's tattered hat, revealing that the top of his bloody skull has a hole in it. Charles instantly pokes his head out of the coach window and throws up as one of the hooded Innocents shoots Rut in the arm. The horses come to a stop and the bandits circle the coach.

The reporters remain huddled inside with the sisters when the door flies open. A young bandit stands rigid, points his gun, and peers through the eye holes of his hood at the frightened passengers.

Meanwhile, two bandits have made their way to top of the coach and are using an iron rod to break loose the strongbox. The other Innocents are standing in front of the coach aiming their guns at Rut, who grins and says, "See ya brought yer tools this time."

The robber snarls. "Shut the fuck up." Rut laughs, so the bandit turns away from Rut and begins to look the sisters over.

Rut growls. "Hurry it up. I don't like being late."

The bandit turns back. "Want me to put another hole in you?"

The young bandit steps forward. "Come on. We don't got all day. Unload the passengers."

The older bandit points his gun at Charles and Michael. "Which one of you assholes was doing all the shooting?"

Charles scowls. "I'll have you know, I've never discharged a firearm in my life."

"That's not what I asked."

Charles points to the dead Mexican cowboy. A third bandit takes charge as he shoves his gun inside the coach. "Get out! All of you." One of the robbers helps the sisters down, while two others yank the reporters out. Charles attempts to free himself, so the outlaw slaps him alongside the head, and the obstinate reporter falls to the ground.

Charles quickly climbs to his feet and points his finger. "There's no need for you to be a ruffian."

The older bandit shoves his gun in Charles's face. "Shut up, Mary! Empty your pockets."

Another bandit grabs the Mexican's hat and tosses it to Michael. "You! Fill it up."

The reporter passes the hat and the sisters pull paper money from their bodices and drop it in the bloodied sombrero. Hazel grins at her younger sister. "Don't worry. We'll get it all back later."

Michael slides over and offers up the collection hat to his traveling companion. Charles removes a gold watch from his vest pocket and clutches it close to his chest. "This was my grandfather's. It's been in my family for years."

Michael prods his partner. "For God's sake, put it in the hat."

Before the reporter can hand it over, the older bandit grabs the watch and shoves it in his pocket. "In my family now, and I'll take that coat."

Charles removes his coat and hands it to the bandit. "I'm gonna catch my death… I hope it doesn't fit." Charles gives up his hat and raises his eyebrows at Michael. "Why you looking at me? They took nothing of yours!"

On top of a hill looking down at the ongoing robbery is Alex Slade. The older bandit spots him, but he can't make out who it is for sure. However, he does recognize the horse the man is on to be none other than Henry Plummer.

Rut guides his coach down Main Street with one arm. Michael, who is sitting next to the driver, is awkwardly holding a shotgun. Inside the coach, Charles is sandwiched between the two sisters. Rut stops at the Saffron Saloon as Jack approaches. Under his coat, the acting sheriff is wearing his homemade red scarf. Jack finally notices Rut's bloody arm. "What the hell happened to you?"

Rut hesitates. "Five Innocents held us up, but I ain't late."

Jack pulls a watch from his pocket and checks the time. "Yep, right on time." He quickly pockets the watch when he sees Charles exit the coach.

As Michael helps Rut down from his driver's seat, Jack slaps the side of the coach. "Better get that arm looked after, Rut."

Charles steps up to Jack. "Constable, those hoodlums killed that poor cowboy in there and pilfered my watch and coat. I'm lucky I didn't soil myself."

Jack locks eyes with the reporters. "Why you two here?"

Michael replies. "We're from the *Sacramento Union*. I'm Michael Roberts and this is Charles Munson. We've come to cover the Plummer trial."

"Ain't that somethin'."

Charles steps forward. "I take it you have a suitable boarding house in this town?"

"Got rooms at the Saffron. Ain't half bad if ya don't mind hearing people drinking and whoring."

Charles turns to the sisters. "Saffron? That's where you ladies said you're going to work, right?" The women step forward and smile. Suddenly shy, Jack turns his attention back to the reporters.

Michael doesn't mince words. "When would it be convenient for us to interview Mr. Plummer?"

"I don't know ... guess when I'm in the mood to let you."

As Jack gawks at the sisters again, Charles interrupts him by poking his arm. "My coat's periwinkle blue and my watch is gold plated ...."

"Yeah. Probably melted down by now."

As Charles starts to leave, he notices Jack's scarf under his coat. "Love the scarf. Did someone make it for you?"

Jack ignores Charles's question. "See you snowflakes later." Without asking, Jack scoops up the sisters' luggage and heads for the saloon as Charles and Michael follow him with their own possessions.

Charles turns to Michael. "Did he just call us snowflakes?"

CHAPTER 28

**"Ladies who play with fire must remember that
smoke gets in their eyes." Mae West**

THE STREETS OF BANNACK are crowded with miners,
merchants, and local citizens going about their business. Still
wearing his red woolen scarf, Jack sits in the outer room of the
sheriff's office with his boots on the desk, knitting yet another
scarf. He yawns, puts his yarn and needles in a leather bag,
removes Electa's brush, and begins to stroke his hair.

Meanwhile, inside the holding area, Charles and Michael sit
uncomfortably on wooden stools outside Henry's jail cell. Charles
eyes Henry. "You really had no choice. He would have skewered
you. And it sounds like Vedder treated Lucy more like a servant
than a wife."

Henry changes the subject. "Can't believe you came all this
way for my trial?"

Michael explains, "Our editor thinks your story is very
compelling."

The jailed sheriff raises his eyebrows. "Compelling?"

Charles adds, "And entertaining. He's all about selling
newspapers."

"Guess it'd be worth a read, if I wasn't in it."

Michael scoots his chair forward. "Have time for a few more
questions?"

"Shit. I'm not going anywhere."

The door opens and Jack strolls in. "Time's up."

Charles argues. "We're not quite finished."

"Won't take me long to dig a hole for two dead bodies." The reporters quickly stand up as Jack chuckles.

As the acting sheriff escorts the newsmen out of the inner cell area, the front door opens and Electa enters carrying a small wicker basket. Jack is delighted to see her, but she ignores him as she looks around the office. As the reporters walk towards the door, Charles does a double take. "Lucy Vedder?"

Electa glares. "No."

Charles apologizes with his eyes. "Sorry, I thought you might be ..."

Electa interrupts. "Lucy Vedder."

Jack pushes the reporters out the door, closes it behind them, and turns to Electa. "Here for my reading lessons?"

"No, I'm here to see Henry."

Jack lowers his jaw, starts for the cell area, and turns back. "He ain't so good. Felt sorry for him last night, so I slipped him a bottle of hooch."

"I'd still like to see him."

"Ya sure? Been fuming all day 'bout you and Lucy bringing him bad fortune ... callin' ya both mantraps."

Electa takes a moment and hands Jack the basket. "I see. If he changes his mind about ... his bad fortune, tell him I'd like to speak with him." She hurries out the door and scurries down the street, crying. Two women see her and whisper to one another.

Back in the sheriff's office, Jack frowns as he carries the basket to the door leading to the inner cell area. He changes his mind, returns to his desk, and puts his feet up. He stares at the basket a moment and then removes a pie from it. He sticks his fingers in the middle of it and sucks the juice off them. Bored, he opens the desk drawer and pulls out Henry's journal. He tries reading it, but gives up and tosses it back in the drawer. He hesitates, dips his entire hand in the pie, and gobbles down a handful of berries.

Alex Slade stands lurking in a dark alley across from the sheriff's office. He watches as Jack exits the building and locks the door. When the lawman is out of sight, Alex puts a hood on his head and exits the alley with a sledgehammer.

When he reaches the office door, he takes a full swing and the door splits open like a ripe watermelon. Alex squeezes his way through the gap in the door and once inside begins to rifle through the desk. From the inner cell area, he hears his brother yell out, "Jack! What's going on out there?" Alex pauses and goes back to looking for a key.

A block from the sheriff's office, Jack stops, slaps a hand to his side, and realizes he's forgotten his knitting bag. He mouths the word "shit" and heads back to the office.

Still searching the sheriff's desk, Alex finally finds the keys, opens the door leading to the inner cell area, races to Henry's cell, and unlocks the door. Henry looks up and says, "What the hell?"

Alex slaps the cell bars. "Go on. Get out of here!" Henry doesn't move, so Alex points his gun and his younger brother exits the cell. When Jack arrives back at the office, he sees the broken door, draws his gun, and crawls inside. As the Plummers vacate the cell area, Jack sees the hooded man and dives behind the desk. Alex fires two warning shots, points his gun at the door, and then at Henry. "Now's your chance ... go!" Henry doesn't budge, so Alex panics, runs to the door, and squeezes his way out.

The fugitive rushes past several locals, who have gathered on the street after hearing the gunshots. Meanwhile, Henry has managed to climb through the broken door, and is watching the intruder as he disappears down an alley two blocks away. Jack joins Henry out front as the bystanders eyeball the freed prisoner and the broken doorway. The acting sheriff's anger gets the best of him and he yells out, "It ain't nothin'! Go home!"

Townsfolk murmur amongst themselves as they wander off. Jack nods and they head back to his jail cell. He opens the cell door and Henry walks back inside. Jack gives his old friend a curious look and says, "What the hell was that all about?"

"Not sure if he wanted to kill me or set me free."

"Probably one of them goons wantin' to hang ya so bad."

Alone in the outer office, Jack looks out the window and sees his reflection. He takes Electa's brush from his leather bag and begins to comb his hair. He hears someone knocking, so he puts the brush in his back pocket, opens the door, and finds a sad-faced Sweet Waters. "The judge is ready for Henry now." Jack shuts the door without a word, grabs the cell keys, and walks in the cell holding area, where he finds Charles and Michael sitting outside of Henry's cell.

Jack nods. "The judge has made up his mind." He opens the cell door and the reporters start to leave.

Michael takes a few steps and looks back. "Good luck."

Once the reporters are gone, Jack enters the cell and dangles a leather strap in front of Henry. The former sheriff wags his head and says, "What the hell?"

"Just doin' my job."

Henry offers up his hands and Jack ties them behind his back. "Why do I get the feeling you're enjoying this?"

The Saffron Saloon is packed with people, who are jabbering away in anticipation of the trial. Ben Girard appears and helps the almost blind territorial judge, who presided over the Spivey case, to a table just in front of the bar counter.

Henry is seated at a small table next to his lawyer and Jack and Dr. Robinson are resting in chairs right behind them. Lucy is situated across the aisle from Charles and Michael, who are busy taking notes. Electa and Sweet are located at the back of the saloon not far from Alex Slade, who is standing near the saloon door with his hat pulled low on his head. Sweet notices the rugged but handsome man and turns and smiles at him. Alex reacts by pulling his hat down even lower and staring at the floor.

Ben interrupts the bar room chatter. "Everyone! Shut the hell up! Judge here's ready to make his ruling." As the judge clears his throat and prepares to speak, he starts to cough. Ben grabs a spittoon and offers it to him. The old man clears his throat again and spits in the cuspidor, so Ben hands him a shot of whiskey and he downs it.

Finally, the judge adjusts his shirt collar, scans the bar, and squints at several bystanders who are talking again. Instantly angry, Ben grabs the gavel and bangs it on the table. "I told you to shut the fuck up! I ain't tellin' you again."

The judge scowls at Ben and grabs his gavel back like it's a stolen toy. He clears his throat once again, lays the gavel carefully down in front of him, and begins. "Armed with a pitchfork or not, John Vedder is dead. Question is what price should Henry Plummer pay for killing a husband who found him in a hayloft with his wife."

Several people chuckle as Lucy jumps to her feet. Ben promptly whispers something in the judge's ear and the old man tries to locate the scorned woman. Finally, he turns to Ben and says, "Where is she?" Ben points to Lucy and the judge looks in her general direction. "What do you want? I've a mind to jail you, too."

"Your honor, John and I weren't married!" People begin to chatter amongst themselves. Ben grabs the gavel before the judge can get it and slams it on the table.

Irritated, the magistrate yanks the gavel from Ben's hand and yells out at Lucy. "How long you live together?"

She thinks about it. "Five years."

The judge smirks. "Have naked relations with him, did ya?"

People laugh as Lucy answers softly, "A few times, early on."

"Young lady, you had yourselves a common law marriage." As Lucy takes a seat, people begin to jeer loudly, so the judge hands Ben his pistol. "Anyone else interrupts me, shoot 'em." Ben points the gun out at various people in the makeshift courtroom and they quiet down.

The judge leans over, spits again, and clears his throat. "Plummer, you claim a pitchfork came your way, so ya shot Vedder. Since I can't ask the pitchfork what happened and a cheating wife's testimony ain't worth shit, here's my rulin'. Where's Plummer?" Ben gently turns the judge, so he's facing Henry.

When people start to giggle, Ben points the gun at them again. The room quiets as the judge sucks in his cheeks and speaks deliberately. "Henry Plummer, I'm sending you to California where you'll be living in the federal prison in San Quentin for ten years."

Several people look disappointed; others cheer and nod in agreement as Henry turns and makes eye contact with Electa. She begins to cry and rushes out of the saloon as Lucy lowers her head and waits for everyone else to leave.

A moment passes and Jack pulls Henry to his feet. He ties his hands together with the leather strap and leads the disgraced lawman out of the saloon.

This is the lowest point in my life. It appears my friendship with Electa, Lucy, and Jack is all but over. Probably just as well, 'cuz I don't think I'm gonna survive a decade behind bars. And even if I do, where will everyone be when I get out?

Main Street is crowded as several people, including Lucy, watch as two prison guards lead Henry, clad in leg irons, out of the jailhouse and into a prison wagon. As the guards fasten Henry to the wagon, Jack stands on the jailhouse steps as Henry looks at the people around him.

At the last moment, Jack hands Henry his journal and says, "Don't do me no good." They stare at one another until Jack turns away. As the wagon rolls off, the crowd disperses, leaving Lucy standing alone in the middle of the street.

When Lucy returns to her store, there are two young boys painting something on the store's front wall. The boys look up, see who it is, and run off. She strides over to the wall and finds in large black letters the misspelled word "hore." She stares at the word a moment and walks inside her store.

Now armed with a bucket and brush, Lucy furiously tries to remove the graffiti from the store's front wall. Two women, who happen to be walking past, cover their mouths and snicker.

CHAPTER 29

"Going to prison is like dying with your eyes open."
Bernard Kerik

SAN QUENTIN FEDERAL PRISON

SEVERAL GRAY-CLAD CONVICTS mill about the prison courtyard talking. The institution itself is bordered by the San Francisco Bay and its brick walls are manned by three guards, who occasionally look down into the enclosure.

Standing alone, Henry looks over and sees Warren Spivey staring at him. The killer takes a moment, totters over to Henry, and spits. "Ain't this somethin'?"

Henry steps forward and looks Warren in the eyes. "Let's get one thing straight. I don't want anything to do with you while I'm here."

"Yeah, well …" Warren grunts. "Ya owe me."

"How you figure that?"

"Crippled my feet. Put me in this hellhole."

"You're where you need to be."

The wrongdoer grins at Henry. "How 'bout us buryin' the hatchet? Got me a plan to get us outta this place. Pitch in and I'll take ya straight to your brother."

Henry takes a moment. "You saying he's above ground?"

Warren smiles. "No, but I can show you where his bones are buried." Henry's countenance darkens and he starts to walk away. The culprit follows. "Come on, I'm just funning with ya. He ain't that far from Bannack."

Henry keeps moving. "Asshole!"

A guard rings a bell and the prisoners head to the main lock-up. Warren, who limps along like an old man, follows Henry through the large iron door.

Judith Green, Lucy's sewing mentor, enters Vedder's General Store and looks around for her good friend. "Lucy? It's Judith. I need some flour. Hello!" She waits a moment and heads for the storage room at the back of the store. She slowly opens the door. "Are you back here?"

Judith covers her face when she sees Lucy's body hanging from a rope attached to a ceiling beam. Her dead friend's face is milk white, and she's wearing the yellow dress made from the fabric Henry gave her.

A young couple strolls past a sign on the city's largest news building that reads: *Sacramento Union*.

Inside the editor's office, Michael and Charles sit across from Felix Blackman, who is reading a copy of the reporters' article on Henry Plummer. Felix looks up and says, "Ten years."

Michael responds. "Sir, Henry's a good man. He just got caught up in his own lust."

Felix looks down at the article again. "Readers are gonna love the hayloft part of this story."

Charles adds. "We were both surprised to find out Lucy and Vedder weren't married."

"Yes, about that. I got word yesterday Lucy Vedder hanged herself in the back of her store."

In unison, Michael and Charles say, "Oh my God!"

"Our readers are going to love the drama of the whole thing. Very Shakespearean."

Michael reacts. "Please, sir..."

"Yeah, I know... but go ahead and add her death to your story before it goes to press."

Charles shifts in his chair. "So that's it? We just forget about him now that he's in prison?"

"Check on him now and again. Have a feeling we haven't heard the last of him. Oh, almost forgot, I need you two to do a story on the Pony Express that's starting up right here in Sacramento."

Michael says, "The horseback mail service?"

"Yes. See Alexander Majors. He's in charge."

As the reporters exit the office, Charles complains. "Good grief, more horses."

The Pony Express headquarters is a complex of the main office, several storage buildings, and dozens of horse-filled stables in a large barn. Alexander Majors exits one of the stables and then the barn with the two *Sacramento Union* reporters close behind.

Charles holds his nose and rubs his eyes as a pony express rider exits the barn behind them, leaving the reporters standing in a cloud of dust. Alexander chuckles to himself as the Sacramento reporters brush off their suit jackets and pants. The express manager pulls out his watch and checks it closely. "Right on time."

Michael writes something on a pad and starts to question Alexander. "Mr. Majors, how long does it take for a letter to get to St. Joseph?"

"Ten days or less."

Michael continues. "And how much do you charge?"

"Five dollars an ounce."

Charles enters the conversation. "That's awful pricey."

"Well, folks are willing to pay top dollar for a timely delivery. Now gentlemen, if you would, I'd like you to observe the swearing in of three of my newest riders."

Inside the Pony Express main office, the reporters watch as Alexander Majors prepares to administer an oath to three new riders. One of the men is the scraggly bearded and even longer-haired Alex Slade.

Alexander puts his right hand in the air and the three riders follow suit. "Do you swear that while employed by the Pony Express, you will under no circumstances use foul language, that you'll abstain from drinking liquor, that you'll refrain from fighting with other employees and conduct yourself honestly and faithfully in order to win the confidence of those seeking the services of the Pony Express? If so, say, 'Yes, so help me God.'"

The riders repeat in unison. "Yes, so help me God."

Michael studies Alex's profile as Alexander hands each of the men a Bible. The men finish signing agreement documents and begin to thumb through their new Bibles.

As the reporters shake Alexander Major's hand, Michael looks at Alex Slade again. "Who's the long-haired man you swore in?"

"Samuel something. Applied two days ago. Don't know much about him. Seems solid though. You know him?"

Michael turns to Charles. "Looks familiar is all."

Charles shrugs. "I can't help you."

From inside the stable, Samuel Plummer (alias Alex Slade) watches as the reporters vacate the express building. He waits a few moments and leaves as the reporters ride off in a one-horse carriage.

Back in Bannack, Jack locks the door of the sheriff's office and sides up to his horse. Clean-shaven and wearing new clothes, he tips his hat to several townspeople who happen to walk his way. He unties his horse from the hitching post and climbs on board.

Inside the Vail cabin, seated at a large dining room table, Electa, Jack, John, Martha Jane, and the two Vail children fill their plates with buffalo meat, corn bread, and sweet potatoes. James smiles, lifts his cup, and toasts Jack. "Nice you could share a meal with us, Brother Cleveland. It's been a long time coming."

"Been here sooner, but you know ... being sheriff and all."

Martha Jane adds, "We understand you have several new obligations, but you're always welcome here."

"Haven't had a free meal, since I ate jail food."

John turns serious. "Spent some time in a lock-up, have you?"

"Yeah. When I was a young buck, I got myself caged for bein' drunk and dishonorable 'bout once a week."

Electa corrects Jack. "I think you meant to say disorderly."

"Yeah, I was that too." Jack smirks and Electa gives him a polite smile.

Martha Jane nods. "You do know that as long as you're willing to reform, the Lord will be gracious enough to forgive you?"

"Gave up sinning once, but every day was dismal. Nights were worse."

John changes the subject. "So, how do you like being sheriff?"

"Gotta say, it's kinda like being the biggest toad in the pond." Everyone laughs, so he tries again. "Croak!" No one reacts this time, so he points at the butter. "Gimme some of that cow grease ... and more of them whistle berries."

Electa doesn't understand. "Butter and ...?"

"Beans."

John passes the butter and beans to Jack and the new sheriff loosens his belt and says, "These britches are starting to get awful familiar. Been a long time since I ate myself this full."

Martha Jane grins. "Eat all you want. We have plenty. But don't forget, we've got pie." She grabs a lemon meringue pie from the counter and puts it on the table in front of Jack.

Instead of cutting a piece for himself, Jack puts his spoon in the middle of the pie and removes a large spoonful. With his mouth full, he mumbles, "Feeling gratification for this meal, but gotta say, the top of this here pie looks like calf slobber."

Electa says, "It's supposed to look like that, Jack. It's a lemon meringue pie."

Jack grins. "Ahhh."

Martha Jane pauses and says, "Okay, well ... I hope you like it?"

Jack takes another spoonful and puts it in his mouth. "Yeah, it's pretty good. Anyone else want some?" In unison, Martha Jane, Electa, and James shake their heads no.

James changes the subject yet again. "Too bad about Lucy Vedder?"

"When I cut her down, her face was as blue as a June sky."

Electa studies Jack's face. "Do you know how Henry is doing?" Jack doesn't respond so she continues, "Thought maybe you might have heard something."

"He's a long way off. How 'bout us havin' another learnin' lesson?"

"Sure, let me help sister clean up, and we'll get started.

Jack leans back. "A,E,I,O,U. I'm chomping at the bit.

CHAPTER 30

**"If I had a flower for every time I thought of you,
I could walk through my garden forever."
Alfred Tennyson**

SAMUEL BLOWS A BUGLE as he approaches Buckland
Station. He brings his horse to a stop, and jumps down as Pete
and Buckie ready a fresh horse. Maria hands Samuel a bag of food
and walks back to the cabin, while Sandra hands him a fresh
canteen. He takes a long drink as Sandra waits for him to come
up for air. He nods at the blushing girl. "It's Sandra ... right?"

"How you know my name? The other riders talking about
me?"

He winks. "Only good talk. My name's Samuel."

Sandra smiles shyly as Buckie, now two inches taller and with
longer hair, watches from a few feet away. He whispers loudly so
everyone can hear. "How many boyfriends do you need?" Sandra
shoves her brother, almost knocking him down, as Pete adjusts
the mailbag on Samuel's new horse and snorts. "See ya in a
week."

"Looking forward to it." Samuel mounts his horse; Pete slaps
the animal's hind quarters, and the express rider speeds away.

The San Quintin courtyard is populated with pockets of
inmates as Henry walks around them. Suddenly, Warren's burly
cellmate, Horace Wilson, approaches and blocks his way. Henry

tries to step around him, but the big man grabs him just as Warren appears. "Change your mind 'bout escaping with me and Horace yet?"

"Why, so can you take revenge for me putting you here?"

"Shit. Why would I wanna kill another Plummer? Sure, ya don't wanna help out now?"

He doesn't respond, so Warren nods and Horace begins to pummel Henry. Two guards look down from the top of the wall, see what's happening, and turn away. Finally, the yard bell rings and all the inmates head inside, except for Henry, who is laying on the ground in the fetal position.

With his pants rolled up to his knees, a bare-footed Henry sits on the bottom cot, battered and bruised, writing in his journal. On the bed above him, his fifty-something cellmate is staring at the ceiling.

Spivey and his underling beat the hell of me today, but that isn't the worst part about being holed up in this prison. It's the isolation and the anger I feel about the time being taken from me. Funny thing is, most of the men here don't seem to mind, probably because they think no one cares about them anymore. Have a feeling I'll be thinking that way myself pretty soon.

Henry coughs and his cellmate looks down at him and says, "If I was you, I'd be doin' whatever that bastard wants."

"I put him here. Sure as hell ain't helpin' him get out."

"Ten years is a long time. Think that gal of yours is gonna wait? Bet she's spreading her legs for some fella right now."

Henry stares at the ceiling. "Just wanna do my time."

Samuel is riding in the direction of Buckland Station when a rattlesnake raises up in front of his horse. His mount takes a turn to the left and throws him hard to the desert sand. He lays flat on his back, afraid to move. Holding his arm and grimacing in pain, he manages to get to his feet. He steadies himself, stumbles over to his horse, and climbs aboard.

The Buckland family is at the dinner table when they hear the muffled sound of a bugle. Pete looks at his watch. "He's running late."

Sandra looks at the front door. "Is it Samuel?"

Buckie mocks his sister. "You know who it is."

Pete and his two children wait at the corral as Samuel rides slowly toward the station. He's slumped over and holding his arm, so Buckie runs and grabs the horse's bridle. The young boy leads the animal and injured rider to the station and Pete helps him down from his horse. Sandra shyly gives the wounded rider her shoulder to lean on.

Pete quizzes Samuel with his eyes and says, "What the hell?"

"Snake spooked my horse."

Pete addresses his two children. "Get him in the house. Careful, I think his arm's broken." Maria exits the cabin and holds the door as Buckie joins his sister and helps steer the wounded rider in the right direction.

Samuel stops. "Wait. That mail's gotta get to the next station."

Pete looks around. "Guess I'm a Pony Express rider."

"You're too fat to ride fast," Buckie says. "You'll wear out the horse. Let me go."

Pete raises up like an exclamation mark. "Hell no!"

"Come on, Carson City is only twelve miles from here."

Maria adds, "He does know the way."

Pete resigns himself to the situation. "Shit."

Buckie mounts a Pony Express horse with gusto. Pete hands the reins to his son and puts his finger on his chest. "I'll hitch up the wagon and meet you in Carson City in a couple hours." Pete puts the mailbag on Buckie's mount and Maria hands him a bag of food and a canteen. Buckie digs his heels into the flanks of the fresh horse and rides off at full speed.

As the Bucklands help Samuel into the cabin, they hear the sound of a bugle blaring, and everyone laughs.

Father and son Buckland roll along in the family wagon headed home as the sun sets. A smile crosses Buckie's face and Pete says, "What you grinning about?"

"Nothin'."

Pete tousles Buckie's hair and laughs. "Nothin', my ass, pony rider."

It's early morning as Pete, Alex, and Buckie work in a rhythmic pattern feeding hay to the horses in the corral. Samuel's right arm is in a sling, but somehow, he's able to manage the pitchfork with his good arm. Maria opens the front door, watches a moment, and says, "Hate to interrupt, but it's time for breakfast." Buckie tosses his fork and runs for the cabin. Pete and Samuel follow close behind.

The Buckland family and their guest are seated at the table eating breakfast. Sandra gets up, takes Samuel's plate, walks to the stove, and fills it with scrambled eggs and fried potatoes. As the family watches, no one says a word or moves until Samuel picks up his fork. Buckie offers his plate, but Sandra sticks her tongue out at him.

Pete finally speaks. "How's the arm?

"It'll be okay in a couple days."

"More like a couple weeks. Bones don't heal that fast."

Buckie qrins. "Especially old bones." Pete threatens Buckie with his fork.

Samuel apologizes. "Don't mean to put you folks out."

Pete smiles at his daughter. "You're no trouble. Right, Sandra?"

Sandra's face turns red and she spouts, "Pa!" Embarrassed, she runs out of the kitchen and into her room.

Maria drops a pancake on her husband's plate and says, "Pete. That was uncalled for."

The room grows quiet until Samuel speaks. "Glad I'm left-handed, so's I don't starve to death."

Pete yells in the direction of Sandra's room. "Sorry, Pumpkin!"

From her room, everyone hears, "I ain't no damn pumpkin!"

Henry strolls through the prison courtyard with his head in the air, staring at the clouds. He comes to a stop and looks up at an armed guard in the tower. Warren approaches and growls. "Ain't too late to get in on our plan."

Henry steps back and puts his hand in the air. "Wind shifted. Ya smell that?"

Warren sniffs the air. "Don't smell anything."

Henry says, "Yeah, you do. It's bullshit." He walks off as Warren bares his teeth and spits.

Samuel finishes pumping water into a bucket, picks it up with his left hand, carries it into the Buckland cabin, and sits it on the kitchen counter. Sandra bounces out of her bedroom carrying a rifle and Samuel reacts. "What's going on?"

"Going hunting."

"You're in a better mood."

"That was yesterday. Come with."

"I don't think so."

"Please. Pa won't mind."

Samuel grins. "Ya even know how to shoot that thing?" Sandra slaps his good arm and pushes him out the cabin door.

Outside, they spot Pete in the corral, shoeing a horse. "Pa, me and Samuel are gonna hunt up some supper."

"All right, just be careful where you're aiming."

As they walk away, Sandra explains. "First time I fired this gun, I almost shot one of Pa's horses."

Pete yells out, "Saw some turkeys west of here."

The couple enters a grove of pine trees, where they hear turkeys gobbling. They instantly kneel down behind a deadfall ponderosa. Sandra offers her rifle to Samuel, but he points to the sling on his arm. She smiles, raises her rifle and waits for a turkey to appear. Samuel whispers. "How many birds have ya shot?"

A turkey gobbles, so she tightens the grip on her rifle and whispers back, "Countin' this one?"

Sandra lowers her rifle. "One." He starts to laugh, so Sandra puts her finger to his lips. She holds it there until Samuel gently pushes it away. She refocuses, raises her rifle again, stares down the barrel, and waits. She grows impatient and tilts her head in the direction of Samuel, who is watching for any sign of a turkey.

Samuel spits on his finger and wipes clean the site at the end of the barrel of Sandra's rifle. Finally, he cups his hands and calls out. "Gobble, gobble. Gobble, gobble."

A moment passes and the couple hears a return gobble, gobble. A turkey appears, so Sandra steadies her rifle and fires. Feathers float through the air and filter to the ground. Sandra laughs as she turns to Samuel and says, "Gobble, gobble."

Still tending to his horses, Pete looks up. In the distance, he sees Samuel toting a turkey by its legs as Sandra marches proudly along with her rifle propped over her shoulder.

CHAPTER 31

"Life goes on, and one should look ahead and not backward." Sonali Bendre

SEATED NEXT TO ELECTA at the Vails' dining room table, the newly appointed Bannack sheriff tries to read from an open Bible: "Oh, gi ... give ... tha ..."

Electa tries to encourage Jack. "Go on. Sound it out."

"Tha ... thanks."

"That's it. Good."

He continues. "Oh, give thanks ... to the Lord."

Electa grows impatient and closes the family Bible. "Better stop for now. I have chores to do. You're doing so well, Jack."

"How 'bout we take a walk along the creek tonight? You can teach me more about them vowels and constants."

"Consonants."

"Yeah, that's them."

"I have plans for the evening. Maybe some other time."

Trying his best to be a sensitive man, Jack compliments Electa. "Ya know, you're 'bout as pretty a gal as I've ever seen."

"Why, thank you. That's sweet of you to say."

He reaches over and pulls her close to him. Surprised by the moment, she lets him kiss her. As Electa pulls away, she touches her mouth and stares at Jack. "I'm sorry."

"Nothin' to be sorry about."

"I shouldn't have let you do that. You need to go." She takes Jack by the arm and leads him to the door. As he puts on his hat, he grins and slaps the door in celebration. When he finally leaves, she leans against the wall, and shakes her head in disbelief.

Sandra carries a bucket of water to the corral, where Pete, Buckie, and Samuel are feeding the horses. After everyone has had a drink, Samuel reaches in the bucket, grabs a handful of water, and throws it at Sandra. She reacts by scooping up some dirt and chasing after him. Not to be outdone, Buckie throws a cupful of water at his pa. Pete retaliates by grabbing the bucket and rushing after him. When Buckie reaches the steps to the cabin, Pete launches the contents of the bucket just as the cabin door opens. The water drenches an open-mouthed Maria. Everyone freezes, waiting for her reaction. Not to be outdone, she grabs a nearby broom and hurries after her husband as Samuel, Sandra, and Buckie laugh. A bugle sounds and they scatter as they prepare for the arrival of the express rider.

Johnny Fry's horse slides to a stop in front of the corral and Pete and Samuel help him change horses. Johnny looks for Sandra, but doesn't see her. Out of time, Johnny jumps on his new mount, gives Samuel a disapproving look, and rides away.

As the noonday sun beats down, father and son help Jane unload feed bags from her wagon. Buckie is wearing Jane's black hat, which covers his whole head. When no one is looking, he reaches over, pulls the cork out of Jane's whiskey jug, lifts it up, and takes a snort. His eyes bulge as he spits the contents from his mouth. He carefully recorks the bottle as Jane laughs heartily.

Not far from Buckland Station, Samuel and Sandra ride along on the open plains. All at once, Samuel pulls his arm from his sling, throws it to the side, digs his heels into his horse's flanks and rides off. He circles back, rejoins Sandra, and lifts his right arm in the air, suggesting that he is fully recovered. Samuel takes the lead back to the station as Sandra falls back with a sad look on her face.

It's the middle of the night and Samuel is asleep in the barn on a makeshift bed of hay and blankets. He awakens when he sees a light shining through the slats of the barn walls. He sits up as the door opens, but the light from a lantern blinds him. As he shades his eyes, he says, "Pete? Everything all right?" Sandra lowers the lantern, revealing that she's holding a blanket. Samuel realizes it's Sandra and says, "It's you. What's going on?"

She offers him the blanket and purrs. "Thought you might be cold."

Still seated, he takes the blanket and wraps it high around his upper torso. "It's the middle of the night. Better get back inside."

"You sure?"

"What you mean? Of course, I'm sure." Samuel's face changes, suggesting he finally understands the young girl's intentions. "Sandra, I'm too old for you."

"Pa's fifteen years older than mother. Sides, you've been making eyes at me since the day we met."

"You know I'm leaving in a few days."

"You don't have to."

"Be back to see you sometime."

"Once a week for two minutes ain't enough."

"Not that often, I'm afraid."

"What do you mean?"

"I'm quitting the Pony Express."

"Why?"

"Got some business to take care of."

"You got a wife, don't you?"

"No."

"A girlfriend?"

"No, I need to help my brother. He's in prison."

"How do you help someone in prison?"

"I haven't figured that out yet."

"You're gonna bust him out, aren't you? Take me with you. I can help."

Samuel smiles. "Listen, a pretty gal like you ... you're gonna find someone else to love as soon as I'm gone."

"Wait. Who says I love you?"

"That's right. You don't even know me."

"I know I love you."

"You just said ..."

"Never said I didn't love you. Just don't want you assuming it is all."

"Love's an awful big word."

"Never felt it with anyone else."

"Not even your family?"

"This ain't no family love I'm feeling." Sandra steps forward and starts unbuttoning her dress.

Samuel steps back. "Whoa now!"

"Not what you think." The young lady reveals she's wearing a heart-shaped necklace, which she removes from her neck. "It's store-bought with my own money. I want you to have it." She tosses the necklace to Samuel and he looks it over. "It'll be our secret."

"I can't take this." Samuel hands the necklace back to her and she reluctantly puts it back around her neck.

Sandra grins. "It's all right. I'm gonna tell everyone you gave it to me. I'm not taking it off until you come back." She slowly buttons her dress again.

"Sandra, I need to tell you something."

Suddenly excited, she asks, "Your last name?"

"Why do you need to know that?"

Sandra's eyes reveal her disappointment, so Samuel says, "All right. It's Plummer, Samuel Plummer."

"Plummer. Sandra Plummer."

"Don't do that."

"Okay, what else were you gonna tell me?"

Samuel chooses his words carefully. "I used to be somebody else."

Sandra reacts smugly. "Nobody used to be somebody else."

"Before I joined the Pony Express, I went by the name of Alex Slade."

"Alex ... Slade. I like that too."

"Listen. Up north in Idaho Territory, I was on the other side of the law, so I run off. Thought I could get back to bein' my old self by movin' to California."

"I don't care what ya call yourself."

"Hear me out. Every time I wake up, I'm still Alex. There's a lot I need to fix to be Samuel again."

"When you were that Alex, did you kill someone?"

"No, but there is a man I would've planted, given half a chance."

"It's not against the law to wanna kill someone."

"Yeah, well, I've done some other bad shit too."

"I don't care. Let's leave, right now."

"I'm a wanted man. The law finds me, they'll hang me for sure."

"Why go back? It makes no sense."

"'Cuz, I need to make things right."

"Then I'll wait here for you to come back and claim me."

"Damn it! I don't want you waiting for me! I'm damaged goods. When I leave, I'll be Alex Slade again. Now, you need to get out of here!"

"You're leaving 'cuz you don't wanna love me." She starts to cry, so Samuel stands up, holds the blanket around his entire body, and wraps his arms around her.

Sandra stops crying, so he leads her to the door. "I'm sorry, I shouldn't have told you all that shit."

"I liked hearing your shit."

"Okay, now go."

"I'm not leaving until you kiss me."

"I don't think that's a good idea."

"Kiss me and you'll see how important I am to you."

Samuel wags his head no.

"I'm staying the night. Pa can shoot you in the morning."

Samuel yields. "One kiss?

"Okay. I'll save the rest of me ... for later."

Samuel pauses and kisses her on the cheek. Sandra promptly steps back. "A proper kiss, not some grandma kiss."

"I'm sorry, but I've never delivered a real one before."

Sandra steps forward and puts the young man's arms on her shoulders. "I don't believe that one bit."

"It's the God's truth." He shrugs and kisses her for real. What starts as a gentle kiss turns passionate. When they come up for air, Samuel backs away and sits down, making sure his blanket fully covers his groin area.

Sandra chuckles. "There's plenty where that came from."

"Yeah, well ... I'm still leaving."

"After a kiss like that?" As Sandra sashays out of the barn, she yells back, "I'm changing my name to Sandra Plummer and there's nothing you can do about it."

CHAPTER 32

"Forget everything you have done. Start over." Marty Rubin

A PRISON GUARD opens the door of Henry's windowless cell and Henry and his cellmate sit up in bed. "Plummer, two odd ducks wantin' to see ya. Warden says it's okay." Henry slowly stands up and his jealous cellmate watches as he exits the cell, the guard following close behind.

In the prison's visiting room, Henry sits at a table across from the two *Sacramento Union* reporters. Charles is the first to speak. "My God! You're skin and bones. And why's your face bruised like that?"

Henry emits a sarcastic grin. "I ran into a fist."

"That's not the least bit amusing. What a horrible place this must be."

"So, what brings you two here?"

Michael smiles. "We have some good news. You're getting out of here."

Henry gives the reporters a look of disbelief. "I know ... in ten years."

Michael continues. "No. Some of your Bannack friends convinced the territorial governor that your sentence doesn't fit the crime. He's agreed to pardon you."

"Don't bullshit me."

Charles adds, "No really. As soon as the warden gets your official paperwork, you'll be free to go."

Henry stares at the reporters as they smile and nod. "What's in this for you?"

Charles grins. "Once you're a free man, our readers will want to hear more about you."

"If what you're saying is true and I get out of here, my life isn't gonna be that interesting."

Michael smiles. "That's all right. We'll embellish it a little bit."

"Embellish?"

"You know, exaggerate, stretch, make it bigger than it is."

"You can do that?"

Michael continues. "A story's not much of a story if it's not overstated a bit."

"If you say so."

Charles adds, "Just so you know, we sold your history to a publishing company in San Francisco. They're going to write a dime novel about you that will make you even more famous."

"Wait. Don't I get a say on who writes about me?"

Charles wags his head. "Afraid not."

Michael changes the subject. "We assume you know about Lucy?"

"No. How's she doing?"

Charles turns to Michael. "I told you."

Michael leans over. "Shortly after you left Bannack, word came that Vedder had abandoned a wife and two kids in Ohio."

Charles continues the story. "People kept gossiping about Lucy being the other woman, first with Vedder and then you. I guess she couldn't take it anymore."

He doesn't react, so Michael says, "Lucy hanged herself."

Henry lowers his head and stares at the floor. "What? Shit!"

There's an awkward moment of silence until Michael says, "Something else. Bannack made Jack Cleveland sheriff."

Henry elicits a fake grin. "Was he one of the ones that talked to the governor on my behalf?"

Michael pauses. "No, Ben Girard and Carl Robinson."

The guard appears and Henry stands. Before he can escort Henry away, Charles taps the blue-coated man on the shoulder and says, "This place is so drab. Why don't you put some curtains on the windows?" The guard ignores the reporter, turns away, and pushes Henry towards the door.

A bell rings and two prison guards approach Warren and Horace's cell. Warren is lying face down on his bunk as is his cellmate above him. The bearded guard rattles the bars impatiently and yells, "Spivey!... Wilson! Wake up! You're on clean-up duty." The prisoners don't move, so the guard yells even louder. "Damn it! Don't make us come in there. We don't have time for none of your shit!"

There's no response, so he nods at his partner, a crooked-toothed man, and they enter the cell yielding large wooden clubs. The crooked-toothed guard reaches up to the top bed and raps Horace on the shoulder with his club. "Hey, asshole! Get down here!" There's no movement, so the guard slaps Horace on the shoulder even harder. "You dead?"

Just under Horace's bunk, the bearded guard reaches down to check on Warren Spivey. Without warning, the scoundrel pops up and hits him across the head with a tin cup. Stunned, the bearded guard topples back and falls to the floor.

As the crooked-toothed guard turns to check on his colleague, his eyes bulge when a wooden shank enters his neck. He instantly slumps to the floor as Horace jumps down from his bunk.

Warren, who is now straddling the bearded guard, slams the tin cup against the defenseless man's head again. Then he puts his hands around the bearded guard's neck and strangles him to death.

Warren and Horace stand in their cell dressed in the prison guards' clothes waiting for the right moment. Behind them are the dead guards, lying face down in the convicts' beds.

Seeing no one in the corridor, Warren and Horace exit their cell and lock the door behind them. They lower their hats, hitch up their pants, and walk past three unsuspecting guards at the end of the cell block.

When the escapees reach the prison gate, Warren waves to the guard on the walkway above, who in turn nods to the gatekeeper on the other side of the prison wall.

The brutes wait nervously until the gate opens. When it does, the wall guard above turns his attention to the courtyard, where a fight has broken out. The escapees see their chance, slip through the gate, and avoid eye contact with the guard by lowering their hats even more.

The gatekeeper nods. "Hey, fellas. Got any chew?" Warren turns and raises his hat. The guard's face reveals that Warren isn't the man he expects him to be. He starts to react, so Warren pulls a shank from his pocket and sticks it in the man's stomach. Warren covers his victim's mouth with his hand and Horace helps him push the gatekeeper up against the exterior prison wall. Warren waits for the man's eyes to dim and lets him sink to the ground. Then he bends down, pulls the shank from the man's stomach, wipes the blood on his victim's coat, and signals his cellmate over to him. Horace picks up the gatekeeper, carries him to a tall stretch of grass, and drops him face down in the muck.

Warren hobbles along behind Horace until they reach a sod house bordered by a small garden and a corral containing two horses. A farmer looks up and sees the prisoners lumbering towards him. He recognizes their gray garb and raises his hands as if to surrender.

The farmer lies in the dirt, his open eyes to the sky, and his throat cut, as his killers ride away on stolen horses.

The next morning Henry is seated across from the warden, who is reading a release document. The suited man lays the paperwork down, pulls a revolver from his desk drawer, and spins the gun barrel. "Pardoned by the governor himself. You must have some powerful friends. Got someplace to go?"

"Oregon Territory. Back to Bannack."

"It's Idaho Territory now."

"Huh. Good to know."

The warden holds up the gun. "Can have this at the gate."

"You're giving me a gun?"

"Yes, but I don't want ya shooting anyone on your way out."

"There's one bastard I wouldn't mind putting a hole in."

"Guess you haven't heard." The Warden hands Henry a handbill and he looks it over.

"Who these fellas supposed to be?"

"Spivey and Wilson. They escaped last night."

"Ya gotta be shitting me."

"Killed three of my guards and a farmer near here."

"Any idea where they're headed?"

"Tracks say north." The warden takes the homemade flier from Henry, writes something on it, and hands it back. "It's a long shot, but what I wrote there gives you the right to kill both those assholes ... or at least see to it they're hanged."

"I was counting on never seeing those bastards again. Sides, I don't have a horse."

"Gonna gift ya one. Find'em and the reward money will get you started again. You're goin' north anyway."

Henry takes a moment and says, "Okay." Then he shakes the warden's hand, takes another look at the handbill, and smiles. "Draw them yourself, did ya?"

The warden grins sheepishly. "Best I could do."

"Other than this piece of paper, how are people gonna know I'm on the right side of the law?"

"Maybe this will help." The warden pulls out a badge and hands it to him. Henry puts it in his pocket and chuckles as he looks at the drawing again.

I was happy to be out of prison, but those six months damaged my soul. I had started to forget about the outside world. But now that I'm free, I'm gonna have to learn to like myself all over again and maybe some of the people I never thought I'd see for ten years.

CHAPTER 33

**"Instead of a man of peace and love, I have become
a man of violence and revenge." Hiawatha**

ELECTA SITS on the bank of Grasshopper Creek with a fishing
pole in her hands. She watches intently as several small fish swim
past her line. The morning silence is broken when she hears a
whistle. She looks around and sees Jack sitting on his horse on the
other side of the creek. Jack waves and yells out, "What ya baitin'
your hook with?"

"Grasshoppers!"

"Try a worm!"

"I don't have one!"

"Dig you a hole!"

Electa shrugs and starts to plow the dirt with her hands. She
finds a worm immediately and holds it up for Jack to see.

"Now, squeeze him on yer hook!"

Electa squirms as she tries to bait the hook. "Ick. So slimy!"
She finishes, throws her line in the water, and watches carefully. A
fish instantly takes the bait and she pulls it to shore. Electa
proudly raises the fish in the air for Jack to see. "You sure know
your fish!" Jack doesn't respond, so she looks across the creek
and discovers he's gone.

Henry rides north on a narrow dirt road skirting the Sacramento River. Just to his right, he spots an old farmer behind a mule plowing his field. He dismounts, walks over to the homesteader, and hands him the wanted poster the warden gave him. The grower studies the handbill, spits tobacco juice downwind, shrugs, and goes back to work.

The three saddle tramps, Red, Swede, and Hombre, ride down Carson City's Main Street, tie their horses to a hitching post, and enter the same saloon where they sparred with Good Time Jane.

Several men are standing at the bar counter, while others are seated at nearby tables. The half-drunk itinerants look around and steps up to the bar. Red, who is front and center, waves the bartender over. He recognizes the troublemakers and reaches under the counter for his shotgun. "Why you cocksuckers back here?"

Before he can raise his weapon, Red draws his gun and holds it to the barman's head. "'Cuz ya run us off 'fore we got our fill." Red jumps over the counter, grabs the shotgun out of the man's hand, tosses it aside, and secures a whisky bottle. He fills three glasses with one hand, while he points his gun with his other. Next, he reaches back and grabs two more bottles. He lines them up on the bar counter, and Swede and Hombre help themselves.

Stumbling drunk, the vagabonds exit the saloon, climb on their horses, and ride off laughing. As Red struggles to stay in his saddle, he tosses an empty bottle to the ground and fires away, missing each time. Frustrated, he leans over to get a closer shot and falls off his horse. As his friends laugh, he climbs back on and the drunk ruffians ride out of town hooting and hollering.

Several miles from Carson City, the saddle tramps share their last bottle of whiskey with one another. In the distance, they notice smoke rising from a Paiute village located by Pyramid Lake, sourced by the Truckee River.

As the men near the encampment, they see two half-clothed Paiute twenty-something women bathing in the river not far from the village. The men start to laugh, shush one another, drop down from their horses, and hide behind some trees.

The voyeurs continue to eye the native women frolicking in the water until Red takes the lead and the three rovers emerge from the trees. As they tiptoe along the river bank, they look around to make sure no one is watching.

When the maiden women look up, they see the outsiders high stepping through the water headed their way. Before they can scream, Hombre and Swede cover their mouths, while Red threatens the frightened women with a large hunting knife.

The ruthless bastards pull their prey out of the water and push them into the trees. There, they tie their hands together and force them on two horses. One of the women bites Swede's hand, and he screams. "Bitch!" Swede slaps her so hard, that she almost falls out of the saddle.

Red and Swede hoot and holler as they ride off with the Paiute females secured to the front of their horses. Not far back, Hombre rides all alone.

Behind a shoreline bush, a Paiute boy watches from a safe distance as the kidnappers and their hostages ride off. When the men ride over a hill, the boy runs to his village, where he tells his mother what he saw. She quickly relays the news to two elderly Paiutes, who immediately spread the word.

Five miles from the Paiute village, Hombre stokes a campfire, trying to ignore Red and Swede, who are laughing in the trees beyond the camp. Frustrated, he cups his hands and yells, "Guárdame un poco! Save some for me!"

As the Mexican backs away from the fire, he looks up and sees a band of ten Paiutes top a hill. Led by Numaga, son of Chief Winnemucca, the warriors are covered in war paint. Hombre instantly drops to the ground, and onto his stomach.

He scoops up a handful of dirt and throws it on the fire. He realizes his mistake when the wood starts to smolder and a small cloud of smoke envelopes the area. "Shit."

The Paiutes see the smoke and head straight for him as he mutters, "Fuck, me!" Hombre jumps to his feet and mounts his unsaddled horse. He rides into the trees, fires a warning shot, and starts to look for Red and Swede. As the terrified Mexican struggles to stay on his horse, he fires another shot and yells, "Paiutes! Run like hell!"

As the Indians close in on Hombre, their war cries disturb the solitude of the forest. Just ahead, Hombre sees a gap in the trees and squeezes through it. There, in an open meadow, he spots his partners, who are desperately trying to put on their clothes. Not far away, the two Paiute women sit naked with their backs against a tree, weeping, and trying to cover themselves.

When Red and Swede see their old friend, the bootless men try to grab hold of his horse, but Hombre kicks them away, and rides off, leaving them to deal with their own fate.

At a safe distance, he turns and watches as the yelping Paiutes enter the meadow and circle the two saddle tramps. Angered by his own cowardice, Hombre spurs his horse and rides off. A moment later, he hears the war cries of the Paiutes and the screams of Red and Swede.

The Mexican rides into Carson City at a fast pace, ties his horse to a hitching post, and rushes into the Carson City Saloon.

The bartender spots him, grabs his shotgun, and points it in his direction. "Ya got some big balls coming back in here!"

Hombre's eyes widen. "De damn Paiutes! Dey bushwacked!"

"Who? You and them asshole friends of yours?"

"Si, I am what is left."

"What ya do to provoke them?"

"What is this pro...voke?"

"How'd you rile them up?"

Hombre pauses as he prepares his lie. "We do nothing. They come to us screaming...el asesinato."

"Assassinated them other two?"

"Si, assassinated."

"What you want me to do about it?"

"Paiutes kill so they can laugh."

The bartender removes his apron and says, "Got a feeling I ain't hearing the full story, but I'll round up some men in the morning and head to Fort Churchill. Colonel Ormsby will know what to do. Nothin' to be done tonight."

Hombre looks the bar over. "I sleep here tonight?"

"Shit. My whiskey wouldn't be safe."

"I have no place."

"Not my problem." The bartender watches as the drifter mopes out the door. Outside the saloon, Hombre looks up and down Main Street looking for options. Finding none, he slumps down, leans his back against the saloon wall and closes his eyes.

FORT CHURCHILL

Headed by Colonel William Ormsby, a stubborn-faced man in his late fifties, the bartender, Hombre, a posse of fifty soldiers, and several Nevada City locals ride away from Fort Churchill.

On the other side of Carson Valley, the posse enters the meadow where Red and Swede were killed. Hombre rides up to Colonel Ormsby and says, "Right here."

The colonel raises his hand. "Hold up, men." The posse halts as the lead officer studies the meadow. Finally, he turns to the saddle tramp. "Sure this is the place?"

Hombre points. "Other side of trees."

"What were they doing there?"

The Mexican thinks twice. "Looking for the dinner."

"Why weren't you with them?"

"I was fixing the fire."

"All right. Lead the way."

The posse follows Hombre past a grove of trees and into the meadow. There, they find the bodies of Red and Swede, who have been scalped, mutilated, and tied to separate trees. Ormsby gives a signal and two soldiers jump off their horses and examine the corpses. One of the men steps away and throws up in the grass. The other soldier scuffs over to the colonel and whispers, "Sir, them fellas got their man parts in their mouths."

Colonel Ormsby dismounts and looks the dead men over. "Paiutes do that when their women folk have been violated." The colonel turns and stares at Hombre. "Were you raping Paiute women? The truth or I'll shoot you myself."

"No. I am fortunato to still have my own pecker."

An older soldier rides up. "We gonna leave them here like this, sir?"

The colonel points to another one of his men and nods at the older soldier. "You two stay here and bury these men. You can catch up to us later." The colonel waves his arm and the posse follows him away from the meadow.

BATTLE OF PYRAMID LAKE

Ormsby and his fifty-man posse ride along the Truckee River headed for Pyramid Lake and the Paiute village.

At the front of his entourage, the colonel turns to one of his young lieutenants and says, "Keep an eye out. Pyramid Lake's just ahead. Their village is near there." As the posse moves forward, a party of six Paiutes top a rocky hill a hundred yards ahead. Ormsby puts a spyglass to his eye, studies the approaching Indians, and waves his men forward.

A few minutes pass, and Ormsby and his men drop down into a ravine. When they bottom out, a hundred Paiutes, most of them on horses, appear at the top of the ravine. Ormsby's jaw drops and he whispers, "Shit."

The Indians create a human circle around the ravine as they yelp and holler, waiting for Numaga to give them the signal to attack.

Members of the posse look to Ormsby for an answer, but the colonel is too busy trying to keep his horse steady. Numaga waves and the Paiutes scream their way down the hill, overwhelming the outnumbered soldiers and volunteers. All hell breaks loose as the Paiutes fire their rifles and shoot arrows at bewildered posse members, who scatter in every direction.

A Carson City volunteer, who has an arrow stuck in his arm and a bloody ear dangling from the side of his head, runs past Ormsby screaming. The colonel yells out, "Form a perimeter!" To the left of Ormsby, a mounted and crazed militia soldier swings his saber wildly as he fends off three Paiutes. When two arrows find their mark in the chest of the soldier's horse, the animal drops to the ground, trapping the man beneath him. As he struggles to free himself, two Paiutes descend on him and pulverize his body with tomahawks. As Ormsby watches the private take his last breath, he hollers out more orders to men who can't hear him. "Stand your ground, men!" He climbs off his horse and surveys the battlefield.

In a flash, a Paiute brave clubs him on the head from behind. The colonel turns, gives the Indian a "how dare you strike an officer" look, and crumbles to the ground. The Paiute grabs the Ormsby by the hair, scalps him with one swing of his knife, holds his trophy high in the air, and screams. "Ahhhhh...! Yut! Yut!"

Seconds later, more Paiutes race down the ravine and attack the remaining militia men and volunteers, who are now in total disarray. Several men stand their ground, while others make their way out of the ravine.

The two men Colonel Ormsby assigned to burial duty exit the trees and stare at the carnage a short distance away. They continue to watch as Paiutes chase and kill their fellow soldiers and posse members. The soldiers gawk at one another a moment and turn and ride back into the trees.

As the Paiutes continue to attack the soldiers and volunteers, Numaga looks across the ravine and sees Hombre. When their eyes meet, the Mexican realizes Numaga recognizes him, so he slaps leather to his horse and rides off. The Paiute leader takes his time, raises his rifle, and shoots Hombre's horse out from under him.

Now on foot, the Mexican tries to run off, but Numaga closes in on him and throws his tomahawk. The hatchet hits the lying saddle tramp square in the back, and he drops to his knees. Numaga jumps off his horse, strides over to the liar, and cuts his throat.

As the remaining militia members and Carson City volunteers fire off the last of their rounds, some of them beg for their lives.

Suddenly, Numaga screams out a victorious war cry, "Hoot! Hoot!" Then he raises his arm and signals his men to stop fighting. The Paiutes back away, mount their horses and leave the few remaining posse members and soldiers dazed and bloodied.

Hearing no more gunfire, the two cowardly soldiers emerge from the trees and ride towards the battlefield. When they arrive, they act surprised by what they see.

CHAPTER 34

**"The whole world can become the enemy
when you lose what you love." Kristina McMorris**

SAMUEL AND PETE finish hitching two horses to a buckboard wagon as Maria, Buckie, and Sandra look on. Pete turns to his wife and says, "Be home as soon as we can."

Buckie hurries to his father and points at Samuel. "Why's he goin' and I'm not?"

Pete winks. "'Cuz, he's leaving in a few days and I wanna get as much work out of him as I can 'fore he goes."

Sandra speaks. "Why can't you wait for Good Time?"

"She ain't coming with the things your mother needs."

Maria raises her eyebrows. "What might those things be?"

Pete displays three fingers, one at a time, and names the items. "Flour, vanilla, sugar for a dozen pies. Speaking of sugar, almost forgot somethin'." He leaps from the wagon and gives Maria a big kiss.

Maria breaks away. "Pete, the children."

Pete laughs as he reaches over to kiss Buckie. His son jumps back, so he shrugs and climbs back in the wagon.

Sandra looks gloomy, so Maria puts an arm around her daughter and whispers, "Don't worry. He's not going to leave without a proper goodbye." Embarrassed, Sandra dashes for the cabin as Maria and Buckie watch the men roll away.

As the wagon heads east, Pete turns to Samuel. "Had enough pony riding, have ya?"

"Yeah, I wanna head back north."

"Gonna look for gold again?"

"Maybe. Got a few debts to pay."

"We'll be missin' you, 'specially that girl of mine."

"Sorry about that."

"It happens. If I was to fit a dress, I'd be sweet on you myself."

Ahead, Good Time Jane approaches with a wagon loaded with bags of grain. She sides up to Pete's wagon and shows her teeth. "Where you two goin' like you mean business?"

"Need some supplies in Carson."

Jane's eyes narrow. "For your horses? I's comin' fast as I can."

"No, you're good. Maria needs makings for pies and I need some other shit."

"Ahh, well, ya got room for this here grain? Save me goin' all the way to your place."

"No, it might pinch us too much. You go on ahead. Hot apple pie for supper. Why don't you plan on spending the night?"

"Married man like you wantin' a good-lookin' woman like me to sleep over? Ain't that something?"

"Good Time, I...."

Jane interrupts. "Not plannin' on sneakin' up on me in the dead of the night are ya?" She laughs and changes her tone. "Naah. Just funning, Mr. Pete. I knows ya got solid gold with the missus. Yes siree, solid gold." She turns to Samuel. "Now, Mr. Samuel here, he don't have to do no sneakin'. I'll be waitin' on his arrival with lovin' arms." Jane laughs and drives off.

As Pete guides his wagon down Carson City's Main Street, the visitors see six posse members nursing their wounds and riding slowly towards them. The bartender is slumped low in his saddle. Behind him, draped over several road weary horses, are the lifeless bodies of six Carson City volunteers.

Pete looks for an explanation. "Jesus Christ! What happened?"

The bartender's face reveals his pain. "Paiutes. Killed Forrester here, Sampson, Pickens, Peabody, Stevens brothers ... and too many militia men to count, even Colonel Ormsby's a goner. Didn't have the horses to bring 'em all back."

"Paiutes? Why they in an uproar?"

"Don't know for sure, but my guess is them three bastards that was in my bar a few days back stole some Paiute women and violated them."

"Why didn't you let the militia handle it?"

"Shit. Didn't know them devils was so many."

Pete's face reddens as he puts the reins to his horses. The bartender thinks of something else and calls out. "Soon as the militia gets some more men, there's gonna be hell to pay!"

Pete pulls up to the General Store, stares at the front window, and turns to Samuel. "Hell with it. We gotta get home!" Pete slaps leather to his horses again, and the wagon lurches forward. With a cloud of dust in their wake, Pete and Samuel race out of town.

Maria is hanging clothes on a rope stretching from the cabin to the barn. She looks up and sees a band of Paiutes, led by Numaga. The natives slowly ride towards the station, as Maria calmly walks to the front door, and goes inside. She watches as Sandra stirs a pot of soup and Buckie plays at the table with his toy soldiers. Maria sighs, leans her back against the front door and matter-of-factly says, "Sandra, take Buckie and get in the cellar."

Sandra stops stirring and says, "Why?"

"Just do as I say. And no matter what happens, don't come out 'til I tell you to or you hear your father's voice. Understand? Do you understand?"

Sandra responds with a sarcastic tone. "Okay. I heard you." When her mother starts to cry, Sandra realizes something is terribly wrong. "I'm sorry, Momma."

"Neither of you can make a sound." Maria drops to her knees and stares into her children's eyes. "I love both of you very much." She hugs her children, stands up, grabs a candle from the fireplace mantle, lights it, and hands it to Sandra.

Next, she leads them into the kitchen, lifts open a trap door, and Buckie and Sandra climb down into the root cellar. Buckie holds his nose as he looks up at his mother. "It stinks down here!"

"What'd I say? Not a peep." As Maria wipes away a tear, she lowers the trap door and then rushes into the living area. She grabs a rug, returns to the kitchen, and covers the trap door. She rushes back to the fireplace, picks up the rifle leaning up against it, and heads for the front door. When she opens it, she sees seven Paiutes seated on their horses fifty feet away. She raises her rifle and aims it at the Paiute leader, Numaga, who slowly expands his chest. Maria cocks the rifle and stares coldly at him.

All at once, a wagon appears on the horizon, so Maria lowers her rifle, waves at what she thinks is Pete and Samuel, and yells out, "Pete!" The Paiutes turn and watch as the wagon makes its way for the Buckland homestead. The Paiutes ride forward, so Maria tightens her jaw and starts to raise her rifle again. But before she can shoulder it, an arrow hits her square in the chest. The mother of two looks down in disbelief. She clutches the arrow with both hands, and falls dead to the ground. Numaga lowers his bow, signals four of his comrades, and they hop off their horses. They hurry into the cabin, while the other two Paiutes wait for the approaching wagon.

Now inside the Buckland home, the Indians toss furniture and smash decorative items against the wall. In Sandra's bedroom, a Paiute finds one of her undergarments, holds it up to his companion and laughs. In the kitchen, another warrior puts a ladle full of soup to his mouth. He takes a gulp, grimaces, and spits the soup out.

In the cellar, Sandra and Buckie hold each other tightly as they listen to the Paiutes ransacking the rooms above them. Careful not to make a sound, Sandra looks at a burlap bag of potatoes, puts her right index finger to her lips, and signals Buckie to stay quiet. She empties the potatoes from the bag, and motions Buckie to climb inside it. Buckie shakes his head no, but changes his mind and crawls into the bag as his sister ties it shut.

The Paiutes finish plundering the cabin and are preparing to leave when they hear a muffled sneeze. In the cellar, Sandra freezes and then puts her hand on the potato bag, trying to keep Buckie from sneezing again. Numaga walks into the kitchen and scans the area. He lifts his nose, sniffs, and points at the floor. One of the other Paiutes drops down and puts his ear on the rug covering the cellar door. The kitchen is silent until Buckie sneezes again.

Numaga kicks the rug away and signals two of his men to open the door leading to the cellar. The Paiutes yank it open and look down into the cellar. They see Sandra, but pay no attention to the bulging burlap bag next to her.

The warriors pull the screaming girl out of the cellar by her hair and hold her up for their leader to see. Numaga touches her hair and skin as Sandra struggles to free herself from the other Paiutes. Irritated, the Paiute slaps Sandra across the face, rips open her bodice, and grins at her partially exposed breasts. He notices her necklace, snatches the jeweled chain from her neck, looks at it briefly, and tosses it to the floor. Numaga nods and one of his men dashes over to the fireplace and grabs a burning log. As the other Paiutes exit the cabin with Sandra, the last Indian lights the kitchen curtains on fire.

Now outside, the intruders watch as the cabin goes up in flames. Sandra screams as the Paiutes take turns trying to hang on to her. Finally, Jane arrives and her wagon comes to a sudden stop in front of the burning cabin. She jumps down and watches as the flames continue to grow. The Paiutes have confused looks on their faces as they study the profile of the large black woman, who is trying to decide what to do about the fire. Sandra breaks free from her captors and rushes over to Jane. "Buckie's still in there!"

Jane screams, "Buckie!" and stomps her way toward the burning cabin as two Paiutes reclaim Sandra. One of the warriors tries to stop Jane, but she tosses him to the ground as if he's a small child. The other Paiutes laugh as the embarrassed man dusts himself off.

Sandra continues to wrestle with her captors as she screams out to Jane. "He's in the kitchen cellar!"

When the big woman reaches the front porch, she pauses when she sees Maria's body. Enraged, she busts her way through the front door and screams, "Buckie!"

With flames all around her, Jane makes her way to the kitchen. Coughing heavily as smoke fills her lungs, she finds the cellar's trap door, rips it off its hinges, tosses it aside, and crawls down inside the opening. When she hears Buckie coughing, she tears open the burlap bag, but only enough to expose the boy's head. Buckie gives her a look of desperation as Jane tries to decide what to do. "Stay safe, honey. Stay safe. Gots to be in this bag a little longer."

Jane makes up her mind and shoves Buckie back into the bag. She ties it shut and carries it out of the cellar as the boy screams, "Damn it! Let me outta here! I can't breathe!"

Jane punches the bag hard and Buckie turns silent. "T's sorry, Buck man. Everything's gonna be okay." When Jane enters the living area, a fiery beam falls in front of her and blocks the path to the door. With flames all around and nowhere to turn, Jane stomps on the floor until it gives way. She pulls away several broken slats and creates a hole big enough for the burlap bag to fit inside. She shoves the bag in the hole, and covers it with her body as the flames engulf Good Time Jane and the Buckland home.

Numaga and his men ride away with Sandra in tow. Two warriors trail behind herding Pete's horses and Jane's mules as the cabin, the barn, and the outbuildings continue to burn.

Almost home, Pete and Samuel see the smoldering cabin in the distance. When they arrive, they pull up to the charred remains of Jane's wagon. Pete jumps down, sizes up the situation, drops to his knees, and grabs his head. "Ahhhhh!" Samuel helps the grief stricken man to his feet, and they make their way to what's left of the cabin.

When Pete sees Maria, he rushes over and pulls his wife's bloodied and blackened body into his arms. He holds her closely, looking for any sign of life as Samuel stands back with his head bowed. Angry, Pete breaks off the arrow lodged in Maria's chest and tosses it as far as he can.

As the men meander through the smoldering rubble, they stumble on the blackened corpse of Good Time Jane. They cover their noses and start to back away when they hear a muffled groan. They look at each other a moment and roll what's left of Jane's body over. In a hole under her corpse is a burlap potato bag. Pete hears another groan, so he pulls the bag out of the hole and rips it open. Dazed and confused, Buckie tries to rid himself of the bag as Pete and Samuel do their best to help. Finally free, Pete grabs his son and holds him tightly until Buckie pushes him away.

When they step away from what's left of the cabin, Samuel looks down and sees Sandra's necklace. He picks it up, looks it over, and hands it to Pete. Sandra's father studies the blackened piece of jewelry until a look of despair crosses his face. He hands it back to Samuel and says, "Might mean she's alive. Never took it off. You keep it for her."

With what's left of Buckland homestead in the background, Pete and Samuel finish burying Maria and Jane. Two makeshift crosses sit on top of their burial plots and not far away, Buckie sits in the wagon crying.

As Samuel and the Bucklands ride along, Pete brings his horses to a stop and gets out of the wagon. He bends down and looks at a series of tracks as Samuel joins him. "We find them, what we gonna do? They won't just hand her over."

"Well, I sure as hell ain't gonna sit around wonderin' what them heathens are doin' with my girl. And I ain't waitin' on no God damn militia to do who knows what."

"I hear you, but we need more firepower."

"Those assholes spooked the Paiutes in the first place ... Got Maria and Jane killed ... and my girl stole."

"Us dying's not gonna help. Let me ride back to Carson City. Maybe the town has a better plan by now."

Pete snarls. "Better plan? Shit!"

"I'll need one of your horses." Samuel head for the front of the wagon to undo a horse. "Be back as soon as I can."

Buckie starts to cry. "I wanna go. I can't stop thinking 'bout Ma bein' in the ground."

"Just hold up. We're all going." Pete slaps the wagon and climbs aboard. Samuel joins them and Pete turns his rig around, headed for Carson City.

CHAPTER 35

"You will never reach your destination if you stop and throw stones at every dog that barks." Winston Churchill

IDAHO TERRITORY

HENRY RIDES down Lewiston's main thoroughfare past several sour-faced merchants and townspeople, who busily go about their business. He spots a saloon named *Molly's Place*, so he jumps off his gifted horse, ties the animal's reins to a hitching post, and wanders inside.

The saloon is filled with ill-fated miners, broke gamblers, and homely hookers. Molly O'Conner, a large-breasted Irish woman, sits on a stool behind the counter pouring a beer. She has a ragged untied bonnet propped on her red-haired head and an unlit cigar in her mouth. Henry sides up to the bar, she winks at him and points to a sign: GIVE UP YOUR GUNS OR GET THE HELL OUT. Henry nods and hands Molly his six-shooter.

Molly grins. "What can I get ya, lad?"

"One beer, Ma'am."

"It's Molly."

"All right. One Molly, Ma'am."

Molly laughs as she pours Henry a beer. "Need one of my gals to keep you company?"

"Don't think they can afford me. I ain't cheap." She laughs again as she hands him his beer. As the saloon keeper turns to wait on another customer, Henry notices the large oil painting of a life-sized red-headed nude above the bar. He stares at it until Molly returns.

She grins and says, "You like?"

"Yeah, is she real?"

"Yes, darlin'. She works here."

Henry looks around, but he doesn't see any red-haired women. He turns back and his eyes light up. "It's you."

Molly smiles. "Twenty years and I haven't changed one bit."

As Henry chuckles, Horace Wilson, who is parked at the far end of the bar staring down at his empty whiskey glass, looks up and spots Henry. He nudges his cellmate and Warren Spivey sits up, gathers himself, and glances in the direction Horace is staring.

Molly walks off as Warren limps over and deliberately bumps into Henry, spilling his beer. "Whoa. Watch it there, partner." Henry sees who it is and his eyes narrow. "If it ain't the devil himself." Warren sucks his teeth and spits on the floor as the warden's deputy continues. "You got a lot of balls hangin' out in a town where ya robbed a bank."

"Shut the fuck up. When'd you bust out?

Henry surveys the room and spots Horace Wilson. "I didn't. Governor pardoned me."

"Shit."

"Just so ya know, the warden gave me the go-ahead to chase you and Wilson down. I didn't think it'd be so easy." Henry flashes his badge. "Only the warden, he don't want ya back."

Warren chuckles. "Good, 'cuz we ain't goin' back."

"Horace your boy now?"

"Shit. That oaf. I like 'em young and tender like your brother."

"You know, Spivey, if you were four times smarter than you are, you'd still be stupid."

Warren growls. "You cocky son of a bitch."

Molly approaches. "Appears you two are in full disagreement, so take your troubles outside. I'll give ya back your guns, so ya can shoot each other."

Warren nods. "Killing's thirsty work. "One more drink?"

The bar owner gives Warren the evil eye. "Bar's closed to the likes of you."

Henry stands up. "Let's go. Been waiting a long time for this."

Warren turns to Horace. "He wants revenge for me killing his pa and stealing his brother. Should thank me. Boy ain't a man 'til his old man's dead and he's an only brother."

"Enough talk. Get your gun." Henry turns his back and reaches his hand out to Molly for his weapon, but when the Irish woman sees Warren reach down in his pants and pull out a pistol, she drops down behind the counter.

Warren grins. "Got me one right handy."

Sensing something is wrong, Henry dives over the bar as Warren fires and misses. Sitting on the floor next to him is Molly. As Warren backs away from the counter, he yells, "Damn you and your ways! Come out from there, ya chickenshit!"

Everyone else in the bar stampedes out the front door, except for Horace, who removes a gun from his boot, flips a table over, and hides behind it. He whispers to Warren. "Got your back!" Still hunkered down behind the bar, Molly hands Henry his gun and the San Quentin deputy tries to decide what he should do next.

As Henry checks his weapon, Warren hollers from the other side of the bar. "Putin' away my shooter. Let's talk." The murderer holsters his pistol and nods to Horace, still hidden behind the table at the ready.

Henry stands, but he keeps his right hand under the counter. "One last time. Where's Samuel?"

Warren shakes his head. "All the time harpin' bout yer damn brother. Truth is, Sam and me had our disagreements, but once the sun went down, we was always real cozy."

Henry raises his gun. "Goodbye, Spivey." Before he can get a shot off, Horace peeks around the table and shoots Henry in his right forearm. Both fugitives fire away, hitting whiskey bottles and a big glass mirror, but somehow they manage to miss their target.

Henry drops back down behind the counter, grabs another gun and fits it to his left hand. On the other side of the bar, Warren gimps over to the table where Horace is still hiding and motions for him to skedaddle. Horace looks Warren straight in the eyes. "Fuck you! Find your own table!" Warren blinks once and shoots Horace square in the chest. The assassin quickly repositions the table and squats behind it.

Still behind the bar counter, Henry checks the chamber of his gun, gathers himself, and pops up. Warren isn't there. Finally, Henry spots a boot sticking out from the overturned table, takes aim, fires, and hits the killer in the foot. He screams, "Jesus Christ! I was just gettin' healed up!"

Warren grimaces in pain as he bunches himself up behind the table, his torso hidden. A moment passes and the villain lifts his pistol above the table and fires twice. The shots miss Henry by inches, leaving splintered holes in the top of the bar behind him.

The barrel of a shotgun raises up from behind the counter. Henry looks down at Molly and she nods for him to take it. He lays his gun down, grabs the shotgun, and waits for Warren to pop up. When he does, Henry blasts a hole in the center of the table, hitting Spivey in the groin.

Warren groans, unfastens his gun belt, and looks down at his blood-soaked pants. "You son of a bitch! You better not have womanized me!" Enraged, Warren hobbles away from the table and charges straight at Henry, his gun cocked and ready. In one motion, Henry drops the shotgun, grabs his pistol from the counter, and shoots Warren between the eyes. As the wrongdoer lifts his hand as if to say something, he falls dead to the floor.

Molly raises up from behind the counter, takes the gun from Henry, and waves away the powdered smoke that fills the room. "Ya bollocks him good, the bloody tosser."

Killing Warren Spivey didn't make me feel as good as I thought it would. And now, I'm gonna have to find Alex Slade, so that bastard can tell me what happened to my brother.

The Lewiston sheriff, Seth Wise, walks to the jail cell and opens it. Henry, seated on a cot writing in his journal, stands up. His right arm is bandaged. Sheriff Wise waves him out of the cell and hands him the handbill the warden gave Henry six weeks earlier.

He follows the sheriff into the office and they sit down. Seth shoves a telegram across his desk and Henry picks it up. "That fancy telegram backs up the paper ya got. Least I won't have to hang them or mail'em back to San Quentin. Did me a big favor."

"Yeah, those assholes needed to be dead."

"Message there says to pay you. I'll make arrangements at the bank. Stop there on your way out of town." Henry moves his bandaged arm and grimaces in pain. Seth chuckles. "Guess you'll be pissing left-handed for a while." Henry coughs deeply as he looks at a wanted poster on the wall. Seth turns and looks at it as well. "Alex Slade, Spivey's partner.

Henry sits up. "Yeah, I know all about him. Seen him lately?"

"No. Never has come around here Could be dead for all I know. Worth some money if he ain't. Suppose you heard about him and Spivey tunneling out of the Dillon jail like two gophers?"

"Yeah, good story, but they did a whole lot of killing and stealing near Bannack when I was there."

"Yeah, think I heard that too."

Henry stares at the poster. "This could be anyone."

"That's old, so I don't know if he's still got long hair or not." The sheriff tears the poster off the wall. "Take it. Ya never know." Henry pockets it and heads for the door.

As Henry rides west on a clear spring day, the gurgle of a nearby river permeates the silence. He comes to a stop, reaches down with his right hand, and removes his pistol.

He fires twice, missing the tin can on the side of the road. He switches the weapon to his left hand and shoots again. This time the can spins as it takes flight. He pulls back on his horse's reins, comes to a stop, and looks up at the moving clouds. A moment passes, he flicks the reins, and rides away.

CHAPTER 36

"When a white army battles Indians and wins, it is called a great victory, but if they lose, it is called a massacre."
Chiksika, Shawnee

JACK'S LIPS move as he silently reads from the Bible propped up on the table in front of him. Electa, seated next to him, is wearing a blue summer dress accessorized by an ivory-carved brooch. "Go ahead. Read it out loud."

"The Lord is my...shep...herd...I shall not want...He make ...eth."

"Sound it out." Electa pulls off her brooch, sets it on the side table near the door, and unbuttons the top button of her blouse.

"He ma ... keth. He maketh me to lie down in green pas ... tures. Funny word that maketh."

"That's enough for today. You're doing so well."

He slaps the Bible shut and grins. "That's 'cuz I got me a good teacher." Electa smiles and leads the new Bannack sheriff to the door. "How 'bout we join up tonight on account of my doing so good?"

"I'm sorry. I have other plans."

"That's okay. We'll find us another time." Electa doesn't react, so he continues. "Ain't forgot our kiss, have ya?"

"You understand that was a moment I wasn't prepared for?"

"Sure would like more of them moments."

He moves toward her, but she backs away and says, "Jack, I care about you, but not in that way."

Jack lowers his shoulders and sighs. "It's okay. We'll build on it, a stone at a time." Electa gives him a sympathetic look and his face darkens. Then he scoffs, "He's still in your head, ain't he?"

When she turns away, Jack grabs her brooch from the side table and stuffs it in his pocket. Then he takes her gently by the shoulders and turns her back to him. "It's okay. Got me ten years to clear your mind."

"I'm never going to ...." Before she can finish, he hurries out the door.

Samuel and the Bucklands roll into Carson City. Pete pulls his wagon to a stop in front of the saloon, where they see dozens of horses and other wagons. He removes a coin from his pocket and tosses it to Buckie. "Go get yourself some candy and meet us back here in a half hour."

"Ma says candy rots my teeth."

Pete raises his head. "Buy somethin' else." Buckie hops off the wagon as several townsmen walk past.

A thin man is headed into the bar when Pete yells at him. "What's going on in there?"

The man doesn't turn back but says, "If yer wantin' to kill Paiutes, we're meetin' right now."

The saloon is filled with local men and several militia soldiers, who are lamenting about the loss of their friends and relatives. Pete and Samuel push their way front and center. Standing next to them is the bar owner and Texas Ranger Colonel John Hays.

The bar owner bangs his gun on the counter and everyone quiets down. "Listen up, everyone! This here's Colonel John Hays of the Texas Rangers. He's Colonel Ormby's replacement."

John takes a step forward and tips his hat. "Listen, I know you're all biting at the bit to get revenge, but I got all the men I need."

The Carson City men yell out and curse loudly, until the bartender raps his gun on the counter again.

"Let the colonel here have his say."

Colonel Hays thanks the bartender with his eyes and continues. "I got two hundred well-trained men out of Sacramento, who are back at Fort Churchill, waitin' my orders.

Pete steps forward. "With all respect sir, either you make room for us or we'll be striking out on our own."

The colonel shakes his head. "I understand, but..."

Pete interrupts. "Two days ago, the Paiutes killed my wife, a good friend, stole my girl, and burned my place to the ground."

The colonel considers what Pete said and continues. "Sorry, but everyone here has lost someone. My men can handle this."

"You being sorry ain't enough. I'm going... and so's my son here." Pete nods at Samuel. "We'll follow behind if we need to."

Another man yells. "Me too! Heathens killed my brother!"

The colonel stares at Pete as the locals talk loudly amongst themselves. Finally, Hays lowers his shoulders and says, "Shit. Pick out twenty men and be at the fort at sunup." Volunteers raise their hands and shove their way towards Pete as Colonel Hays and his militia men walk out of the bar.

Pete, Samuel, and Buckie are sitting in their wagon in front of the local church. Buckie is wearing a red straw hat, bought with the money his father gave him. Angered by the news he is being left behind, Buckie says, "Ain't leaving me in this shithole town!"

"I told you. We only got two horses."

"That's a lie. You can find me a horse and you know it."

"Buckie, you're just a boy. We're going to war."

"You left Mom and Sandra alone and now they're dead."

"Watch your mouth, young man!"

Buckie points at Samuel. "Why's he going? She's my sister."

"You're staying at this church and that's final."

"Ya can't make me, if I don't wanna."

Pete makes eye contact with Samuel. "Get him!"

The two men grab Buckie, wrestle him out of the wagon, and pull him towards the church.

Reverend Jonas Brown stands looking at Buckie, who is tied to a chair inside the church. Pete gently shoves his son and says, "When the Reverend here unties you, you're gonna stay put, right?"

Buckie scowls. "Soon as I'm loose, I'm stealing a horse and finding Sandra myself."

Pete turns to Reverend Brown. "If he tries to run off, take him to the jail and have the sheriff lock him up."

SECOND BATTLE OF PYRAMID LAKE

Led by Colonel John Hays, a regiment of two hundred Texas Rangers and militia men ride away from Fort Churchill. Behind them are Ben, Samuel, the bartender, and eighteen other Carson City volunteers.

As Colonel Hays and his entourage approach Pyramid Lake, not far from the Truckee River, the bartender points at the spot where the first battle took place.

Two scouts ride over the hill and join the colonel. The oldest one, clad in deerskin leather, says, "Paiute village just over the hill. Looks awful quiet."

Hays sits up in his saddle. "Well, we're about to change that." He signals fifty militia men on his right flank and fifty men on his left to spread out. As the men fan out, he signals the Carson City volunteers to move forward.

When Hays and his men top a hill, they see two Paiute boys playing along the banks of the Truckee River. The boys spot the soldiers and take off in the direction of their village.

Colonel Hays gives another signal and his militia men ride down the hill past the boys with bayonets raised. Several Paiutes see the soldiers coming and run for their weapons.

When Hays and his men reach the village, they fire away and torch several teepees, some still occupied by women and children. The outnumbered Paiutes scatter as the soldiers surround and occupy the village.

Pete and Samuel dodge arrows and try to stay on their horses as several Indian braves attack them. Other natives mount their own horses in an effort to compete with the overwhelming number of horse soldiers.

As Pete scans the village for any sign of Sandra, an arrow hits him in the leg. He falls to the ground, and a tall Paiute sees he's vulnerable. The warrior runs toward Pete, his knife drawn, but just as he raises his knife to stab him, Samuel shoots the Indian in the back.

Soldiers continue to chase down and kill Paiutes, until very few warriors are left standing. As the battle subsides, Samuel takes stock of the dead militia men and fallen Indians all around him. Not far away, Colonel Hays and his men hoot and holler, celebrating their victory, while other men pilfer Paiute tents, looking for treasure.

In the distance, Samuel spots Numaga on a horse with Sandra positioned awkwardly in front of him. As the Indian and his captive ride away, Samuel locks eyes with Pete. His mentor tosses him his rifle, and the former Pony Express rider hurries off at a full gallop.

Samuel searches the banks along the Truckee River, looking for any sign of Numaga and Sandra. Up ahead, behind a large pine tree in a small meadow, the Paiute steadies his horse as Sandra sits uncomfortably in front of him. Numaga sees Samuel coming, puts a knife to Sandra's neck with one hand, and covers her mouth with the other. Unaware that he is closing in on the escapees, Samuel sees an opening in the trees. He rides through it and into the clearing.

Numaga spots the white man, sheathes his knife, and grabs his rifle. While still holding his hostage's mouth shut with his other hand, he shoulders his weapon with his free arm, and prepares to fire at Samuel. Sandra sees what he is about to do and bites his hand. The Indian promptly shoves her off his horse and aims his rifle point blank at the frightened young woman. Sandra reacts by making herself small and covering her head.

All at once, a shot rings out and the top of the Paiute's head explodes, covering Sandra with blood. She looks up and sees that part of Numaga's skull is missing, replaced by a bloody mass. The Indian's shoulders sag and he falls backward off his horse.

Numaga, now sitting tilted against the tree, looks like a creature who has fallen from the sky. His mouth is open and he has an evil jack o' lantern smile on his face.

Samuel rides along; trailing behind him on Numaga's horse is Sandra, whose face is expressionless. When the young couple appear on the outskirts of Carson City, Sandra's father and brother see them and Buckie takes off running. When he arrives, he grabs the bridle of his sister's horse. Sandra climbs down from her horse, Pete limps over, and the Bucklands embrace.

Back home, Sandra looks down at her mother's grave as Pete, Samuel, Rut, and Buckie fit logs together for a new cabin, which is not far from the blackened and gutted barn that is barely standing. Rut's coach is parked between the remains of the old cabin and a makeshift corral filled with the driver's eight horses.

When Rut and Samuel finish wrestling a log in place, they look over at Pete, who is staring at his despondent daughter. Rut joins Pete as Samuel and Buckie sit down on a log. The coach driver struggles with what to say to his old friend. "Maria was a good woman, but you'll get through this."

Buckie shuffles over and gives his father a big hug. "Sorry for bein' such an asshole in Carson City." Pete runs his hands through Buckie's hair and joins Sandra in front of Maria's grave.

Rut stands and says, "I'd best hook up the horses."

Samuel jumps to his feet and follows him. "I'll help you."

As Samuel and Rut hitch up the horses, Pete, Sandra, and Buckie stand in front of Maria's grave holding one another. Samuel turns to Rut. "You going back to Sacramento?"

"Yeah, still got me toting people to Idaho Territory and back."

"Might see you. Going there myself."

"Not planning on holding up any coaches, are ya?"

"Ya never know."

"Know what they say, ya can't trust a man who don't wanna steal somethin'."

"Who said that?"

"Don't know. I might've made it up."

PART FOUR: VIGILANTE JUSTICE

CHAPTER 37

"No man ever steps in the same river twice, for it is not the same river and he is not the same man." Heraclitis

WITH HIS FEET PROPPED UP on the desk, Jack sucks the last smattering of whiskey from a bottle. Then he reaches in his pocket, removes Electa's brooch, smells it, and tries to pin it on his chest. He thinks better of it, puts it in his desk drawer, and vacates the office. Right away, he spots Henry riding down Main Street headed his way. He spits on the ground, adjusts the badge on his chest, and shuffles towards his old friend.

Henry unhorses and extends his hand, but Jack steps back and pretends not to see his friendly gesture. Henry senses his coldness, retreats, and tries again. "What's this I hear 'bout Bannack getting themselves a new sheriff?"

Jack ignores the question. "That's a short ten years."

"Got myself pardoned. Figured ya knew."

"I knew all right. Just didn't think you'd come back here."

"Well, here I am."

"Why?"

"'Cuz this is the place I know."

"Lots of changes. Peaceful now."

"You must be doin' one hell of a job. Curious, any sign of Alex Slade lately?"

"No. Spivey? See him in Quentin?"

"Yeah, he was there."

"And?"

"He escaped, but got himself beefed in Lewiston a couple weeks ago."

"Ain't that something."

Henry hesitates. "How's Electa doing?"

"She's mine now."

Henry chuckles. "Really? Does she know that?"

"Don't start. Got us somethin' good goin'. How long?"

"How long what?"

Jack grumbles. "How long ya stayin'?"

"Think I'll stick around awhile. See if Slade shows up again. He's the only one who might know what happened to Samuel."

"You still don't get it. Your brother's dead!"

Henry changes the subject. "How bout we team up and look for some gold like old times?" Jack rubs his badge and Henry grins. "Awwh. You being sheriff does change things."

"Yeah. Them things are to my liking and I plan on keepin' 'em that way." Jack walks off without saying another word.

Henry rides up to Gus's livery stable, where he finds the blacksmith in a corral, shoeing a horse. Gus looks up, sees who it is, and says, "What the hell!"

Henry climbs off his horse, holds out his hand, and hollers, "Gus!"

Gus jogs over, shakes his old friend's hand vigorously, and steps back. "Goddamn, it's good to see you. Heard they cut you loose."

"Ya think maybe I could hole up in your hayloft a few days?"

Gus chuckles. "Why not. You know that place better than I do." The blacksmith puts his arm around Henry's shoulder and they walk towards the front door of the livery stable.

Henry struts down the street, wearing a bright yellow store-bought shirt and carrying a thin metal pole. Townspeople smile as Bannack's former sheriff passes them. When he reaches his old office, he knocks lightly. No one answers, so he cracks open the door and looks inside. He grins when he sees Jack behind his desk knitting another red scarf. "Is it safe for me to come in here?"

Before the new sheriff can answer, Henry slips inside. Jack puts his knitting away as Henry pulls up a chair and sits. "How 'bout we start over ... talk about old times?

Jack stares at Henry's fishing pole and his new shirt. "Thought you hated fish?"

"The fishing part relaxes me."

"That's some fancy pole?"

"Gus made it for me. I'm sleeping in his hayloft you know."

"Suits you. Why ya all gussied?"

"Heard fish were attracted to yellow."

"Bullshit. Where ya fishin'?"

"Grasshopper Creek. No other place."

"Let me guess, near the Vail place?"

"Yeah, Gus says they're biting there."

"How long did you say you were stayin again'?"

"Day longer than when ya asked me yesterday."

Jack stares at him, so Henry shakes his fishing pole, stands up, and starts to leave. Without warning, Jack throws his tin coffee cup at the door. Bang. Henry turns back. "What the hell?"

"You ain't fishing for no fuckin' fish, ya sneaky bastard!" Henry turns to leave again and Jack explodes. "How many times I need to tell you? I gotta claim on Electa?"

"If I see her, she can tell me that herself."

"I'm tired bein' second to you and your ways!... always wantin' to get 'tween her legs."

"That's awful rough talk."

"I'll talk any damn way I please."

Henry softens his voice. "After sitting in prison for six months, I'm seeing things a lot different."

"Bullshit! You're still wantin' to steal things that ain't yours."

"If you're talking about Electa, she makes her own choices."

"Ya think you're really somethin', don't ya? Well, your shit stinks just like everyone else's."

"You're making it awful hard to stay friends." Henry heads out the door as Jack grits his teeth and yells, "Beware of pitchforks, pretty boy!"

My friendship with Jack has always been a disagreeable one, but the fact that we both love Electa appears to be an obstacle we're never gonna get over.

Henry rides along on the bank of Grasshopper Creek, gripping his new fishing pole. He dismounts, leads his horse into a grove of aspens, and looks through the trees at the Vail cabin. He moves a branch and sees Electa hoeing in the garden. His horse neighs, so he covers the animal's mouth with his hand.

Now sitting on the bank of the creek fishing, Henry's pants are rolled up to his knees and his boots are resting next to him. Sensing someone's presence, he turns and sees Electa approaching. For some reason, he turns his eyes back to the creek.

As he stares at the water, he matter-of-factly says, "Still gathering berries, I see."

Startled by Henry's voice, Electa drops her basket and takes a deep breath. "Oh my God! What are you doing here?"

"Been back a couple days now."

"I saw Jack last night. He never mentioned you."

"Does that surprise you? Are the two of you a couple now?"

"He thinks we are, but we're not."

There's an awkward silence as Electa turns her back. Henry lays his pole down, hops up, and approaches her. "You've been on my mind every day since the time I left."

"Did you escape from prison or what?"

"No. The governor set me free." Electa turns back to Henry and he says, "I didn't know if I'd ever get to tell you this, but Miss Bryan, I love you."

There's a moment of silence as Electa stares at Henry. "I guess I should say something."

"It's all right if you don't love me. I'm in no hurry."

"I sat right here thinking about you almost every day, even though I didn't want to. One day, I gave up and started trying to see the world without you. And now ..." Electa turns and starts to walk away.

"Now you're just gonna walk away?"

She turns back, sits on a log, and puts her face in her hands. "This is all so confusing." Henry slides over, sits down next to her, and puts his arm around her waist. She finally notices that it's bandaged. "What happened?"

"I'll tell you later. I've got other things on my mind."

Electa lays her head back on his shoulder, but he lifts her chin and kisses her fully on the mouth. She leans back, looks deep into Henry's eyes, and sighs, "God help me. I do love you."

CHAPTER 38

"Life consists not in holding good cards but in playing those you hold well." Josh Billings

BUCKLAND STATION has been rebuilt. It's a roughshod version of the original complex, and the ground around it is still black from the fire. The outbuildings, including the barn, are a blend of both old and new materials, and the workmanship is shoddy.

Sandra exits the cabin carrying a bucket, looks around, but she doesn't see anyone. As she pumps water into the wooden pail, she grabs her stomach, bends over, and throws up. She checks again to see if anyone is watching and hurries back to the cabin. Samuel, hidden behind two horses, waits for her to leave and goes back to feeding the livestock.

The early morning sun lights the station, as Sandra sneaks out of the cabin, strolls to the barn, opens the door, and peeks inside. Samuel raises up from his makeshift bed as the young woman speaks. "Is it true, you're leaving tomorrow?"

Samuel stands, holding the blanket around his full body. "Yeah, I've been putting it off."

"My brother didn't eat his supper 'cuz of you."

"I never meant to ..."

Sandra interrupts. "Why didn't you find me sooner?"

"We did the best we could, Sandra."

"I was saving myself for you."

"I'm sorry."

She starts to cry, so Samuel steps closer and gently takes her in his arms. "Everything's gonna be okay."

Sandra breaks free. "No, it's not! Nothing's ever gonna be the same." She rushes out of the barn as Samuel bows his head. His mind wanders as he picks up a bag and begins to put clothes in it. When he finishes packing, he pulls Sandra's necklace from his pocket, studies it, and puts it back. Then he walks over to the barn's only window and stares at his reflection.

Pete and Buckie are sitting at the table as Sandra readies to serve them breakfast. When Samuel walks through the front door, everyone stares, because he's clean-shaven and his hair has been cut short. Sandra looks at him a moment and slams a pot of porridge on the table. Pete asks, "Everything all right, Pumpkin?"

"No! It's not all right!" She turns to Samuel and gives him a look of disdain. "Can hardly wait until you're gone!"

Pete raises his voice. "Sandra, that's enough!"

She ignores her father. "Go on. Get the hell out of here! We don't need you anymore! You're nothing but a hired hand!"

Pete reacts. "Sandra!"

Her words strike home and Samuel reacts. "I'm leaving right now. Just wanted to say goodbye." He reaches in his pocket, pulls out the necklace she lost in the fire and tries to hand it to her. "Wanted to give this back. Your pa and I found it."

Sandra cries out, "Oh my God!" and storms to her bedroom.

Pete nods. "She'll be okay." He limps to his daughter's bedroom door and knocks. "Young lady, come out here and apologize. You need to give Samuel a proper goodbye."

There is silence until Samuel says, "It's okay. Leave her be."

He steps forward and tries to hand Pete the necklace, but he waves him off and says, "I'll get your horse ready."

"No, I'll do that …" Before Samuel can finish, Pete exits the cabin, so he turns his attention to a cold-faced Buckie.

Buckie sputters, "Ya don't have to leave. Ya just wanna."

"I got a life to get back to."

"Why aren't we your life?"

"You'll always be a part of my life."

"Not enough for you to stay."

"Sandra's right. I'm nothing but a hired hand whose time is up."

"You're a liar and a cocksucker!"

"Buckie."

"Got lots of other bad words I could say if I wanted to." Samuel's shoulders sag as Buckie hurries to his room.

Pete holds Samuel's horse as the soon-to-be traveler tightens his saddle. When he reaches to shake Pete's hand, Pete grabs him and gives him a bear hug. "Counting on seeing you again real soon."

"That'd be good. Listen, sorry about Sandra and Buckie."

"They'll be all right. I'll tell them you said goodbye."

The cabin door flies open and Buckie runs out. He sprints over and grabs the horse's reins out of his father's hand. Samuel peers at Buckie, assuming he's trying to stop him from leaving. Instead, Buckie pushes him over to his horse. "Climb up slow. Don't want you breaking another arm, so you have to stay longer." Samuel takes the reins and Buckie cups his hand to his mouth. Samuel leans over and Buckie whispers. "Sorry, for what I said. And Sandra … she just loves you."

He whispers back, "Take care of her. She's special." Buckie steps away and Samuel mounts his horse. "Guess this is it."

Pete grins. "Be safe now." He pulls a package from his pocket and tries to hand it to Samuel.

Samuel leans back. "What's that?"

"Wages for helpin' out."

"Hell no. I'm the one that should be paying you."

Pete stuffs the package into Samuel's saddle bag and slaps Samuel's horse. Pete and son watch as their special guest rides off at a fast gallop. In the distance, they hear the sound of a bugle. Pete ruffles Buckie's hair, and they head back to the cabin.

Henry and Electa stroll along on the bank of Grasshopper Creek on a cool summer evening. Electa is wearing a white spring dress and her hair is piled high on her head. Henry has on a new white shirt, a leather vest, and he's clean-shaven and hatless. Henry breaks the silence. "So, you really don't think we're a match?"

"It's just that we're so different."

"Well, I'm not lookin' to marry myself."

"You know what I mean."

"You did say you loved me?"

"I was having a weak moment."

Henry turns quiet and begins to stare up at the moon.

Electa loses patience. "Are you still with me?"

"Yeah, I'm just waiting for another weak moment."

Electa punches him in the arm. "I don't know. The whole thing with Lucy… and you going to prison for killing John Vedder. You're so …"

"Damn…?"

"Yes, so damn complicated."

"But you're crazy about me, right?"

"I'm just afraid you might be like some bee that goes from flower to flower?"

"You're the only flower I want."

Electa turns serious. "Other than Vedder and Spivey, how many other men have you killed?"

Henry counts the fingers on both hands as Electa watches. He laughs. "I'm just funning with you. That's it. Wait, I forgot about the Gunderson boy."

"I don't think taking another person's life is a laughing matter."

"All three drew on me first. What was I supposed to do?"

"And then there's your obsession with trying to find that Alex Slade… and your brother."

"Okay. I've had some problems, but I'm ready to settle down and take care of you."

"I'm not looking for someone to take care of me."

"Wait. If we were married and I got sick, you'd help me out, right?"

"Maybe."

"And if I was on my death bed, you'd cook me up some chicken and dumplings, right?"

"Sure, and after you died, I'd bake a cake for your funeral."

They laugh and then Henry turns serious. "So, what do ya say? Let's get married. We'll start a new life and leave all that other shit behind."

"You're persistent. I'll give you that much." She pauses a moment and continues. "If we were to get married, there'd be no secrets between us, right?"

"You'll be hearin' everything I'm thinkin'."

"Will you give me some time before I give you an answer?"

"Rather wait for the right answer than hear the wrong one now."

"I promise I'll weigh my choices very carefully." Henry pulls Electa close and kisses her passionately.

As she gently pulls away, she adds, "Very carefully." She stands and straightens her dress. "Now, go back to your hayloft."

Henry walks down Main Street, stops, and looks through the window of a haberdashery shop. The shop owner waves him inside. On the other side of the street, Jack happens to see Henry enter the store. He takes a moment, lights a cigarette and crosses the street. When he peers through the window, he sees the shop owner helping Henry put on one suit coat after another.

Henry exits the shop carrying a large package and spots Jack on the corner looking his way. He takes a step in his direction, but before he can take another, his rival is gone.

Samuel rides up to two guards manning their posts in front of San Quentin Prison. On top of the prison wall looking down at him is a third guard, who watches carefully as the visitor climbs off his horse. The wall guard aims his rifle down at him, so Samuel lifts his arms in the air. As all three men keep the outsider in their sights, the gate guards stroll over with their rifles at the ready. Samuel looks up at the wall guard and slowly lowers his arms. A moment passes and the two sentries chuckle, turn in unison and point north. Samuel promptly climbs back on his horse and rides off.

On a peaceful Sunday morning, James Vail faces Henry and Electa as they exchange vows on the bank of Grasshopper Creek. Barefooted Electa, wearing a calico dress, and barefooted Henry, dressed in his new black suit, hold hands and smile at one another.

The ceremony ends and James shakes Henry's hand, while Martha Jane hugs her sister. Mary and Harvey Vail stare at the married couple briefly and then run for home giggling.

Not far away, Jack watches from behind a tree with a whiskey bottle in his hand. He takes a drink and reaches in his pocket. He pulls out Electa's brooch, throws it to the ground, and stomps on it.

Jack thinks I'm a claim jumper and maybe I am. But Electa chose me, and I'm ready to get started with the rest of my life. I don't want anything to do with my past. What I do want is to grow old with the most beautiful I've ever known…and she's smart to boot.

The newlyweds drive their wagon up to a small white house, not far from the center of Bannack. Mrs. Plummer turns to her husband. "Looks like a nice place, Henry."

"Best I could find … for better or worse."

Electa smiles. "I'm counting on better." Henry begins to cough and she gives him a look of concern. "That's not getting any better. When did you last see Dr. Robinson?"

"It's been a while."

"Don't be stubborn. Go see him."

"Wait. Did I just hear someone wantin' to take care of me?" Electa gives Henry a gentle shove.

CHAPTER 39

"Come, let's be a comfortable couple and take care of each other! How glad we shall be, that we have somebody we are fond of always, to talk to and sit with." Charles Dickens

HENRY ARRIVES HOME, his clothes covered in dirt and mud. He walks into the kitchen, kisses Electa on the cheek, and watches as she puts the finishing touches on dinner. He begins to cough and she points her finger and frowns. "Henry?"

"What? I stopped by Dr. Robinson's office yesterday, but he was at the Jorgensen place delivering a baby."

"Good for the Jorgensens."

"Not really. Hired girl's having it."

"Oh dear. Who's the father?"

"Nobody knows for sure. If it's old man Jorgensen's, Hugh Junior's got a new brother. But if it's junior's baby, his old man's a grandfather."

"That poor child. Any luck today?"

"Nothing to brag about."

"Hate to ask, but how's Jack doing?"

"He's drinking a lot. Town's ready to give him the boot."

"It's my fault, isn't it?"

"Don't think like that. He goes his own way."

"I'm sorry you're not finding very much gold. You've been working so hard."

"Gold's not something to be earned; ya gotta be in the right place."

"Your luck will turn. I feel it."

Henry touches Electa's stomach lightly. "Not feeling something else, are ya?"

She shoves him away as Henry pulls a pearl necklace from his pocket and dangles it in front of Electa's face. Taken by surprise, she says, "What pray tell ...?" He hands his wife the necklace and helps her put it on. "We can't afford this! Where did you ...?"

"Shush. It's a secret."

"Henry, we agreed ... no secrets."

"Been putting aside a few flakes for a while. Do I smell supper?"

"It can wait." Electa pulls Henry into the bedroom.

TWO MONTHS LATER

On a dirt road leading to Bannack, Rut's stagecoach comes to a stop. From his driver's seat, he watches as two bandits frisk three frightened passengers. The dust-covered travelers empty their pockets and hand over the little bit of money and the few trinkets they have as the robbers lick their lips nervously. Next to the seasoned driver, two other bandits busy themselves trying to open the strong box. Rut grins. "Nothin' in there ya want."

An older bandit points his gun at the driver. "Shut the hell up!

"Suit yourself. Wasting your time."

A younger bandit shoots the lock off the metal chest. He opens it, but he only finds a few paper documents inside. "Shit!"

Rut complains. "Damn it! Ruined a perfectly good lock."

Frustrated, the younger bandit fires a hole into the strong box. "Tell that boss of yours the next time we find nothing, we'll be killing you, your passengers, and your horses."

As the bandits ride away, Rut nods to the travelers. "Don't listen to them. They'd never kill my horses."

Samuel rides into Dillon and tethers his horse to a Main Street hitching post. He looks around, sees no one on the street, so he enters the Dillon bank. He immediately recognizes Buxton Bailey, who is standing behind the teller window. The bank manager looks up and smiles as the former robber approaches. Samuel lays the bag of money Pete gave him on the counter. Buxton's smile turns to a look of curiosity. "What you got here?"

Samuel pushes the bag forward. "Take it. Money in there is for the trouble I caused you a while back."

Buxton stares at Samuel and then turns and looks at a wanted poster on the wall with the names Alex Slade and Warren Spivey on it. When Samuel turns to see what he's looking at, the banker grabs a shotgun from under the counter and aims it at Samuel. "Hair or no hair, I know you." Buxton cocks the shotgun and shoves it forward. "Don't move. This thing makes an awful big hole."

"You don't understand. I came here to make things right."

"Put your damn arms in the air."

Samuel raises his arms.

Henry sits barefooted on his front porch writing in his journal as three drunken drifters ride past firing their guns. He stands, reaches for his gun, but he doesn't have one. He continues to watch as the ruffians arrive at the Saffron and stumble inside.

Like a lot of married couples, Electa and I enjoy each other's company. We go fishing, eat dinner together, and even though she probably doesn't like it, she lets me wander off to the bar once in a while. Problem is, I'm restless. Hate to admit it, but I kinda miss Jack's smartass talk and the danger that comes with bein' a sheriff.

Henry sits back down, stares at his journal, and tosses it aside. He slaps the arm of his chair, stands up again, and heads down Main Street.

Henry enters the Saffron Saloon, gives Sweet gives a big smile, and takes a seat at the bar next to Ezra. Sweet pours him a beer without asking as he turns to Ezra and says, "What's it like burying the dead?"

The former sheriff's question piques the undertaker's interest. "Well, it's kinda like I'm a doctor, but 'stead of bringin' people into the world, I send 'em out ... and so forth."

Henry pulls a wanted flyer from his pocket and unfolds it. "Ever see this fella?"

The undertaker studies the poster. "Don't bother yerself lookin' for him."

"Why's that?"

"Got himself caught a couple weeks ago in Dillon."

"How you know that?"

"Town had me measure him and two others for coffins last week. Set to hang any day now."

Henry grimaces. "Any day?"

"Yeah, but that drawing ain't him no more. Hair's short, beard's gone, has a big scar on his neck too."

"Scar?"

"Yeah, like he's already been hanged or something?"

Henry's eyes open wide and he lowers his head. "Or maybe branded?"

"Could be. You all right, and so forth?"

"They give him a trial?"

"Nope. Dillon's gone straight to hanging. Hanged the other two already. Be stretchin' Slade anytime soon… and so forth."

Jack enters the bar followed by Ben Girard and three other townsmen. He spots Henry and sits on the other side of Ezra, while Ben slips behind the bar to talk to Sweet.

Jack looks past Ezra and says, "See yer woman let ya outta yer cage."

"Electa doesn't mind me bein' here."

Jack grunts. "Got no one bitchin' me."

Ben grabs a bottle of whiskey and four glasses, hands it all to the townsmen, and they head for the back room. Ben comes out from behind the bar and Henry nods at him. "What's going on?"

"Got us a meeting to try and put a stop to them asshole Innocents."

Henry looks over at Jack. "Isn't that his job?"

The saloon man pulls Henry aside and whispers as Jack watches. "He ain't sheriff no more … on account of him being all the time pickled."

Henry whispers back. "You lookin' to replace him?"

Ben takes a moment as they continue to whisper. "Why? You offerin'?"

"Need to check with the boss."

Ben takes the badge from inside his vest and slips it in Henry's pocket. "Wear it when you're ready." Ben heads for the back room and Henry exits the bar.

Jack picks up the wanted poster on the counter in front of Ezra and looks it over. He turns to the grave digger. "Him again? How much he worth now?"

"Nothin'. He's fixing to be hanged in Dillon and so forth."

"Shit! Could've used the money. Henry see this?"

"Yeah. He ain't pleased." Jack wads up the flyer and tosses it over the bar. Sweet picks it up, unfolds it, and looks it over.

The bedroom is dark as Henry lays staring at the ceiling, while his wife sleeps. A few seconds pass and he climbs out of bed. Electa awakens and sits up as her husband finishes putting on his boots. "What is it? What's wrong?"

Henry whispers, "Go back to sleep. I gotta go to Dillon. Be back as soon as I can."

"It's the middle of the night. I don't understand." As Henry exits the bedroom, she calls out, "Can't you wait until morning?"

From the living room, Henry says, "Goin' now…and just so you know, I'm back to bein' sheriff."

Electa stiffens her back. "What? No." She waits for a response, but all she hears is the front door open and shut.

Henry rides off into the dark of the night, a second horse trailing behind him packed with other belongings.

CHAPTER 40

"Life is short, break the rules, forgive quickly, kiss slowly, love truly, laugh uncontrollably, and never regret anything that makes you smile." Mark Twain

DAWN IS BREAKING as Henry rides into Dillon, where the streets are empty. When he passes the local general store, he sees three pine boxes. Two contain the dead bodies of two recently hanged men, but the middle box is empty. He slows his horse, jumps down, and studies the profiles of the men, stares at the empty coffin a moment, and then climbs back in the saddle.

Henry tethers his two horses to a hitching post in front of the sheriff's office, pulls the badge Ben gave him out of his pocket, puts it on, and opens the front door.

He stops in the doorway when he sees Dillon sheriff, Hewitt Feger, asleep on a cot. Henry clears his throat and Hewitt, dressed in dirty red long johns, snorts himself awake. He sits up, adjusts his crotch, and looks at Henry. "Jesus. How long you been standing there?" The old sheriff puts on his well-worn hat, wobbles over to a pot-bellied stove, and pours himself a cup of coffee.

Henry takes a step forward. "Understand you have Alex Slade holed up here."

"Yep. In there breathing his last."

"Well, I'm here to take him off your hands. Bannack wants to hang him."

Hewitt cackles as he yawns. "Oh, they would, would they? And who the hell are you?"

"Bannack sheriff, Henry Plummer." He shows his badge and Hewitt squints at it. "So, if you'll just hand him over ..."

"Slow yerself down. Plummer, hmm. You the one that planted that Spivey fella in Lewiston?"

"That's right."

"Bannack sent you to San Quentin."

"Yeah, well I'm back."

The sheriff returns the badge to Henry. "Town must have a short memory. So, why the hell should I hand Slade over to you?"

"'Cuz he's done our town more harm than yours."

"Might be pretty to think so, but that bastard robbed our bank and made me look like an ass when he tunneled outta here."

Henry pulls out a bag of gold and hands it to the sheriff. "Gold in there covers the reward money and yer trouble."

Hewitt lifts the bag, checking its weight. "Folks gonna be mad as hell if they don't get another hanging." Hewitt struggles to his feet. "People come from miles around. Some even spend the night." He reopens the bag of gold and stares at Henry. "Makes no sense, you buying a hanging, but I guess it'll save me the trouble."

Hewitt grabs a small rope from his desk drawer and leads Henry to the cell area. Samuel, who has started another beard, stares sullenly through the bars at his brother. Henry turns his head and wipes away a tear as he is overcome with emotion. He regains his composure when the Dillon sheriff opens the cell door and nods at Samuel. "Appears Bannack wants to hang you more than we do." Hewitt ties the prisoner's hands behind his back and pushes him out of the cell and into the outer office.

Before the brothers walk out the door, the sheriff holds up a pocket watch and Sandra's necklace. "He had these on him. Likely stolen. I'm keepin' them." Henry guffaws, reaches in his pocket, pulls out a five-dollar gold piece and offers it to the sheriff. Hewitt grins and says, "Nah, that don't cut it."

Henry reaches back in his pocket, removes a wad of paper money, and lays it on the desk. The lawman gives Henry a curious look and hands him the watch and necklace. Still not satisfied, the Dillon sheriff says, "Suppose you'll be wanting his horse, too?"

Henry looks at Samuel and gets the answer he's looking for. He reaches in his pocket for a third time, pulls out several gold coins, and hands them over. "That's all I got. I'll kick in the extra horse and saddle I brought." As the sheriff weighs the coins in his hand, Henry scoffs. "Ya wantin' me to buy his clothes, too?"

Hewitt snickers. "Naw, you're good."

Sheriff Feger and the Plummer brothers stand outside the office waiting for the stable boy, who finally arrives leading a coal black horse with a white speckled rump. It's obvious the stolen horse is Henry Plummer. The Bannack sheriff shakes his head and stares at Samuel, whose hands are still tied behind his back. He helps his brother on the horse and the Plummers ride out of Dillon at a slow trot.

Now a few miles out of town, the brothers keep silent until Henry coughs deeply. He discreetly pulls out a handkerchief and spits into it as Samuel breaks the silence. "Out of prison and wearing a badge. Why you taking me to Bannack?"

"Maybe. Haven't figured that out yet." Henry changes the subject. "Where'd ya get the horse?"

"One of a kind, ain't he? Won him in a poker game ... filled an inside straight."

"Bullshit! You stole him from a young gal in Bannack."

"Hear that, Lucky? Guess, I'm gonna have to change your name."

"His name's Henry Plummer."

Samuel laughs. "You gotta be shitting me."

Henry turns serious. "Samuel, do you know how long I've been searching for you?"

"Name's Alex. I'm not the one you're looking for?"

Henry reaches over and pulls down the collar of Samuel's shirt, revealing the brand on his neck. "You don't think I know my own brother?"

"Don't be a prick. I didn't know for a long time if you were dead or alive either."

"The difference is when ya did find out, you let me go on thinkin' you were dead." Samuel flicks his gaze away as Henry continues. "And why the hell were you in cahoots with Spivey so long? How's something like that work?"

"Stop judging me!"

Henry hesitates and says, "Why the name Alex Slade?"

"'Cuz, Alex was Spivey's partner, the one who tied us to the tree. Spivey forced his name on me after he killed him."

"You let him do that?"

"Shut the hell up! I was a kid. You don't know all the ugly shit that bastard did. Took the boy right out of me." Henry stares at his brother a moment and Samuel continues, "How'd you come to figure me out?"

Henry hesitates and then says, "Always been something about you."

"Why didn't you want that posse to hang Spivey?"

"Thought I needed him to tell what happened to you."

"Ya know, that bastard damaged a lot of people after that."

Henry argues, "You're the one that came to his rescue."

"'Cuz, I wanted to kill him myself."

"Well, he's dead now. Busted out of Quentin and got himself beefed."

Samuel studies Henry's face. "You killed him, didn't you?" Henry turns away as Samuel continues. "All these years waiting for my chance and you stole it."

"You had your opportunities...all those years ridin' with that asshole. Sides, I got my own right. He killed Pa."

"I killed Pa."

"Samuel, you killed a fuckin' cow."

"I pointed him to an empty gun. Try carrying that around all these years."

"That wasn't your fault." He removes a bullet from his pants and tosses it to Samuel.

"What's this?"

"When you gave me pa's gun and left me alone, I got curious. I removed a cartridge 'cuz I thought it would be fun to look at. When I heard you coming back, I panicked and put the bullet in my pocket. You fired five times. One more bullet might have saved Pa's life."

Samuel tosses the bullet aside. "More bullshit. I'm the one who stole his gun and emptied it."

Henry changes the subject. "Where ya been hiding so long?"

"California, Nevada. Riding mail for the Pony Express."

"Why'd you come back here?"

Ignoring his brother's question, Samuel says, "I stopped by San Quentin, but you were gone."

"You what?"

"Yeah, the guards told me you'd been let go and was chasing after Spivey and Wilson."

"Why would a wanted man stop by a prison?"

"'Cuz, I thought I could bust you out and kill Spivey."

"And you figured they'd just let you walk in there?"

"In my head, San Quentin was a lot smaller. When that didn't work out, I came back here to set things right."

"By robbing a bank?"

"You don't understand. I went back to make amends."

"I think you've gone soft in the head."

"Could be."

"Go somewhere else. Buy some dirt and start over."

"I tried that, except for the dirt part."

"Well, try harder. Nobody knows you're my brother, but you stick around here, I'll have to hang you myself."

"I've hurt too many people. Stood by and watched Spivey kill and rape. I need to fix what I done."

"There's that soft-headed thinking again! Ya robbed a few banks and held up some coaches. Get over it. Go back to Maine. Ma would give worlds to see you."

"Case you haven't heard, there's a big war going on out east that I sure as hell don't wanna get caught up in."

The Plummer brothers ride along gnawing on chunks of bread as the late afternoon sun breaks through the trees. Henry pulls Samuel's watch and Sandra's necklace out of his pocket and holds them out. "These are yours."

Samuel takes the necklace but leaves Henry the watch. "Keep it. Maybe it'll bring ya luck. It ain't done nothin' for me."

Henry puts the watch in his vest and reaches in his pants pocket and pulls out Samuel's childhood knife and begins to cut the rope still around his brother's wrists. "Samuel ... Alex ... call yourself whatever you want, but I know who you are. Now, ride your ass out of this territory, so you don't get hanged." After he frees his brother, Henry ties the rope to his saddle horn and hands him the knife. "Loaned it to me, remember?"

Samuel looks it over. "Your pockets are full of surprises. Anything else I don't know about?"

Henry forces a grin. "Been married two months."

"Well, ain't that a daisy."

Henry pulls out two peppermint sticks, puts one in his mouth, and offers the other to his brother. Samuel takes it, pops it in his mouth, and smiles. Henry points. "South is that way. Go!"

"You sure about this?"

"Yes, damn it! Go!"

Just as Samuel turns his horse to ride away, Ben Girard comes over the hill with three other Bannack men. Samuel recognizes Ben and heads back to Henry. "Shit! Change of plan, little brother."

Ben looks confused as he rides up. Henry speaks first. "Hey, Ben. What's going on?"

"We're lookin' for them damn Innocents. Robbed another coach not far from here."

"Don't say."

Ben sits up a little taller. "Electa come to me all worried like. Said you was headed to Dillon."

"Yeah, didn't have time to explain my intentions."

"Went there to see Slade hang didn't you?"

"Yeah, but things went a little sideways."

"How so?"

Henry hesitates. "Here's the thing; this here is Alex Slade."

Samuel smiles and reaches out to shake Ben's hand, but saloon man turns to Henry and wags his head. "What the hell?"

"We've been trying to chase this asshole down for so long, I figured Bannack deserved to see him hang, so I talked the sheriff into letting me have him."

"And he just handed him over?"

Henry points to the badge on his chest. "Took you up on your offer about me being sheriff again."

"Yeah, Electa told me."

Ben eyeballs Samuel, who grins and says, "I can't help it if everyone wants to hang me."

Ben gives Henry a curious look and says. "If this don't beat all? Why ain't he tied up?"

Henry agrees. "Yeah. That's probably a good idea." He removes the small rope from his saddle horn and ties Samuel's hands behind his back as his brother chuckles. Henry pokes Samuel in his side and whispers, "Shut up, 'fore ya get us both hanged."

No matter how much time goes by or what the circumstances bring, blood is blood and a brother is a brother.

CHAPTER 41

"What strange creatures brothers are!" Jane Austin

IT'S EARLY EVENING when the Plummer brothers, Ben Girard, and his two men, ride down Main Street. The saloon owner and his underlings peel off and head for home, while Henry and his prisoner keep riding, headed for Gus's livery stable. A few people stop and stare at Samuel, who trails Henry with his hands still tied.

When they reach the stable, they find Gus out front, shoeing a horse. The brothers dismount and Henry hands the reins of all three horses to Gus, who studies the horse Samuel was on. "Well, if it isn't Henry Plummer." Gus chuckles and turns to the new sheriff. "And Henry Plummer." The new sheriff takes his brother by the arm and they head in the direction of the jailhouse.

Henry enters his house, finds Electa, and says. "You tell Ben I rode off to Dillon?"

"I was worried about you."

"Worry about someone else."

She recoils. "What did you say?"

"You heard me."

"I don't understand. You…" Henry walks away, leaving his wife alone with her thoughts.

Two Innocents, flour bags on their heads, sneak around the corner of the Bannack Mining Office. They enter the building, pistols drawn. The office manager, Felix Ragway, who is standing behind the counter, looks up and raises his hands in the air as the younger bandit hands him a large sack. "Fill it up!"

The spectacled man gives the robber a curious look and asks, "Notes or gold?"

The young bandit barks. "Don't be funny, asshole! Everything ya got!" Felix fills the sack with small bags of gold, coins, and currency. When the young bandit turns away, Felix purposely drops one of the bags and kicks it under the counter. The older bandit notices and cocks his pistol. "Think that bag is worth dying for, do you?"

Felix stammers. "I didn't figure… you would ..."

Without another word, he clubs Felix on the head. Stunned by the blow, the manager touches the crown of his head, looks at the blood, and crumples to the floor. The older bandit scoffs. "Guess ya figured wrong."

The younger bandit turns to his partner and says, "You didn't have to do that." He ignores him, crawls under the counter, grabs the last bag of gold, and the thieves slip out the door.

Inside the sheriff's office, Ben is sitting behind the desk adjusting the glove on his left hand when Henry rushes through the door. The disheveled sheriff is out of breath and he coughs deeply.

Ben nods. "Where ya been?"

"Mining office was just held up."

"Shit. The Innocents?"

"Maybe, but only two of them. Watch Slade for me, will ya?"

"What?"

"Got no one else. Gotta round up a posse."

Henry exits the door as Ben yells out. "Wait. We need to talk." He doesn't respond, so Ben walks to the inner cell door. He opens it a crack and looks at Samuel, who appears to be sound

asleep. "Shit. I wouldn't be wasting what time I had left sleeping."
When Ben closes the door, Samuel opens his eyes and stares at
the ceiling.

Electa tends to her chores as Henry follows her around the
house. He goes into the kitchen, pours two cups of coffee, finds
Electa in the bedroom making a bed, and holds a cup out to her.
"Coffee ... with an apology?"

Electa takes the cup. "I'll take the coffee."

"Just hear me out."

"Now you want to talk? Ever since that trip to Dillon, you've
hardly spoken to me."

"I've had a lot on my mind."

"Before we married, we agreed there'd be no secrets."

"Right, so let's talk." She gives him permission with her eyes,
so he continues. "I know you're not happy about me being
sheriff."

"Because you promised we'd start a new life. Being a sheriff
again is your old life."

"It's only until they find someone else. The town needs me."

"I need you ... alive!"

"I could die looking for gold just as easy as wearing some
badge."

Electa moves Henry's vest aside, revealing his badge. "So,
what else haven't you told me?"

"Give me a day or two and I'll reveal everything."

"What's wrong with now?"

Henry smiles, so Electa purses her lips and says, "All right.
You do what you have to do, but don't expect me to like it."

"It'll grow on you. I promise."

"What if you get shot?"

"Not gonna happen unless you do it."

"Don't tempt me."

"Come on, give me a smile." She gives him a half-hearted smile. He doesn't give up. "No, a real smile."

"Your dinner is getting cold."

Henry grins. "It can wait."

He tries to pull her close, but she resists and steps back. "So can you. I haven't forgiven you yet." She turns and walks into the kitchen.

From the other room, Electa hears Henry's angry voice. "The hell with it!" She takes a moment, thinks about the situation, and moves to the living room. She gets there just in time to see the front door slam shut.

I know I'm an ass for not telling Electa about Samuel, but I don't know if she would understand with him being in jail. We're in a dark place right now, but I'm sure we'll find our way out of it sooner or later.

Rut helps an older woman into his coach as the Sacramento reporters, Charles Munson and Michael Roberts, exit the Buckland cabin along with Pete, Buckie, Sandra, and her three-month-old baby.

Charles looks at Rut and tips his hat to Pete. "Mr. Buckland, that was a fine meal. I just hope I can keep it down."

As they make their way to the coach, Michael says, "A simple thank you would have been sufficient, Charles."

"Well, that crazy driver needs to know."

Pete addresses his daughter as they near the coach. "You know, I'm against this."

"Don't start again, Pa."

Pete wags his head. "I know. Just thought I'd try one last time." He helps Sandra in the coach and Michael and Charles get in after Sandra and the baby are settled. Then he takes one last look at his daughter and grandchild and turns to Rut. "Slow as you go. That's precious cargo you're carrying."

Buckie looks through the coach's window at the reporters. "I'm an uncle." Michael and Charles smile politely as the baby starts to cry.

Pete yells, "Be safe now!" as Rut slaps the reins to the horses. The coach lurches forward and away as Charles and Michael hang onto their hats. Inside the coach, the older woman stares at Sandra's dark-skinned baby a little too long, so Sandra cradles her child close to her and turns away.

It's mid-morning as Jack exits the Saffron and staggers down the street. His clothes are disheveled and he has a five-day beard. He manages to make his way to the sheriff's office, where he comes to a stop and stares at the building. He removes his pistol from his holster and aims it at the door.

Henry looks up from his desk as the former sheriff wobbles in and looks around. Henry nods. "Go on. Say what ya gotta say."

Jack slurs his words. "Stole my job, my woman, my whole damn life! Anyone says different is a fuckin' liar!"

Henry snarls. "Can't help it if we want the same things."

"Eat shit, Pretty Boy! I'm tired of losing to the likes of you." Jack spots a makeshift bed in the corner of the room. "You sleeping here?" Henry doesn't respond, so Jack takes a flask from his back pocket and takes a drink.

"Kinda early to be getting soaked, isn't it?"

"Can't drink all day if I don't start early."

"Why ya here?"

"Heard ya got that asshole Slade back there." Henry doesn't answer, so Jack continues. "Why didn't Dillon hang him?"

"Talked them into letting me do it."

"You're a fuckin' weird duck, ya know that?" Jack stumbles into the cell area, looks at a sleeping Samuel, and comes out again. "Think hangin' Slade's gonna make you some kind of saint? Well, it won't ... not after I tell all the dirt I got on you."

"Only dirt you have are bald-faced lies. Maybe you should try keepin' your mouth shut for a while."

Jack heads for the door but turns back. "Don't be tellin' me what to do, you flannel-mouthed dickhead." After his old friend stumbles out the door, Henry opens his desk drawer, removes a bottle of laudanum, takes a drink, and begins to write in his journal.

I can't stop Jack from telling lies and I probably won't be able to change people's minds if they choose to believe them. I just hope anyone who cares about me will wanna hear my side of the story.

STINKING WATER RIVER

Not far from Bannack, smoke filters from the chimney of a log cabin near a fast-moving mountain stream, which is surrounded by several ponderosa pines. Four Innocents, hooded with flour sacks, walk their horses to a small corral and tether them to hitching posts by George Dempsey's mining camp.

The older bandit, wearing Charles Munson's coat, takes the lead as the intruders burst into the cabin with guns drawn. Seated at a table playing poker, George and four of his men look up, appraise the situation, and drop their cards.

Two of the bandits cover George and his men, while the other two search the cabin for valuables. One of the intruders sees a board that doesn't match the rest of the flooring, so he smashes it with the heel of his boot. He reaches into the newly made hole and removes three bags of gold. George Dempsey speaks up. "How ya know where my gold's hidin'?" He squints hard at the bandit holding his gold. "Red, that you? I know them squirrely eyes of yours." Red stands frozen a moment and turns away. Two other Innocents finish tying Dempsey and his men to their chairs in one large configuration and all four robbers rush out of the cabin.

Outside, two Innocents chase Dempsey's horses away as Red faces the cabin and lights a torch. The older bandit steps up. "What ya doin'?"

Red booms, "Dempsey named me. I ain't safe." The older man grabs at the torch, but Red pushes him off and throws the flaming stick through the window. Instantly, the Innocents hear George and his men scream as smoke and flames fill the cabin.

Ben rushes into the sheriff's office and finds Henry washing his hands in a white metal bowl. "There's a fire burning east of here. We need to check it out." Henry doesn't respond, so Ben leaves him standing. Henry thinks about what Ben said, grabs his hat, and exits his office.

Ben, Henry and three local Bannack men ride in the direction of a large billow of smoke in the eastern sky. When the five men arrive at Dempsey's camp, they find the miner's cabin burnt to the ground. Ben sits up in his saddle and announces, "This is George Dempsey's place." He points to the three local Bannack men. "Look around."

Henry drops from his saddle and begins to traipse through the smoldering ashes until he finds several blackened skeletons slumped over in a circle. He yells out, "Ben!" Ben arrives and Henry points at the charred remains of five men.

Ben swallows. "Jesus Christ."

"Kinda like they was sitting around when the fire broke out."

"Why didn't they get out?"

"Maybe they were already dead." Henry sifts his hands through the ashes. "Dempsey have a family?"

"No, just his hired men."

The three men ride up with three of Dempsey's horses. One of the men sides up to Ben. "They was scattered in the trees."

Ben sizes up the situation as Henry reaches down in the ashes again and removes some small pieces of burnt rope. He holds them up for Ben to see. "They were tied up."

Ben snarls. "God damn Innocents."

As the posse rides back to Bannack, Ben turns to Henry. "Town wants to know when we're gonna hang Slade?"

"Why do they care?"

"Looking to be amused I guess."

Henry is quick to respond. "Vultures."

Ben waits for Henry's comment to settle and says, "You figure Slade's an Innocent?

"Strikes me as a loner."

"I'll find some men to build a gallows. We'll hang him Monday morning."

Jack stands hidden in the shadow of a tree near the Plummer house smoking. He stomps out his cigarette, walks around to the back of the house, looks in the bedroom window, but it's too dark for him to see anything. He waits a moment and lights a match. He holds it up to the window and sees Electa asleep in bed. He lights a second match and stares at her. His eyes narrow as he pulls a pistol from his holster, cocks it, and points it at her.

Electa awakens as if from a bad dream. She turns to the window and watches as a small light goes out. "Henry? Is that you?" Not far from the window, Jack stands frozen behind a tree.

She puts on a robe, exits the house, and walks over to side of the house. She leans down, picks up a couple of burnt match sticks, and rolls them in her fingers. She steps over and stares through the bedroom window at her own bed.

When the sun's rays break through the jailhouse window and shine into Henry's eyes, he sits up in his makeshift bed. He rubs his face and walks to the holding area. He opens the door and watches Samuel, who is sitting on the edge of his bed examining Sandra's necklace. "Someone special?"

Startled by his brother's voice, Samuel looks through the crack of the door and grunts. "Maybe."

Henry opens the door fully. "We got two days to figure somethin' out 'fore they hang you."

Samuel wags his head. "Don't understand people wantin' to hang one another. A bullet to the head is a hell of a lot easier."

"Ain't no joke. Don't know how I'm gonna save your ass."

"You already tried. Let's just get it over with."

"And that's it? You're just gonna let it happen?"

"Truth is, I'm a thief. How many coaches you robbed?"

"Believin' Jack's lies too? No one's seen me steal anything."

"You saying a thief's not a thief until someone sees his face?"

Henry backs away from the door and says, "Since you know so much, figure your own way outta here." Henry leaves the cell door open, but as he walks to the outer office, he begins to cough. He bends over, pulls out a handkerchief, and spits blood into it.

Samuel stands up and yells out, "What's that all about?!" There's no response, so he hollers even louder. "Fess up!"

From the outer office, Henry finally says, "Consumption ... tuberculosis! I don't have that long to live myself!"

"Bullshit! Find you a big city and get some help!"

"Won't matter if they string us both up!"

"Why would they do that?!"

"'Cuz, if I don't come up with a plan, I'm turning you loose."

"Well, I sure as hell ain't let 'em hang you 'stead of me!"

"Better than chokin' to death on my own blood! We got til Monday morning!"

CHAPTER 42

"Depend on it, sir, when a man knows he is to be hanged in a fortnight, it concentrates his mind wonderfully."
Samuel Johnson

THREE BANNACK CARPENTERS finish their work on the gallows and climb down from the scaffolding as several townspeople look on.

In front of the Saffron Saloon, Henry waits for the stagecoach to arrive. Finally, it rolls up and stops right in front of him. Rut slaps the dust from his hat and nods at Henry. "Your friends are back." The reporters exit the stagecoach and assist Sandra Buckland and her baby. Somehow, Charles ends up with the baby's bottle, which he looks at with a great deal of curiosity. Rut hops down from the coach, picks up Sandra's bag, and escorts her and her baby to the front of the Saffron Saloon. The child starts to cry, so Rut grabs the bottle out of Charles' hand and gives it to Sandra. She smiles at her old friend. "He's okay. Stomach's upset is all."

Rut frowns. "Tried not to drive my usual fast.

"I know. I appreciate that."

"Be headin' south in a week, if ya wanna go back home."

"Thanks. I'll keep that in mind."

Rut shuffles over to Charles and Michael. "You fellas keep an eye on that gal. She's a special friend of mine."

Michael nods. "We'll be happy to do that." The reporters doff their hats at Sandra as Rut climbs into the driver's box. Michael turns to Sandra. "Miss, if you leave your bag right here, I'll take care of it for you. We just want to ask Sheriff Plummer here a few questions."

Sandra points. "Is that him over there?"

"That's right."

"You've been talking about him so much, I feel like I know him." Sandra studies the sheriff's profile, while the reporters approach him.

All at once, Rut tosses down a bundle of newspapers that land at Michael and Charles' feet. "Don't forget the rest of your shit."

Rut pulls the strongbox from a compartment under his driver's seat as Henry watches. He throws the box over his shoulder, hops down, and gimps past as Henry asks the reporters, "What brings you two back here?"

Michael explains. "We're following up on your story."

"I already told you. My story's over. Ya got it all."

Charles grins. "Don't worry. We'll find something."

"I'm sure you will."

Charles continues. "Love the shirt. You look so rugged." Henry gives Charles a curious look as the sheriff removes his hat and reshapes the crease.

Michael interjects. "We were told you settled down and got married."

"Married, yes. Settled, not so much."

Charles says, "Also heard you've still got a crime spree going on here. That's why I wore this old coat."

"Yeah, there's been some trouble."

Michael asks, "How's Jack?"

"Let's just say he's not happy with me being sheriff again."

Charles chuckles. "See, another story." He continues, "Saffron Saloon still the only place to stay?"

"It is, if ya wanna sleep in a bed." Henry notices Sandra looking his way, so he tips his hat. "Who's the young gal?"

Michael smiles at her as well. "Miss Sandra Buckland. She and her baby joined us in Nevada." The reporters shuffle over and join Sandra again. Michael picks up her bag and carries it into the saloon. Right behind him, Charles struggles with their two suitcases and the stack of newspapers. Somehow, he manages to fumble his way through the door.

Henry sits alone at the bar finishing a beer. Sweet walks over and takes his empty mug and says, "Go home."

Slightly tipsy, Henry replies, "Not somewhere I care to be right now. Bring me another."

"Got plenty of rooms upstairs ... and some of them come with a shine." Her eyes sparkle as she pours Henry another beer.

Henry chuckles as Sweet hands him his drink. "Yeah, think I'll just keep sleeping in my office." He hears laughter and looks over and sees a young man and the two sister hookers, Hazel and Bernice White, at the end of the bar. They cackle as they take turns gawking at a dime store novel. Henry raises his voice and calls out, "What's so funny?"

The older sister, Hazel, laughs. "It's all about you, Sweetie."

Henry winks at Sweet, takes a sip of beer, and stands up. "I'll be right back." He walks over to the threesome and holds out his hand. Hazel hands him the small book, he studies the cover, and reads the title aloud: "THE LIFE AND TIMES OF SHERIFF HENRY PLUMMER." He looks at the sisters. "What the hell? Where'd ya get this?" Henry doesn't wait for an answer. He opens the book and begins to read.

The younger sister, Bernice, giggles and says, "One of them backward Bobby reporters give it to us."

Henry reads awhile longer and hands the book back to Hazel. "It's all horseshit. None of it's who I am."

Hazel straightens her back. "Sure would like to know who you are. Wouldn't we, sister?"

Bernice grins ear to ear and adds, "For free."

Embarrassed, Henry smirks. "My mind's a wonder." The sisters giggle as Henry walks back to his beer.

I miss Electa a lot, but we're both too stubborn for one of us to draw first. I think she still loves me, but the problem is I'm sure she can carry on without me and be just fine.

Henry is seated at his desk, slightly hungover. He starts to write something in his journal, but he hears the door open. He looks up and sees Sandra standing in the entry with her baby. She walks over and announces herself. "My name's Sandra Buckland."

Henry puts his journal away and nods. "You came in on the stage this morning."

She gives the sheriff a sincere look. "I'm here to see Samuel."

Henry looks her over. "Got no one here by that name."

"Okay, how about Alex Slade?"

"How do you know him?"

"He lived with me and my family for three months".

Henry looks at Sandra and her baby. "The baby his?"

She ignores the question. "May I see him or not?"

Henry stands, takes the keys out of his desk drawer, and walks toward the cell area. Before entering, he carefully pats Sandra down. He even looks under the baby's blanket. The Nevada girl follows him into the cell area. When they reach the cell block, Henry yells at his sleeping brother. "Got you a visitor!"

Henry places a chair in front of the cell as Samuel sits up and tries to focus. Sandra promptly sits on the chair and Henry leaves. The prisoner realizes who it is and his eyes open wide. "What the hell? What you doing here?"

Sandra grabs one of the cell bars with her free hand and squeezes it. "I want you in my life."

Samuel takes his time. "Too late; they're set to hang me."

"But it makes no sense."

"We've been through this."

"I know, but it's not right. You haven't even killed anyone."

"I killed that baby's father."

"That was no crime."

"Listen, the asshole I rode with killed a lot of people while I stood by and did nothin'. The law doesn't care who pulls the trigger." Sandra watches carefully as Samuel looks the baby over. He nods and says, "Boy or girl?"

"His name is Samuel."

"You didn't?"

"I didn't know if I'd ever see you again."

"What's your pa think, you naming him after me when he ain't mine?"

"He thought it was a great idea."

"My name isn't yours to give."

She begins to cry and Samuel softens. "Sorry. I shouldn't talk so tough."

Sandra looks down at little Samuel. "I tried not to love him, but I do."

"He's a fine-looking boy."

Sandra starts to cry again. "I tried fending him off, but he ... he was too strong."

"It wasn't your fault."

Samuel reaches through the bars to try and comfort her, but she leans back and away. "I didn't come all this way for you to feel sorry for me."

"You need to go home. I don't want you to see me hang."

"Your brother's the sheriff? Why doesn't he do something?"

"It's complicated?"

She waits for an explanation.

"Look, if he lets me go or they find out he's my brother, they'll hang the both of us. He and his wife have their own lives to live."

"What about your life, Samuel?"

"It's not Samuel they're gonna hang, it's Alex."

"Stop it! You're not two people."

He lowers his shirt and shows Sandra the brand on his lower neck. "See this? The asshole I rode with gave it to me. Changed me into Alex Slade ... Made me someone I never thought I'd be."

"But you're not him anymore."

"Tell that to the law."

Sandra looks again and sees her necklace around Samuel's neck. She smiles and says, "That's my necklace."

Embarrassed, he raises his shirt back up around his neck and says, "Thought it might bring me some luck."

"So, you have been thinking about me. Once your brother lets you out of here, we'll run off and start a new life."

"I told you if Henry frees me, they'll just hang him. Sides, one Samuel is all you need."

Sandra starts to cry again, so the condemned man takes a moment, reaches through the bars, and takes both her hand and the baby's hand. Sandra squeezes back. "I'm not giving up, even if I have to break you out of here myself."

The doomed man sits up straight. "Supposin' I was to get myself free. How would it be with you, me raising this little guy as my own?"

"Would I be there?"

Samuel grins. "Boy's gotta have a mother."

"By then you'll have told me you loved me, right?"

Samuel's mood shifts. "Ya know, it ain't easy tellin' someone you love them for the first time when yer about to be hanged."

"So, you're going to the grave not saying it?"

"Okay. I love you. You happy now?"

"Very happy."

Henry strides in and interrupts their moment. "Time's up. You need to go."

Sandra's face glows as she leaves. At the door, she turns to the sheriff. "This baby and me are counting on you doing the right thing." Henry purses his lips, but he doesn't say anything. As Sandra opens the door, she looks down at her young son and says, "That's your Uncle Henry, Samuel."

CHAPTER 43

**"If a relationship is to evolve, it must go through
a series of endings." Christopher Morley**

CHARLES AND MICHAEL sit upright in their Saffron room
listening to the couple in the next room having noisy sex. A
woman screams, so Charles opens the door leading to the
hallway. He sees a naked cowboy, wearing nothing but a hat and
boots, chasing the scantily clad Bernice, one of the sisters he met
during his first trip to Bannack. As she scampers past him, she
waves, grins and yells: "Hey, Charlie!" He starts to wave back but
thinks better of it. As he's about to shut the door, a boot blocks
the way. Obviously drunk, Jack pushes past him and stumbles
into the reporters' room. Michael immediately jumps out of bed
and crawls into his pants as Jack checks out the room.

"Listen up, you Nancies. I got a big secret to tell for yer
newspaper."

Michael adjusts his suspenders and asks, "Couldn't it wait
until morning?"

Jack ignores the reporter and gloats. "Ain't gonna bandy no
words."

Charles finishes buttoning his shirt and says, "Have you been
drinking, Mr. Cleveland?"

"I always drink, ya odd stick. Now, shut the hell up! Ya know
about the Innocents, right?"

Michael turns up the flame on a kerosene fueled lamp and says, "The ruffians that held us up the first time we came here?"

"That's right. Well, Plummer's their leader."

Michael narrows his eyes. "You and Henry aren't exactly friends right now."

"Don't matter. Truth's the truth. Him and four more are the gang; wait, make that three."

Charles holds up his hand. "What happened to number four?"

"Changed his ways … on the straight and narrow now."

Michael continues. "Henry couldn't have been one of the ones that robbed us. He was in jail."

"You gonna let me finish my fuckin' story or not?"

The reporters nod and the informer goes on. "What ya don't know is Plummer's a sly dog. After he killed Vedder and the town put me in charge, his gang waited 'til I left for the day …"

Charles interrupts. "You left him all alone?"

"Shut the hell up! So, after a long day, I went to drinkin' at the Saffron and the other Innocents busted him loose. Chased down your coach and stole all they wanted." Jack nods at Charles. "Took yer coat and pocket watch too. Next morning, when I got back to the office, pretty boy was sleepin' like nothin' happened."

Charles continues. "They put him back in jail?"

Jack kicks the heel of his boot on the floor. "Like nothin' happened."

"How you know all of this if you weren't there?" Michael asks.

Jack hesitates. "Thought ya might say that. Henry got stewed one night and got ta braggin' 'bout all the robbin' and killin' he's done! Listed them off one by one."

Charles says, "Still can't get over them putting him back in jail. Why didn't they just let him ride off?"

"'Cuz, nobody figured he'd have to pay for killin' Vedder."

Michael continues to probe. "Who are the other Innocents?"

"Keepin' them names to myself ... ya ball eaters!"

Charles reacts. "Such filthy talk."

Jack turns to Michael. "Why ain't ya writin' my words down?"

Michael says, "We'll remember, but we will have to verify your story."

"Ain't I verified enough?"

Michael shows Jack to the door. "These are serious accusations. Give us a little time."

"Better hurry, I'm about to tell the fuckin' world." Without another word, the stone-faced schemer stumbles out the door.

Henry is seated at the bar next to Ezra drinking a beer and drawing something on a cloth napkin. A few feet away, Jack sits alone at a nearby table. Restless, he downs his drink and staggers over to the bar counter. He sees Sweet cleaning a shot glass, grabs it out of her hand, and gives it back to her. "Gimme some more coffin varnish."

Sweet manages to remain calm. "Been hitting it awful hard. Don't you think you've had enough?"

Jack grits his teeth. "If you're askin' for trouble, I can be yer trouble." Sweet walks away and he responds by shattering his glass on the bar room floor. "Don't be walkin' away from me, bitch."

Henry, who's been watching, says, "Easy there, partner."

"Fuck you. If I want any of yer shit, I'll squeeze it outta ya."

"Just settle down."

"How 'bout I settle down by tellin' everyone yer big secret?"

"You're drunk. Go upstairs and sleep it off."

"Everyone all the time tellin' me I'm drunk. Damn it! I know I'm drunk!" Jack draws his gun. Before Henry can react, his old friend holds the pistol to the sheriff's head. "Think I'll stay a little longer." He removes Henry's gun from his holster and tosses it over the bar. Henry stands frozen as Jack waves his gun erratically and yammers. "Everyone … listen up!"

Henry warns. "Somebody's gonna get hurt."

The *Sacramento Union* reporters enter the bar just as several miners and hookers rush out. As they look around, Charles says, "Where's everybody going?" They finally notice that Jack is holding a gun to Henry's head and Charles lets out a high-pitched, "Ahhh." Both men turn and start back to the saloon entrance as Charles says, "You know, we're really not that thirsty."

Jack points his gun at the befuddled men. "Sit your asses down! Henry here is about to verify my story. That's what ya need, right? Verification?"

"I don't think a forced confession counts. Right, Michael?"

Jack cocks his pistol and the reporters immediately plop themselves down in two chairs. He puts his gun back to Henry's head and the sheriff reacts by reaching behind his back. He pulls a derringer from his pants and aims it at the drunken man's foot.

Jack surveys the bar and begins his story. "Listen up! I got somethin' to tell. You see when Pretty Boy here ain't bein' sheriff, he's gratifying himself by headin' up…."

Suddenly, his speech is interrupted by the sound of a gunshot. Confused, he looks down at his foot, drops his pistol, and bends over in pain. "Ahh! You son of a bitch!"

Henry steps back and points the derringer at Jack. Unafraid, his old friend collects himself, picks up his revolver, and points it at Henry, daring him to shoot. "Purse gun ain't got but one shot."

Henry cocks the small pistol. "It has two. Put it away."

Jack scowls. "You look worried. Is it my gun or my words?"

All at once, Sweet sneaks up behind Jack with a whiskey bottle and smashes it over the drunk's head. Jack staggers a moment and falls to the floor. Henry waves two men over, hands one of them Jack's gun, and they help him to his feet. "Have Doc tend to him. Then bring him over to the jail."

Ben enters as the two men assist Jack out of the saloon. Henry follows close behind and Ben gives him a curious look. The sheriff doesn't say anything and keeps walking, so Ben turns to Sweet for an answer. "What'd I miss?"

She rolls her eyes. "It's a long story."

Ben pauses and says, "I got time."

The reporters are seated across from Henry, who is rearranging a stack of papers on his desk. Michael breaks the silence. "How's he doing?"

Henry nods. "He'll be all right. He's in the back sleeping it off."

Michael pulls an envelope from his jacket. "Almost forgot, I found this in front of your door when we got here."

Henry takes the envelope and removes the piece of paper inside it. His face turns pale as his lips shape the words he is reading. He finishes and lays the letter carefully on his desk. Michael looks to Henry for a response but doesn't get one, so he says, "You okay?"

Henry smirks. "Yeah, everything's good."

Michael continues. "Need to tell you something. Jack came to our room last night claiming you're the leader of the Innocents."

Charles cuts in. "Pretty sure that was his big announcement before you shot him.

"Yeah, he's been spreading a lot of lies lately. The thing is, the more lies he tells, the more he thinks he's telling the truth."

Michael softens his voice. "You were such good friends. What changed?"

"Me marrying Electa ... him thinking I stole his job."

Michael continues. "That can't be an easy thing to deal with in a new marriage."

Henry snaps. "My marriage is my business."

Michael nods. "Of course, it is.

Charles notices a coat hanging in the corner and points. "That looks like my old garment."

"That coat's been here a while."

"May I look at it?"

Henry grabs the coat and tosses it to Charles, who examines it closely. "This is mine."

Michael asks, "How do you know for sure?"

Charles shows Michael the lapel. "Right here. My mother sewed my initials in it." Charles tries to show Henry, but the sheriff picks up a piece of paper and looks it over.

"Ain't that something."

Charles stares at Henry. "Do you happen to have the time?"

Henry pulls out the pocket watch Samuel gave him and checks the time as the reporters observe carefully. "It's ten o'clock."

As Charles looks at Michael from the corner of his eye, he says, "Nice watch."

"Yeah, I like it."

"May I see it?

"No, I gotta go. I got things to do at home." He stows the time piece in his pocket and coughs. Then he takes a bottle of laudanum from his desk, takes a swig, and picks up the envelope. He stands and quickly ushers Charles and Michael to the front door. He gently pushes the reporters out, exits the office himself, and locks the door behind him.

Losing a friend because he dies or moves away is a lot easier than having to see him every day. It was bad luck with me and Jack falling in love with Electa and with us wanting the same fame and fortune, but those are the cards we were dealt.

Back in the jail's holding area, Jack wakes up, looks down at his wounded foot, and touches the bandage on his head. He sits up and spots Samuel in the cell next to him. "That son of a bitch put me in here with the likes of you?"

Samuel smiles. "Gotta admit, I kinda enjoy watching the two of you jailing each other."

"Why ain't you hanged yet?"

"Been trying to figure that out myself."

"Soon as I verify Plummer being an Innocent, he'll be joining you."

"I'd be careful naming too many of them seeings you're one of them."

"You don't know shit."

"If they hang my brother, you won't be far behind." Samuel realizes his mistake and says, "Shit. I meant to say is if they hang Plummer." Jack takes in what Samuel said and lays back in his cot.

CHAPTER 44

"Well, heaven forgive him! and forgive us all! Some rise by sin, and some by virtue fall: Some run from brakes of ice, and answer none: And some condemned for a fault alone." William Shakespeare

ELECTA IS DRESSED and ready to travel. Henry watches as she finishes packing her belongings in a large leather satchel. He lifts the letter she wrote high in the air and says, "You're set to leave and you weren't even gonna say goodbye."

"Because, I knew you would try and talk me out of it."

Henry lifts his chin. "You're right. Let's talk."

"You haven't been home for two days and I find out you shot Jack."

"He's fine. I shot him in the foot."

"I can't live with all this drama."

"It's almost over."

"You keep saying that and I hope for your sake it is, but it's too late for us. I'm leaving this godless town before they hang you."

"Really think they're gonna hang me?"

"Those reporters you know came by and asked me some questions this morning. They said Jack is claiming you're the leader of the Innocents."

"Jack's a liar and those two are dealing with backward facts."

"Backward facts?"

"You think that's who I am ... some kind of thief? I admit, I've hidden a few things, but stealing gold and killing people is not one of them."

"I don't know who or what to believe anymore."

"Electa! I'm not a fucking Innocent!"

"Those reporters told me Girard and his men are ready to take the law in their own hands and hang anyone they think might be one. They said Jack told them ..."

Henry interrupts. "What Jack says and what's true are two different things."

"If what you're saying is right, come with me." Electa watches as Henry struggles to say something.

"I can't. I need to save Samuel."

"That's never going to happen."

"Yes, it is. He's in my jail."

"What? I thought Alex Slade ..."

"Alex Slade's my brother. He's Samuel."

Electa's eyes open wide. "My God!"

"That's why I went to Dillon ... to keep him from being hanged. Before I could free him, Ben came along."

"So now what are you going to do?"

"I have a plan."

Electa stares at Henry for a moment. "A plan? You mean another secret." She picks up her bag. "I'm happy you found your brother."

She walks stiffly towards the door as Henry says, "I'll come for you when this is all over. You'll be at your sister's, right?"

At the door, she turns back. "I'm going home to Indiana on the afternoon stage."

Henry pleads. "Don't do that. Give me a little more time."

She pauses. "All the time you spent looking for your brother, you should've been looking for yourself. You're the one who's lost."

There aren't many things worse than a woman leaving you when it's not your choice. They say letting go is what you're supposed to do next, but I'll never do that. I need to figure out a way to win her back.

The Overland stagecoach sits in front of the Saffron Saloon. Rut puts Electa's leather bag in the rear boot and scampers over and opens the door for his only passenger. Once inside, Electa breaks down and cries.

Suddenly, Sandra appears at the coach window holding her baby. Electa grabs her chest. "My God! You frightened me."

"I'm sorry. I didn't mean to... it's Electa, right?" Henry's wife wipes her eyes as Sandra continues, "I need to speak with you a moment." She signals Rut to be patient and gets in the coach with Electa.

Rut leans down and looks in the window. "Sandra, this coach ain't goin' to Nevada."

"I know. I won't be long."

Stubborn sits nervously checking his watch, while the women talk inside the coach.

Electa and her new friend stand next to the coach waiting as Rut removes her bag from the boot and hands it to her. As they walk away, Electa turns to Sandra and says, "We can stay with my sister until we figure something out." Rut shakes his head as he watches the two women walk away. He whistles, slaps leather to his horses, and drives off.

Henry opens Jack's cell door as Samuel watches from his own cage. Henry escorts the crippled man to the front door and says, "Do yourself a favor and don't tell any more lies."

Jack spews. "Ya say that like it's some kinda warning."

Henry chooses his words carefully. "Think whatever you want; time will tell my story."

As Jack limps away, he spits and says, "Eat shit, Pretty Boy!"

Ezra is seated at the bar when Henry enters and parks next to him. Sweet hands Henry a beer as the door to the back room opens and Charles and Michael approach. Henry raises his hand and stops the reporters. "Heard you had a visit with my wife."

Charles apologizes. "Sorry, we didn't mean…"

Henry grins sarcastically. "Now, ya can add to your story Electa left me and I became a drunk."

Michael says, "I need to tell you something. Jack took an oath back there claiming you and some of your friends are Innocents."

"Did he name himself?"

"No, but they gave him clemency for naming everyone else."

Henry nods. "Clemency? Ain't that a daisy."

"Good news is Ben Girard says they need a lot more evidence to go along with everything he told them."

"Yeah, Jack's gotten good at using half a truth to tell lies. Kinda like you two."

The reporters question Henry with their eyes as he continues. "Remember what you said at Quentin? 'Sometimes a story's not much of a story if it's not overstated.'"

Ezra chuckles. "Kinda like getting your pole halfway polished. Half a polish is worse than no polish at all."

Henry smirks. "Yeah, something like that."

The reporters stand aside as Ben and his heavily armed men approach the front of the bar. Henry turns to Ben. "Hey. I'm drunk."

"I see that."

"I've never been drunk. I kind of like it." Henry begins to slur his words. "I hear Jack's been naming names. Either way, I'm an innocent man, right?"

"That's not funny. If what he's sayin' is true, we ain't takin' it lightly. Why don't you come with us."

"Gonna stay here. Bringing everyone back for a trial, right?"

Ben ignores Henry. "Hangin' Slade soon as we get back."

Henry scoffs. "Can't miss that." As Ben and his men exit the bar, the reporters follow with sheepish looks on their faces.

Henry turns to Sweet and snickers. "Am I in trouble?"

Sweet takes his empty beer mug. "Get you another?"

"Give me some of that tarantula juice Jack's always drinking."

"You don't even like whiskey."

"Not drinking it for the taste." Henry coughs deeply as Sweet pours his drink. He gulps it down and shakes his head.

Sweet leans over the bar counter. "Ya know, Ben's giving you a big chance to get your ass down the road."

"I know, but I wanna see how everything plays out."

"Why are you so damn stubborn?"

Ezra speaks up. "The tick tock is on."

They sit in silence until Jack limps out of the back room. It's obvious that he's been drinking. As he walks past, Henry holds up his whiskey glass and toasts his nemesis. "To friendship gone bad." Jack doesn't respond as he shuffles out the door. Henry slumps over the bar as the liquor takes its toll. "Yer the only friend I got, Ezra."

CHAPTER 45

"A hanging typically occurs after someone is found guilty in the eyes of the law and irredeemable in the eyes of society. A lynching is the killing of an individual for how they look and what they represent to a vigilante mob."
Stewart Stafford

SEATED ON THE STEPS of the Saffron, Jack watches as Ben Girard and ten other vigilantes ride hard out of town. Trailing behind them on borrowed horses are Charles and Michael, who are trying their best to keep up.

As the dust settles, Jack pulls a half-full bottle of whiskey from his pocket and gulps it down with gusto. He tosses the bottle, struggles to his feet, and steps in a pile of dog shit. "Goddamn it!" As he tries to scrape the shit from his boot, he sees a dog looking his way. Angry, he draws his gun and fires at the stray. The hound jumps aside, whines, and runs off.

Jack tries sliding his boot in the dirt again, but he loses his balance and plops down in the middle of the street. He looks around to see if anyone is looking, cups his hands, and screams, "Plummer!"

Henry, still in the bar with Ezra, hears Jack howl his name, but he doesn't react. The undertaker starts to stand up, but Henry gently places his hand on his shoulder. "Leave him be." A moment passes and Henry takes a wad of money from his coat and puts it in Ezra's pocket. Sweet gives Henry a suspicious look as he whispers something in Ezra's ear. Then the sheriff turns back to Sweet and grins. "Paying my way ahead. He's gonna get it anyway."

Ezra lifts his glass. "To business ... and so forth."

Henry mimics the black-suited man. "And so forth."

Ezra downs his drink and stands. "Well, that's today's hole dug."

The mortician heads for the door as the sheriff raises up and says, "Where you going?"

Ezra doesn't look back but says, "Red Yeager's place."

Henry lifts his glass. "More tarantula juice."

The worst way to end a friendship or a marriage for that matter is to drink it to death. Having never been much of a drinker, I decided to make up for lost time.

Michael and Charles struggle to keep up with the vigilantes, who are a hundred yards ahead of them. Not far from Red Yeager's Rattlesnake Ranch, Ben and his men bring their horses to a stop and begin to drink from their canteens. The exhausted reporters finally arrive, come to a sudden stop, and almost fall off their horses. Ben chuckles and points to a path leading to the Red's place.

When Ben and his men arrive at Red's Yeager's homestead, they see two of his children playing in the dirt in front of the family's sod house. The kids see the well-armed vigilantes and run inside. Red's wife, Teresa Mae, steps out onto the front porch, just as her frightened husband runs out the back door.

Two lanky vigilantes chase Red down, tie his arms behind him, and put a rope around his neck. A third man fastens the other end of the rope to his saddle horn and tightens the slack. Teresa sees what the man is about to do, so she charges him, and pulls him off his horse. One of the lanky vigilantes rushes over, slaps Teresa with the side of his rifle, and she falls to the ground in a heap. The fallen vigilante dusts himself off and climbs back on his horse, while the other men snicker.

Red stumbles along behind his captors' horses until Ben spots a large pine tree. One of the men throws a rope around a tree limb, while another puts Red on his horse and leads him to the tree. Everyone turns in unison, when they hear Ezra's death wagon roll over the top of the hill. When it comes to a stop, Ben drops a noose around their victim's neck and waits for him to talk. Finally, the boss man says, "Who are the others?"

With fire in his eyes, Red mouths a diatribe directed at Ben and all the men around him. "You fucking assholes! Ain't done nothin' you all ain't done! Get this fuckin' rope off my neck!"

Ben signals and one of the vigilantes pushes Red's horse a step forward, making the rope so tight that Red begins to gag. Ben signals the vigilante again and he pushes the horse one step back, releasing the tension. Ben looks down and sees that Red has wet his pants. Desperate, the condemned man leans over and whispers in Ben's ear. Getting the answer he's been waiting for, Ben slaps the horse and it runs off, leaving Red dangling from the tree. As the frantic man's eyes bulge, he kicks wildly, struggling to breathe. Finally, he yields to the rope's pressure and goes limp.

Not far away, Charles leans over his horse and throws up as Ezra walks over to Ben and asks, "He tell you anything?"

Ben clenches his teeth. "Told me all I need to know." Before Ezra can respond, Red's wife appears at the top of a ridge. She sees her husband hanging from the tree, rides down the hill, jumps off her horse, and tries to lift his body enough to relieve the pressure of the rope. Two posse members pull her away and toss her to the ground.

Ezra steps up and cuts the hanging rope. He signals Charles and Michael and they carry Red's corpse to the wagon. Before they get very far, Teresa knocks the reporters down and reclaims her dead husband. Ben looks down and says, "Leave her be."

As the posse leaves, Teresa, who is cradling her husband in her arms, screams, "You monsters!"

The reporters ride along in Ezra's wagon, seated next to him. Their horses are tied to the back. Ezra slaps leather and tries to catch up with the posse as the reporters hang on for dear life. When Charles turns back, he sees Red's bereaved wife still seated under the tree weeping, her husband's head resting in her lap.

Henry carries two trays of food to Samuel cell, pulls up a chair, and the brothers begin to eat. Samuel snickers. "My last meal?

Henry frowns. "Could be mine too."

"Why's Jack out to get you so hard?"

"'Cuz, he thinks I stole his woman."

Samuel perks up as he changes the subject. "You said Ben and his gang are outta town. Why we here? Let's go. . . you, me, Electa, Sandra, and the baby?"

"They'd track us down in no time. I got a plan I think's gonna work."

"You think? What kind of plan is it?"

"I'll lay it out when I get back." Samuel looks puzzled as Henry takes his tray and walks off.

Abe Gunderson stands in his rundown corral with Gus Franklin, who is shoeing one of Abe's horses. Both men look up and see Ben and the other vigilantes riding their way. Gus realizes what's happening and starts to run, but Ben rides after him and shoots the blacksmith in the leg. Two vigilantes yank Gus to his feet and lead him to the hayloft of the Gunderson barn. One man throws a rope over an exterior beam, while another one ties Gus's hands together. A third man drops a noose around his neck and without a word, all three men push him out of the barn.

The executioners ride off, leaving Gus swinging from the front of Abe's barn.

Abe is staring at Gus's body when Ezra and the reporters pull up. The undertaker jumps out of his wagon and looks at the blacksmith's corpse suspended high above. He scratches his head, jumps back in his wagon and drives off, leaving Abe to deal with Gus's dead body.

The vigilant committee members near the entrance of a local church in a rural community. Monty Montgomery exits the church with his wife and two boys and Ben signals him to come over and whispers something in his ear. The family man returns to his wife and kids, hugs them, climbs on his horse, and rides away with Ben and his men.

Ezra and the reporters drive past the local church and see Monty's wife and her sons holding each other and crying. A few minutes later, the three men approach Ben and his men, who are staring at Monty's lifeless body which is still hanging from a pine tree.

As Ben and his gang start to ride off, Ben waves Ezra away and says, "Leave him hang. We need to show people we mean business."

"What about my business?" Ben ignores him and Ezra slumps back to his wagon.

His head and foot still bandaged, Jack watches from the alley as Henry exits his office and locks the door. Jack limps across the street and tries to open the door, but it won't budge. He reaches in his pocket, pulls out a knitting needle, pokes it into the lock, moves it from side to side, and the door opens.

The deposed sheriff enters the office, removes two keys from the desk drawer, and uses one of them to open the cell block. Once inside, he fits a second key and unlocks Samuel's cell door. Startled, the prisoner wakes from a deep sleep and sits up. "What the hell?"

Jack draws his gun. "I know who you are. I ain't stupid."

Samuel scoffs. "Go ahead. Fish in a barrel."

Jack waves his gun. "Get out!"

"What? I'm not going anywhere."

The crippled man cocks his gun, points it at Samuel's head, and scoffs. "Don't matter to me."

Samuel thinks it over, stands, and heads to the outer office. Jack opens the door, looks out to make sure no one is looking and pushes his prisoner outside. When he turns to shut the door, Samuel grabs a handful of dirt and hides it behind his back.

When Jack turns back, he yells, "Run, you asshole!" Samuel doesn't move, so Jack hobbles over and raises his gun. Before he can fire, Samuel tosses the dirt in the wrongdoer's eyes. Then he whips around and grabs the gun out of his hand. As Jack tries to clear his eyes, Samuel slams the heel of the gun against culprit's forehead and the misanthrope crumbles to the ground.

Samuel scans the street and starts for Gus's Livery Stable. When he arrives, he sneaks inside, finds Henry Plummer, the horse, grabs a saddle, and throws it on the animal's back.

Back on the street, Jack staggers to his feet. He clears his head, looks down the street, and sees Samuel riding out of town on the often stolen horse, Henry Plummer.

Two vigilantes creep their way towards an old log cabin surrounded by pine trees. The other men, including Ezra,

Michael, and Charles, watch from a distance as two of their own push the door open. Seeing no one, they take their chances and step inside.

Lou Chavez, alias "The Greaser," who is hiding in the darkness behind an overturned table, fires two shots. A bullet hits one of the vigilantes in the chest and the other one hits the second man in the hip. The vigilante with the chest wound stumbles out the door, collapses and dies, while his friend hobbles back to his comrades.

Three men react to their friend's death by grabbing two powder kegs from Ezra's wagon. They run to the cabin, put one against the front wall, and toss the other one on the roof. They signal one another and fire simultaneously at the kegs.

The first explosion decimates the front wall of the cabin and the second one destroys the chimney and most of the roof. As the dust settles, several men enter the cabin and find "The Greaser" lying dead on the dirt floor. The vigilante with the hip wound limps over to "The Greaser" and empties his revolver into the man's lifeless body. Still not satisfied, three men carry Lou's Chavez's body to a nearby tree, wrap a rope around his neck, and hang him from the largest branch. As the cabin burns behind them, six vigilantes fire dozens of shots at Lou's body. Slowly, the corpse begins to swing from the rope like a Mexican piñata.

When the shooting stops, two men walk over, cut the Mexican's body down, and throw it in a large fire. The carcass smolders and turns black as several men hold their noses.

The vigilantes ride away as Charles and Michael sit in the wagon and watch Ezra sifting through the smoldering ashes of "The Greaser's" remains. Charles grimaces as he covers his mouth and addresses Ezra. "What in God's name?"

Ezra measures his words. "Gold in his teeth... and so forth."

CHAPTER 46

"Death is the last enemy: Once we've got past that, I think everything will be alright." Alice Thomas Ellis

BEN AND HIS ENTOURAGE RIDE down Bannack's Main Street. Their shoulders are drooped and their eyes reveal a darkness that can only come from the guilt and shame of having ended so many men's lives.

Not far behind them, at the edge of town, Ezra Simpson's death wagon approaches. Two horses are tied to the back of it, and the reporters are seated next to the undertaker on a blanket. With every rut the wagon goes over, Charles and Michael grimace in pain. As Ezra reflects on the events of the day, he turns back and shakes his head in disgust at the empty bed of his wagon.

As Henry starts to unlock his office door, he spots Ben and his men come to a stop in front of the Saffron Saloon. He continues to watch as most of the men peel off and ride for home. He puts the key in the door, only to discover it isn't locked. He shrugs, pushes the door open, and walks in. Henry sits down, pulls out his journal and begins to write.

Life has gone faster than I ever thought it would, but I guess that tends to happen when you're never quite sure how much time you have left. Ben and his men have caught the scent now, and I think it's me they'll be comin' for next.

Henry coughs deeply and his blood splatters on the open page. He pushes the journal aside, grabs a rag from his pocket, and holds it to his mouth. When he looks at the soiled cloth, he sees a blotch of blood on it.

Back on Main Street, Jack limps across the street and meets up with Ben and three other vigilantes. They talk a moment and then make their way to the sheriff's office. When they reach the door, Ben notices a change in the size of the bandage under Jack's hat and his bruised forehead. "Take your hat off."

"Why?"

"Take it off!"

Jack removes his hat and Ben sees an even larger bandage on his head than the one he had before Ben left town. "That ain't from Sweet clubbin' you on the head."

Jack guffaws. "A horse kicked me."

"Shit. You got no luck."

Ben opens the office door and the five men stroll inside. Henry looks up, obviously hung over. Ben scowls. "Why you still here?"

"Thought you might be bringin' me some prisoners." Henry looks over and sees the large bandage under Jack's hat.

Ben notices the look. "Claims a horse kicked him."

Henry smiles. "Hope he knocked some sense into you."

Jack seethes. "Shut your pie hole!"

Ben interrupts their moment. "Got some bad news. Red Yeager named you leader of the Innocents."

"Let me guess. There was a rope around his neck."

Ben stares at Henry until Jack speaks. "No more talk. I say we hang 'em both ... Slade and Plummer."

Ben turns to Henry. "Hold on. Ya got anything to say?"

"I know it's not your style, but I deserve a trial, and I promised Slade he'd have one more day."

"I don't give a fuck about Slade. And as for you, you an Innocent or not?"

"Give me a day and I'll prove Red and Jack wrong."

Jack grabs the keys off the desk and limps to the cell block as Ben reacts to Henry's request. "I've already given Slade more time than he deserves and as for you…."

Jack returns and interrupts. "Slade ain't there."

Henry hops to his feet. "What do you mean he's not there?"

"You heard me; he ain't there!"

Henry hurries back to the cell area and Ben follows. "I just fed him two hours ago!" When they return, their faces reveal that Jack is right.

Jack sees his chance for revenge. "What more verification we need? Didn't walk out of here on his own. Told you, they're both Innocents."

Ben's face turns dark as he stares into the sheriff's eyes. "You was set to let him ride off outside Dillon, wasn't ya?" Henry stares blankly until Ben says, "Yer face tells me all I need to know."

Henry shrugs. "Don't matter. You've made up your mind."

Ben nods and the two vigilantes grab Henry. "Let's get this over with. We can hunt down Slade later." Jack steps up and tears the badge from Henry's shirt, but Ben grabs it out of Jack's hand. "No more sheriffs." As Ben pockets the badge, Henry bends over and starts to take off a boot. Ben reacts. "What the hell you doing?"

"Let me do this one odd thing." Henry finishes pulling off his boots and removes his journal from his desk as Ben and his men usher him out the front door in his bare feet.

Electa and Sandra sit on a bench in front of the Vail house. Little Samuel is at Sandra's feet, asleep in a wooden cradle. Sandra looks at the sky and turns to Electa. "It's not right. How can they hang a man for stealing, especially if he tries to give it back?"

"Ben Girard and his men do whatever they want."

"Think if we told them they are brothers, it would help?"

"It might make it worse."

"If they're planning on hanging Samuel in the morning, I think I should go back to Bannack."

"Henry said he has a plan."

"I don't care. I wanna go now."

Sandra leans down and takes Samuel out of his cradle. "Think the Vails will let me borrow that wagon?"

Electa thinks for a moment and points at the Vail cabin. "You can leave your son with Martha Jane. I'll go with you."

James Vail finishes hitching two horses to his wagon and the two women climb on board. Martha Jane, who is standing on the front porch with little Samuel in her arms, waves the little boy's hand as if he is saying goodbye as the women head for Bannack.

Henry, Ben, Jack and the other vigilantes walk towards the gallows as several townspeople follow close behind. Henry spots the Sacramento men on the other side of the street and waves them over. Still saddle sore, they limp their way across the street. Henry turns to Ben and pleads with his eyes and Ben motions his men to step back, giving the accused lawman a moment alone with the reporters. Henry smirks. "Not the way you were expecting it to end is it boys?"

Charles panics. "No, you're not going to hang this man?"

Jack chortles. "We can hardly wait." Suddenly, Charles charges Jack, but before he can reach him, two vigilantes grab the reporter and toss him to the ground.

Charles sits up and snarls. "Excuse my language, but you're an asshole, Cleveland." Jack grins as the reporter crawls to his feet and dusts himself off.

Michael steps forward and offers his hand to Henry, but the fated man pushes his hand away and bear hugs both reporters. Then he steps back and gives Michael his journal. "Most of my story is in there. Read it when you get a chance. Might explain a few things. And I gotta favor to ask."

Charles' voice quivers. "Anything you want."

Henry hands the reporter his boots. "Those are for Ezra."

Michael interrupts. "You sure you don't want us to give all of this to Electa?"

"No, she's on her way to Indiana."

Jack's eyes open wide. "Indiana?"

Henry ignores Jack. "Anyway, it looks like I'm not gonna get a chance to say goodbye. So, if you should see her, let her know I was thinking about her 'til the end." He coughs and turns to Ben, "Make sure these two get a good view. They're trying to make me famous."

Ben takes Henry's arm. "Enough talk." He pushes Henry in the direction of the gallows, while the reporters trail a few steps behind.

On the edge of town, dozens of people have already gathered at the gallows. Jack is hidden at the back of the crowd, staring at the noose that is gently swinging in the breeze. Michael and Charles are standing in the front with their hats in their hands as more people arrive. Charles nods at Michael and says, "That didn't take long. People must sit around all day waiting for a hanging." To the reporters' right, Ben and Ezra walk the barefooted sheriff, his hands tied behind his back, to the top of the gallows.

Unaware of what is happening on the other side of town, an unarmed Samuel rides down a back alley, not far from the sheriff's office. He tethers his horse to a drain pipe, walks across the street, and enters the jailhouse with his hands in the air.

Henry is now positioned on the scaffold next to Ben and Ezra as they prepare to execute him. Ezra looks nervous as he addresses Ben. "Thought we was hangin' Slade ... and so forth."

Ben grunts. "Plummer's taking his place."

Ezra steps back and whispers to Henry. "This ain't in the plan. The undertaker takes his time prepping Henry as townspeople squeeze their way to the front of the gallows. Henry looks out and sees Sweet Water standing in the back row crying. Overwhelmed by what's about to happen, the barmaid rushes off.

Samuel exits the sheriff's office with a lost look on his face as Sweet rounds the corner. She stops in her tracks when she sees Henry's brother. She points. "You'd better hurry. They're about to hang him." As Samuel starts to run, he hears the crowd jeering and loud talking in the distance.

The reporters, their heads bowed, look up at the gallows when Henry begins to speak. "Sure ya got the right man?" Ben doesn't respond, so he continues. "Hope you sleep well tonight; I know I will."

Ben removes a Bible from his coat, opens it, and begins to read: "You shall not steal, nor deal falsely, nor lie to one another..."

Henry interrupts. "You really think reading a few words is gonna excuse what you're about to do?" Ben stops and closes his Bible as Henry stares at him. "Got one request." Ben doesn't say anything, so he continues. "Don't display my body on the street like I'm some curiosity."

Ben nods. "Simpson?"

The undertaker agrees. "Fair enough."

Electa steers the horses at a fast pace in the direction of Bannack as Sandra hangs on for dear life. In the distance, the women see the outline of a man standing on the scaffold readying to be hanged. Sandra cries out, "Samuel! No! Dear God no!"

Electa slaps the reins to the horses and heads straight for the gallows. "I thought you said it was tomorrow."

Henry makes eye contact with Abe Gunderson, who is standing front and center, with a blank look on his face. Henry shifts his eyes to the reporters and grins as Ezra places a canvas bag over his head. The undertaker takes his time, carefully fitting the noose around the lower part of the bag.

Ben clears his throat. "Let's get this done." Ezra adjusts the noose one more time and nods to Ben. All at once, Samuel flies around the corner and stops in his tracks when he sees the raucous crowd in front of him. He spots the hooded man at the top of the gallows and frantically nudges the old man next to him. "They can't hang him. He hasn't done anything wrong."

The old man chuckles. "Apparently, they think otherwise."

Samuel fights his way through the crowd as Ben takes Henry by the arm and guides him to the edge of the drop hole on the gallows platform. From a few rows back, Samuel screams, "Stop! I'm the one you wanna hang!"

Ben looks at the fugitive and sneers. "Get him! He's next."

Three of Ben's men weave their way through the crowd with guns drawn as Henry sees what's happening and hollers, "Run, Samuel! Run!" Before Samuel can react, Ben gives Henry a shove and he drops to the bottom of the gallows with a thud. Several members of the crowd let out a collective sigh and push their way to the front to get a better look at the sheriff's body.

Two bystanders grab Samuel and try to hold him back, but he breaks free, takes a cane from an old lady, and holds everyone at bay. The vigilantes, who are still trying to reach him, aim their guns, but they don't have a clear shot. Samuel stops swinging the cane, turns to the gallows, and watches as his brother's body sways from side to side before coming to a sudden stop. He screams. "Arggh!" Samuel tosses the cane and tries to grab a large man's rifle, but the big man pushes him away as Ben's men arrive. Outnumbered, he darts off, ducking and weaving his way through the crowd. When he reaches the alley near the jailhouse, he jumps on his horse and rides off. The three vigilantes round a corner and fire several shots, just missing him.

Electa and Sandra's wagon slides to a stop and both of them stare at what they think is Samuel's body hanging from the scaffold. Electa tries to comfort Sandra, who is crying hysterically.

Under the gallows, Ezra checks his friend's body for any sign of life. The undertaker removes his hat and signals Ben that Henry is indeed dead. Ezra cuts the hanging rope and Henry's body drops to the ground. As Ezra and Ben start to carry his body to the death wagon, the reporters appear, and Charles hands Ezra Henry's boots. "He wanted you to have these." Ezra looks at them a moment and tosses them in his wagon. Charles continues. "I know it's unusual, but could I see his watch?"

Ezra looks irritated. "His pocket goods belong to me and so forth."

"I'll give it back."

Ezra fishes the watch from Henry's pocket and hands it to Charles, who looks it over and hands it to Michael. "Looks like someone scratched off a name or something. It's not mine."

As Charles starts to hand the watch back to Ezra, Sandra and Electa appear. Charles pulls the timepiece away from Ezra's waiting hand and offers it to Electa instead. "You should have this."

Electa looks puzzled but takes the watch anyway and says, "This is Henry's."

Charles removes his hat. "We're sorry for your loss, Ma'am."

"My loss? What are you talking about?" Electa's mind spins as she steps to the wagon to get a closer look at what she thought was Samuel's body. Electa instantly tries to pull the hood from Henry's head, but Ezra gently pushes the grieving woman away. "Henry don't look so good right now, but I'll fix him up and so forth."

Electa drops the watch and covers her mouth as she sags to the ground. "Oh my God!" The reporters give her a moment and help the panic-stricken woman to her feet. When no one is looking, Ezra picks up Henry's watch and puts it in his pocket.

The crowd has dispersed and only a few bystanders remain. Electa and Sandra sit in their wagon as Ezra rolls away with Henry's body in the bed of his death wagon.

As Sandra grips the horses' reins, she bends down and whispers to Charles. "What about Alex Slade?"

Charles whispers back, "He's on the run, but don't you worry. Ben and his men will track him down." Sandra slaps leather to the horses, and the wagon lurches forward and away.

CHAPTER 47

**"There is nothing wrong with changing a plan
when the situation changes." Seneca the Younger**

IN THE BACK ROOM of his funeral parlor, lit by candlelight,
Ezra finishes putting a man's corpse in a pine box. As he nails the
coffin lid shut, Henry approaches from the shadows wearing his
old boots. "Who'd you put in there?

Ezra grins. "Some no-name drifter who drank himself to
death last week. Had no kin, and so forth."

Henry coughs deeply, rubs his neck, and nods at Ezra. "Ya
know, I almost moved when you started to pull that bag off my
head. What was that all about?"

"That wasn't me." Henry questions the undertaker with his
eyes and Ezra continues. "Your woman done it."

"Electa was there? She saw me hang?"

Ezra smirks. "She's gonna be in a loud mood when she sees
you again, and so forth."

"Samuel? He get away clean?"

"Yeah, he done flew the coop."

Henry pats Ezra on the back. "We did it. We pulled it off."

"I almost shit my pants when I saw it was you and not your
brother I was about to hang." Henry chuckles as Ezra holds up a
leather collar and says, "This contraption sure held its own."

TWO DAYS EARLIER

In the parlor's back room, Ezra finishes stitching a thick leather collar to the inside of a white bag. He yanks on it, testing its strength, picks up the bag, puts it on his head, and adjusts it to fit. Next, he puts a rope around the bag and tightens it on his neck. He coughs and looks in a mirror. "Boo!"

Henry walks in and laughs when he sees Ezra with the bag and rope on his head. The undertaker chuckles, removes the bag, and hands it to his co-conspirator. Henry checks the leather insert carefully and says, "Sure hope this thing works."

"It better. We got nothin' else. Hope your brother knows what's in store for him, and so forth?"

"Not yet."

"Better tell him soon. He needs to practice looking dead."

Ezra slaps Henry on the back and gloats. "Gotta say, I'm kinda proud of myself. Never fake hanged anyone before."

"Thank God everything worked out."

Henry turns for the door, but Ezra grabs his arm. He hands him his pocket watch. He takes a close look at it, holds it in the air, and toasts Ezra. "To another day above ground."

On the bank of Grasshopper Creek, Electa throws her line in the water and waits patiently for a fish to bite. A shadow appears in the water in front of her as Henry's voice interrupts her tranquility. "Catching anything?"

Electa turns and sees Henry standing on top of the creek bank holding the reins of his horse. "Lord Jesus! Oh my God!" She drops her fishing pole in the water and covers her face. "Stay right there. I thought you were dead."

Henry takes a step in her direction. "Maybe you should make sure I'm not."

Electa lowers her hands, scampers up the bank of the creek and hugs Henry. "Why do you keep doing this to me? My heart can't take it."

The Plummers are sitting next to each other on the creek's bank looking out at the water, when Electa turns to Henry with disapproval in her eyes. "Well, you certainly had me fooled."

As Henry removes his boots, he explains his plan. "I couldn't figure out any other way. When Samuel escaped, things got complicated."

"I'm sorry, but that was way beyond complicated." Henry begins to cough, so he pulls out a handkerchief and wipes his mouth. Electa sees the blood on it and reacts. "My God!"

"Yeah, I'm going to San Francisco to get checked out."

"San Francisco?"

Henry stares stoically in the distance. "You were right. I'm done here. We'll go together and start a new life."

"Aren't you forgetting something?" Henry looks at Electa for the answer. "The town thinks they hanged you. When they find out…"

Henry butts in. "You and Ezra are the only ones that know. They won't be looking for a dead man. We can ride off, free and clear … settle down in California."

"When have I heard that before?"

"When we get to San Francisco, I'm gonna get me a gentleman's job. You haven't heard that before."

"You're buttering the wrong bread." Electa lowers her voice and continues. "Shooting Jack, being hanged … not being hanged. It's all too much."

Henry looks her in the eyes. "We're still married … aren't we?"

"Barely."

Henry persists as puts on his boots. "Get yourself ready. Soon as I find Samuel, we'll head south."

"Wait. You're going to look for him again?"

"I need to find him before Ben does."

"This is never going to end."

"Yes, it is. When I find him, we'll team up and head south— you, me, Samuel, Sandra, and the baby. One big family."

"Saving him once almost cost you your life. Isn't that enough?"

Henry shakes his head and climbs on his horse. "Don't need to save him, only find him. Be back for you, soon as I can."

As he turns to ride away, Electa yells out, "I won't be here!"

"Yeah, you will!" Henry pulls up on the reins of his horse, stops, and looks back at Electa. "Sorry, I can't fetch that pole for you."

Electa wades into the water, grabs the pole, and heaves it to the other side of the creek. She turns back, but Henry's gone.

CHAPTER 48

"Great is the art of the beginning, but greater is the art of ending." Henry Wadsworth Longfellow

THE CROWN OF A BLAZING SUN tops the dark gray of the Bitterroot Mountains on a cloudless fall morning. Majestic ponderosa pines diffuse the sun's rays, revealing a heavy morning dew and the low-lying surface rocks that sculpt the area.

Samuel finishes attaching his bedroll to Hank and gazes into the distance, shading his eyes from the level shafts of the new-risen sun. He peeks over the horse's ears and sees two turkey vultures fly from a tree limb and circle above him.

As his campfire smolders, Samuel climbs in the saddle. With his left hand, he pulls his gun and aims at the scavenger birds. He thinks better of it, lowers his weapon, and holsters it. Restless, he removes a peppermint stick from his saddle bag, takes a bite, and puts the remaining piece in his pocket.

In the distance, the outlaw notices a cloud of dust. He shifts nervously in his saddle and hears the sound of approaching horses. He immediately sets Hank's head north, rides out of the ravine, and onto the flat prairie ground. When he pivots back, he sees Ben and twelve other vigilantes bearing down on him. Several of the men fire away and the chase is on.

After putting some distance between himself and the posse, Samuel enters a dark forest filled with pine trees. He dodges limbs, stumbles over rocks, and battles the rough terrain. When he looks back, he doesn't see anyone, so he climbs down and begins to pull Hank up the side of a hill. All at once, he hears voices in the distance, so he looks up the hill and spots a cavern on the ridge above. When he reaches the top, he leads his horse into the pitch-black cave and sits down.

He instantly hears hissing and rattling, so he strikes a match, revealing a large den of rattlesnakes. Somehow, he manages to control Hank as he scrambles out of the cave and resumes his trek up the hill. With the horse in tow, he reaches the summit, remounts, and heads for the light coming from a break in the trees ahead. Once he exits the forest, Samuel sits back in his saddle and lets out a sigh of relief.

Suddenly, multiple shots ring out. When he looks back, he sees Jack Cleveland and several other men aiming their rifles at him. Jack fires and removes the horn from his saddle. Samuel quickly turns Hank's head and rides in the opposite direction.

As he speeds his way upwards into a narrow box canyon, Samuel comes to a stop at the edge of a buffalo jump. When he looks down, he sees four Blackfeet women skinning a fallen buffalo. He spins Hank away from the cliff, only to be abruptly greeted by the vigilantes, who surround him. Samuel raises his arms and Ben takes the gun out of his holster and pockets it.

Another vigilante grabs Hank's reins and leads the way as the other men follow close behind. A few seconds later, Samuel reaches into his pocket, removes a peppermint stick, puts it to his mouth, and bites down hard on it. Jack sides up to Samuel and slaps the candy out of his mouth.

The morning sun peeks through the branches of a huge cottonwood tree. It's the only one in the meadow and is bordered by a mound of large rocks. Samuel stands in a hole under the conifer digging his own grave, while Ben and his men share a bottle of whiskey and wait for their prisoner to finish his task.

In the distance, perched on top of a small cliff, Henry watches nervously as Ben's pre-hanging ritual plays itself out. As he tries to decide what to do, Henry sees his brother throw a shovel full of dirt that hits Jack in the face. Three of Ben's men draw their guns and Samuel starts to dig again. Henry chuckles, mounts his horse, and readies his pistol for action.

Now hidden behind the rocks not far from the hanging tree, Henry sees his older brother mounted on Hank, his hands tied behind his back.

Jack tosses a rope over a large branch and puts the noose around Samuel's neck. He pauses when he sees the scar below Samuel's shirt collar, but regains his focus and ties the end of the rope to his saddle.

As Ben opens his Bible and prepares to read, he hears coughing in the nearby rocks. He draws his gun and hollers, "Whoever you are, come outta there!"

Henry yells back. "Let him go!" He coughs again, tries to catch his breath, and covers his mouth with a handkerchief.

Ben growls. "Show yourself, asshole!" Several vigilantes dismount, draw their guns, and wait for further orders.

As Henry watches from a small opening in the rocks, he removes the handkerchief from his face and spits a mouthful of blood to the ground. He looks up at the sky and the moving clouds and tries to strike a bargain with God. "I'm thinking it's been you up there all along trying to get my attention. I know it's selfish of me to ask so late, but if you exist…and I'm choosing to believe you do, please help me free my brother…and let Electa move on with her life without me?"

Ravens circle above as Henry bends down, puts his hands in the dirt. and rubs them together. Ben points and three vigilantes start for the rocks. Henry braces himself and fires at the men, who dive for cover. He turns his attention to the two vigilantes guarding Samuel and blasts away at them. The two men panic and ride off, leaving Samuel all alone. While Henry reloads his gun, Samuel begins to untie the rope binding his hands.

After he finishes reloading, Henry fires away at Ben and his men as they desperately try to control their horses. Samuel sees his chance to escape, removes the noose from his neck, and rides off. Two men leap from their hiding places and prepare to fire at the run-away, so Henry pops up and shoots both of them in their legs. Having ridden to the top of a nearby hill, Samuel watches as several vigilantes advance on the man hidden behind the rocks.

Down to his last bullet, Henry's hands shake as he aims and shoots Ben in the chest. Ben falls from his horse, hops to his feet, dusts himself off, removes his Bible from his coat, and looks it over. When he sees that it's mutilated, he tosses it aside.

Out of ammo, the barefooted former sheriff steps out from behind the rocks. He tosses his gun at Jack, who ducks out of the way. Henry approaches with his hands raised. Everyone is shocked to see who it is, especially his brother who is watching from a distance.

Samuel screams. "What the hell, Henry!?"

Ben growls. "What the fuck?"

Jack scoffs. "Why ain't you dead?"

Several of the other men retreat as Henry takes another step forward. When he looks up the hill in search of his brother, Jack follows his eyes and sees Samuel as well. Henry realizes his brother is not out of danger and yells, "Get the hell out of here!"

Jack grabs his rifle and aims at Samuel, who sits up in his saddle as if daring the villain to shoot him. Henry tries to reason with his old friend. "That's my brother."

Ben is nonplussed. "Brother? What the hell?"

The rogue lowers his rifle and stares at Henry. "I know who it is. I ain't stupid." Then Jack turns his rifle and aims it at Henry.

Ben sees what's happening and holds up his arm. "No! We'll hang Plummer for good this time."

As Ben tries to decide what to do next, in the distance, he and his men hear, "Gobble gobble! Gobble gobble!"

Jack lifts his rifle again and takes aim at Samuel. Henry eyes his old friend and calmly says, "Don't do it."

"Yer brother ain't no more." Before he can get a shot off, Henry leans down, pulls his derringer from his boot, and shoots his old friend in the stomach. Jack raises his arm, studies the expanding red spot on his shirt and moans. "I'm a gut-shot rabbit."

As Henry rolls off his horse, two vigilantes grab him and take his small gun. A third man checks on Jack, who raises up briefly and falls back again. With one last surge of energy, he reaches out to Henry and gasps, "Ya fuckin' claim jumper ... I ain't old enough to die." Jack's eyes go blank as his spirit leaves his body. His eyes remain open, so the vigilante rakes his hand across his face, closing the jealous man's eyes forever.

Henry sits on his horse beneath the hanging tree with his hands tied behind his back and a noose around his neck. Still a safe distance away, Samuel watches helplessly.

Desperate to save his brother, Samuel cups his hands and yells, "Henry! What you want me to do?!"

Henry turns his head as far as he can and yells. "Stay put!"

Samuel searches his saddle for a rifle he knows isn't there and screams again. "I ain't got no fuckin' way to help you!"

Henry yells again. "God damn it, Samuel! Ride!"

Ben tightens the noose around Henry's neck and says, "Never had to hang a man twice." Henry looks up at the clouds, studies them one last time, and lowers his head. Ben hesitates, slaps Henry's horse, and the animal steps away. The ex-sheriff slides from his saddle, the noose tightens around his neck, and his legs swing from side to side as he struggles to breathe.

Armed with a lap full of rocks, Samuel charges down the hill in the direction of the hanging tree. The vigilantes fire away as the desperate man throws the rocks at them. Realizing his attempt to rescue his brother is futile, he turns around and rides back up the hill. Several vigilantes mount up and start to go after the renegade, but Ben holds up his hand. "We'll chase him down later. Had my fill of death for one day." Ben signals one of his vigilantes and the man cuts the rope. Henry's body falls in the hole meant for Samuel with a thud.

The wind picks up as Ezra and the reporters approach in Ezra's death wagon. The three men stare at the hanging tree and the vigilantes, while they put the final touches on Henry's grave.

Ezra climbs down from his wagon and studies the mound of dirt as Ben scoffs. "Too late. He's in the ground."

"Slade?"

Ben points to Samuel at the top of the hill. "Slade's up there."

Ezra looks up and sees Samuel, who sits rigid in his saddle. He stares at Ben. "Who ya got in the ground, and so forth?"

"Slade's brother, Henry. Ezra, you owe me a big talk when we get back."

Charles chirps. "I'm confused."

Ezra tries to explain. "A man can only avoid bein' hanged so many times." Ben nods and four men load Jack's body and two other dead vigilantes in the back of Ezra's wagon.

Michael's jaw drops. "Wait. That's Jack Cleveland."

Ben responds. "One less problem I gotta deal with."

Michael and Charles walk over and stand at Henry's grave until the wind picks up. Ben and his men quickly climb on their horses and ride off holding their hats. As the reporters make their way back to the wagon, they look up at the hill again and see Samuel still watching them. A moment passes and the surviving Plummer brother rides away.

The dirt on the grave swirls in the wind as the hanging rope sways back and forth. In the distance, Ezra's wagon tops a hill and disappears.

Two miles outside of Bannack, Ezra and the reporters roll along. Charles breaks the silence. "We're looking forward to hearing your story as to how Henry survived being hanged."

Ezra instantly pulls his wagon to a stop, jumps down, and unhitches one of his horses. "This is as far as I go." Charles and Michael look at each other as the undertaker climbs on the unhitched horse. "Wagon and that good horse is yours."

Charles looks confused as he says, "Did I ask the wrong question?"

"Every town has its dead. Time for me to move on, and so forth." Ezra slaps the reins to his horse and rides off.

Charles hollers. "Wait! What about these dead bodies?"

Ezra doesn't bother to look back. "Bury them deep!"

Michael takes the reins attached to the remaining horse and says, "Strange man."

Charles shakes his head. "And so forth."

EPILOGUE

"Farewell! God knows when we shall meet again."
William Shakespeare

SAMUEL ARRIVES at the Vail house and slides off of Hank. He knocks on the door and waits patiently until Electa opens it. Behind her stands James and Martha Jane Vail. Electa looks at Samuel, hoping for the best, but his eyes reveal something is wrong. He clears his throat and says, "Henry saved my life."

Electa's lips tighten. "And? They hanged him, didn't they?"

Samuel lowers his head. "It should have been me."

The new widow wipes away a tear as her voice remains stoic. "Where's his body?"

"Five miles north of Bannack in a large open meadow, under a lone cottonwood tree. Take ya there if ya want."

Electa pauses and says, "No, you and Sandra need to get as far away from here as possible."

Hearing her name, Sandra steps to the door and rushes over and hugs Samuel. They hold each other until Henry's brother turns back to Electa. "If there's anything I can do."

Electa holds her head high. "Live a good life. That's all Henry ever wanted for you." She steps back and leaves the couple to themselves.

Electa, Martha Jane, and James walk out of the cabin as Samuel and Sandra continue to hold each other tightly. Martha

Jane tries to console her sister, but Electa stiffens and moves away.

Samuel and his new family ride off in a two horse-drawn wagon. Hank, trails behind, tied to the back of the wagon. Samuel looks back at Hank and nods at Sandra. "I got one stop to make." Electa watches until the couple and their baby are out of sight. She raises her head, wipes away a tear, and walks back to the house.

The Bannack girl that Henry gave the special horse to walks out to the family barn, opens the door, and finds Hank tied to a post. She can't believe her eyes. "Hank! You're back."

At a safe distance from Bannack, Samuel, Sandra, and little Samuel roll along in the wagon at a fast clip. All of a sudden, Samuel stops the wagon, climbs down, and picks a daisy. He climbs back in the wagon and hands the flower to Sandra. She smiles and kisses Samuel on the cheek.

In the meadow near the tree where Henry is buried, the wind picks up and the newly dug dirt covering his makeshift grave begins to swirl. Without warning, Henry's hand, followed by his arm, raise out of the ground and reaches for the sky.

Electa, asleep on the bank of Grasshopper Creek, awakens with a start and sits up. She takes a moment, stands, and looks at the clouds high above her. She takes a step, but hears something behind her. When she turns, a rabbit stares at her for a few seconds and hops off. She grabs her fishing pole, tosses it in creek, and watches as it disappears in the water.

The sun shines through the window of the *Sacramento Union* newsroom as Charles lays the Plummer article in front of Michael. When he doesn't look up, Charles slaps the desk. "Blackman wants fewer hangings and more romance."

Michael sits up. "We're not changing a damn thing."

Charles steps back. "What's come over you?"

"I'm not Blackman's word whore."

Charles chuckles. "Aren't you something?"

"We wrote the truth and his own words need to be heard.."

"You're right. I'm going in there and give the old man hell." Charles takes a few steps and stops in his tracks. "Or maybe after lunch. They say you should never make an important decision on an empty stomach."

Charles struts away as Michael picks up Henry's journal and begins to read.

Ben and his boys will be here soon. I'm not afraid of dying. When I saw my father killed and I lost my brother, I wanted them back. But now, I realize we're all on a wheel that spins around until it's our turn to get off. Who knows what the mystery of life and death hold for us. Maybe my plan will work and Electa and I will find happiness in California.

Charles lays the journal down, walks over to the window and stares down at the street as people go about their busy lives.

Pete and Buckie are feeding their horses. When they look up, they see a wagon approaching in the distance. Pete strains his eyes and grabs Buckie by the arm when he realizes the wagon's passengers are Samuel, Sandra, and his grandson. Buckie tosses his pitchfork and runs toward the wagon, while Pete stands waiting with a big smile on his face.

AFTERWORD

Over the course of a month, Montana vigilantes hunted down and executed more than twenty men. Sheriff Henry Plummer was hanged on January 10th, 1864. Some say he was the victim of vicious rumors. Others claim justice was served.

On May 26th, 1864, President Abraham Lincoln signed a bill that realigned Idaho Territory, thus creating what would become the state of Montana. The town of Bannack, which is now a state park, was named the first territorial capital.

After Henry Plummer's death, Electa Bryan Plummer moved to Vermillion, South Dakota, where she married a widower named James Maxwell. She helped raise his two daughters and the couple had two sons of their own. Up until her death in 1912, Electa maintained that Henry Plummer was an innocent man.

THE REAL HENRY PLUMMER

Sheriff Henry Plummer (1832-1864) is one of the most colorful characters of the American West. During his short life, Plummer's rumored unlawful exploits resulted in his being hanged in Bannack by the newly formed Montana vigilantes. Whether Henry Plummer really carried out the crimes he was accused of remains a mystery to this day.

For over a century, many people accepted the accounts of Montana writer and vigilante member Thomas Dimsdale (*The Vigilantes of Montana*). In his book, published shortly after the vigilante lynching spree of 1864, Dimsdale concluded that Henry Plummer was both a respected sheriff and the secret leader of a gang of road agents called "The Innocents."

Dimsdale claimed Plummer and his gang committed dozens of murders and numerous robberies throughout the gold camps of the Idaho Territory. When several local leaders decided enough was enough, they formed a vigilance committee. Some of the first men that they hanged included Henry Plummer and several other supposed members of "The Innocents."

ABOUT THE AUTHOR

Daniel Landes retired from South Dakota State University in 2011, where he served as an Assistant Dean of Arts and Sciences and as a professor of English.

Originally from Williston, North Dakota, Dan grew up in Great Falls, Montana and graduated from C.M. Russell High School. He went on to earn an undergraduate degree in History at Minot State University, a Masters in English at Bemidji State University and a Ph.D. in English from the University of North Dakota. He and his wife Martha live in Rio Rancho, New Mexico, where Dan continues to pursue his love of writing, film production, bicycling, and coaching. Dan is currently serving as a cross country and track coach at a local high school in nearby Albuquerque.

www.hangtheinnocent.com

To see the short film, "The Innocents," based on the opening of this novel, click on this code and access it through google drive.

Made in the USA
Middletown, DE
05 November 2022

14060463R00203